Very naughty . . . a jumbo-sized belly laugh . . . the most riotously readable ribaldry on the market.
Penthouse

Monstrously funny.
Illustrated London News

If you are shockable, steer cle
Punch

Calls for a loud cheer.
The Observer

Fascinating to read.
Desmond Morris. (*Author of* The Naked Ape) *on B.B.C.*

Patrick Skene Catling

The Experiment

A Panther Book

A Panther Book

First published in Great Britain by Anthony Blond Limited
1967. Reprinted 1967. Panther edition published 1968. Reprinted 1969. Copyright © Patrick Skene Catling 1967.
This book is published at a net price and is supplied subject
to the Publishers Association Standard Conditions of Sale
registered under the Restrictive Trade Practices Act, 1956.
*Printed in Great Britain by C. Nicholls & Company Ltd.,
The Philips Park Press, Manchester, and published by Panther
Books, 3 Upper James Street, London, W.1*

ONE

"ORGASM?" anxiously repeated the President of Digby College. "Surely you didn't say . . .?"

When important members of the Board of Trustees suddenly changed the subject from the weather of the Middle West, the flora of the Digby campus, and the prospect for next fall's football team, Dr. Frank Essen, Ph.D., always assumed that the time had come to discuss money.

The dark walnut paneling, the crystal chandelier, the red-leather-covered desk, the rose Aubusson carpet, the prospect through the leaded panes of the mullioned windows – everything that lay sumptuously about him recalled the prosperity of Digby yesterday or the day before, when the railroad shares of the college's rich nineteenth-century Wesleyan endowment still really meant something. Today the case was altered.

The campus was still generally regarded as one of the prettiest in southern Ohio, "surrounded by gently rolling hills", as the prospectus pointed out. "With its bosky arboretum, its nine-hole golf course, and the white frame dwellings and stores of its friendly township (pop. 4,264 – good neighbors all with the faculty and student body), Digby reminds many a percipient visitor of the sort of gracious, small New England communities from which our distinguished Founder sprang." The splendid buildings were still there, neo-Georgian, neo-Gothic, neo-Byzantine, representing sizable portions of several family fortunes at the turn of the century. But during the fifty years or so since the seminary had closed, since the college had become nonsectarian and the first young lady undergraduates and the first scientists had been admitted, there had been a gradual, steady financial decline. The Administration had certainly done its utmost to keep in step with other progressive, imaginative liberal arts colleges, even while striving at the same time to uphold Digby's tradition of scholarship and service. For example, Digby was one of the first colleges to offer a bachelor's degree in television script writing, yet Digby continued to support one of

7

southern Ohio's most highly-respected *a cappella* choirs, which gave weekly public concerts of inspirational songs of all faiths in the old Wesleyan chapel. The academic scope of the curriculum had been ever broadened as the students had been taken from an increasing variety of social, economic and ethnic origins, Free Chinese, Nicaraguans, even a few American Negroes of exceptional athletic prowess. It was now the college's just boast that at Digby one could find just about any kind of person studying just about anything. But even so, year after year, the treasurer's report made doleful reading. When Turner Symington, one of the pharmaceutical Symingtons, and therefore probably the wealthiest member of the Board of Trustees, had written to Dr. Essen for an urgent meeting, the President had automatically agreed to receive him immediately, though he could not imagine what good could come of another discussion of ways and means of fund raising. The alumni were already quite obviously becoming impatient with all the nagging letters of appeal.

"Surely I did say," Symington said. He was a fiercely fit-looking man of about fifty, with a white crew cut, an expensively massaged plump red face and bright blue eyes. When he spoke he seemed as vigorously authoritative as a flag flapping in a fresh breeze. "Orgasm, I said. O-R-G-A-S-M. Orgasm."

"But, Mr. Symington!" Dr. Essen said. He tried hard, with a short barking guffaw, to suggest the manly tolerance, the wicked complicity, that he imagined some of the heartier alumni remembered from locker rooms long ago. But seeing Symington's hard expression, Dr. Essen realized that he might be serious and that in any event the laughter was premature. He abruptly concealed it in a cough. "I mean," Dr. Essen said, "I don't quite see –"

"I used the word advisedly," Symington said. "As you know, Dr. Essen, I am a practical man." The President weakly smiled in complimentary deference. "I run a big enterprise, Dr. Essen. Right?"

"Of course, Mr. Symington. We at Digby have often had reason to feel grateful –"

"We're not the biggest," Symington said. "But we're big. And we stay big." Dr. Essen's face spastically flinched from the implied rebuke. "We stay big," Symington went on,

8

"because we stay ahead. And how do we stay ahead?" He didn't wait for the ritual respectful request for him to answer his own question. "We stay ahead because we use up-to-date methods, not only in manufacture, packaging and sales, but before all that, when it really counts."

"The name of Symington is a byword," Dr. Essen humbly acknowledged. "Your cough syrup, your soaps and sundries –"

"All right, never mind the flattery," Symington said, waving a beautifully manicured hairy ham of a hand. "I'm here to tell you how Digby can be put back on its feet and on top of the heap, where it belongs. Where it used to be."

"Any suggestion you may care to make," Dr. Essen said, "would, of course, be gratefully considered." Inwardly, he shuddered, expecting the usual trustee's recommendation to hire a live-wire new football coach.

"We do a lot with motivation research," Symington said. "And I could kick myself sometimes. We hire these motivation research people, pay them a lot of money, and they come up with things that should be obvious to any grown man of the world, such as you or I."

Dr. Essen winced only slightly. He somehow sensed that Symington, in his own good time, had something to say. First he must be allowed his moment of triumph, his little lecture.

"What is our society really working for?" Symington demanded. "What's its real goal?" Again the hesitation was merely for histrionic effect. "In this day and age, they're not worrying about a chicken in every pot, two cars in every garage, are they?"

"I suppose we have gotten beyond that," Dr. Essen agreed.

"Everyone has his split-level home, his summer place, his boat," Symington went on. "By everyone, I'm talking about the kind of person who's been to a school like Digby. This is a period when people have just about everything you can think of that makes life feel secure and comfortable. You'll go along with that, won't you?"

Dr. Essen nodded.

"There's only one area of uncertainty and deprivation," Mr. Symington said. "Even hardship." He looked fiercely into Dr. Essen's tired eyes. "That's why I said *orgasm*.

9

That's the key word. That's the one thing left that people aren't sure of. The outfit that can guarantee that has got it made."

Dr. Essen was not wholly unaccustomed to fanatics. There had been a woman only last week – a woman who, having pledged a large sum for construction of a new women's dormitory building, unfortunately could not be disregarded – who had lectured him for two hours on the importance of supplying the dining halls with bread made with unrefined flour. But he had never thought of Mr. Symington as anything but a practical man, insistently practical, and here he was talking about sex. However, as Dr. Essen was only too well aware, at a certain unpredictable age – it varied from person to person – one became mysteriously prone to morbid fantasies, and in their more obsessional forms these fantasies could intrude themselves into otherwise rational conscious thought, impelling hitherto most respectable men and women to blurt out indiscretions and absurdities, in spite of all past responsibility and dignity, even in the offices of college presidents. The trend of Dr. Essen's rationalization caused his face to relax and then to recompose itself in an expression of noncommittal sympathy.

"Yes," he said.

"I can see you're not getting it," Symington said impatiently. He could ill abide obtuseness. Otherwise promising executives had been tossed out on their ears for giving signs of being slow on the uptake at company meetings. With patent medicines as competitive as they were, the lame and the halt soon fell by the wayside. But Dr. Essen was not one of his employees, not really, so Symington took a tranquilizing deep breath.

"The orgasm is a kind of symbol for a whole lot more," he explained. "It represents the ultimate self-expression," he added, quoting a mimeographed manifesto in the pigskin briefcase beside him, "total personal fulfillment, the absolute merging of the individual with the infinite, the timeless moment of truth, the . . ." His memory failed him and he spoke more characteristically for himself. "Hell, Doctor, it's the best thing in life, isn't it?"

"Release from tension," Dr. Essen suggested helpfully.

"That's an outmoded concept," Symington snapped,

10

"Negative. Recent studies in the field indicate that the orgasm is, in fact, a positive factor in both physical and mental health. I've seen statistics that convince me that orgasms actually revitalize. Graphs have been drawn showing the correlation between sexual outlets and muscle tone, retardation of the build-up of fatty tissue around the heart — longevity, Dr. Essen. In short, the more orgasms you have, the healthier you are, the longer you live. All other things being equal of course."

"That's very interesting," Dr. Essen said with sincere regret for the self-inflicted inhibitory cold showers of his adolescence and his years at teachers' college. "But I have to say, Mr. Symington, that the health-giving properties of sexual indulgence do not come within the scope of this office. What has all this got to do with the educational program at Digby? If you could only give me some idea ..."

"I'm coming to that," Symington said severely. Dr. Essen looked properly chastened, leaned back again in his padded swivel chair and with pious solemnity conjoined the tips of his thumbs and slowly, one by one, his fingers. Symington, nodding his approval, leaned masterfully, confidentially, forward.

"You want to get this school out of the red, don't you?" he said. Dr. Essen gravely inclined his head to signify assent. "All right then. I'll tell you. What Digby has to do is take a few leaves out of the books of Kinsey, Goodspeed, and Masters and Johnson. What Digby has to do if it wants to re-establish itself in the vanguard of American education, with all the rewards as well as the duties that such a position entails, is set up a first-class, up-to-the-minute department of sexual research."

"Oh, really, Mr. Symington!" Dr. Essen protested, sitting forward again as Symington complacently rested.

"Yes, really, Dr. Essen. Take a look at the record. Consider what the public wants. And imagine the future. Do you take *The New York Times*?"

"I am an educator," Dr. Essen said primly. "Naturally I keep myself informed."

"Then you see the Sunday book-review section. You've noticed, perhaps, that during the past fifteen years or so no books have won such universal attention and acclaim

11

as Kinsey's and –" The turn the conversation was taking emboldened Dr. Essen sufficiently to enable him to interrupt.

"Dr. Kinsey's work was highly controversial," he reminded his visitor. "Digby has a special reputation to consider. Anyway, what do you mean, a *department* of sexual research?"

"Kinsey *was* controversial," Symington said. "Some city folk were shocked by the notion that so many of our American farm boys spent so much of their time feeling up the pigs and sheep."

"*Please,* Mr. Symington!" Dr. Essen implored. "My secretary's in the next room. I must ask you to keep your voice a little lower."

"You don't think she's read Kinsey?" Symington retorted, smiling banteringly. "Your grandchildren probably have a copy in their playroom, along with *Lady Chatterley* and *Fanny Hill.* Kinsey isn't controversial any more. Not any more than Freud is, or that character that got the Bible Belt in an uproar – you know, the Scopes trial – Darwin. The American people want the facts even if they hurt. You remember the hundred best books? I do. I have 'em in my office, the whole set, leather-bound. They're great. But there ought to be at least a hundred and two or three. How about Goodspeed? He carried on from where Kinsey left off. He was the first to publish legitimate photographs of men and women on the job. And then Masters and Johnson. The Reproductive Biology Research Foundation of St. Louis, Missouri. You've got to hand it to them. Somebody had to think of it, and they were the first to do something about it."

"The names do sound vaguely familiar," Dr. Essen said in some bewilderment.

"Are you kidding?" Symington asked.

"They wrote another of those books, didn't they?" Dr. Essen hazarded.

"A very highly respected work," Symington heartily affirmed. "And it has sold like LSD. It was their brilliant, long-overdue scheme to study, by direct observation, how men and women respond to various methods of sexual stimulation. They spent eleven years conscientiously and systematically examining, scrutinizing, measuring, testing, recording every detail of male and female physique before, during and after performing every imaginable sexual act. The medical profession, most of it, and the entire reading public hailed them as pioneers. 'A major breakthrough,' their publisher called their first book, *Human Sexual Response,* and that was even before it hit the best-seller lists."

"I suppose I should have read it," Dr. Essen mumbled fretfully. "But if you only knew the amount of paper work, the number of documents and letters that pass across my desk every day of the week."

"You shouldn't talk like that," Symington said in a voice of gentle menace. "It's all right for me to hear. But if the word got around among some of the less sympathetic trustees ... 'Poor old Doc. Essen. Too bad he doesn't delegate more of the mechanical administrative chores. Too bad he doesn't have enough time and energy left over for creative thinking.' You know?"

"I devote my whole life to consideration of Digby's future," Dr. Essen said, but his voice noticeably trembled as he said it, as though he recognized that Symington in his crude manner was expressing a criticism that Dr. Essen had already addressed to the shaving mirror.

"Sure you do," Symington agreed. "All I want to do is help you help yourself, and help my old alma mater as well. We're a team, aren't we?"

"Oh, most assuredly," Dr. Essen hastily confirmed. "As I often say to my wife, the time has long since passed when the senior administrator of a seat of higher learning can be expected or can expect to live the life of a scholar, shielding himself from the practical demands of the new era. I always say the value of the trustees resides in their going about in the great world of industry and commerce, those stalwart twins of pragmatism –"

"Good, good," Symington said. "I'm glad we see eye to eye. What's good for you is good for Digby. What's good for Digby is good for the trustees."

"What's good for the trustees is good for me," Dr. Essen said. It was his gallant little joke.

Symington didn't notice it. "So," he said. "What to do? You authorize the establishment of a new department. We can call it The Digby Institute – dignified and it doesn't give anything away. It'll eventually need its own new build-

13

ing. Casting modesty aside for a moment, frankly I'd like to see it called The Symington Building. For five million we ought to be able to put up something in very good taste."

The mention of money had come at last, as Dr. Essen had known it must, and all the familiar feelings of anxiety bubbled up again to the surface of his mind.

"Five million dollars!" he said. Symington looked dismayed.

"Five approximately," he said. "That's a rough estimate. You know how difficult it is nowadays, the way costs keep going up."

"Where on earth do you think we're going to lay our hands on that kind of money? I thought you came here to propose a new source of income. Even the most successful of textbooks can hardly be expected to earn the college five million dollars."

Symington patiently waited for the tiny outburst to come to an end. He then calmly proceeded.

"I know you're very hard-worked, Dr. Essen," he said soothingly, "but that's a real naïve-type thing to say. Are you forgetting the foundations? Are you forgetting the conscience of American industry? Come now, Dr. Essen; I'm talking about the big time."

"Everyone says, 'Go to the foundations'," Dr. Essen said. "They seem to think that all you have to do is ask the foundations and they give. I'm not without experience in this matter of fund raising," Dr. Essen said with a faint smile. "The foundations are very sophisticated organizations and very hard-boiled, if I may use plain language. They, like everyone else, expect a return for their money, even if only that most evanescent of intangibles, prestige. Money without strings is the most difficult of all to get hold of. With strings, you can pull."

"Let's put the financing aside for a while," Symington said airily. "Let me provide the answer to that one. But hypothetically, you haven't any objection to setting up an Institute, have you, if it's guaranteed to show a handsome net gain to the college? And eventually brings us in some very favorable publicity?"

"Of course not," Dr. Essen replied, and then added, somewhat more cautiously, "that is to say, if we could be

14

sure that the publicity would be favorable. It seems to me that in the case of ... due to the intrinsic nature of the research you suggest, there would be a very real and present danger that the whole thing might prove quite embarrassing, even dangerous. Many of our parents are conservative by nature. It only takes –"

"I've thought of all that," Symington said. "I have come prepared. First of all, possibly for the first two or three years, at least until we were ready for publication, the work of the Institute would be secret. Since the war, the world war, more and more campuses have become accustomed to the presence of major research projects of a secret nature. A college doesn't have to be any M.I.T. to get its share of top-secret government research contracts. Not that I'm suggesting for one moment that we should allow Washington in on this. Don't worry. I feel the same as you do about Federal interference. Besides, no government could be expected to allow itself to get mixed up with sex, election year or no election year. I considered and rejected it. No, it's easier than that. One of this country's leading pharmaceutical houses will be willing to underwrite the whole deal."

Symington beamed. Dr. Essen softly bit his lower lip while squeezing and releasing the top of his ballpoint pen, sure symptoms of repressed excitement.

"How far have you gone?" Dr. Essen asked.

"The talks have all been quite informal," Symington said. "There's nothing in writing yet but, believe me, it's as good as in the bag." He paused. "I have several cards up my sleeve, Essen. One of them is that we live in an age of consolidation. Big business, you see, is getting bigger. Huge corporations, like certain species of large predatory fish, are ever on the lookout for smaller fish to gobble up. I'm one of them, and Buckeye Pharmaceutical has already made a couple of passes. They've been buying up our stock on the sly – or so they think. Not that I mind, by the way. There are worse things than mergers. Far better that my estate pay long term capital gains than shell it out in one hunk. Besides, I'm of an age where I'd not be averse to taking it a little easier. Let the other fellow do the worrying, I say. Oh, Buckeye will go along with us, Dr. Essen, have no worry on that score."

15

"But what do they want in return?" Dr. Essen wanted to know.

"There's a new pill they're developing," Symington said. "A new kind of birth-control pill. Once our institute has been established as the foremost organization of its kind in the United States – in the world – its seal of approval could be very valuable. Some of the freer-thinking directors of the company are also talking – they're just at the talking stage, kicking the idea around – about possibly coming up with some sort of aphrodisiac pill, a harmless little pill that anyone could buy, like chewing gum, out of a vending machine. As the nation matures in its thinking about sex, there's bound to be a great demand for drugs that'll safely improve our physical performance, prolong and strengthen our sexual vigor. We're none of us getting any younger."

"I think aphrodisiacs might be going a little far," Dr. Essen said, trying not to brighten too visibly. "But it is undeniable that the world needs to regulate its population growth. That is certainly a cause beyond reproach. Let me say at this stage, Mr. Symington, that I am most appreciative of all the efforts that you have evidently been making on Digby's behalf."

"We all have to do what we can," Symington said modestly. "And now you must be wondering where we go from here. I've taken the liberty of having some plans drawn up for a building. Beautiful, Dr. Essen, really quite imposing. Better to have something to show Buckeye, you know. I've chosen an excellent firm in Washington, one of the best, and I should warn you one of their young architects, Richard Doughty, may pop out here to look around and start things rolling, I hope. Interesting boy, Doughty, quite well connected. As a matter of fact, his father, who's got a sort of strangle hold on the construction of highways, has made an imposing bit of money since the war. Won't hurt, you know, the boy does the building, who knows but what the old man might feel grateful enough to want to give a bit to the old endowment fund. We'll have to help the boy all we can. And I'm also working on a Greek by the rather improbable name of Philopoulos – or should I say Greek-American; I never can remember. All those minority fellows are touchy about that, rich or poor, and

16

this one's rich as Midas. Owns most of Buckeye Pharma-ceutical and a lot of other large corporations all over the world, though he seems to spend most of his time aboard his yacht having at movie starlets. Well, when you've got more of it than is buried too, in Fort Knox I guess you can afford to. So, I want to get Mr. P. here, possibly for the laying of the cornerstone around Commencement. Show him around the Institute a bit, you know; no harm in shaking the plum tree."

"It has occurred to me," Dr. Essen said, "that there would be a need, if this project did, after all, prove feasible, there would be a need for a full-time, dedicated, ah, direc-tor of the Institute. Medicine is not my subject, as you know. I would have to cast about. You mustn't be impa-tient with me, Mr. Symington. Whether or not we could decide to go ahead would depend to a great extent on whether or not the right man was available for the task."

"The director is here, Dr. Essen," Symington said, his hand sweeping in an arc as melodramatically as a magi-cian's. He gestured toward the closed door. "I was confi-dent that you would see things my way and wish to meet our prospective savior. But it isn't a man, Dr. Essen. The director will be a woman."

TWO

At the age of thirty-six, Dr. Beatrice Schumann was no longer merely pretty. She was handsome, almost majestic. Unfashionably buxom, she ignored fashion and transcended it. Sitting, waiting, reading her own copy of the *Journal of American Medical Association* in an armchair in Dr. Essen's outer reception room, she was wearing a classically tailored dark-gray suit of somber dignity – somber but not severe. The white lace of her blouse was ornately pleated and ruffled. Her legs were crossed in an attitude of relaxed grace; the stockings, flesh-colored, were imperceptible but for a sheen that was finer than human, and her black shoes were plainly elegant, with slender spike heels. Her long, dark-auburn hair was brushed upward at the neck and arranged in a sleek, serpentine coil of dramatic simplicity on top of her head. An almost horizontal beam of late-winter sunshine, like an amber spotlight through the window, lighted one side of her hair as red as flame. She wore no makeup, no jewelry, and no other adornment, except a quaintly old-maidenly wide band of black velvet around her white neck. She gave an impression of striking simplicity, of sublime serenity, of high electric potential quietly at rest.

Dr. Essen's secretary-receptionist, in contrast, a flaxen-haired young lady in her early twenties, seated at a Scandinavian glass desk that half barred the way to the inner office, was hardly ever still. Dressed like any undergraduate coed in a tight pink cashmere sweater, a matching pink cashmere cardigan, open, a single strand of artificial pearls, and a dark-green-and-blue-plaid skirt, she moved about like an ornamental cage bird, pecking with brightly manicured fingernails at the typewriter, picking up the telephone, plucking at plastic cables in the switchboard, pushing buttons on the console of the intercom.

"Dr. Schumann," the secretary said, with the lilting, impersonal friendliness of a charm school, "Dr. Essen says for you to kindly step in now."

Dr. Schumann looked calmly at the exquisite miniature

gold watch on her wrist, unhurriedly uncrossed her legs, placed the *Journal* in her large, simple black-leather handbag, and rose to her feet. In spite of the high heels and the tall coiffure, she was a surprisingly short woman, but formidable nonetheless.

"Thank you," she said, pleasantly nodding.

The inner door opened. Turner Symington was standing there, his face ruddier than ever, his blue eyes shining, beckoning to her with controlled excitement.

"Come on in, Dr. Schumann," he said. "I've already told Dr. Essen a lot about you."

Beatrice Schumann went in.

For nearly an hour, Dr. Schumann did most of the talking, outlining the aims and methods of her proposed research program as nontechnically as she was able. In accordance with Symington's private briefing earlier, she plied the soft pedal of euphemism; her sales pitch was so dulcetly pianissimo that several times Dr. Essen found it necessary to coax her to be more outspokenly explicit, and even at last to assure her that the academic climate nowadays had become so liberal, "freshened by invigorating drafts of enlightened public opinion," that no investigation of genuine usefulness need be cramped through fear of the interference of bigoted pressure groups.

"Who was it who said that the proper study of man is man himself?" Dr. Essen asked them. He was not quite sure of the exact quotation, and, neither of the others remembered it at all, but the point was well taken. As Symington jovially and rightly observed, "That takes in a lot of territory!" and Dr. Schumann, who had been sitting stiffly upright during her dissertation, bent a little and smiled.

"Academic freedom is without meaning unless it is exercised," Dr. Essen said piously. "Exercised to the full. You may rest assured, Dr. Schumann, if this project works out as we all hope – and I am sure that it will – I myself, as President of Digby College, will protect you and the Institute against any critics."

"That's a fine sentiment, well expressed," Symington said, nodding his head appreciatively and with a token flourish of a fist indicating his full support.

19

"All the same," Dr. Schumann said, decisively straightening again into an upright posture of authoritative determination, "there are certain aspects of the program that lay persons, inadequately informed, might misunderstand. It would be better for everyone concerned if, at first, they were not informed at all."

"A little learning is a dangerous thing," Dr. Essen vivaciously agreed. "That's true!"

"This is a public-relations problem," Symington said. "I've got some people who can help with that."

"Once the Institute is properly established," Dr. Schumann said, "once we have assembled our team and recruited our research-study population group, once we have conducted a sufficient number of in-depth sexual personality probes, once we have collated our laboratory observations, then we shall be able to reach conclusions that may enable us to offer the public at large practical guidance of incalculable human value."

"That's where the books'll come in," Symington said.

"Precisely," Dr. Schumann assented. "Publication is essential. My colleague and I shall publish our findings in the learned journals. We shall present papers before the A.M.A. at our annual convention."

"That's a public meeting," Symington interjected. "The wire services cover it."

"Yes, I know," Dr. Essen said.

"And then, of course," Dr. Schumann said, "there will be the books. I recommend that we found a Digby Institute Press. We want to be sure that we retain control of the entire process."

"An excellent notion," Dr. Essen said.

"Great," Symington agreed. "You say you already have a colleague picked out?"

"Nothing definite could be settled before this meeting," Dr. Schumann courteously conceded, "but I have every reason to hope that we may be able to persuade one of this country's ablest young sociologists to participate with us. He's really a psychologist. He majored in psychology at Ohio State. But he has been applying his psychology sociologically. I have been watching his progress with great interest."

"What's this person's name?" Dr. Essen asked. "Not that I would allow myself to encroach in any way upon your domain."

"He has a Ph.D. from State," Dr. Schumann said. "His thesis was on the psychology of industrial absenteeism. A remarkable probe into the nature of withdrawal. It made a real contribution. His name is Porter. Dr. Louis Porter."

Agreement in principle having been so harmoniously reached, the conversation drifted amicably to other subjects – to the weather of the Middle West, the flora of the Digby campus, and the prospects for next fall's football team.

Dr. Schumann and Turner Symington made their adieus. Symington offered Dr. Schumann a lift to the railroad station, she accepted the offer, and they left Dr. Essen's office together.

When they had gone, Dr. Essen, walking with an uncommonly sprightly bounce, hurried out to his secretary.

"Things are looking up at Digby!" he told her. " 'Dig! Dig! Dig! for dear old Digby'!" he sang, only a little out of tune. "You may take the rest of the afternoon off. I'm going out."

His secretary looked blankly at him as he put on his coat and hat and left the room.

"Thanks," she said, recovering from her surprise. "Thanks a lot, Dr. Essen!" she said to the closing door. She shrugged her shoulders, grinned, and pulled the plastic cover over her electric typewriter.

In a Cadillac gliding out between the Grecian marble gateposts of the entrance to the Administration block, Symington turned to Dr. Schumann with a smile of candid delight.

"This is a great day!" he exclaimed.

"It seems almost too good to be true," she said. "After all these years of planning to fix it all as easily as that."

"It wasn't all that easy," he said, his face serious. "But I have my contacts. Where there's a will there's a way, as Dr. Essen would say."

21

"I'm very grateful to you, Turner," Beatrice Schumann said. "I really am."

"It's a pleasure to be of help," he said. "This institute's really going to put Digby on the map."

"I'm sure it can," Dr. Schumann said.

THREE

HAVING established himself as one of the Middle West's foremost authorities on the psychological causes of industrial absenteeism, a lesser man than Dr. Louis Porter might have rested on his laurels.

At thirty-three, he was an associate professor of sociology in a large and rapidly expanding college of arts and sciences in upstate New York. If he stayed there and kept his nose clean, he had a good chance of promotion to a full professorship within the next five years, which would mean security of tenure and a degree of academic autonomy that many a scholar fifteen years his senior might envy. But, for Dr. Porter, security and autonomy, though necessary, were not enough. He aspired to greatness. He wanted to achieve some sort of theoretical breakthrough that would assure him a place in academic history. He wanted to be cited in textbooks as the Einstein of psychological sociology. And after all, as he kept asking himself, why not? With his determined, single-minded devotion to self-improvement, he had already come a long way from the slums of Cincinnati. A mathematical prodigy in junior high school, he had earned his escape from poverty and squalor. By means of a succession of scholarships and part-time jobs, he had put himself through college entirely unaided by his parents. As newspaper delivery boy, bowling alley pin boy (he antedated automation), dormitory furnace tender, dining-hall dishwasher and waiter, assistant librarian and laboratory technician, he had dedicated all his energies to work, until work had become a habit, a way of life, almost a philosophy. Any activity that neither earned money nor added to his capacity for absorbing knowledge was strictly eschewed. He felt sorry for fellow students who wasted precious hours on frivolity. He soon left his contemporaries behind. He entered college at the age of sixteen, got his bachelor's degree at nineteen (he attended summer school every year) and his master's the following year.

Even his years of military service were not entirely lost,

When he was drafted, shortly after the Korean War, he resolved to approach the experience constructively. He was commissioned as an education and information officer in the Engineers and sent to a base near Frankfurt, Germany, to organize its library, its motion-picture theater, and its university extension-course lecture series. While other junior officers spent every off-duty hour in orgiastic self-indulgence in the bars, nightclubs and brothels of nearby towns, Louis Porter saved his money and undertook an ambitious program of self-instruction in German, especially scientific German, which enabled him to read many classic psychiatric works in their original form, adding immeasurably to his fund of academic jargon, investing his professional writing with an elevated, turgid prose style and a rarefied air of dispassionate, omniscient grandeur, and enriching his understanding of the use of the footnote.

Like many other intellectuals, he was an ectomorph, underweight, wiry, quivering with nervous energy, burning up nourishment as fast as he took it in, without any noticeable accretion of extra flesh. Unlike many other intellectuals, he tried to improve his physique, with vitamin pills and daily exercise in the base gymnasium and with regularly scheduled walks to places of architectural, historic and botanic significance. After his daily morning exercises in his small, monastic cell in the bachelor officers' quarters, push-ups, sit-ups and deep-knee-bends in time to popular music on the radio, he examined himself in the mirror with scientific objectivity, and believed, not without real justification, that he detected small indications of physical development. He was one of those hairy, pale, gaunt, cadaverous, durable men that begin to go bald in their twenties, look middle-aged at thirty, and then never change until extreme old age. Porter kept his thinning black hair neatly trimmed; shaved and talcumed his thin, blue chin twice a day; had his shirts starched, his uniforms pressed and his shoes polished with obsessional frequency; and with the aid of *Playboy* magazine and a jar of lubricant petroleum jelly, which were secreted in the drawer of his bedside table, he masturbated once every morning before he got out of bed, and once every evening upon retiring. He did so without the fleeting illusory joy of romantic fantasy and without any morbid sense of guilt or despair.

24

He masturbated with unemotional briskness, with efficiency and for the sake of efficiency, in the cause of physical and mental hygiene, thus freeing himself, he felt confident, from time- and money-wasting sexual distractions during the working day.

When his two years of military service came to an end, while his fellows reluctantly faced the difficulties of re-adjustment to the rigors of Stateside civilian life, Porter returned to his academic career with savings of $5,200, an additional language, and a reinforced certainty that he had nothing to fear from competition.

He was confident but not complacent. He was aware that he still required a great idea, a hypothesis, a research project worthy of his ambition and his powers of application.

When Beatrice Schumann telephoned him after all these years and offered him the post of assistant research director of the forthcoming Digby Institute, he recognized the authentic voice of fate. After hearing her persuasive presentation of the proposed goals and ways and means of the Institute, he asked her a few succinct, practical questions about his own responsibilities, opportunities and rewards, and her answers were, to put it mildly, encouraging.

"There's just one thing I'm not happy about though, Dr. Schumann," he said.

"What's that?" she asked solicitously. "It's essential that we work together in close harmony right from the start."

"It's a question of status," he said. "I don't feel quite comfortable about the title 'assistant'. Don't you think *associate* director would be more appropriate?"

"I see your point," she said magnanimously. "Of course we wouldn't want to seem to be imparting to the direction any sort of female bias. Agreed – *associate director*. That would be quite suitable. And please, Louis, do call me Bea. We have known each other for a long time, haven't we?"

As if he could ever forget that childhood incident! If he'd been of less stern stuff it might have blighted his whole life. It was not merely the sexual debacle, though that had been traumatic enough, God knows. But even as a girl Beatrice Schumann had shown a nasty aptitude for getting her own way, and from all he'd heard the years had merely whetted her ambitions and the techniques for satisfying them. It was a good thing he'd grown into the sort of man who knew how to handle such a woman.

"Don't be offended," he said, "but it's very important, in my opinion, especially in a project of this nature, to establish a working relationship that not only *is* professionally correct, but is *manifestly* correct. I think it would be better if we leaned over backward to indicate our professionalism. I'd better call you Dr. Schumann."

"All right, Louis," she said. "As you wish."

"And I'd appreciate it if you'd address me as Dr. Porter," he said. "That may be overcautious, but I think things'll work out better that way."

"Right, Dr. Porter," she said solemnly. "I look forward to a very productive association."

"Thank you, Dr. Schumann. And thank you for thinking of me."

"I often do," she said. They said goodbye, there was a click and his telephone was silent. Dr. Porter thoughtfully stroked his chin. That night he did not resort to the companionship of the month's pink, pneumatic center-fold Playmate. In the circumstances, on the threshold of academic distinction, such behavior might have seemed undignified.

"Dr. Louis Porter, Ph.D.," he said aloud in his empty room. "Associate Research Director of Digby Institute." And somehow he felt impelled to go one step farther: "Dr. Louis Porter," he intoned, "Director of Digby Institute." He liked the sound of it. He didn't see how he could miss.

FOUR

LOYALTY, greed and fear – at least greed and fear.
These, in their simplest terms, were the forces that Dr.
Schumann was counting on to preserve the security of the
Digby Institute. Thanks to Turner Symington and the
Buckeye Pharmaceutical Manufacturing Company, Inc.,
her budget was an ample and flexible one, and she was free
to deploy the Institute's resources at her own discretion.
She decided that necessary secrecy could be maintained
most surely if she kept the research team and laboratory
staff as small as possible, paid them exceptionally generously (with thirty-three and a third of their salaries with-
held to be paid only upon satisfactory fulfillment of the
requirements of their contracts), and warned them that anybody who discussed the nature of the organization and its
work program would be subject, on apprehension, to instant dismissal.

As Dr. Schumann realized, there is no more gossipy
social microcosm than the faculty of a coeducational college. Life on the campus is as concentratedly introverted
as life in the monastery of a contemplative order of monks,
but the academics are not conversationally held in check
by any sacred fraternal vows or charitable discipline. They
spy intimately upon one another and exchange their observations and deductions as avidly as savages swapping
their birthright for mirrors, beads, rotgut booze and gunpowder.

During their first conference, over small glasses of Tio
Pepe, in the pleasantly old-fashioned dimness of the Faculty Club lounge late one February afternoon, Dr. Schumann sketched out her dream of the Institute's potential
and warned Dr. Porter of the danger against which, above
all others, they must always be on guard.

"The program, the Institute itself, our whole mission
here would be placed in jeopardy if someone prematurely
disclosed what we are trying to achieve," she emphasized.

"No independent publication," he promised.

"Absolutely not," she agreed, glancing rather sharply at

27

him for even having thought of such a thing. "Everything must be planned. First we have to be sure we have gathered enough data to ensure that our pronouncements are scientifically beyond reproach. These days, fortunately, anything irreproachable scientifically is inviolate on every other level as well. And every pronouncement must come from the Institute as an institution; sexual research is not a matter for personalities."

"I couldn't agree more," Dr. Porter said. "Too many unqualified people have written about sex in the past. Sex is too important for amateurishness. We must be able to offer the public the final word, and they must be able to recognize it as such."

"And so there must be no scandal," Dr. Schumann said. "Not a breath of scandal. Not even a hint of it. There are certain laymen, even some other scientists, who would be only too glad to smear us if they got an idea of our intentions before they could be carried out and so vindicated. We couldn't really expect them to understand the essentially constructive humanitarianism of the Institute's program if they only got a distorted picture of our clinical investigations."

"They might get the wrong idea," he agreed, nodding sagely. "Even scholars are sometimes inclined to be ... petty when judging other people's projects. And with this kind of money involved –"

"Quite," Dr. Schumann said dismissively.

"Jealousy breeds cynicism," Dr. Porter said. "There are cynics everywhere." He sighed and took a righteous sip of sherry.

"But they can be confounded," Dr. Schumann said. "I foresee a day in the not-so-distant future when married couples of all ages will thank Schumann and Porter for hitherto only dreamed-of technological know-how on the marital couch. There's no reason to doubt we could enable married couples to attain orgasmic gratification on virtually every occasion of mutual arousal. I know it sounds like pie in the sky, but with the right erogenous-zone analysis and stimulus-pattern profiling, there isn't a couple in the world – within reasonable relative dimensional limits, of course, in good health and adequately fed – that couldn't have their love play programed to hit the target every time. Between you and me, I'd even say that the time might not be too far off when we could help the average couple to become habitually multi orgasmic."

There was a moment of silence.

"Dr. Schumann," Dr. Porter said humbly. "I'm very proud to be working with you. I mean that."

"Let's shoot for the stars!" Dr. Schumann urged.

"Sure," he said. "The stars!" He raised his tiny goblet and sipped to it. "They laughed at Galileo, but he showed them."

"You have very good fact retention," Dr. Schumann said. She offered him a second sherry, but he held up his hand and smiled a firm no. He explained that he wasn't a drinking man, and they adjourned until the following day.

The next morning, having recovered from the strangely debilitating exhilaration of their first encounter since childhood, Dr. Schumann and Dr. Porter met in the suite of offices and laboratories that had been set aside for them in the Zoology Building, a white concrete two-story rectangular structure decorated with frosted glass and chromium trim in the streamlined style of 1938 Federal. The Institute was to have almost half the ground floor, which could be cut off from the rest of the building, and to which access could then be gained only through its own doorway.

Dr. Schumann showed her younger colleague around the premises.

"It's not magnificent," she said modestly. "But it should be quite adequate for temporary use. Mr. Symington expects the plans for our own building any day now. Construction is scheduled to begin this semester and should be finished by the end of the summer. In fact, the architect, a Mr. Doughty, is due to arrive before the end of the month from Washington, D.C. He'll be staying at the Digby Lodge until he finds an apartment. We'll arrange a dinner for him. Mr. Symington says he seems a very bright young man. I'm sure it'll be quite a building. Anyway, let's get things organized here and now. This will be my office." She led him through a light, airy room with cork flooring and blue fluorescent-light fixtures suspended from the ceiling.

"Mmm!" he said,

"And here's yours," she said. "Through here." She opened a connecting door that led into a considerably smaller room without windows. "It'll be very convenient," she said. "And don't worry; it's all going to be redecorated. We can pick out the colors and furniture after lunch. I said I thought a soft, warm pastel beige would probably be right for the observation lab, but I'd consult you about that. Psychologically speaking, what do you think of beige? I think it should be reassuring, even encouraging, but not unduly overstimulating. What do you think?"

Engaging his interest and appealing to his professional vanity in this way, Dr. Schumann eased him quickly in and out of his future office. They walked along a short hall and into a small auditorium with steeply tiered rows of wooden chairs.

"This was one of the zoology lecture halls," she said. "We're having it converted into a motion-picture projection room. Much of our work will be concerned with films."

"Won't that mean a technician?" Dr. Porter asked warily.

"It's all right, I've got just the man for the job," she said. "He's had a great deal of experience making training films for the Physical Education Department. Everything from huge spectacles like football games down to the more artistic and intimate studies, like gymnastic and folk dancing by classes or individual coeds. He's really surprisingly good, Louis, and we're fortunate to have found him."

"But all you said about security," Dr. Porter said. "Don't you think a man of that sort . . .?"

"Don't worry about that side of it," Dr. Schumann said cheerfully. "I checked. His wife has some kind of nervous complaint. Paralyzed from the waist down. They've spent a fortune on surgeons. There's a ninety-per-cent mortgage on his house. The college holds the mortgage. He's loyal to the core. Ah, and here's the main lab. This is where history will be made. It needs quite a few minor structural alterations and refinements, but I think if you use your imagination you'll see that it can be easily adapted to our special needs."

The laboratory, a commodious room with work counters, sinks, cupboards and shelves running the entire length of three walls, still smelled sharply of formaldehyde. Dr. Porter noticed with squeamish distaste, and Dr. Schumann noticed with nostalgia, a grayish-green frog, spread-eagled, cut open, eviscerated, flayed, and pinned open on a dissection board.

Pale miniature monsters floated inanimate in alcohol in specimen jars on the shelves. At one end of the room, a human skeleton dangled beside a full-scale chart of a man stripped down to his muscles.

"You can imagine how popular we are with the Zoology Department," Dr. Schumann said. "They have to get all this stuff out by the end of the week."

"This smell!" Dr. Porter said with a wry grimace.

Dr. Schumann beamed. "I'm surprised you never went through with your childhood plan to become a doctor," she said.

"I never planned to," he said. "That was your idea." His voice had assumed the slightly whining quality that she remembered from nearly a quarter of a century ago, and she smiled reminiscently.

"Anatomy is the basic science," she said. "The human body is the center of our universe. However hard we may try, we cannot objectify that fact away. Here we are, inside our solitary physical selves looking out. Sometimes I think we scientists try too hard to forget the natural measures of things, the human pulse rate, the fingers and toes, the height of the average man, the range of the normal eye. Everything else should be considered in those fundamental units."

"I thought the great thing about science was supposed to be that it enables man to go beyond his own small physical limitations," Dr. Porter said. "I thought you'd be one of the people who say, What's the good of rockets to the moon and electronic computers if we're going to sit on the ground counting on our fingers and toes?"

"You'll get to know me better during the months ahead," she said. "I won't be dogmatic. Let's go into this project broadmindedly. Let's not argue, Louis."

"O.K.," he said. He smiled boyishly. The innocence and vulnerability of the smile made her feel strangely secure.

"The guided tour's almost over," Dr. Schumann said brightly. "Let me show you where we're putting the auxili-

31

ary rooms – the interview rooms, the records room, the disrobing rooms, the showers and toilets, the personnel orientation chamber. You see, there'll be plenty of room where the pathology lab used to be. There won't even be much need for additional plumbing. You're looking pale. Let's go back to my office and have some Nescafé and we'll look through some of the student files. We need a completely reliable, intelligent, cooperative undergraduate woman lab assistant. Once the project gets rolling there'll be a lot of repetitive chores that we'll want to delegate to someone else."

FIVE

RICHARD W. DOUGHTY, JR., was a perfectly pleasant amiable young American male. His physical coordination was good; his reflexes were quick. He was moderately interested in almost everything, enthusiastic about many things, concerned about a few, worried about none.

His father was a civil engineer, a small builder who had become a big builder and had then gone into highway construction. Richard junior was brought up just below the Mason-Dixon Line, in Maryland, first in Baltimore and later, as the family prospered, in a series of larger and larger houses, farther and farther from the center of the city. Having been born during the Second World War and raised during an era of full employment and rising production, he had an economically carefree childhood. As a high-school senior he helped to circulate petitions for the United Nations Association, Americans for Democratic Action, and even the Civil Liberties Union. His father – quite rightly, as it turned out – let him go ahead. The phase did not last long. Richard junior settled down to a mellow orthodoxy by the time he was a freshman at the University of Maryland. There he easily breezed through all the required courses with plenty of energy left over to make his mark, just short of the front rank, as an athlete. And as sport had distracted him from scholarship, so the innocently rowdy social life of his fraternity house distracted him from sport. He discovered girls and he proved surprisingly adept at having his way with them; indeed, he had never encountered one that he couldn't wheedle into the feathers so long as he was truly interested and put his mind to it. He was a useful all-rounder, a man who cheerfully pulled his weight, a good companion. His father was very pleased with him.

There was a narrow escape in Vietnam. After gradua-tion, he enlisted in the Army, and was sent to Saigon in the early days of the big build-up. Because of his engineering degree, he was assigned, as a second lieutenant, to a con-struction battalion engaged in bulldozing new roads and building bridges around the capital. Lieutenant Doughty's military career ended abruptly during a counterattack against one of the routine VC ambushes of his Caterpillar tractors. Splashing across rice paddies, he stumbled into one of the enemy's primitive but effective booby traps: a sharp bamboo stake impaled his left foot. As he was told afterward, only prompt first aid and removal by helicopter to a field hospital purified the wound in time to save his foot from amputation. He arrived home a few weeks later, still in uniform, hobbling with a crutch, and enjoyed a gala reception. He applied to return to duty in spite of his mother's argument that he had already done his fair share; however, the Army discharged him, and probably would have done so even if his father had not telephoned some people he knew on Capitol Hill. Now, many months later, Richard limped slightly, almost imperceptibly and only when he was overtired.

He experienced one of his few difficulties with his father when the time came to decide about a job. Taking for granted his ability to earn a sufficiency of money, Richard was not interested in money itself. Although he had never questioned the family assumption that he would become a builder of some sort, he resisted his father's proposal that he should join his father's company, even though he could have become a vice-president after a token period of apprenticeship. Richard hurt his father's feelings by saying that he would rather design one good building than pour a billion cubic yards of concrete for highways. "You could do both," his father pointed out. "Making money's nothing to be ashamed of."

Richard countered – a trifle sulkily, his father thought – by attending several meetings of a local society for urban renewal and becoming interested in plans for low-cost, low-rent housing.

"Some people would turn the Taj Mahal into a slum," his father said. Richard replied that he thought the Taj Mahal was one of the world's really great bad buildings. The quality of the debate deteriorated.

As often before, Richard's mother intervened, and because he was devoted to her, he accepted her arbitration. The compromise was vague enough to satisfy both Richard and his father. Richard was to go out on his own as an architect, completely independently, to gain experience. In five years he would become a consultant to his father's company in order to become able eventually to administer it, at least part of the time, when his father wanted to retire. Richard's father was in excellent health and Richard could not conceive of his ever retiring. Richard's father was surprisingly meekly acquiescent to the scheme. Of course there was no way for Richard to know that his father, through Turner Symington's help, had got him the commission to collaborate with Ben Wicksteed, one of Washington's most distinguished, successful architectural hacks, in making the drawings for the projected Symington Building in Digby, Ohio. Richard thought he got the commission on his own merit, by chance, after having been introduced to Wicksteed at a cocktail party in Georgetown. Such things sometimes really do happen, though not very often. That carefully engineered accidental encounter took place the week before Richard's twenty-fourth birthday.

During the next couple of months Richard did more work than ever before in his life and on the whole very much enjoyed it. Wicksteed, having initially briefed him, gave Richard a remarkably free hand, allowing him to do most of the creative work and all the routine practical planning that more or less automatically followed. Richard had not expected nearly so much responsibility on his first commission and rose to it with zeal. Some of his more ambitiously imaginative preliminary sketches were summarily rejected.

"We're not designing a tropical embassy," his senior colleague told him firmly but not unkindly. "Digby is a solid old school in Ohio. They want to build something that'll last. Take it easy on the sculpture, courts and water gardens. Look at this patio! Ask yourself, is this patio really necessary? The answer is obvious. And this glass wall! Very dramatic, but think of the maintenance costs. Your building would need half a dozen full-time window-cleaners. Try something more moderate. I know how you feel; I used to try to imitate Frank Lloyd Wright myself. But they're not about to spend five or six million dollars to satisfy your desire to fabricate eccentric doodles. A building this modern would be old-fashioned before completion...."

And so on.

Richard mentally squirmed during the lecture but grudgingly recognized that the old man might know what he was talking about, at least from a practical point of view. When Richard went away and produced some almost sarcastic roughs for a building that could have been a nineteenth-century shoe factory he was quite properly reprimanded.

"Functionalism doesn't have to be a prison," his mentor said. "This is supposed to be an applied-biology building. I don't know what that means any more than you do. Apparently, according to Symington, this one's something very secret. That first thing you did was about as secret as the Hollywood Bowl. This, as you undoubtedly intended, goes to the opposite extreme. Let us charitably give these biologists the benefit of the doubt and assume that they are human beings. They require shelter, but you can let in *some* light and air. Can you imagine working in a box like this?" Richard was suitably ashamed.

"Don't forget that you can afford to spread out a bit," Wicksteed added encouragingly. "The college owns plenty of land. This isn't supposed to be a Park Avenue office building. Give them something horizontal and they'll feel they're getting more for their money. Don't worry; you'll get it all right. I can see you have talent; all you need is patience and experience. Come and have lunch with me at the Cosmos."

Richard's third try was a success.

"I like it," Wicksteed said, after long, silent scrutiny. "Yes, this is what they want – and it's good. It's dignified and stable, and yet there's a youthful boldness about it. Perhaps when you do the finished projections, though, you'd better put in a few trees with luxuriant foliage and some of those elegantly elongated *Vogue* models on the entrance steps. *You* know. And of course a very long Cadillac in the driveway. Always helpful. Symington will go for this in a big way and no doubt suggest you run out there to have a look around. I heartily approve. Two weeks, possibly a month, take your time – within reason, of course. Do no harm to get things started, get to know our clients and all that. Digby College. Not a bad sort of place I hear. Coeducational, too. Girls, my boy. God bless them. Wish I were a bit younger. Might go in your place."

He got at it with gusto. As Wicksteed had predicted, Symington was rhapsodic. He wanted the marble foyer enlarged; but that was the only alteration. Richard was summoned and arrived in Digby by airline and taxi, eager to break ground.

There was a cordial enough welcome, two or three dinner parties to introduce him to "the Digby family"; he was shown the surveyor's report and taken to the recommended site; he entered into correspondence with the contractor; and now he was waiting.

March gave its usual false promise of an early spring. There were some bright, gusty days that melted the snow on the ground and dried the mud. Richard went for some drives in the surrounding countryside, but there were few signs of life. The farmers knew their land and its climate and remained indoors, drinking beer and watching television.

Richard went for walks across the campus and into the town. It consisted of little more than a Main Street and a Center Street, forming a nuclear crossroads, with stores rapidly dwindling away in all four directions, and a grid of smaller streets where the townspeople lived. There were half a dozen small churches, half a dozen gas stations, two hotels, two drugstores, a movie theater, an old pool hall and a new bowling alley, and a couple of supermarkets; a dozen restaurants, bars and grills, and bars without grills; a police station, a fire station, a school, a public library, a weekly newspaper office and job-printing shop; an American Legion Post and an Elks' Lodge, a post office, a Western Union office, a Hertz Rent-A-Car agency, a Coca-Cola bottling plant, and a funeral parlor. It was Smalltown, U.S.A. Confronted by the nationally familiar pop art of its posters and by the usual neon exhortations to go, stop, eat, drink, fill up, buy and enjoy, Richard felt an alien. The girls seemed to him corn-fed and strangely unappealing. His walks were lonely.

April was gentler right from the start. After the annually unexpected unseasonable final downpour of sleet, the weather became almost balmy. The black-and-white steel engraving of the frozen months became a light-blue-and-green aquatint. Buds began to swell and open in the soft,

37

moist, amorous air. Students took off their Arctic clothing, the hooded anoraks and ski pants and enormous rubber overshoes that had weighed them down since Thanksgiving.

As soon as he felt the leaden burden of the old season lifting, Richard resolved that he really must do something about getting an apartment of his own. The Digby Inn, a gloomy institution that smelled of radiators, dusty carpets and furniture polish, was inhabited principally by unmarried faculty members resigned to lazy discomfort, by students' visiting parents, and traveling salesmen. Richard was tired of dining alone, tired of reading, tired of watching television in his bedroom. His interest suddenly revived.

After breakfast one particularly bright and promising morning, he went out early, had a haircut, and walked over to the Administration building to remind them of his need for someplace to live. Their response was so hopeful that he walked across the awakening campus feeling glad to be alive and sure that something wonderfully exciting was going to happen to him. And so, of course, it did. Within half an hour he met Camilla. It was in the John Wesley Memorial Library of Digby College that he first encountered her. In danger of being late for her next class, at that moment she seemed outwardly careless and clumsy, rounding a tall, green-lacquered metal bookcase in the stacks, with a pile of books in her arms and her head down so that her chin pressed upon the top volume. The collision caught Richard by surprise. He was knocked off balance; he slipped on the highly polished linoleum and found himself on his hands and knees, lacking poise and serenity. The pile of books was scattered all over the place. The young woman stood in the middle of them and crossly wrung her hands.

"Gosh!" she said. "Look what you made me do! Now I'll be late for my ten o'clock!"

Richard made a great show of controlling his anger, performing the classic pantomime of the slow burn, as if thus silently to force her recognition that the mishap had been her fault and that she owed him an apology. The effectiveness of this attempt was impaired by the obvious inferiority of his posture, and she couldn't help laughing even as she frowned and tried to glare down at him.

"You look like a dog down there," she said. She laughed

so naturally and looked so lovely with the electric light of the aisle glowing in a golden nimbus around her yellow hair, that he realized his position was untenable, and not worth holding anyway, and he got to his feet.

"I'm sorry," she said, smiling, and then impatiently frowned again. "Look, please help! I'm going to be late!"

He crouched down with her and started collecting the books, but he wasn't in a hurry.

"Cut the class," he suggested.

The idea froze her motionless and she looked profoundly shocked.

"What did you say?" she asked.

"I said why don't you just not go? Let's go and get a cup of coffee. That's what I used to do if I was late."

"We're only allowed six cuts a semester," she said agitatedly, reaching for a loose-leaf notebook lying open, face down on the floor.

"How many cuts have you taken?" he asked.

"None," she said. "Hey, did you bump into me on purpose or something?"

"The vanity!" he said. "But, after all, now that the accident has happened, why not relax and enjoy it?"

"I think you're being very silly," she said. She was now completely in control of herself and her belongings. Politely she thanked him and started moving quietly, quickly, away.

"Just a minute," he said, following her and holding her arm above the elbow. "Please. Not so fast."

"Let me go," she said sternly. "At once." She wrenched her arm free.

"Take it easy," he said. "What's your name?"

A spinsterish male librarian raised his eyebrows in a silent rebuke and pointed to the sign on the wall requesting silence.

During the moment of distraction, she got away. Richard hurried after her.

"What's your *name*?" he asked again. The loud theatrical whisper got the librarian out from behind his desk in a veritable tizzy of outrage.

"I must ask you to observe the silence rule," he demanded. "People are trying to work."

"O.K., O.K.," Richard said, weary in defeat. He noticed

her push her way through the revolving doors in a determined rush.

Considering how annoying she was, he was quite surprised to find something stirring uneasily within his lower
abdomen. He recognized the symptom and smiled. Perhaps
he had been wrong; this was different.

SIX

"WOULD you want a daughter of yours to marry a man who ejaculates prematurely?" Dr. Schumann demanded.

"The question could hardly arise," Dr. Porter replied. They were sitting in Dr. Schumann's lavishly redecorated office, talking, as they talked so often, of the work that lay ahead.

"The question is hypothetical in your case," she conceded. "But think of all the millions of parents who should really consider the sexual qualifications, or disqualifications, of their offsprings' prospective marriage partners. Community of interests may be desirable, but sexual compatibility is a *sine qua non*. Even in your case," she added, "the question could become of immediate, real consequence, couldn't it?"

"Sure it could," he said. "Some day."

"Well, then. Don't you agree that even in this age of new enlightenment too many parents are inordinately concerned, even preoccupied to the exclusion of all other considerations, with outward appearances and with the social and economic suitability of their children's partners? Whereas it is generally recognized that the number one factor governing the duration of a marital liaison is sexual harmony or lack of it."

"Everyone knows that," he said.

"And yet even today the father-in-law-to-be is primarily interested in whether his daughter's fiancé is going to be able to provide for his girl the material security and comforts to which she has been accustomed."

"You wouldn't expect the father to ask the young man point-blank how he and the girl get along in bed?"

"I wouldn't expect it," she said. "No. But, of course, you are suggesting that today's questions must be posed in yesterday's interview situation. I don't think you're applying your scientific principles as you should."

"I think I'm with you," Dr. Porter assured her. "You

41

mean the young couple could be analyzed by a properly qualified consultant."

"Of course. Tested individually and together. I'm just thinking out loud, Dr. Porter, throwing out the ideas as they come to me, but I think that one of the most valuable contributions that our program can eventually make is to help eliminate the sexual risk in marriage. Regional clinics could be established in population centers all over. Young men and women, on presentation of certificates of parental authorization, could then get a thorough premarital physical checkup, a psychosexual interview and, under expert professional observation, a dual sexual performance rating. All the tests could be graded both quantitatively and qualitatively, numerically and critically, finally arriving at conclusions of the probable sexual viability of the proposed union. Recommendations to seek other, more suitable partners would undoubtedly save millions of impetuous young persons from finding themselves involved with incompatible mates. Billions of wasted sex hours!

"In borderline cases," Dr. Schumann went on, "or in cases in which for various reasons the couples were insistent on going ahead against the analysts' prognoses, and even in more promising cases, the chances of success could be improved by means of custom-tailored constructive sexual criticism and detailed personalized technical advice. After betrothal, but before the formal marriage ritual, couples could attend a series of practical seminars, sort of sexual workshop sessions, with chalk talks, slide lectures, panel discussions, group therapy, self-criticism, and just good, honest-to-God supervised practice. That would take the interrogation points out of the honeymoon.

"It seems to me that we have within our reach an opportunity to revolutionize sexual selection. There's hardly any limit to what we may be able to do. Individuals' sexual characteristics could be observed and recorded annually from puberty on. The characteristics could be symbolized and computerized. There could be a great national bank of personal sexual statistics, as readily available as financial credit ratings, within the reach of every telephone."

"Don't you think some people might object to having such intimate information made public?" Dr. Porter said uneasily.

Dr. Schumann casually waved the objection aside. "We have to consider and decide what would offer the most help to the greatest number of people," she said. "There would have to be certain controls. There are many details that have to be worked out. The A.M.A. naturally would be the ultimate authority. At the moment, though, I'm only talking off the top of my head, in ideal terms."

"It certainly would be wonderful to be the ones to have initiated the system," Dr. Porter said.

"Perhaps one of my troubles has always been that I'm too much of an idealist," she went on, chiding herself with a rueful chuckle. "I'm counting on you to keep your feet on the ground. You've taken some courses in business administration, haven't you?"

"Just a couple of introductory courses," Dr. Porter replied modestly. "Electives. They've given me one or two useful insights into corporate behavior." He frowned slightly. "How did you know?"

"Digby insisted on my obtaining a transcript of your academic credits," she said. "They had to be sure of your fitness for work in such a sensitive area. You would expect them to be careful."

"Of course, Dr. Schumann," he said.

"But I was just wondering, between you and me. . . ."

"Yes?" he said.

"With the mass of material that we are about to gather, once we get started . . . It seems to me that we shall be in a very strong position. That is to say . . . Let me explain. I was thinking the other night about the difficulty that many parents experience when their children ask them questions about sex. My own mother, for example, found it impossible to answer my questions." Her face clouded for a moment, and cleared. "My father did his best. But it wasn't easy."

Dr. Schumann sat back in her padded-leather Eames contour chair and stared out the window with thoughtful, narrowed eyes. The rain had stopped and a bough close to the window was gleaming with water.

"Hey, Beatrice! Beatrice, honey. Open up! It's me." The hoarse, conspiratorial whisper was her father's. She turned and raised herself on one elbow. "Come on, Bea, sweetie, I

43

want to talk to you." She wondered whether to let him in. He didn't sound very drunk. She got off the bed. She was barefoot and silent. She stood close to the door and listened. She thought she could hear him breathing. He must be pressed right up against the door.

"Pops?" she whispered. "What d'you want?" She loved him, but she didn't really want to have anything to do with him right then. She knew why he was there.

"Just want to have a visit with my little honey-Bea," he loudly whispered back. He was quite drunk, she realized. He wasn't slurring his words badly, but there was a special kind of desperation in his voice. She could imagine the redness of his eyes. He was a tall, strong, handsome, absolutely hopeless man. An electrician. He had had a small shop of his own and had sold electric stoves and refrigerators and so on, but a few years ago he had lost it and gone to work for another shop.

"All right," she whispered. "Wait a minute." She moved to one side and the door opened.

"Shhh!" he warned her, and although Beatrice could see him only as a dark shape in the obscurity of the doorway, she knew that he was holding an unsteady forefinger up against his red mustache in an exaggerated pantomime of caution.

"Where's Ma?" Beatrice whispered.

"Gone to her room," he said, forgetting to whisper.

"Shhh!" Beatrice warned him.

"Gone to her room," he whispered. "Let's shut the door. I want to talk to you. What about this Porter kid? Has he been messing with you?"

"Oh, Pops! Honestly! He's only nine and a half years old, for heaven's sakes!"

"But what was going on in there? The way your mother told it, it sounded pretty bad."

"All it was, was he went into my dolls' house."

"Yeah?" Beatrice's father said. "I'm listening, honey." He took one of her hands in one of his and softly stroked it with the other.

"I was in the yard clearing up a few things, you know all that junk Ma throws out there? She's always yelling for me to help."

44

"I know you help, Bea." He gave her hand another little squeeze of approval.

"Well, I was just trying to straighten things up when I heard that little creep – Louis – in my dolls' house. I've told him a million times to stay away from it."

Beatrice's father gently scratched the palm of her hand.

"Well, what do you think he was doing?" she asked.

"What was he doing?"

"He had all his clothes off, and he was *peeing*, right on the floor where I play with my dolls."

"Beatrice!" His voice sounded deeply shocked and distressed. He released her hand and waited for her to go on.

"That was all there was to it, really. I bawled him out and told him how disgusting he was, and of course he burst out crying. I was about to tell him to get properly dressed and get out of there, when Ma came stomping in, yelling and screaming and beating me up and everything. She didn't give me a chance to explain."

There was no sound but his breathing, and Beatrice thought for a moment that he had gone to sleep. He hadn't.

"My little Bea," he whispered thickly. "You've had a rough time, haven't you? Come here and let me hold you, sweetie. She doesn't understand."

Beatrice snuggled with her cheek against his work shirt. His chest was warm through the shirt, and she could feel rather than hear the strong, slow thud of his heart.

She came back to the present with a start.

"Schools have assumed the burden of informing the nation's young in this most vital of subjects. All public-school systems, except the most backward or reactionary ones, have courses in sexual hygiene, sometimes together with general biology. The teachers do their best, and I'm not criticizing them. But their best is hardly ever good enough. Most children are unsatisfied by the cross-sectional anatomical diagrams that illustrate their sexual textbooks. They find it difficult to relate the experienced reality of their own genitalia with the forbidding drawings in black and white. Why not use photographs? Why not color photographs? And then I asked myself: Why not pictures that move?"

"But think of the outcry!" Dr. Porter exclaimed. "Think
45

of the angry complaints at the meetings of parent-teacher associations!" He shook his head regretfully and clicked his tongue.

"I wondered about that," Dr. Schumann admitted. "But it's so illogical. No modern parent would dare go to a school and say he or she wanted to withhold sexual information from children. That would be ridiculous. Obviously, the more they know the better. No sane person would deny that. All right, then what reasonable objection can be made to using all the tools that facilitate instruction? Any teacher will tell you that visual aids are the most effective of all. Any teacher will tell you that motion pictures make a far bigger impact than illustrations in a book.

"At first," Dr. Schumann continued, "I considered the possible advantages of animated drawings in color. Like the films that Disney made during World War Two to help instruct men in the armed forces. Disney-style sexual-instruction movies would disarm critics who might have aesthetic objections to movies depicting actual persons. But I had to face up to the fact that teen-agers tend to identify cartoons with comedy and violence, or violent comedy. Cats and mice beating each other up, and so forth. We wouldn't want any of that to rub off on sexual hygiene, would we? So at last, by inexorable logic, I concluded that the only thing would be to show the kids movies in color, with sound, showing the male and female genitalia and all the ways they can be combined for the sake of gratification and, when wished for, reproduction. And to make the lessons as acceptable and creditable as possible, I decided that the male and female roles should be performed by members of the teen-agers' peer group, that is to say by teen-agers like themselves, in the familiar settings of their daily lives."

"Motels and drive-in movies?" Dr. Porter said.

"Why not?" Dr. Schumann said. "Education is supposed to communicate. Let's communicate! I'm interested in *results.*"

Dr. Porter fingered his jaw reflectively.

"Y-e-s. . ." he said. "I suppose you're right."

"Of course I'm right. That's elementary. Anyway, that wasn't the end of my train of thought. I'll leave the teen-agers to their teachers. I was wondering whether we shouldn't consider the possibility of sexual-instruction films for adults. Made properly, under medical auspices, and licensed with the seal of approval of some appropriate body – the Digby Institute, for example – educational movies of this nature could be a boon to the unaware, the timid and the stale. I can imagine tastefully filmed scenes of knowledgeable sexual practitioners, enacting the lessons of the classic manuals, being shown in the privacy of the home and doing much more good than all the books that have ever been published."

"But we will be publishing our findings, won't we?" Dr. Porter asked.

"Most certainly, yes. Mainly, of course, for members of the medical profession, though we might perhaps run off a few hundred thousand extra copies for interested laymen. I'm talking about the logical progress beyond publication. Sexual-education films on pay TV. Sexual-education films at neighborhood sex clinics. A sexual-education film-of-the-month club. There's no such thing as a couple that knows all there is to know. And even when they believe they do – films on sexual geriatrics! I haven't been sitting by idly while the decorators have been in."

"The long-range potential is terrific," Dr. Porter said admiringly. "But we must be careful not to risk being accused of having any sort of commercial interests in what we're doing."

"That had me worried, too," Dr. Schumann said. "I've been consulting Mr. Symington about that. He said he'd get his lawyers and accountants to work something out. A foundation of some sort. A trust fund. I'm no good at money matters, but I'm sure they'll devise a formula that will protect our professional status. Anyway, there's nothing unethical about receiving fees and royalties from the Buckeye people, is there? There's nothing about that kind of thing in the Hippocratic oath. We'd be benefiting humanity, wouldn't we?"

"It's very exciting," Dr. Porter said, "and I don't want to throw cold water on anything. But I've been thinking a lot myself recently. Not so much about the final applications – though, of course, they are what will really count in the end. I'm thinking about what we should do immediately. I mean, to put it in words of one syllable, just how do we start?"

"I'm glad you reminded me," Dr. Schumann said. "That's what I call being practical. I meant to bring it up myself. We've been so concerned with getting the work-rooms and the electrical equipment set up that we haven't got our immediate work program squared away, have we?"

"No, we haven't," Dr. Porter said. "That's what I was wondering about. Here it is April already and I don't feel that I've really done anything."

"Well, it isn't all that complicated," Dr. Schumann assured him. "But it will be hard work, and I'm going to have to lean heavily on you to help do it. What we have to do now is recruit the pilot group of our study population."

"Get some people for the laboratory ... activities?"

"Exactly," Dr. Schumann said. "We need some people who know their subject, whose cooperation can be requested as and when we need it, and who are willing, for the right remuneration, to undertake even the most strenuous, awkward and bizarre sexual trials while we work out some of the fundamentals of our program. What is normal, for instance? We want people who will let us interview them exhaustively about the most intimate details of their sexual habits, and then demonstrate them for medical observation and recording. We need a baseline for our graphs. There are technical problems – lighting, cameras, tape recorders, et cetera. For this preliminary survey, we must employ people who are not easily disturbed."

"Whom do you think we ought to approach?"

"Well, that's your first assignment, Dr. Porter," she said, addressing him now with all the hearty fervor of an Air Force general wishing a bomber crew good luck on an essential, hazardous mission. "Dr. Porter, I'm counting on you to go out and round up thirty prostitutes."

SEVEN

How does one go about recruiting thirty prostitutes? Dr. Porter had never engaged the services of even one, but in conversation with Dr. Schumann he evaded confirming or denying the fact. Although he disapproved of prostitution in principle, he was reluctant, like many other men, to seem priggish about the subject. Prostitutes belonged to the world of manly good fellowship, Legion conventions, stag smokers, fraternal singsongs and barroom dirty jokes. Laughing about prostitutes proclaimed that you were one of the boys, an initiate, a regular guy, a sport. Dr. Porter scorned the tradition, but he kept his scorn secret; he did not wish to flaunt his nonconformity.

The tradition was an old one, a heritage from the Old Frontier. You worked hard, fought hard, gambled hard, drank hard, and finished up late at night in one of the cribs above the dance hall. The prostitutes themselves were all right at heart, believers in the code of the Old West, rough but fair; they demanded no more than their due; they expected no less, and they held their own when it came to swapping badinage with cheating bullies. The relationships between the men and women in the old cattle and mining towns were simpler than the relationships between men and women today. Then as now commerce was predominant, but it seemed somehow less hypocritical then, more straightforward and friendlier. Prostitutes still maintained the old, simple values, still offered good, solid vice, C.O.D., even if the cattlemen and miners had gone soft, sold out, and got wives and houses in the suburbs. Dr. Porter recalled Hemingway, O'Hara and Mailer, and felt that he was about to go in search of a myth. He hoped the search wouldn't be dangerous.

He rapidly packed a suitcase, drew two hundred dollars in traveler's checks in small denominations from the bank, caught a bus north, registered at a large, medium-price commercial hotel in a city on the shore of Lake Erie, went to his room and picked up the telephone.

"Good evening! At your service!" a woman said.

"Good evening," he said. "This is Dr. Porter in twelve-sixteen. May I speak with the bell captain?"

"The bell captain's line is busy at the present time," she said brightly. "May *I* help you?"

"Oh, no!" he said with more emphasis than he had really intended. "I mean, no thanks. I'll call again. No – could you give me valet service, please?"

"Surely, Dr. Porter," she sang, and he wished she didn't know his name. He should have registered under a false name, he thought. He should have left his credit cards at Digby, brought cash, and done the whole thing pseudonymously. It was too late to think of that now. He could imagine the operator speaking to the operator next to her: "That was Dr. Porter. Educated voice. But he wanted the bell captain. Couldn't tell me what he wanted. You know what *that* means. A ball. Let's check with the front desk, get his address. Should be good for a laugh. And – who knows? – maybe he's worth something. . . ." Dr. Porter was sweating profusely by the time the valet answered. He said he'd come up right away to pick up Dr. Porter's suits for pressing.

Dr. Porter sat on the edge of one of the two single beds, crossing and uncrossing and recrossing his legs, leafing through "What's On." The advertisements for nightclubs looked formidably respectable, but there was one Polynesian restaurant evidently staffed by Gauguin maidens wearing nothing but orchids. Artistic license, he presumed. He tried the Yellow Pages. But he really couldn't just telephone a physician, he decided, call from out of the blue, explain that he was doing some scientific research – sorry, he couldn't say specifically what it was – and he needed thirty prostitutes. He would probably score low marks for credibility.

The buzzer sounded at the door.

The valet was a stunted, thin man, not young, with a red-veined, fleshy Punchinello nose, a soft beak with large nostrils, which he tilted back as though testing the air of the room, assessing the situation before speaking. His oily, sparse black hair was parted in the middle and brushed back. There was oil on the upper tips of his large, red ears. The red of his complexion clashed with the maroon of his uniform. He smiled a lot, but his smile was crafty, his

50

teeth unconvincingly blue-white, and Dr. Porter felt disinclined to confide in him.

"Press only?" the valet said, taking the two suits that were handed to him. "When do you want them?"

"I'd like one back right away," Dr. Porter said, speaking in the firm, almost harsh manner that often characterizes men who are shy.

"You mean this evening?"

"If you can. I want to change before dinner. I have to go out."

"Impossible," the valet said. He tilted his head again, shrewdly. "I'm off at five. I'd have to stay late." Dr. Porter frowned anxiously. "I'd like to help you out though," the valet said. "Maybe if . . ." The suggestion was plain enough. His watery little eyes approvingly followed Dr. Porter's hand to his billfold. "Thanks a lot, mister," the valet said, drawing back his lips in a smile that disclosed horribly pretty pink gums. Dr. Porter disliked the thought of the man's hands on his clothes. The valet made his agreement to work a few minutes overtime seem like an illicit pact between them. Dr. Porter was quite certain that the valet was the sort of person who could direct him to any number of prostitutes. But the request stuck in his throat, and the door closed leaving him alone again and undecisive.

What would he say to a prostitute if he managed to find one? The thought of a prostitute looking curiously into his eyes made the palms of his hands damp. He wondered how any man could actually accompany a strange woman into an unknown building, into an alien bedroom. How could he begin the procedure of sexual foreplay, opening gambits as extraordinary, when one came to think of them, as the courtship ritual of baboons or fireflies? Were the prostitute and her customer utterly matter-of-fact, like a surgical team preparing to operate? Or was there usually some sort of social pretense, an attempt to make the encounter seem something like the communion of a man and woman who knew, understood, admired, loved each other? Dr. Porter prickled with curiosity, yet his imagination flinched from the pictures it created. Identifying with the blank-faced man in his mind, he thought of himself undressing while a woman watched him and thought contemptuous thoughts about what he revealed to her. He shut his eyes tight in a vain attempt to obliterate the terrible moment. How he hated Beatrice! Why didn't he stand up to her? Why had he agreed to collaborate with her? He could imagine that eternally jeering, immortal, twelve-year-old girl laughing at him, Dr. Porter, scaredy-cat Dr. Porter, afraid to venture into the streets of the city. He resented the fact that Beatrice Schumann, Dr. Schumann, by remote control was again forcing him to expose himself. He was sweating with shame. Why then, he wondered, did he also feel the warm pulsation of growing excitement?

His hands were trembling slightly as he unpacked his suitcase. He unzipped his leather toilet case and removed a jar of petroleum jelly. He undressed and went into the bathroom. A little later, when the valet returned with the suit, Dr. Porter was calmly composed. He whistled while he dressed and while he descended in the automatic elevator to the lobby.

The lobby was crowded with middle-aged men wearing identification cards on their lapels. They were delegates to a national sales conference. The lectures and discussions were over for the day, and the delegates, having just left the ballroom-auditorium, were chatting as animatedly as boys coming away from school.

Dr. Porter passed through the throng and sought the cocktail bar. He felt that a drink would embolden him sufficiently to press his inquiries. It was absurd to hesitate any further. After all, he had the academic credentials of one of the state's most respected institutions of higher learning, the title of doctor of philosophy, the prestige of associate director of the Digby Institute, the financial power of the great Buckeye drug empire. Why should he not command attention, respect and cooperation? He tightened the knot of his white-polka-dot navy-blue silk tie, adjusted the cuffs of his white shirt so that a decent length of them was displayed at the end of each sleeve, smoothed with his hand his slightly errant short forelock, and walked into a dimly lighted oak-paneled room called The Tudor Pubbe.

The bar was already filling up, mostly with conference delegates, and Dr. Porter had to wait to be served. There was a pleasant clamor of conversation and laughter, and he felt for a moment the familiar melancholy of being an outsider. Other men seemed so naturally outgoing, so cheerfully confident that their small talk would be heard gladly, as they accepted the jovially proffered trivialities of others.

"There's a priest, a rabbi, and a Presbyterian minister. Huh? O.K., he's an Episcopalian. Anyway, they're the only survivors of World War Three, in a deep shelter in the Rockies, along with this fabulous blonde. She's really stacked. Well –"

"The Olds may have better pick-up, but for looks –"

"The first week is tough, but I lost thirteen pounds already. I had to have my pants taken in."

"Believe me, once you've had a Japanese girl –"

"You're not a Catholic, are you? Well, did you hear the one –"

"And I say zero to sixty in nine seconds. Want to bet?"

"He was screwing the ass off her."

"That's a great necktie, Chuck. I really like it. Do you mind if I ask what you gave for it?"

"My wife said –"

"The trouble with bourbon sours –"

"I still say the Buick –"

"Hey, J.B., where's a fella get laid in this town?"

"Put up or shut up! Here's twenty bucks that says –"

"So I told my wife –"

"What time's the first session in the morning?"

"Hell, have another! Are you a man or a mouse?"

"Have you driven the new Corvette?"

"She said –"

"I –"

Dr. Porter noticed, with the usual pang of envy, that even their aggressiveness was friendly.

"What's it going to be?" the bartender asked him. The bartender was one of Them, extroverted, affably boorish, direct.

"Oh," Dr. Porter said, rather flustered. "A Manhattan, please." The bartender looked unimpressed, but tolerant. "A double. With dry vermouth." The bartender began automatically to mix the drink, very fast and deftly. "On the rocks," Dr. Porter said. "Please."

He stood close to the bar, moving first one way and then

the other in deference to the hearty, rubescent men who kept pushing their way to the counter to order drinks, but he never wholly surrendered his position, for he felt that he was close to the heart of masculine life, that there he might overhear some fragment of conversation that would give him a clue to the best way to proceed on his quest.

But, after twenty minutes or so of prudent sipping and eavesdropping, he noticed the crescendo of noisy bonhomie reach a sudden climax, and then there was a lot of defeatist talk about going up to get ready for the banquet. The group began to break up almost as quickly as it had formed; it began to seem that the cross-talk at the bar had been an end in itself. When Dr. Porter raised a forefinger to attract the bartender's attention he succeeded almost immediately.

"Bartender," Dr. Porter began, setting down his glass as a talisman.

"Yes, sir? Dry Manhattan on the rocks?"

"I wanted to ask you –" Dr. Porter began again. "Yes, all right, I'll have the same again."

Within a few seconds, it seemed, the large old-fashioned glass, a glass tub full of ice cubes and dark amber fluid, was placed in front of him. The bartender, no longer hard-pushed, twisted the strip of lemon peel with a flamboyant little flourish, and performed a ceremony of solicitude, giving Dr. Porter a fresh paper napkin and moving pewter dishes of salted peanuts and stuffed olives within convenient reach. He was encouraged by this show of willingness to serve. When the bartender returned from the cash register, Dr. Porter, after the most casual of sips, casually spoke.

"I imagine you know the city well, don't you, bartender?"

"Been here nearly three years," the bartender said with due pride.

"I was wondering ..." Dr. Porter said. He took a judicious sip. "This is a very good Manhattan," he said.

"Nothing but the best!" the bartender said cheerfully. "You're not with the conference?"

"No," Dr. Porter said.

"Quite a bunch of guys," the bartender said, shaking his head with a wry smile of admiring disapproval. "They

54

come here twice a year." He sociably wiped the bar where not a drop of drink marred its polish. "Three days, four nights. Wow! What a time they have! Real spenders! You have to hand it to them though. They put in three long days of work. The last night is the payoff. You earn a lot, you spend a lot, right?"

"They seemed to be having quite a time," Dr. Porter said.

"That's nothing," the bartender said. "With them, four, five martinis before dinner, that's only the warm-up. They leave the little woman at home, minding the kids. It's only twice a year. You know what I mean?"

"That's what I wanted you to tell me about," Dr. Porter said, smiling a bit stiffly. He took a large sip, almost a gulp. "What does someone do here — where do they go? Afterward."

The bartender looked briefly to his left and his right. The bar was now almost deserted. He leaned closer to Dr. Porter.

"This is a hell of a town, if you know your way around," the bartender said. He nodded and winked. "You can get anything here, if you don't mind spending. Don't let the look of it fool you." He went away for a couple of minutes to give someone a drink. When he came back, Dr. Porter self-consciously handed him a folded five-dollar bill.

"Have a drink," Dr. Porter said.

"Thanks," the bartender said, tucking the money into the gold-braid-encrusted breast pocket of his maroon mess-jacket. "I'll have one later. What was it you were looking for? A real snappy nightclub? A class joint?"

"Well . . ." Dr. Porter said doubtfully. He drank.

"This town's come up a lot since I came here," the bartender said. "Some say you have to go to Chicago or New York. Don't you believe it. There's a lot of money in this place, a lot of action."

"I'm sure there is," Dr. Porter said. "I don't doubt it for a minute. But I'm looking for something . . . a little special."

The bartender looked attentive.

"Let me explain," Dr. Porter said.

"I'll be right with you," the bartender said. He went and served one of the few other remaining customers and hurried back. Dr. Porter finished his drink as though it had been medicine and gestured with his empty glass for replenishment.

"Another double?" the bartender said. Dr. Porter nodded, breathing somewhat harder than usual.

"I'm a sociologist," Dr. Porter said.

"Sure," the bartender said. "We get a lot of college people here. Is that one dry enough for you? I made you a special one."

"Very good," Dr. Porter said, feeling the straight whisky gently searing the lining of his alimentary tract. "I'm conducting a very important research project."

"Is that right?" the bartender said pleasantly. "Good for you!" He looked uncomfortable for a moment, his professional antennae having picked up an early warning of boredom. "We get a lot of very distinguished guests at the hotel," he said. "Last week we had an ambassador. Came from one of those South American countries."

"I have to ask you to keep this to yourself," Dr. Porter said, swaying slightly. "Confi – confidential."

"The Dominican Republic!" the bartender exclaimed, as pleased as though he had answered a question in a quiz program. "You don't have to worry about what you say in this bar," he said. "I get to hear talk about some very big deals. This is as far as it goes."

"Thirty ... women," Dr. Porter said, staring tragically into his empty glass. "That's what I need. Bartender! Where'm I going to find thirty of them? I've got to. Gimme another drink, please, bartender. Dry Manhattan on the rocks."

The bartender looked apprehensively around the room before answering.

"Look, buddy," he said.

"Porter," Dr. Porter said, tipping ice cubes into his hand and onto the carpet in an effort to capture the whisky-soaked lemon peel. "Dr. Porter."

"Dr. Porter, I've got just the spot for you. Very exotic. You'll be crazy about it. Look. Take this card. Show it to the man at the door. Say Louis sent you. He'll take care of you."

"Funny," Dr. Porter said. "That's *my* name, Louis." He grinned stupidly. "Dr. Louis Porter. P ... H, D."

56

"Is that right?" the bartender said, signaling to a bell-boy near the lobby entrance to the bar, indicating that Dr. Porter wanted him. "No kidding, Dr. Porter. Maybe we're brothers or something. Look, he'll get you a cab. The fresh air'll feel good."

"Couldn't be brothers," Dr. Porter said, shaking his head gravely. "Not logical. Anyway, I don't have a brother."

"Goodbye now!" the bartender said, smiling cordially as Dr. Porter was escorted out. "Go have yourself a ball. Don't do anything I wouldn't do!" The bartender turned to a silent customer and said, as though commenting on the weather, "He must've had a few before he got here."

"Vodka and tonic," the man said.

"One vodka and tonic coming right up!" the bartender confirmed.

The evening air outside the hotel was cool and fresh, but the taxi driver's cigar and the loud music on the car radio were confusing.

"Where to, Mac?" the driver asked. Dr. Porter gave him the card.

"Louis sent me," he said.

The rest of the evening was a series of colour slides, increasingly abstract, mostly red. A montage of laughing faces, bartenders and waiters and others. An unexpected scene in which he was standing beside a large, shallow box lined with green baize, and everybody was watching him, and a man was saying, "Come on and shoot then. Roll the dice!" People close around him. The lights swung rapidly in parallel arcs and there was a severe jolt. Somebody said, "Oh, leave him alone. He's drunk." A taxi. Revolving purple, red and orange lights. A woman with ostrich feathers on her head slowly walked to and fro. Syrupy music. Purple, red and orange buttocks; purple, red and orange breasts. A small circle of white light. A man's teeth and hands clapping at the microphone. "I'm sorry," someone said. "I think you've had enough." Applause. He was in a toilet that smelled of carnations. He was in a taxi. He was at a bar. Bottles. Mirrors. Mirror-bottles. Mirror-mirror-bottles. A cork popped. "The professor's buying!" someone said. His hand holding a pen, gripping it hard, trying to move it to form the letter *L*. Another taxi. An-

57

other bar. "Get that bum out of here!" someone said. A woman's face. His name was Dr. Porter. Bubbles in his nose. Acid. Money. Inside his cheek there was a lump that tasted of blood. Sick somewhere. "Where are you staying?" someone patiently kept asking. He could not move his head. "Where are you staying? Where are you staying? Are you staying in a hotel? What's the name of your hotel?" The coffee burned his lips. It was too hot to drink. "You'd better come home with me, dear," someone said.

EIGHT

"IF you could imagine a mixture of Paul Newman and Tony Perkins," Camilla Fairbank said to her roommate. "Oh, he's so difficult to describe."

"A tough poet, sort of? A kind of sweet boxer?"

"Mary, cut it out. This is no joke. Won't you be serious?"

"I'm serious, silly. But your powers of description haven't as yet quite done justice to this great meeting."

"It wasn't a proper meeting, Mary. That's the trouble. I told you. He just bumped into me."

"An impetuous booklover."

"I don't even know his name," Camilla said. "He asked me mine and I wouldn't tell him."

"You're nuts then. Why?"

"I don't know," Camilla said. "I didn't want to give him the idea that I was just dying to know who he was. Anyway, I wasn't. I was in a hurry. It wasn't till halfway through zoology, when I was asked a question about polychaetes, and I suddenly realized I hadn't been listening, that I found I was thinking about his face. He has a very nice face."

"Well, sweet dreams. Maybe he'll be there, in Dreamland." Mary turned out the light beside her bed and the bedroom was dark. "Good night, Camilla."

"Good night, Mary."

There was silence, except for an occasional late car leaving or arriving at the dormitory parking lot.

"Camilla?"

"Yes?"

"You're not going to sleep, are you?"

"Of course I'm going to sleep."

"No you're not. I can hear you thinking from here. The whole room's jangled with your thoughts." Mary's bedside light came on again.

Camilla sat up, her eyes half shut against the light and one white silk shoulder strap falling off her shoulder. "Have you any cigarettes?" she asked. "No, I'd better not. I'm always smoking your cigarettes."

"Big deal!" Mary said, throwing back the blanket. She got out of bed. She was wearing a Baby Doll shortie nightgown. Pink. She walked over to the shelf they used as a kitchen. There was a hot plate on it, a saucepan, a toaster and an electric percolator, and some odds and ends in bottles and jars. Quite a cosy, domestic array, on a small scale. There was a package of filter cigarettes amidst this litter and she threw them over to Camilla's bed.

"There," she said.

"I wish I had legs like yours," Camilla said peevishly.

"Oh, God! Now what's wrong with you? Have you been taking inventory again?"

"My legs are too skinny," Camilla said in a voice of doom.

"You sound as though the doctor had just given you six months to live," Mary said. "Mine are too fat." She demonstrated their fatness by slapping the outside of a thigh. It made a solid, meaty sound.

"Men like well-rounded girls, don't they though?" Camilla said. "I know they do."

"They like thin girls and thick girls, giants and dwarfs, girls with single Cyclops eyes, girls with green hair and twelve thumbs. If you try to change yourself to please them, you're mad. All a girl needs is one velvet trap, in reasonable working order. But if you must know, why don't you ask him?"

"He seemed quite eager to get to know me," Camilla said doubtfully. "But it couldn't have been *me* he wanted to know. He doesn't know anything about me."

"For that matter, you don't know anything about him. He might have a wife in every state. He might be a member of the Ku Klux Klan."

"Not with eyes like his! He could be married though, I suppose. He's old enough. He looked quite old."

"An *old* Paul Newman."

"Relatively old. Compared with all these ridiculous boys."

"How old?"

"Twenty-five or six."

"Camilla, love, you're such an idiot," Mary said, getting back into bed.

"But he's got a sense of humor," Camilla said,

60

"Growing old gracefully."

"I don't think he's married," Camilla said. "He didn't seem married."

"There's one easy way of finding out," Mary said.

"How?"

"Ask him."

"But I don't know his *name*, I keep telling you."

"All right, all right. Keep calm."

"How can I keep calm? It's already been three days."

"Ca-*milla*! This is wonderful. I thought all you cared about was staying on the Dean's List and making Phi Beta Kappa and stuff like that. It must be spring."

"Of course I care about 'stuff like that'," Camilla said. "That's what we're here for, isn't it? But I care about lots of things."

"Have you finished?"

"Yes. But I had to tell you. I'm not going to let it throw me or anything. I just wonder . . . *you* know. I just . . ."

Mary turned out the light again.

"Don't worry," she said, yawning. "Digby isn't a very big place. Everyone ends up with the person she deserves."

There was another silence.

"Mary," Camilla said.

"Yes, what is it now?"

"I've got a nine-o'clock. Make sure I'm up before you go, won't you?"

NINE

Dr. Louis Porter's eyelids opened heavily and slowly, like a chameleon's. He lay on his back, not daring at first to move, trying without any success to deduce from the ceiling some theory on his present whereabouts. His mind was a warm porridge of emotions that were strange to him, a thick, stodgy muddle of guilt, remorse and dread. His superego had returned, having been absent for several hours, to find the place a mess – and not knowing what had happened, was unable to do any more than fume and fuss and complain in the vaguest general terms.

Cautiously moving his tongue within his mouth, he perceived that it was cloacally impure. His forehead hurt, his cheek hurt, his teeth hurt, his back hurt, his legs hurt, and he could feel that he had socks on.

The curtains were drawn, but there were narrow, vertical gaps that glared like strips of white-hot steel. Morning had come. Where had it come? He looked around the dim room and gradually gathered evidence that he was lying on a sofa in somebody's apartment. He heard a door open and close, not far away; then the hiss of a shower. The hiss stopped. He heard the knock of wooden shower-sandals approaching along a short, tiled corridor. Dr. Porter quickly pulled the sheet up to his eyes and looked fearfully over the hem, watching the door handle. The door opened.

"You're *alive*, lover!" exclaimed a man in a kimono made of a pale-blue toweling. "*That's* a relief. A little while ago you looked as though you were dead." He was a neatly compact fellow of about fifty, with smooth skin tanned sienna, gray hair trimmed short to show a clever, round skull, clearly delineated black eyebrows, now raised in mock surprise, and a triangular tuft of gray beard.

"Don't look so horrified," the man said to Dr. Porter. "You were marvelous, once we got you home. You were so pompous! You were adorable."

" 'We'?" Dr. Porter echoed faintly. "Was there a woman here?"

The man laughed good-naturedly.

"You've got a thing about women, haven't you?"

"I apologize if I was a nuisance," Dr. Porter said cravenly. "I'm very sorry. I'm afraid I wasn't quite myself. I think there was something wrong with one of my drinks. I don't drink much. I have a weak head."

"Weak?" the man said. "That wasn't the way *I* heard it. You told us you had the highest I.Q. in your class. Practically a genius – *Dr*. Porter. It was so wild we just had to turn on the tape recorder."

"Tape recorder!" Dr. Porter said.

"Take it easy. Everything's going to be just fine. You were very, very funny. Who's this Dr. Schumann? She must be a living doll."

"How did I get here?" Dr. Porter asked, trying to keep the panic from showing, but unable to. "What did I say?"

"I'd play back the whole tape," the man said. "But it's so *long*. Parts of it might embarrass you in your present delicate state. Anyway, I'm hopeless with mechanical things. The tape recorder is Lawrence's department."

"Who's Lawrence?"

"Louis! Don't tell me you've forgotten Lawrence! He'd be so hurt. He's my friend. He's out shopping. We decided the best thing would be bloody Mary's." The man raised a prohibitive hand. "Don't say you won't stay for lunch, because we *insist*. And anyway it's already past two o'clock. Now I must dress and get busy in the kitchen. The bathroom's all yours. It's all right: I won't *look*. There are some guest toothbrushes – the little ones in Cellophane. You can use our shaving things. And God knows there are plenty of clothes. You'd better not take any of Lawrence's though. He wouldn't be amused. Anything from the black and white bedroom's O.K."

Dr. Porter felt feeble, dizzy and confused, but his host's briskly decisive manner gave him an unaccustomed sensation of relief from responsibility. Years of proud, even stubborn, self-reliance had exhausted the innermost energetic reserves of his psyche. Although there seemed to be a certain malice, a teasing suggestiveness, in the unknown man's remarks, it was a bright, cheerful malice, unlike the sour envy and veiled criticism of Dr. Porter's academic acquaintances.

Dr. Porter smiled.

"That's the boy!" the man said, and gaily bustled out.

Dr. Porter got to his feet and was assailed by a sudden black wave of nausea. It passed, though, and he tottered to the bathroom with the careful, slow gait of an elderly invalid allowed up for the first time after a serious illness.

Naked, round-shouldered, he stood in the pink shower stall and alternately scalded and froze himself as he fumbled slowly with the chromium controls, until at last he succeeded in producing a mixture slightly warmer than blood. He stood under the spray for a long time. Gradually, the gentle needling stimulated his scalp and the skin on his neck, his shoulders, his back, his buttocks; suddenly, he felt better. At the washbasin, he wiped a circle of clarity in the center of the condensed steam on the mirror. Peering closely, he surveyed the personal wreckage and realized, with new hope, that he might be able to reconstruct a plausible face. He brushed his teeth with punitive severity, gargled with peppermint mouthwash, scrubbed his tongue with a pink facecloth, shaved with the exquisite, coolly devoted skill of a brain surgeon, blew his nose in pink Kleenex, rinsed his eyeballs in a soothing eye bath, helped himself to a couple of large, prettily striped vitamin capsules from a jar in the medicine cabinet, and found that he was able to believe, in principle, in the possibility of survival.

Once the elemental question of life and death had been thus encouragingly answered, however, he was stricken by fresh awareness of his unexplained immediate surroundings and company. The situation remained, at best, enigmatic. He groped through the debris of his mind for clues that would enable him to compose an orderly account of the latter stages of the previous evening, but his memory was like a short horror film that always broke, no matter how carefully he threaded it through the projector, and ended in darkness just before the appearance of the mad scientists and bloodsucking vampires that he knew must be imminent. He didn't want to see the horrible climax, but he was afraid to turn his back on it. Knowledge, no matter how repugnant, was an indispensable prerequisite for exorcism. He reviewed his incomplete recollections again and again, hoping that they might once gather enough momentum to continue to finality. Again and again, as he dressed in his wrinkled clothes, as he polished the scuffed fronts of his shoes on the backs of his trouser-legs, as he rearranged the handkerchief in his breast pocket, again as he combed his hair, again as he wound his watch and listened to the calm regularity of its familiar tick, he saw the hotel bar, the bartender, the succession of bartenders, the episodes in bars and taxis and bars, and then the increasingly spasmodic close-ups of objects that turned into faces and faces that became things. Again and again he reached the total obscurity of the abyss, the void; again and again he heard the first words of the morning, "You're *alive, lover*!"

"*Lover!*" The word terrified him. Dr. Porter felt quite odd.

He was nervously picking his nose in the empty living room, an impersonal room with chalk-white walls and department-store modern furniture, decorated here and there with ornamental antique-shop assertions of individuality, when he was startled by another, a younger voice.

"Oh, you're up."

Dr. Porter turned guiltily, and ostentatiously scratched the outside of his nose, to give the impression that he had been doing only that before. A man of about twenty, wearing an Irish fisherman's coarsely knitted off-white sweater, exceptionally tight fawn jeans, white woolen socks and beautifully polished dark-brown loafers with small leather tassels, stood inside the front doorway, hugging an A. & P. bag to his stomach. He had the elaborately disorderly, silkily gleaming bleached-blond hair, long at the sides and neck, and the sulky-cherub look of a pop singer. There was a wide, smooth gap between his eyebrows. His complexion was white and almost flawless. Beside his classic Greek-sculptural lips there was a single red bump, a tiny organic volcano, an incipient pustule, which afforded Dr. Porter a minor, inadequate consolation for his renewed sense of inferiority and vulnerability.

"You must be Lawrence," Dr. Porter said appeasingly. The young man's smile was nasty, as though to notify Dr. Porter that he wasn't going to get off easily.

"Yeah," the young man said. "Boy, were you stoned last night! Out of your *mind*." He walked in the direction of the kitchen. "Rollo!" he called, raising his whining, nasal voice, sounding like Jerry Lewis in distress. "That crummy delicatessen doesn't even *have* Lea and Perrin's. I had to go to three places."

"It was very kind of you, letting me stay overnight," Dr. Porter said with breathless, false eagerness, trying to gain Lawrence's good will before he left the room. Dr. Porter hated the thought of the young man and his elder in the kitchen together intimately finding fault with him. Lawrence stopped at the door and shifted the big paper bag so that it rested on one hip. He raised an eyebrow in the theatrically ironic manner of a dandy disdainfully staring through a quizzing glass.

"The pleasure," he said, "was all *ours*." Dr. Porter winced inside, but bravely smiled. He decided that one had better use psychology, ask the young man a favor, get him on one's side.

"It's silly, Lawrence," he confided, "but I can't quite remember your friend's name – Rollo's surname. What did he say it was?"

"He didn't," Lawrence said. He smiled again. "Everything was very informal." He left the room, leaving Dr. Porter in uncomfortable speculation. He could hear voices from the kitchen but he couldn't hear what they were saying. There was a metallic scream, the hysterical mechanical uproar of an electric blender pulverizing ice cubes. Then, a minute or two later, footsteps returned along the hall.

Rollo was carrying a circular silver tray. There were three large glass tankards and a streamlined Swedish glass jug on it. The jug was frosty.

"I hope you like your bloody Marys with everything in them," Rollo said solicitously. "Lawrence likes his terribly *tabasco-y*." He made the word sound naughty, and looked at the young man fondly, with a smile of maternal pride in his young taste buds' precocious affinity for hot spiciness. "The lime juice counteracts the tabasco, the Cayenne pepper and the Worcestershire sauce. Fresh limes. Lots and lots of ice. Our own tomato juice. Lawrence won't *touch* canned juice. We strain it through muslin." Lawrence, sitting with his feet tucked beneath him in a purple-velveteen-covered armchair, began to fidget petulantly.

"You should like *Good Housekeeping*," he said. "How about a drink?"

66

"Lawrence is just crazy about *vodka*, too," Rollo said, unperturbed. There was a hint of menace in his expression, just a *soupçon*, suggesting that the balance of power, Rollo's and Lawrence's, was nicely poised in equilibrium. Lawrence smiled a genuine, boyish smile in acknowledgment of a point scored against him. Rollo smiled tolerantly, rather archly, back, and passed around the tray.

The drinks were extremely cold and had a good, strong, complicated taste. After the first cautious sips, Dr. Porter felt himself relax a bit. He held the cold, wet glass gratefully against his forehead.

"Well," Rollo said with quiet geniality. "That's better, isn't it?"

"Wonderful," Dr. Porter said.

Lawrence got up and topped up the glasses.

"And now," Rollo said, "let us get down to business."

"Business?" Dr. Porter said, feeling his innards drop with fright.

Rollo smiled reassuringly. "We're going to help you," he said. "You *need* help. You kept saying so yourself, didn't he, Lawrence?"

"He sure did," Lawrence agreed, smiling again. Rollo frowned at him, and Lawrence stopped smiling.

"We *love* the idea of the Digby Institute," Rollo said. "We think it's great."

"Was I talking about the Institute?" Dr. Porter said. "I wasn't sober. I couldn't have been making any sense. There isn't any Institute."

Rollo waved a kindergarten teacher's admonitory finger, chiding the wicked fibber.

"Now, Louis!" Rollo said. "*In vino veritas!* Do I have to play the whole tape? Please not. We will if you make us, but it would be such a *drag*. Believe me, Louis, you told all. It's amazing how the brain keeps going, isn't it? Even when the part that usually remembers things is *paralyzed*."

"How much money do you want to keep quiet?" Dr. Porter asked dully. He had a substantial amount in the bank.

"*Louis!*" Rollo protested. "That's no way to talk. We're your *friends*."

"Your buddies," Lawrence confirmed. "True blue,

67

through and through. Till the end of time." Rollo gave him a sharp look of reprimand.

"Louis isn't in the mood for fooling around," Rollo said. "Are you, Louis? Now look, Louis. If you really have pulled a blank. You *said* you wondered how on *earth* you were going to find thirty whores. And I admit it does sound *frantic*, when you put it like that. As though you were searching for thirty rare species of fungus. In this hygienic city, too."

Dr. Porter's knuckles whitened as his fingers tightened around the handle of the glass tankard. After all that Dr. Schumann had said about security. . . .

" 'Prostitutes,' you called them," Rollo went on. "I don't think I'm *especially* squeamish, but I just *hate* that word. So old-*fashioned*. It makes me think of some old melodrama. You know: painted women, selling their rotten old *bodies*. All those *germs*. Things are better now, thank *God*. Let's say you need thirty people able to help you with your research, and you're willing to pay them very, very well."

"What do you want?" Dr. Porter implored. "I can let you have anything I have. Anything within reason. I'm not a rich man. You don't look like blackmailers."

"*Thank* you, dear," Rollo said.

"What do blackmailers look like?" Lawrence asked. "What do blackmailers look like, Rollo?"

"Hush, Lawrence," Rollo said. "Mother's very busy." Rollo turned earnestly to Dr. Porter.

"Please, Louis," Rollo said. "You must stop *worrying*. We can't settle *anything* if you won't calm down. We're not going to spoil anything for you. We're not going to embarrass you in any way. Really, Louis. We might even be able to save you from some embarrassment, if you agree to handle things our way. You have to *trust* us. Trust is very important. Will you do that?"

"Our research at Digby is still in the earliest formative stage," Dr. Porter said. "Naturally we're concerned about possible leaks. And you talk about tape recorders. What do you expect me to think?"

"We're all civilized people," Rollo said teasingly. He looked at Lawrence and smiled. "Civilized*ish*."

"I'd be very grateful if you'd keep anything I said last

night strictly confidential," Dr. Porter said. "Not that ordinary people would be at all interested."

"*Wouldn't* they though?" Rollo said. He made a solemn face. "'Strictly confidential'," he said, gloomily lowering the tone of his voice. He turned again to Lawrence. "Don't you *love* the way he talks?"

"Now who's kidding around?" Lawrence said peevishly.

"*Touché*," Rollo said. "You jealous thing. All right, Louis. We'll put you out of your agony. All we want, Lawrence and I, is to be members of the team."

"Members of the team!" Dr. Porter exclaimed.

"Members of the team," Rollo agreed.

"But that's impossible!" Dr. Porter said. "You know it is. How could I possibly fix that? You aren't qualified scientists, are you?"

"No, sweet," Rollo said. "But we are qualified."

"I don't get it." Dr. Porter said.

"When your Dr. Schumann told you to come here and collect thirty prostitutes, she couldn't have meant thirty *women*, could she? You'd look silly going back without any men, wouldn't you? The Institute's supposed to cover all kinds of sex, isn't it?"

Dr. Porter suddenly felt a buoyant surge of relief.

"Yes, it is," he said. "Of course. We're going to need as many men as women before we're through. Perhaps there should be some men right from the start."

"Of course there should."

"Cocks are all the rage," Lawrence said.

"But," Dr. Porter said, anxious again, "Dr. Schumann stressed the point that we should start off with prostitutes. Professionals. People that could be expected to discuss and demonstrate various sexual practices professionally, as a job."

Rollo's expression was half-pitying, half-wistful. "You've led a very sheltered life, haven't you, Louis?"

"I was in the Army in Germany," Dr. Porter said defensively.

"Then you should know that prostitute is just a *word*. There are prostitutes and prostitutes. It's a relative term. There's some prostitute, more or less, in almost everyone. Someone pays you to do something you really don't want to do, and you do it. Maybe they pay you in cash; maybe in something else. Some people get paid well, some not so well. Some sell more of themselves, more valuable parts of themselves, than others. Think of being in *commercials* or *television*. Think of being married to an insurance sales-man. Frankly, I prefer earning money by going down on some stranger I picked up in a bar. At least I'm independ-ent to *choose*. The hours are good. Sometimes it's *fun*."

Dr. Porter smiled nervously. "You're speaking meta-phorically, of course," he said. Rollo leaned over towards Lawrence and tweaked his cheek so hard that the pain made him yelp.

"You cute little figure of speech, you!" Rollo said to him.

"Cut it out, Goddammit!" Lawrence complained. Rollo ignored him. He spoke to Dr. Porter.

"The trouble with you, Louis," Rollo said, "is that you're probably not capable of recognizing reality when you *see* it. What did you think your fallen women were going to *look* like? Bette Davis at the end of Of Human Bondage? Most call girls look like the girl next door who made *good*. They know how to dress better and use make-up better and walk better and even talk better than nine housewives out of ten, and ten out of ten social workers."

"Then you mean that you and Lawrence. . . . ?"

"Oh, no, Louis! We're not *prostitutes*! But we often do unconventional little favours for unconventional people, and they reward us for our services. They give us presents, don't they, Lawrence? Where do you think Lawrence got that *vulgarly* large diamond ring he's wearing? No, I mustn't tell you. We have our ethics, haven't we, Law-rence?"

Lawrence histrionically sighed, like a teen-ager whose parents are always nagging.

"He hasn't forgiven me because it's a real one, and I said it was paste," Lawrence said. He twisted the ring on his finger and smiled when its scintillating glitter made Rollo scowl.

"Perhaps it's a sign of middle age," Rollo said to Dr. Porter, "but I must say the idea of spending the spring in Southern Ohio has a certain charm – and a lump of cash at the end. And Lawrence had better come along, because he'd only get into *trouble* without a manager, and *ill* without a housekeeper. And not only that. He'll tell your Dr. Schumann things about sex in the Middle West that'll make her *toes* curl."

"In some ways," Dr. Porter conceded, "it's a good idea. I'll talk to Dr. Schumann about it. I'll let you know."

"Tut, tut, Louis!" Rollo said, shaking his head from side to side. "No, no, no. This has to be *definite*. You're a full associate director of the Institute, aren't you? You seemed proud to be, last night. You have enough authority to write out a guarantee here and now. Let's make it a *letter,* shall we? A formal invitation to Messrs. Roland Hawkins and Lawrence Da Silva. In return, we'll let you have the tape. I'm sure you'll enjoy playing back some of your childhood reminiscences about Beatrice Schumann. *We* certainly enjoyed that bit."

That did it. Dr. Porter wrote to Rollo's dictation.

When the document was duly signed and safely put away in Rollo's pocket, Rollo got Lawrence to pour out the remainder of the bloody Marys and proposed a toast to the success of the Digby Institute. "Here's to letting all those quaint, backward members of the public know how it's really done!" he said. "The poor square darlings!"

Dr. Porter was now quite obviously longing to leave, but as he was rising uncertainly to his feet Rollo gently pressed him to stay a bit longer. "Don't forget the other twenty-eight," Rollo said. "You still don't know how to get *them,* do you?"

Dr. Porter recognized that he had no idea.

"Now you'll see how fortunate it was that you happened to fall into such good hands," Rollo said. "I know you'll be thrilled to hear that we have access to the names and addresses of every known . . . prostitute in this city."

"You have?" Dr. Porter said.

Lawrence uttered a spluttering giggle, and this time Rollo seemed inclined to join in.

"Some of our city police are much more human than many people think," Rollo said, his eyes merrily atwinkle.

"I'll say!" Lawrence said, again, at the very thought of them, exploding with laughter.

"A very good friend of ours is a sergeant on the Vice Squad," Rollo said. Lawrence nodded, hooting in delight.

"It's true!" he said. "It's really true!" Rollo composed himself. Business was business.

"Sergeant O'Halloran," Rollo said. "He's *priceless*. A collectors' item. I'm sure there can't be many faggoty Irish police sergeants in town."

"Can't be many," Lawrence said.

"And he's on the *Vice* Squad?" Dr. Porter said.

"Can you think of a *better* place for him?" Rollo said. "From his point of view. That's why he *joined,* to get on the squad. It's the quickest way there is to meet people, make friends. Interesting people. He'd done very well."

"Until one night –" Lawrence began.

"He was careless," Rollo said. "Indiscreet. There was a party. A couple of City Councilors were involved. But we don't want to bore you with all the details. Anyway, Lawrence happened to have taken the tape recorder along. It's one of those miniature ones. In short, we were able to smooth things over. O'Halloran owes us a favor."

"He keeps owing us favors," Lawrence said.

"We still have the tape," Rollo explained. "So I'm sure he'll be glad to put you in touch with any number of people of the kind you need. Men and women. Black and white."

"Penthouse and bargain basement," Lawrence said.

"Are you sure it's quite safe?" Dr. Porter said. "Isn't it possible that he might take offense?"

"Leave it to us," Rollo said. "I'll tell you what. I'll call him now. We'll have him over for a drink. He *adores* bloody Marys. You'll like him, Louis. He's got those marvelous Irish eyes – pale blue, with the *blackest* lashes."

"Oh, no!" Lawrence said. "Not the eye bit. I can't stand going through all that again."

"Lawrence thinks he's the *only* good-looking man in the *world,*" Rollo observed tartly. He picked up the telephone, and, without having to look up the number, began to dial.

While they were waiting for Sergeant O'Halloran, Rollo mixed another batch of drinks.

"Not for me," Dr. Porter said. "I'm not a drinking man. Oh, all right. Perhaps just one. If this sergeant can help us as simply as that, my work here is as good as finished."

72

A little later, Dr. Porter spoke again. "Rollo," he said.

"Yes?" Rollo said.

"Last night," Dr. Porter said. "Nothing actually ... happened, did it?"

"Of course not," Rollo assured him.

"In *your* condition?" Lawrence said.

Dr. Porter made no comment, but he looked thoughtful.

TEN

As the lull continued before the beginning of construction of The Symington Building, Richard Doughty often thought of his brief encounter with the fair-haired girl in the library. The college found him an apartment, the whole second floor of a faculty widow's white frame house on Maple Street, overlooking the trees and lawns of the campus; but getting settled there occupied his mind for only a couple of days. His accommodations were more than adequate, overfurnished quite comfortably – a rudimentary kitchen, a bathroom, a bedroom, and, in the front of the house, a large, high-ceilinged sitting room, with two bay windows and window seats, a fireplace occupied by a vase of dried flowers, and two walls lined with books, the overflow from the late professor's study downstairs. He had been an archaeologist, a specialist in the Mayan Indians of Central America. Most of the books had dusty, dark covers, as though they themselves had been excavated from old tombs. Richard went to the college bookshop and bought an inexpensive framed reproduction of a Dufy water color of some tenuous race horses in a sunny paddock at Maisons-Laffitte. The picture looked flimsy and silly against the faded mauve geometry of the widow's wallpaper. The contrast was depressing.

He felt that there must be some systematic way of searching for the girl with the golden hair or some other girl. But the passage of time was making her more and more radiantly alluring. There were only about twelve hundred undergraduates registered at Digby, no more than half of them girls. Six hundred girls. Two hundred blondes? Hardly. And of those, how many could be called beautiful, or even good-looking? Twenty would have been a generous estimate. Which of the twenty had classes at ten o'clock on Wednesday mornings? (They had met on Wednesday.) A high proportion. A popular hour for lectures. Fifteen girls, say. But he wanted this girl. Even though she was an unknown stranger, she seemed special, possibly unique. He had to have her.

In the Student Union recreation hall one evening, he saw a girl in a blue sweater and jeans bowed over the selection panel on the juke box. She had her back to him. The bottom seemed just right, and the hair was right. He hurried toward her just as she turned around. Her heavy eyebrows and thick glasses, the total wrongness of her face, struck him like a discordant fanfare of trombones.

He saw another blonde, bicycling along Center Street in the rain. He ran after her. He saw her dismount, shove the front wheel of the bicycle into a sidewalk parking rack, and go into a restaurant. He crossed the road and followed her inside, in time to see her pass through a back doorway. He sat at a table, pretending to study the menu, for nearly ten minutes. When she returned, her eyes and mouth were painted like a doll's and she was wearing the uniform of a waitress.

He then went to the registrar's office and persuaded a secretary to type him a list of all the classes that began on Wednesdays at ten o'clock. The list took surprisingly long to prepare. When he got it he saw why. Almost every department had classes in session at that time. There were courses in everything from Archery to Zoology, almost everything imaginable, and many in almost unimaginable subjects he had never before considered, such as Automotive Traffic Control, Institutional Flower Arrangement and Pet Obedience Training. Even if he kept watch at a different classroom door at the beginning and end of every Wednesday ten o'clock from then until the end of the semester, he wouldn't have a chance to get around to them all.

He walked across the campus to Main Street, and along it to the Elite Drug Store. The prescription department counter was jammed with students buying their medical supplies for the weekend, mostly pills supposed to extend and invigorate consciousness, to counteract the mildly barbituric placebos that had enabled the boys and girls tranquilly to endure the tedium of the week. A few of the younger freshmen, those who had not as yet effected reliable arrangements with suitably equipped girls, were buying packets of condoms. These transactions were conducted in a deliberately ostentatiously furtive manner that made Richard feel his years.

The soda fountain too was crowded. But he found an empty bench in a booth near the back of the room. He sat down. A waitress brought him a thick cup of very hot, weak coffee. He slowly drank it, while examining the cryptic list of ten-o'clocks, trying to decide, by eliminating, where he might have the best chance.

And then he saw her. She was standing a few yards away, idly revolving a circular stand of paperback books. Her long, straight, yellow hair, her downcast eyes and grave seriousness gave her face the appearance of an angel's. She was wearing a camel's-hair coat, a gray cashmere cardigan, a gray tweed skirt, and brown shoes with low heels.

For a moment, Richard simply sat there, enraptured. But then she took a book from the stand. Fearing that she might be ready to leave, he quickly went over to her. "How about that cup of coffee?" he asked brightly.

She looked up at him and smiled as though they had been friends. Then she realized that they weren't, and the smile evaporated. "Oh, hello," she said. "I'm sorry I was so rude the other day."

"That's all right," he said. "Come and sit down."

"The thing is," she said, "I'm always like that before a quizz. I was almost late for zoology. He starts every single session with a quizz. You wouldn't think anyone would treat seniors like that, would you? He's furious if you miss one, and I'm a zo. major, so I really should get an A in genetics even if he is corny. Anyway, I'm sorry."

After her speech, she was slightly breathless, and blushing a little and looked almost unbearably lovely.

"Zoology!" Richard said. "I'd never have guessed."

"What?"

"I would have thought English lit, or perhaps philosophy."

"What are you talking about?"

"I was trying to work out which ten-o'clock you could have cared about so much. I mean, someone who looks like you. You're not my idea of a zoologist somehow. What's your name?"

"Camilla Fairbanks," she said. "If you know about English literature and things like that, maybe you'll help me." She showed him the cover of the book in her hand. "Do you know anything about Saul Bellow? Would he be easy to write a term paper on? I've got to get at least a B-plus, but I haven't much time."

"I'll tell you how to get an A-minus if you'll come and sit down with me. My name's Richard Doughty. I'm a lonely newcomer to Digby and my coffee's getting cold."

Camilla looked at her watch.

"All right," she said. "I have ten minutes. Thanks a lot, that is. My roommate says I ought to relax. How are you supposed to get everything done and relax, I'd like to know? Are you a transfer student? What department are you in? You're not a member of the faculty or something are you? Could I have a lemon Coke?"

They sat in the booth for over an hour. She didn't mind cutting a piano lesson. By lunchtime Richard had learned that she was the third of three sisters born in Elyria, Ohio, and was going to be a teacher and loved swimming and Debussy and the color gray and differential calculus and lemon-meringue pie and the Rockefeller Center in winter and most of the Impressionists and the Peace Corps and Jacques Tati and Edna St. Vincent Millay and dissection and Digby, Digby, Digby, Digby.

She seemed unbelievably square.

But he asked her to dinner and she said yes.

ELEVEN

Marcia Daventry, though she had been one of the most enterprising and sought-after hustlers between Lorain and Ashtabula in her day, was, in her middle age, becoming a little bit lazy, and more than a little anxious. She needed frequent reassurance. It was easy enough to get it at night. The days were more difficult. Sometimes she was almost afraid to get out of bed. Billie, the maid, tried to make things easier.

"Beautiful sunny morning!" she announced, pulling a cord that opened the theatrical double curtains, disclosing the CinemaScope picture window, the terrace, and the parkway and the lake eighteen floors below. The great silk-canopied four-poster bed was elevated on a dais – a bed with a marvelous view of the waterfront and beyond. But Marcia burrowed deeper under the silken electric quilt, the mohair blankets and silk sheets. Only the top of her head was visible. Her voice of reproach was muffled.

"Billie!" she said. "*Please!*"

"You said eleven, honey," the maid said, continuing to pull the curtain cord until the pale-blue-and-oyster-gray Louis Quatorze room was bright with daylight. "Come on now. I filled your bath."

Marcia raised her head a few inches, frowned at the sunshine, and let her head drop again.

"Eleven already?" she said. "I only just got to sleep a few minutes ago." She artificially groaned. "Has Mr. Allen gone?"

"Wasn't nobody here when I arrived," Billie said. "Sure did leave the bathroom in a state though, whoever he was."

"Sorry, Billie," Marcia said, sitting up and yawning. "I guess he was kind of loaded. He's not a bad guy when he's sober."

"You're too easy on them," Billie said. As an old retainer, she was privileged to criticize Miss Marcia and her clientele. "That's the trouble with you, honey. You're a whole *lot* too easy on them. Who do they think they are? Inch deep in water! Towels laying there! Whisky glass on the

78

basin! They take advantage of you, honey, I swear!"

The maid's familiar ritual grumbling and her Deep Southern affectionate slavishness began to work their daily magic. Marcia smiled at her.

"You're a doll, Billie," she said. She looked at the golden sun-burst clock on the pale-blue watered-silk wall. "Is that the right time?"

"You always ask that," Billie said. "It always is. Sure it's the right time. D'you want me to call Antoine's and tell them you'll be a half hour late?"

Marcia lifted a loose wave of her ash-blonde hair and contemptuously let it fall.

"You'd better," she said. "He's got to do something with it if I'm going to go out this evening. And I have to go out this evening. And tomorrow evening. And the evening after that. Oh, Billie . . ."

"You'll feel better after your bath," the maid said, picking up a full ash tray from a glass-topped gilded cane table beside the bed. "I put some of that new Milady in it. Smells real elegant."

"Thank you, Billie," Marcia said. "Bless you." She got out of bed, automatically assuming the negligee that Billie held out for her. The black gossamer accentuated the whiteness of her overripe Rubenesque curves. She was a woman of opulent convexities, a rich harmony of round-nesses and dimples. Her breasts were so round that they softly pressed against each other. Her navel was small, neat, deeply sunken. She had a belly-dancer's cushioned stomach. The luxuriant triangle of curly black fleece embellishing her statuesque mount of Venus lurked between her plump white thighs like a furry beast in ambush, the animal under the lace.

"Those pills are great," Marcia said. "But the night goes by like nothing. I could sleep another twelve hours."

"If I had a figure like yours, honey, I'd want to go out and show it off," Billie said with sincere fervor. "A new hairdo, a little lunch in a fancy restaurant, a walk along the avenue, window-shopping. What's so bad about that? I'll go fix your coffee, so it's ready when you are."

"Thanks, Billie. It's funny, isn't it? I've always wished I was small like you. All the new clothes look better on petite models."

"I don't call it petite, honey. I call it pathetic."

"You're lovely, Billie."

Marcia yawned and walked indolently into the steam of the bathroom. She shed the negligee and let it fall, floating slowly down to form a puddle of silk on the shaggy white bathroom carpet. She carefully stepped over the low white-marble side of the bath and slowly subsided into the scented pale-pink froth of bubbles, the hot embrace of the water. She lay there for a long time, blissfully unthinking, until the bathroom door opened and Billie started fondly scolding her again.

"I'll only get up if you do my back," Marcia said.

"Now, honey, it's getting late, honest, I'm not kidding," Billie said, but she rolled up her uniform sleeves and picked up a soft, lathery soap mitt. "You know sometimes, honey, you just plain *bad*."

Marcia looked around at her and smiled.

"You know you like it as much as I do," she said.

The curtains had been closed again, not quite all the way, and there was a faint, aqueous half-light on the nude bodies on the bed.

Marcia was supine, spread-eagled, with the back of one hand across her eyes. Her lips were parted and the tip of her tongue kept licking the outside of them, incessantly slipping wetly around the outside of her lips. Then her tongue went in and she started softly chewing her glistening lower lip. Her head rolled helplessly from side to side beneath the back of her hand. Her hand moved down to her open mouth and she gnawed the knuckle of her fore-finger. Her head tilted back, pressing into the pillows. Her eyes were squeezed tight shut and her mouth was open in a silent scream as she gave birth to a huge, excruciating joy.

The telephone began ringing. It was unheard.

Marcia sighed.

"Oh, Billie. What do you do to me? That was wonder-ful."

"M-m-m."

About ten minutes later, the telephone rang again. This

time Marcia awoke with a twitch of worry. "Oh, hell, get that Billie, will you?"

Billie, however, was in another room. Marcia leaned over and picked up the golden telephone. "Miss Daventry's residence," she said. "Who's speaking, please? ... Sergeant O'Halloran? For Christ's sake, Terry, it isn't twelve o'clock yet. I haven't even had my coffee.... Huh, Terry? This afternoon? What for? ... Yeah, I bet it's urgent. Look, Terry, I don't care if J. Edgar Hoover's in town personally. I don't owe anything.... I *am* calm.... All right, so tell me.... A *holiday*! Terry, are you drinking? ... You sound serious.... O.K., O.K.... Right, Terry. The Berkeley-Carlton.... Yes, Terry.... Have I ever let you down when you really needed help?"

TWELVE

WITH all the expert assistance that Dr. Porter was being given, recruitment for the Digby Institute initial research team proceeded apace. Rollo Hawkins proved to be a most efficient secretary. Right from the beginning, it seemed to be tacitly understood that his status was special, that of a non-commissioned leader, an intermediary, an interpreter.

He set up a series of interview appointments with candidates in Dr. Porter's suite at the Berkeley-Carlton Hotel. All afternoon and evening they kept arriving, one every fifteen minutes, blondes, brunettes and red heads, apprehensive apprentices, mature men and women in the prime of their careers, strained veterans. Members of the hotel staff who had an eye for that class of visitors began to raise their eyebrows and exchange incredulous murmurs, one with another, as the procession steadily continued. What sort of man could he be, they wondered, the occupant of twelve-sixteen?

Rollo acted as a receptionist in the drawing room. He was acquainted with many of the candidates, at least by sight, and he was able to put at ease even those who were strangers to him. His informally friendly, courteous manner immediately soothed any feelings that had been ruffled by Sergeant O'Halloran's brusque, peremptory summonses. By the time Rollo had outlined to each the terms of prospective employment in his merrily pithy professional vernacular, most of the candidates felt that he had let them in on a good deal, a combination of creativity, profit and prestige rare in their line of work. Most of them were relaxed and smiling by the time they went on to the bedroom, where Dr. Porter, wearing spectacles and an expression of grave responsibility, sat at a writing table with a pen and a loose-leaf notebook, prepared to make final decisions. His conversation with Marcia Daventry was one of the more cautious ones.

She was dressed simply but strikingly, in all white – a hat, or headdress, of white feathers, a white fur cape, a low-cut, *very* low-cut, white silk sheath, white gloves, white shoes, and a broad bracelet that scintillated like a dance hall's revolving mirrored globe of lights, throwing out rainbow gleams and sudden glints of electric brilliance.

Dr. Porter stared at the bracelet. He stared at the overflowing cornucopia of her décolletage. He took off his glasses and put them on again, coughed, and manfully looked up into her eyes. "Miss ...?" He looked down at his notes. "Miss Daventry?"

"That's right," she said. "Listen, Dr. Porter, excuse me if I'm out of line, but I get some screwy calls. Was that really Sergeant O'Halloran, so help you? Are you on the level? Or is this some kind of sick joke?"

"Please sit down, Miss Daventry," he said. She sat warily on the edge of a straight-backed chair, with the desk between them. "Will you have a cigarette?" he asked. He held out a pack, but she shook her head. "I assure you, Miss Daventry, that we are one hundred per cent ... 'on the level.' This is a bona fide scientific project, under the auspices of one of the finest institutions of its kind in this part of the country. Digby is a very old school, Miss Daventry."

"I don't doubt it," she said doubtfully.

"Didn't Mr. Hawkins explain our program?" Dr. Porter asked.

"The money sounds good," she said. "And I could use a little fresh air. I haven't been feeling too good the last couple of months. But what's the catch? Sergeant O'Halloran and Rollo are not the kind of team you expect to win the Nobel Prize, you got to admit."

Dr. Porter flushed a bit, coughed again, smiled, frowned, eased his button-down blue collar with a forefinger, and otherwise registered awkward, ingenuous, good-natured sincerity. The amateurishness of the performance was disarming.

"O.K.," she said. "Don't be offended. But people don't come along the pike every day making offers like this. A person could get herself into trouble if she doesn't watch out. That's one thing I don't need, trouble. Frankly."

"There are many safeguards," Dr. Porter assured her. "You have my word, I guarantee. The Institute has the personal blessing of Dr. Essen himself. Dr. Essen," he explained in a reverently hushed tone, "is the president of Digby College. He's a very respected educator. He's in *Who's Who in America*."

"I'm not too brainy," Marcia said. "I read magazines a lot. I see a lot of TV. I'm well informed. I've been around. But I didn't have much schooling. What are we going to have to do down there in Digby? If there's a lot of forms to fill in, forget it; I'll mess them up for sure."

"It won't be like that," Dr. Porter said. "We believe that you are an expert on certain aspects of relations between men and women." He smiled broad-mindedly. "Sexual relations. We want to ask you some questions about various practices, methods, techniques, and reactions to them."

"Everyone knows that stuff," she said.

"You'd be surprised," he said. "Even today there are areas of mystery and misgivings. You could help a lot. And then," he added hurriedly, "there'll be the demonstrations."

"What demonstrations?"

Dr. Porter smiled nervously and waved a nonchalant hand.

"Oh, all sorts of demonstrations, Miss Daventry. Nothing that you won't be able to take in your stride. Dr. Schumann will explain it all when you get settled in your quarters in Digby. It'll be easier, I think, if she tells you. She's a very respected doctor of medicine. She's my associate director."

"A lady doctor!" Marcia said.

"Yes. Beatrice Schumann. I'm sure you'll get along with her like a house on fire."

"All right, Dr. Porter," she said. "It's a deal. Let me have that cigarette."

THIRTEEN

AFTER lunch, Richard Doughty went to one of the local used-car lots and rented a dark-gray Chevrolet sedan, so that he could drive over to Camilla's dormitory to pick her up for dinner. But when he telephoned her she told him not to bother; she had one or two things to do outside, and she wasn't quite sure how long they would take; it would be simpler if they met where they were going to eat. He was not dismayed, he needed a car anyway, and he had taken it on a weekly basis, being unsure, actually, how much entertaining he would be able to manage on the widow's premises, especially of Digby undergraduates of the opposite sex. He had already found that Ohio small-town morals were decidedly more demanding than Washington's.

Richard got to the Digby Inn at six fifty-eight. They were due to meet in the lobby at seven. He sat in a rocking chair close to a chintz-curtained window and looked through advertisements in an old *New Yorker*, but couldn't really concentrate on them. Every time somebody walked across the lobby, he looked up. The minutes ticked by heavily. He was so impatient to see her that her lateness began to irritate him, and then worry him. Perhaps she had been hit by a truck. When he saw her walking in through the front door of the hotel, he felt relieved, cross, sulky, and then, as she stood indecisively in the middle of the lobby with a hand comically pressed to the top of her head, he felt quite simply delighted. He threw the magazine at a table and missed and leaped up, leaving the chair rocking.

"Here you are!" he exclaimed.

Her smile was dazzling. "Have you been waiting long?" she politely inquired.

"Hours," he said. He looked at his watch. She was nearly five minutes late. "I hope you're hungry. You have to be hungry here. But there isn't anywhere else."

"It's the Waldorf after the dining hall," she said. "I'm starving."

85

He managerially guided her into the dining room. The head waitress, a Grant Wood pioneer grandmother, led them to the table he had reserved, which had the negative virtue of being as far away as possible from the swinging doors that admitted gusts of noise and heat and the smell of hot fat from the kitchen. He held Camilla's chair for her and ceremonially scraped it forward an inch or two as she murmured her gratitude.

The table was small, made of brightly varnished pine, against a dark Williamsburg-green wall decorated with Audubon birds posing self-consciously on branches. There were plastic-lace table mats and a small plastic-parchment lampshade and a plastic rose in a bud vase between them. Hardly the Colony, but he had made out in far worse.

The moment of wordless anticipatory communion was ended by a waitress in a mauve nylon smock bearing two enormous handwritten menus.

"Would you care for a cocktail from the bar before I take your dinner order?" she asked, in the unctuously encouraging manner of a progressive mortician.

"I don't think so," Richard said. "I mean, yes, of course. What will you have, Camilla?"

"Nothing for me, thank you," she said, smiling broad-mindedly. "You have one though."

"I'll have one if you will," he urged.

"No, honestly. But please do. I'll have some fruit juice."

"But this is an historic occasion," he said, laughingly adamant. "Have at least a sherry."

"All right," she said.

Richard turned to the cataleptic figure by their side.

"That's one sherry," he said. "Dry?" he asked Camilla, "medium? Medium-dry?"

"You choose," she said.

"Dry," he said. "And for me – I'll have the same."

"Dry for you, too?"

"Yes, please."

The waitress silently handed them the newspaper-size menus and silently withdrew. Richard felt that he had not adequately asserted himself about cocktails. Still, ordering meals in restaurants was one of modern man's few public opportunities of proving his masculinity. He sat up a bit straighter. Camilla smiled and waited for him to lead.

86

"It's always the same," he said, gruffly apologetic. "I lived here before I moved to Maple Street. The steaks are not bad though, if you like steak."

"I love steak," she said. He surreptitiously watched her search through the card for steaks, and then glance to the right-hand column of prices. "But I think perhaps something lighter. I've been eating like a pig. My roommate is a compulsive candy-eater. She leads me astray."

"Is she nice, your roommate?"

"Mary? Oh, she's wonderful. I don't know what I'd do without her. Lose my mind, I suppose. She's practical without being boring about it. You know?"

Richard nodded and smiled. "Steak isn't too filling," he said. "A steak and a salad. The sirloin. Even they do it quite well. Let's begin with a shrimp cocktail." The inevitable meal assumed its familiar shape. "Afterwards," he suggested, "you should try a pear Helene. People say their pear Helenes are really good."

"That sounds marvelous," she said. "What is it?" She smiled. He smiled modestly and explained.

"Is that what you recommend to all your girls?" she asked. "That's very adolescent of me, isn't it?" Richard was delighted.

"If you want to know," he said. "The only people I've taken out to dinner since I came to Digby were a Mr. Symington and a couple of building contractors."

"You have a perfect right to take out anyone you want," Camilla said earnestly, then the waitress, like a referee, came between them with the sherry.

"I think I'd like the Southern-fried chicken and pineapple ring," Camilla said. "Or Yankee pot roast."

"This is beginning to sound like the War between the States," Richard said.

"The Civil War," she corrected him.

"We'd better not get into that," he said. "Let's both have steak."

"You order then," Camilla said. "I'm no good at it. I've led a sheltered life."

Richard assumed command, and everything went quite smoothly, except for the objections, doubts, concessions and queries about table wine. The waitress sighed and went away. There was silence as they sipped their sherry.

"I've been looking forward to dinner all day," Camilla said.

"Have you really?" Richard said. "So have I."

"If I'm not exactly the life and soul of the party," she said, "it's not because of anything to do with you. I'm a bit worried." She looked into his face and smiled. "It's nothing very bad," she assured him. He relaxed visibly. "But I have to make a decision, and it may be important. I hate making decisions, don't you? You know you have to turn either right or left, and both turns look about the same, but you know that the whole rest of your life is going to be changed, and you'll never know for sure whether it mightn't've been better if you'd gone the other way."

"Or it might have been worse," he pointed out consolingly. "If you thought about every decision that way you'd soon end up paralyzed."

"I feel a little paralyzed," she said. She broke a small piece off her roll and broke the small piece into halves and one of the halves in turn into halves, and then noticed what she was doing and brushed the crumbs aside as though they were to blame.

"A nervous wreck!" she said. She smiled. He smiled.

"For a nervous wreck, you have the most wonderful smile," he said. "How could someone like you have anything to worry about? Is it something to do with your family?"

"It's nothing like that," she said. "It's something annoyingly petty, in one way. But I can't not talk about it. I've already talked Mary's ear almost right off. Do you mind if I ask you what you think? It'll probably ruin our dinner and you'll never want to see me again."

"Go on," Richard said calmly.

"Well, I don't know if you took zoology," she began grimly. "It doesn't matter. But anyway there's a class of creatures called Nemertinea." Richard judiciously sipped his sherry and tried to look sympathetically receptive.

"Yes," he said.

"Now you won't laugh at me, will you?" Camilla said. "Sometimes Mary does, and it's infuriating. She doesn't care about college as much as I do. She doesn't have to."

"Go on," Richard said quietly.

"The Nemertine ribbon worms are long, soft-bodied, and unsegmented. Very long, some of them." She looked up at him, and he recognized the shining zeal of scholarship in her eyes; awareness of her own knowledge obviously excited her. "There's a marine worm called the *Lineus marinus*, or sea snake, that's said to be the longest animal in the world."

He nodded in acceptance of this curiosity.

"They're only about as thick as spaghetti," she said, "or as thin, but they sometimes reach a length of a hundred feet or more."

"Really?" he said. "That's amazing."

"Their bodies are as soft as velvet and a sort of purplish color. Quite beautiful. Not very amazing though – except, in a way, I suppose, *everything's* amazing, isn't it, when you think about it?"

"But how," he asked mildly, "does this astonishingly long worm inconvenience you?"

As he asked the question, the waitress arrived with two small dishes on pedestals. They contained an opaque pale orange sauce in which strips of lettuce and a few shrimps were almost entirely immersed. The waitress looked at Richard with resentful menopausal distrust. Camilla laughed, and the waitress looked at her too and then went away again.

"I got off the track," Camilla said. "I usually do. I love zoology – everything about it. I could go on for hours. Even the simplest, most rudimentary protozoa fascinate me. They really do. My mother thinks it's just a phase. But they're *life,* aren't they? Some people think everything's based on mathematics, but I don't. Mathematical laws may seem very fundamental, and they are, in a way, but, gosh, they're really only ways of describing things that are already there, aren't they? Things or forces or states of being. These shrimps are good, aren't they? My father always takes me out for a sea-food dinner when I go home. Poor man. I just eat and eat and eat till I almost pass out."

Richard gave her a kindly, paternalistic smile. It was pleasant to watch her face animatedly changing as the thoughts burbled out. She had a tiny piece of shrimp on her lower lip. The pink tip of her tongue tidily removed it, and she went on talking.

"The more elementary a thing is," she said, "the more exciting, in a way. I mean if you want to try to discover what everything's all about. But academically you have to consider other goals as well, don't you? I mean, you can't mess around with worms all your life, can you?"

"No," Richard said, trying to echo her indignation convincingly. "But you're not stuck, are you? You're a senior. You'll graduate in June, won't you?"

"Yes, I'll graduate," she said. "I'm on the Dean's List. I'm not bragging about it; it's just a fact, and I'm proud of it. But I want to graduate better than anyone in the department's ever graduated before. I told you this morning that I wanted to be a teacher, didn't I?"

"Yes."

"Now I'm not so sure. You see, we haven't very much money. We have enough, but no more than enough. I've had to have jobs all the way through Digby. I don't mind. I really don't. I think jobs can be meaningful experiences, in a way. But this afternoon I almost felt like giving up. I was thinking about all we talked about at the Elite."

"I've been thinking about nothing else," Richard said.

"Unfortunately I had to," Camilla said. "This pill I've been working for. The character who gives all the ridiculous quizzes. He's my employer, too."

Richard rather wished she'd get on with it.

"I've got this ghastly boring bunch of chores to do in his lab," she said. "He seems to take a fiendish pleasure in giving me the most horribly dull things to prepare. I think if I see another section of *Lineus marinus* on a slide I'll – I'll scream!"

Richard's hand reached forward and touched hers on the table. Her eyes were glittering with tears. She blinked and smiled.

"It's all right," she said. "I'm not going to cause a scene. I know I'm being unreasonable."

"Not at all unreasonable."

"I've been studying too hard probably. But it isn't completely unreasonable to almost go out of your mind if you have to do the same sort of chores day after day, is it? He says I've got to stay with the elementary classes be-

cause the schedules have already all been made out and
it's too complicated to switch them around, and anyway
I can't have a job during my own class hours. He's right,
of course. That's one of the most annoying things about
him."

"What sort of man is he?"

"Oh, he's about a hundred and ten years old," Camilla
said. "He smells of stale cigarettes."

"It's only for a few more months," he said. He paused.
"Look," he said. "Why don't you quit? I'd be glad to let
you have some money. It could be a loan, if you want.
You could pay me back one day. There wouldn't be any
hurry."

"Oh, no!" Camilla exclaimed, looking quite alarmed. "I
couldn't do that. I mean, thanks, thanks a lot; it's very
nice of you. But I've never borrowed a cent from anybody.
No, here's the thing. I've just been offered another job, and
I don't know whether I should take it or not."

"What is it?"

"It's in the Biology Department," Camilla said. "A lot of
the kids have already been interviewed for it. I was told
this afternoon by someone who works in the office that
my name is at the head of the list. It's mostly a matter of
grades, but not only grades. I may not seem very systematic to you in this mood I'm in, but I really am a very efficient lab technician. I just am. Everyone in the department
knows that."

Richard looked admiringly at her slender, smooth, white
fingers, the beautiful fingernails, pink and white under a
demurely colorless varnish. It was difficult to imagine them
slicing worms, but not impossible. They were supple-look-
ing hands, but they handled the tools of the dining room
quite authoritatively.

"Would the work be interesting?" Richard asked. Camilla hesitated and looked down at her plate before answering.

"I'm not sure," she said. "I mean, I don't really know. I
don't even know what it would be exactly, except that it's
a job in a lab. The project is under the direction of someone I hadn't heard of before. She just arrived here, like
you. Dr. Schumann her name is. I looked her up and she's
very well qualified. It's a new research project of some

kind. She didn't tell me much, so I can't tell you." She looked into Richard's face and looked down again. She cut at her remaining piece of steak but then abandoned it. "It's one of those madly secret research things," she said brightly. "She said she was quite sure I'd find the work invaluable. She even said that if I did well at it she felt it might lead to a really important graduate school appointment. She said I'd have my master's thesis practically all ready-made. I might even want to go on to medical school, she said."

"Did you like her?"

"Well, she was very flattering about my record, and that's always nice to hear, let's face it. She said she'd take me more fully into her confidence after I signed the contract. There's a security clause. I asked her if . . ."

"What?"

"Oh, it doesn't matter."

"Maybe it's something to do with biological warfare," Richard said with a forced smile.

Camilla laughed. "I don't think so," she said. She smiled at him. "I'm sorry to come and cry on your shoulder like this."

"Any time," he said. "Try and eat some more of your steak. Drink some wine. Everything will be all right."

"Do you think so?" Camilla said, intently searching his face for guarantees. "I said I couldn't possibly sign a contract until she told me more about the job. What I myself would have to do. And she kept saying I was worrying unnecessarily; I had to have faith. The job was very important. Selection for it was a great honour and all that jazz. She seemed very dedicated though. I was impressed, but we seemed to have reached an impasse. Then she told me the salary. It's nearly three times what I'm getting now."

"How did you leave things then?"

"I said I'd like to think about it. She said she must have my decision tomorrow. There's some element of urgency. They want to get started by the beginning of next week, she said."

"I think you should take it," Richard said. "It'd be a change from what you've been doing."

"Yes, I suppose so," Camilla said plaintively. "It seems

a very unscientific basis for decision-making though, doesn't it?"

"Science isn't everything," Richard said.

The heresy startled Camilla. She looked at him to see whether he was joking and decided to give him the benefit of the doubt.

They sat talking for a long time over coffee, until the waitress began clearing up around them more and more ostentatiously.

"I'll drive you home," Richard said.

"There's no need to do that," she said quickly. "I've had a wonderful evening, but the walk would do me good. It's only a couple of minutes across the campus. There's no need to drive all the way around."

"Come on," Richard said masterfully.

In the car, she reluctantly gave him directions.

"I don't belong to a sorority," she confessed.

Richard lightly kissed her cheek. "Silly," he said.

On the way, Camilla casually asked him how long he was planning to stay in Digby, and vehemently he replied that he was going to stay as long as possible.

At the dormitory, Richard began to open his door, but Camilla asked him to stay in the car.

"Please," she said. "I loved every minute, and you've been a big help."

He sat and watched her hurry along the flagstone pathway and run up the dormitory's floodlighted front steps where other couples were saying good night. Just before entering the building, Camilla turned and waved. Richard sounded the horn and drove away. He felt that the evening, if not an unqualified success, had been a start.

FOURTEEN

THE Digby Institute Pilot Research Population Group, twenty-two white adult females and eight white adult males, assembled in the renovated zoology lecture room in the Biology Building the following Monday morning.

Like so many others engaged more or less successfully in prostitution these days, when not actively on duty they were practically undistinguishable in appearance and behavior from any ordinary group of citizens of their age and income brackets, between eighteen and fifty years old and $6,000 and $20,000 a year. There had been no need for Dr. Porter to give them cautionary instructions about the proper mode of dress for visitors to a college campus. Both the men and women were wearing those well-cut, conservatively fashionable, unexceptionably dull suits or non athletic sport clothes that set the majority of Americans apart from the flamboyantly, eccentrically or shabbily costumed persons of other lands. If any of the whores erred, most of them did so on the side of conspicuously exaggerated respectability. Having taken Dr. Porter's timid injunctions too literally, some of the younger women had arrived at Digby wearing no facial make-up whatsoever. The tightest skirt, the lowest neckline and most vivacious cosmetics were worn by a voluptuous brunette in her mid-thirties who had attended Sarah Lawrence College, studying the theater, before discovering her true métier. Her name was Pru Griswolde, and there was an aggressive ostentation about the sensuality of her gait that caused some of her colleagues to look slightly embarrassed.

Generally, however, the group looked as natural and wholesome and discreetly outgoing as members of a new suburban country club attending their first committee meeting. As usual in any inaugural gathering of cooperative strangers, a few individuals, especially some of the men, perhaps because they were in a minority, sat quietly apart, content at first only to look on and listen as the others chatted inconsequentially about the sunshine, the traffic conditions they had experienced on the way down, and the attractive spaciousness of the small college town, compared with the big city they had all just left.

Lawrence Da Silva, who was wearing a chocolate-brown vicuña hacking jacket, a pale-beige cashmere sweater and fawn cavalry-twill trousers, sat with his exquisitely coiffed fair head bowed attentively over an emery board with which he was shaping his nails, until Rollo Hawkins gave him an almost invisible but severe little nudge and whispered a few words. Lawrence histrionically sighed, but put the emery board away in his pocket and sat up straighter. Dr. Schumann, followed by Dr. Porter, had entered the room.

Dr. Schumann's face was composed in a calm expression of dignity and confidence. Dr. Porter's smile to the audience was one of proprietary approval. Dr. Schumann had been very pleased with the speed and success of Dr. Porter's recruitment expedition. When she had asked him how he had managed so well, he had been suitably modestly vague, and she had been most favorably impressed. He was in a good mood.

They mounted the steps at the side of the lecture platform. Dr. Porter sat down on one of the chairs behind the lectern and looked at the men and women gathered together in front of him. By chance, he caught Rollo's eye. Rollo winked it at him, and Dr. Porter quickly looked away, pretending that he had not noticed, but blushing. Dr. Schumann, in a simple dark-purple woolen suit that strikingly complemented the gleaming dark copper of her hair, walked to the lectern, placed both her hands on it in an attitude of presidential authority, and cleared her throat. The room was absolutely silent.

"Good morning," she said cordially. "Welcome to Digby. I'm not going to bother to use this microphone. Why don't those of you in the back move on down to fill the seats in front? We are all going to be working very closely together during the weeks ahead. Let's get acquainted right from the start." There were scrapings of chairs against the tiered floor and polite murmurs of "Excuse me" and "Thanks a lot" and "You're welcome," and soon the audience had rearranged itself more compactly, in the center of the front three rows.

"That's better," Dr. Schumann said. "Now. I want to tell you about your role in our program here. Dr. Porter and I appreciate your having decided to participate, and I want to make sure that you too appreciate your opportunities to help make medical and social history. Yours is the way of the pioneers. You are the pathfinders. Where you are about to lead, Mr. and Mrs. America will follow. I want you to think about what that means. But first, to facilitate your personal orientation, to make you feel at home here in Digby, we're going to see a short movie. As Dr. Porter knows, I'm a great believer in the visual. So sit back and make yourselves comfortable. This ... is Digby." Dr. Schumann looked up toward the projection booth at the back of the auditorium, nodded and smiled. "Any time you're ready!" she called.

A beam of dusty blue-white light illuminated the large screen behind and above the lectern and the room was suddenly full of the inspirational loud brazen fanfare and clashes and rattles and thuds of the Digby Drum and Bugle Corps.

"The Digby Story," proclaimed the title, spelled out in ardent crimson and yellow Gothic letters. A squad of drum majorettes in red-plumed white shakos, white blouses and red-tasseled white miniskirts proudly strutted toward the camera, raising their knees high and twirling silver batons like airplane propellers. The drum majorettes faded out, like spiritual giantesses marching across the blue sky, as an aerial view of the Digby stadium faded in, crowded with cheering students on a gloriously bright autumn afternoon. Then the cheers faded, the stadium faded, and there was a shot of the campus, the trees, the lawns, the white Doric columns of the library, and a handsome young man and a pretty young woman with books under their arms, walking down the broad white stone steps. "Digby College, Ohio," said a roundly euphonious disembodied voice. "A fun place – and a work place, too! Yes, Digby has come a long, long way since 1893, when a God-fearing New Englander by the name of Ebenezer Digby first dreamed a dream...." There was a glimpse of an actor wearing an old-fashioned suit and long side whiskers, and then a montage of white-coated scientists peering intently at test tubes and retorts, through microscopes, at a cyclotron, and at an interplanetary rocket blasting off. "Digby is tradition, to be sure. But Digby is more than that. Digby is a promise of a better life tomorrow!" There was a lot more along the same lines. When the film was over there was a spontaneous outburst of applause, Marcia Daventry's eyes were glittering with tears, and even Rollo's smile seemed to lack cynical conviction.

Then Dr. Schumann told them, in some detail, about their accommodations on campus, the recreational facilities to which they would have special limited access, and their duties.

FIFTEEN

"NATURALLY there are limits to the overlap of our interests," Camilla reported to her roommate. "But the overlap is there, I'm sure. It's very encouraging. Richard is wonderfully open-minded about everything. I've never met anyone quite like him before."

"Sort of a Renaissance man?" Mary suggested. She was standing by the hot plate, waiting for the percolator to finish bubbling.

"I'm not really one-hundred-per-cent sure that he was absolutely entirely interested when I went on and on about zoology," Camilla said. "But he listened. He really listened. He didn't just kid me about it."

"You mean not like a certain English Lit major who from now on shall be nameless?"

"There never was anything between me and Dwight."

"This is the real thing," Mary said.

"You always make everything sound like a movie star arriving at an airport," Camilla complained. " 'This time it's for keeps'."

"Black or white?" Mary asked, pouring coffee.

"White, please," Camilla said, frowning at herself in the dressing-table mirror. "I wish I could put on about ten pounds. Maybe I ought to start eating breakfasts."

"He seems to hunger for a more ample blubberiness than you offer?"

"We talked about architecture," Camilla said aloofly. "His architecture. And music, and how they're both related to mathematics."

"And that got you back to where you came in. Back to the good old lab."

"I admitted that Digby's stronger in the sciences," Camilla said. "Most places are. They have to be. But I pointed out that the people in the sciences and the people in the humanities are making a real effort to meet each other halfway. And if you met Richard at a party I bet you wouldn't be able to guess right off whether he was a chemical engineer or a linguist ... or anything. He's great about listening, but he isn't just passive. I know he was really thinking. I could feel it."

"He can say yes with feeling."

"There you go again!"

"No," Mary said. "He sounds fine. I wish you'd let me know if you stumble into another one like him. One for me."

"I don't believe in fate, of course," Camilla said. "But it was lucky, wasn't it? Someone I can really talk to. Someone really interesting. I even asked him for advice about the job."

"And he said?"

"He said take it."

"That's what you'd already planned to do anyway."

"Well, yes, probably. But I cared about his reaction. He seems to be an idealist, but practical. His opinions matter to me."

"And he just happens to be fantastically good-looking."

"Yes," Camilla said matter-of-factly. Dreamily she sipped coffee and smiled. "He is."

"But that's incidental," Mary said. "It's the meeting of minds that counts, right?"

"In the long run," Camilla said defensively. "Yes. Certainly."

"And you think this looks like it's set for a long run?"

Camilla only took another sip.

"But I assume he hasn't as yet made any lunges?" Mary said.

" 'Lunges'!" Camilla said. "Honestly, Mary!"

Mary impatiently snorted.

"Now that you've told an outsider about the new job, can you possibly see your way clear to telling me?"

"It's so technical, Mary," Camilla said. "I didn't bore him with it. I won't bore you. It's just another lab. You're always accusing me of putting men off with lab talk. Richard and I switched back to architecture. He's doing very well, considering he's only just begun. They're breaking ground for his building within a week or two. He's very excited about it. He explained about functionalism and ornament, and composition and design, and how you achieve balance in painting and sculpture. And architecture."

99

"Did you take notes?"

"Very funny," Camilla said. "Scientists aren't inhuman. I listened to everything he said. But sometimes I was looking at him talking, more than listening to the actual content."

"Did he kiss you?"

"Oh Mary!"

"Did he? In the car? Did he walk you to the door? Right up to the searchlights and machine guns? Did he kiss you good night?"

"Sometimes, Mary . . ."

"When are you seeing him again?"

"Tomorrow afternoon," Camilla said. "After work. We're going to the art gallery. He promised to explain things."

"You're the one that's soon going to have to do some explaining," Mary said. "Sometimes, Camilla, love, you make me think of a Pilgrim fresh off the Mayflower."

"Is that so bad? I don't know what you expect me to tell you. We had dinner. We talked. There's nothing wrong with reticence about some things."

"Maybe there was nothing wrong with chastity belts, too, in their day," Mary said. "Though I think they must have been horribly uncomfortable."

"Why do you have to always go through the same old argument?" Camilla said.

"Argument?" Mary said. "What argument?"

"I'm sure you don't really disagree with me," Camilla coaxingly insisted. "Not in principle, deep down. You always make me feel so *square*."

"Seven out of ten college girls really do disagree with you," Mary said. "And I'm not so sure about the other three."

"Some surveys claim those statistics are 'way off," Camilla said.

"O.K., O.K.," Mary said. "You're right and I'm wrong. Let's not make a Federal case out of it. It's something personal that everyone has to figure out for herself. Right? Let's leave it at that. I believe in peaceful coexistence."

"I like you a lot," Camilla said. "You know that, don't you?"

"Thanks, Mary," Camilla said. "Good night," She turned over onto her side in the dark and immediately went to sleep.

"All right, stupid. Good night. And I hope you have a ball at the gallery. I mean it."

SIXTEEN

AFTER their day of familiarisation and indoctrination, touring the campus, getting settled in their various rooming houses, and attending an informal get-acquainted mixer in a private reception parlor in the Digby Inn, most of the thirty research subjects were glad to retire early for the night.

"It seems like a nice place," Marcia told her maid. Billie was going to stay with her in Digby, though there was not going to be much for her to do in their small two-room apartment, except, as Marcia put it, "boost morale." In the living room, a convertible sofa had been made up as an extra bed. Billie had tested the springs skeptically with a strong, probing hand, and had been pleasantly surprised by their soft resilience.

"It'll make a nice rest," she said. "My! I wish some of your gentlemen friends could see you now – Miss Marcia Daventry back at college!"

"What do you mean, 'back'?" Marcia said, smiling. The smile disappeared. "You know, Billie, when I was watching that film today – they showed a Technicolor film, all about the history of Digby College – I couldn't help thinking to myself, shit, it must be a good deal, getting an education."

"What's such a good deal about that?" Billie demanded loyally. "You talk a whole lot more sense than some of those college men who sometimes come around. You got an educated *body*. That other stuff anyone can pick up any time, that book knowledge, out of books. You can buy books."

"No, Billie. It kind of gets you. That atmosphere. It made me wish . . ."

As she spoke, Marcia slowly undressed, throwing her clothes casually over chairs and onto her bed, while Billie followed her and automatically gathered the fallen garments to fold and hang up or to launder. When Marcia reached her hands behind her back and fumbled with the clasp of her brassière, Billie stood still and gazed with reverent expectancy, waiting for the release of the pale-

102

brown-tipped round white breasts. They slumped plumply free, rubberily bouncing, until Marcia captured them in her cupped hands and held them up like two prizes and looked down at them. The shiny circles of smooth dark skin around the nipples began to pucker, as her nipples reddened, and became more pointedly prominent, like small red-rubber erasers.

"Think what it would be like to have a fabulous vocabulary and general knowledge and talk about things you know," Marcia said, absent-mindedly gratifying her breasts by slowly kneading the two handfuls of flesh. "Think of people calling me 'Dr. Daventry.' Wouldn't that be wild?"

"Do you want me to fix you a drink or something?" Billie asked.

"It'd be too much, Billie. 'Dr. Daventry.' That'd impress Joanna and her European friends, wouldn't it?" She smiled mockingly with heavy eyelids at the thought, and then became aware of the warmth in her hands. "Billie, go to my cosmetics case, will you? Fetch me that bottle of skin conditioner from Paris, France. It's the pink, oily one with that crazy perfume, Billie."

"But it's early yet. Don't you want a cocktail and a bite to eat?"

"The oil, Billie. I had a couple of vodkas at the reception. Billie, I feel kind of sexy."

"I swear," Billie said, "when the time comes you don't feel kind of sexy – that'll be the day!"

Disapprovingly clicking her tongue, but then unable to repress a smile of marveling admiration, Billie went to the bathroom, while Marcia, more hurriedly now, removed her black suspender belt and gray silk stockings, ripped aside the blankets and sprawled heavily on the bed.

A few minutes later, Billie tip-toed back into the dim room. She was naked, carrying only a pink bottle. Standing beside the bed, she unscrewed the plastic cap, carefully placed it on the glass-topped table next to the head of the bed, poured some of a viscous, sweet-smelling fluid into the palm of her hand and leaned solicitously forward.

"Great!" Marcia murmured. "Oh, God, Billie, that's great. I've been thinking about it all day."

For minutes, the only sounds in the room were the sounds of laborious breathing and the rhythmical slushy friction of oily flesh against flesh. Occasionally there were whispers, whimpers and cries of admiration, exhortation, gratitude and appeal. "A little higher, Billie. There, Billie. Not too fast. Easy. Easy, Billie. That's it. Yes. Yes. Yes, Billie! Oh, yes!"

Then there were incoherent guttural sobs and squeals. Then only a deep, slow, irregular panting. Then, after some minutes of silence, Marcia spoke again.

"Maybe Dr. Schumann could fix it so I could take a couple of courses. That'd shake Joanna, wouldn't it? If I wrote her and said I was at Digby Institute, huh?"

"I don't want to seem selfish," Billie said with ponderous irony, "but do you mind if we talk about your starlet daughter after a while? How about yours truly?"

"I'm sorry, honey," Marcia said. "I was just thinking. Turn around the other way."

Adjustments were made.

"Wouldn't it be just too much though?" Marcia insisted, before settling down with a will to her democratic task.

SEVENTEEN

"And so to work!" said Dr. Schumann, smiling over the top of her reading glasses as encouragingly as a Girl Scout den mother. "You've found your accommodation quite comfortable, I trust? You're sleeping well?"

"Just fine," Pru Griswolde replied, sitting on the edge of the visitor's chair in front of the desk in Dr. Schumann's office. "I haven't slept this well in ages. Not as long either." But the question had been rhetorical, a mere pleasantry. Dr. Schumann, seated stiffly upright behind her desk, was looking through papers in a manila folder. "It can be a positive pleasure, can't it?" Pru said. "Unconsciousness, I mean."

"What?" Dr. Schumann said, looking up again. "Oh, yes. Good. Very good. You've completed the initial questionnaire very well indeed. I see that you're a Sarah Lawrence alumna. That's very interesting."

"It's not so unusual," Pru said defensively. "Some of my best friends are literate."

"I suppose educational standards in your field have risen generally," Dr. Schumann acknowledged. "Even so, I consider the Institute fortunate to have your cooperation. Articulate subjects such as yourself will be of inestimable value in formulating the standards by which less eloquent verbal responses can be measured."

"Groovy," Pru said sarcastically. Dr. Schumann gave her a sharp look of reproof.

"Sorry," Pru said. "I was only kidding. You reminded me of my mother. I really am interested though. Otherwise I wouldn't be here, would I?"

"This is a serious enterprise," Dr. Schumann said. "I'm relying on you to help set the tone." She relented a little and smiled. "I'm sure we're all a bit tense today. It'll all get easier, no doubt, as we progess. For the first few days we'll be carrying out the preliminary medical examinations and the case-history interrogations. All in private, of course. We respect the fact that the individual personality is sacrosanct. You won't be Prudence Griswolde on the record. You will be Subject A. I assure you that the public will never learn Subject A's identity."

"Right," Pru said. "So what do I do?"

"Our Miss Fairbank will conduct you to the wardrobe department and assign you a personal locker. It will be perfectly secure. You may leave your valuables there during the day. And your clothes, of course."

"My clothes?"

"Of course. On arrival for each session, thirty minutes before the time of your appointment, you will check in at the locker room, have a shower, don your laboratory costume, and rest in the lounge until called for. We want you to shed your outside persona here, and relax, and be *yourself*."

"Starting today?"

"Starting right now, Miss Griswolde – that is, Subject A. If you'll excuse me now, I have some paper work to attend to." Dr. Schumann smiled reassuringly and pressed a switch on the desk intercom console.

"Yes, Dr. Schumann?" asked a small, nasal voice.

"Subject A is ready," Dr. Schumann said. "Please have Miss Fairbank step this way." She snapped off the intercom and turned again to Pru. "I wish you a very rewarding stay here," Dr. Schumann said. "If you have any questions or comments, please don't hesitate to let me know."

"Thank you," Pru said.

"You're entirely welcome." In answer to a knock on the door, Dr. Schumann said, in her commanding professional voice, "Come in. Ah, Miss Fairbank. Please. Subject A to wardrobe."

Camilla was dressed in a nurse's white coat, white stockings and white shoes, which made her face look more radiantly peachy than ever. She nodded gravely, like a conscientious young actress playing her first big part.

"Right away, Dr. Schumann," Camilla said. She turned toward Pru with a courteous inclination of the head and murmured, "Follow me, please." With an almost imperceptible shrug of the shoulders, Pru followed her out of the office.

They walked along the pinkish-gray-carpeted corridor with businesslike rapidity, in silence except for the creak of Camilla's new shoes and the brisk swish of nylon.

106

"Hey, slow down a little, can't you?" Pru protested. "Where's the fire?"

"Excuse me," Camilla said, slackening her pace, enabling Pru to catch up and walk beside her. "Dr. Schumann said it was important to keep to the schedule of appointments. It's going to be a real busy day."

"What's a nice girl like you doing in a place like this?" Pru asked with a strange twisted smile.

"What?" Camilla echoed, blushing and smiling perplexedly.

"You know the old gag," Pru said impatiently. "I get it all the time. Male customer to whore with books and paintings and a Vassar pennant on her bedroom wall. You're supposed to answer, 'Just lucky, I guess'."

Camilla looked blank. She tried to laugh politely but only coughed instead.

"When it comes to jokes like that," she confessed candidly, "my roommate says you have to draw me a diagram. But anyway, we're all here cooperating for the sake of science, aren't we? That's the important thing. As long as you remember that then I don't think backgrounds matter, do you?"

"Well, goody-goody," Pru said nastily. "That's a load off my mind." Camilla flinched as though she had been slapped in the face.

"Here are the dressing rooms," she said resolutely. "You can have any one of these lockers, as you're the first. The showers and toilet facilities are through that door. Here's a whole stack of smocks – all sizes – and some slippers. If you'll just ring the bell by the door when you're ready, I'll take you to the examination room."

"Thanks, kid," Pru said. "Is this your first day, too?"

"Yes," Camilla said. She shyly smiled.

"Take it easy. It's going to be a gas. Something to tell your grandchildren. And I bet you're the kind that'll have grandchildren by the dozen." Again, Camilla's cheeks prettily pinkened.

"Ring if there's anything you need," she said. She wasn't quite sure whether Pru was hostile or wanted to be friendly. However, Camilla decided, it would probably be better in the end for all concerned, in the circumstances, if the relationship were kept meticulously impersonally correct,

107

"Dr. Schumann expects you in fifteen minutes."

"Dr. Schumann?"

"She's doing the physical," Camilla said. "Dr. Porter will do the case-history interview."

"Big deal," Pru said.

"All right then?"

"All right."

Camilla left the room, closing the door behind her.

Alone, Pru seemed less self-assured. She looked apprehensively around the windowless pale-pink Female Dressing Room and began slowly to undress. She began to look younger as her clothes came off. Some of the voluptuousness was synthetic – padded breasts, a tightly cinched waist, and padded hips. The body itself was modestly lithe. She peered closely into the full-length mirror inside her open locker door and ran her hands lightly down over her ribs, her flat abdomen and her long, slender thighs, as though seeking for reassurance, in vain. There was a tender vulnerability, a pathos even, about her delicate collarbones, her small, pale nipples, and the mousy, light-brown, triangular tuft of pubic hair. The gleaming dark-brown hair on her head was, of course, dyed.

"Oh, hell," she said to the brightly made-up face in the mirror. "What the hell are you doing here? What the hell are you trying to prove?" She stuck out the pointed pink tip of her tongue and scowled in a grimace of girlish defiance, so that it wouldn't seem to herself that she was taking herself too seriously.

She stayed a long time under the shower, stretching under hot spray, soaping herself unnecessarily thoroughly, washing away the lather, and soaping herself again. The warm, scented foam made her breasts feel more significant than they had looked. She washed and washed and washed between her legs with puritanical zeal that gradually turned into a glow of self-appreciation. She washed all the cosmetic colour from her face. Then after drying herself, she got her pocketbook from the locker shelf, and carefully repainted herself. She lightly rouged her nipples, rigid points, and felt better. She brushed her hair until her wrist ached. She examined herself again in the mirror, and she thought she looked O.K. She donned a female laboratory smock, a pink nylon Mother Hubbard shift with

DIGBY INSTITUTE embroidered in small capital letters over the left breast, and felt another qualm of inadequacy. She was chewing her lower lip pensively when the dressing-room door opened.

"Are you all right?" Camilla gently inquired.

"Huh? Me? Oh, sure. Let's go," Pru said gaily. "Lead on." She stuck her feet into a pair of heelless woolly pink slippers and followed Camilla along another silent corridor. Camilla opened a door and ushered Pru inside.

The room was fitted out as an orthodox medical clinic, with a hard white rubbery floor, several gray steel cabinets, a tubular-steel-legged table and chairs, a gray plastic-topped examination table with a large adjustable overhead spotlight, and a large stainless-steel basin beside a stainless-steel counter cluttered with brightly glittering, sharply inquisitive-looking metal and glass instruments.

"Here you are!" Dr. Schumann genially exclaimed. She was now wearing a surgeon's green cap and gown and corpse-gray thin rubber gloves. "Thank you, Miss Fairbank. I'll buzz if I need you. Well, Subject A, I want you to consider yourself anonymous. Let's get you up on the table, shall we? Let's have a good look at you."

Pru felt afraid. Her smile was especially jaunty. "Do you want me to take this thing off?" she asked.

"Oh, yes, certainly. Everything off. We have to take inventory. You see, our sexual behavior is to a considerable extent regulated by our physiology. Not altogether by any means, but largely. Our file on Subject A would be almost meaningless without a complete physiological survey in your normal state of sexual nonarousal. Or relative nonarousal, I should say." Dr. Schumann chuckled good-humoredly. "Really, there's no such state as absolute non-arousal. Baby boys are sometimes born with their little penises in erection; old men's penises have been known to ejaculate at the moment of the death rattle. Did you know that? Asleep and awake, from the cradle to the grave, we're always being subjected to more or less sexual stimulation, aren't we? It's the human condition. But I mustn't get going on my pet theme just now. Will you please – that's it. Off with the smock! Jump up! Lie back. Tha-a-at's the girl. That's the way. That's fine. Fine. Hmmm. *Very* interesting. Very nice...."

109

Softly humming a cheerful though tuneless little song, Dr. Schumann busily pottered about, like a dentist investigating a nether mouth.

Pru lay rigidly still on her back. The hot light shone bright orange through her tightly closed eyelids. She felt Dr. Schumann's adroit rubber-clad fingers moving about with delicate yet firm precision. There was a faint clink of metal against glass. Pru felt something cold against one thigh. There was an intrusive thrust, and it seemed as though a tiny umbrella were being opened inside her. It didn't hurt, but the thought that suddenly it might caused Pru to gasp out aloud, and sweat to trickle down from her armpits.

"There, there!" Dr. Schumann reassured her. "This part doesn't take long. It's very important.... There. That didn't take long, did it? You didn't feel any discomfort, did you?"

"No," Pru said. "It's just that ..."

"Of course not. Lie back and relax. There's nothing to worry about. Do you manipulate yourself violently for prolonged periods?"

Pru said nothing. There was a moment of electric silence.

"Never mind," Dr. Schumann said casually. "There seems to be a slight hypertrophy.... But don't worry. It's not uncommon. It's quite all right. Relax...."

The examination continued, with clippers and tape measure, with thermometer and optical lenses, with syringe and needle, with rubber bulb and tubing, with scissors and probe, with X-ray camera and microscope slide, but always with clever hands and expressionless, unblinking eyes. Pru's upper arm was bound and tightened so that Dr. Schumann could read her blood pressure. Pru was asked to breathe deeply while her chest and back were softly thumped and sounded. Her pulse rate was counted. Her vision and hearing were tested. Every personal orifice was mechanically penetrated and inspected. All the time, Dr. Schumann almost inaudibly muttered numbers and descriptive medical phrases to herself and jotted them down on a printed form for Pru's dossier.

"These abdominal striations," Dr. Schumann said pleasantly, as though chatting about the weather. "So-called 'stretch marks.' Tell me – how many children?"

Pru hesitated.

"It's perfectly all right," Dr. Schumann assured her. "Childbirth doesn't disqualify you. We want all sorts of subjects."

"One," Pru said.

"Where does he or she live?" Dr. Schumann asked.

"It's dead."

Dr. Schumann asked Pru about her diet ("Everything," Pru said), her use of tobacco ("two packs of filter-tips a day"), and her consumption of alcohol ("Average, I guess.")

"How much?"

"I'm a social drinker – you know, a couple of cocktails, a few highballs." Pru laughed harshly. "Except when I get stoned."

"Intoxicated?" Dr. Schumann asked.

"Yeah," Pru said. "You could call it that."

"And how often does that happen?"

"When I'm with a man I don't like."

"I suppose that occurrence must be not infrequent?"

"You can say that again," Pru said.

"But you have no drinking problem?" Dr. Schumann insisted.

"No, that's not my problem," Pru said.

"It's really amazing," Dr. Schumann said. "The muscle tone is excellent. In fact, in general, you're in very good shape."

Pru sat up. "I am?"

"Yes, very."

"No kidding," Pru said.

"The human body is not a joke," Dr. Schumann said austerely. She frowned, but resolutely composed her face into a tolerant, calm, professional smile. "The answer is exercise, I suppose. You must take a good deal of regular exercise. What do you do?"

Pru grinned venomously. "Whatever they pay for."

Again a cloud passed across Dr. Schumann's face, but again she controlled herself. After all, it was to be expected that most, if not all, of the pilot group would manifest personality problems of one sort or another; their trade itself was one such manifestation. Dr. Schumann swallowed and smiled again. "I want to thank you again

111

for your cooperation," she said. "I'm sure I must be imposing quite a severe nervous strain on you."

"I've had other clients who were more difficult," Pru said sincerely. "Believe me. My nerves are in great shape."

"Subconsciously though," Dr. Schumann dogmatically insisted, "inevitably there must be certain residual feelings of resentment and resistance. To you, I must represent authority. A parent, perhaps, or a professor, or a police magistrate."

"To me you represent a doctor," Pru said. "No hard feelings. I just twitch a little. Doesn't everyone at the doctor's?"

"I assure you," Dr. Schumann said, "I'm not unprepared for hostility of this nature."

"It isn't anything personal," Pru began.

But Dr. Schumann, totally dominant now, raised a silencing hand. "Please," she said. "I'm going to give you something that will make you feel immediately much more relaxed. Naturally, you are perfectly free to activate the escape clause in your contract and resign from participation in the program at any time you choose. We'd be sorry to see you go; and, from your point of view, of course, there would be a considerable financial sacrifice. Your bonus. But we want you to feel absolutely free. A cooperative volunteer, not an employee. I think that once you feel more tranquil, more at home, you'll be able to see the Institute for what it is. In the meantime, let's just try this. . . ." Dr. Schumann turned away briefly, and turned back, holding a small cotton swab.

"Give me your arm," Dr. Schumann said. Pru automatically obeyed. Dr. Schumann sterilized a small patch of skin close to Pru's shoulder, returned to the counter, and brought back a large hypodermic syringe. Pru looked down at her arm and then nervously looked away. Hypodermic syringes have irresistible authority in the present epoch.

"There!" Dr. Schumann said, breathing out a moment later. "You didn't even feel it, did you?"

"What was it?" Pru asked, hypochondriac curiosity overcoming hypochondriac docility.

"Something to make your interview go more easily," Dr. Schumann said. "I won't bother you with a lot of technicalities. But I'm sure it'll help, almost immediately. You probably feel better already, don't you? Now: gown on, please. I'll get Miss Fairbank to show you the way."

Pru did, indeed, begin to feel pleasantly relaxed, glowingly numb. Dr. Schumann had injected into her a massive shot of a serum popularly known as a "truth drug".

Another corridor, another door. Camilla quietly withdrew again.

"Hi!" said Dr. Porter, holding out a glad hand. "Good morning!"

"Good morning," Pru said. She held out her hand. His fingers were warm and soft and moist.

"Subject A," he said. "This is quite a historic moment. I'm Dr. Porter. I'm sure we'll get along fine. Would you care for a cigarette?"

"No, thanks."

"Mind if I do?"

"Make it!"

"Well," Dr. Porter said, puffing smoke out through his nostrils. His forehead was shiny with sweat. "Let me tell you the way we're going to work. The possibilities. We can sit here in these armchairs – a face-to-face confrontation – for our chat about your background. Or we can have you talk in what we call our ... confessional. You're not a Catholic, are you?"

"No," Pru said.

"Not that it would matter if you were," Dr. Porter said. "I'm not saying a word against them. Those priests knew a thing or two, psychologically speaking. We have installed two side-by-side booths, visually isolated from each other but with audio two-way communication. Any interviewee who feels any initial bashfulness may elect to go into a booth."

"I feel fine," Pru said.

"You're sure?" Dr. Porter said. He took a handkerchief out of his pocket and mopped his brow. This wasn't going to be easy. "Well, we may as well sit here then. But if you change your mind at any time don't hesitate to let me know."

They sat down, on opposite sides of a coffee table. Dr. Porter switched on a tape recorder, and coughed a couple of times, told the machine the date, and the interview began.

"Now," Dr. Porter said, looking down at the interview form on his lap. "Miss A."

"Why don't you call me Pru?"

"That's very gracious of you," Dr. Porter said, squirming desperately from buttock to buttock. "But I think perhaps we had better abide by the ground rules."

Pru shrugged casually.

"So," Dr. Porter said, frowning. "Let me say first of all that while we would like you to answer all the questions as freely and fully as possible, you are always permitted to skip any question that you wish to."

Pru nodded and looked around the room. Beige wall-to-wall carpeting, a paler-beige wall. Van Gogh sunflowers instead of a window. A bookcase of new reference books that looked as if they had been chosen by an interior decorator.

"Your date of birth?" Dr. Porter was repeating.

"I'm thirty-four," Pru said.

"The exact birth date, please."

She gave it, and Dr. Porter smiled gratefully.

"Place of birth?"

"New York."

"New York City?"

"East Sixty-eighth Street, between Fifth and Madison," she said. "Or do you want the name of the hospital?"

"No, that's fine," he said. "The residential section is more significant." He made a note. "What is your father's occupation?"

"Bum," Pru said. She noticed Dr. Porter's expression of anguish and added: "He was an investor."

"Was?" Dr. Porter said, his voice down an octave and muted with the fake sympathy of an undertaker.

"He died when I was a kid. A dizzy spell on the Merritt Parkway. I was fourteen."

"I see. And what did your mother do then?"

"What she'd be doing. Organizing charity balls. Traveling. New York in the fall, Palm Beach in winter, Europe in the spring, Long Island in summer. You know — drinking and screwing."

Dr. Porter brusquely cleared his throat.

"Do you have any brothers and sisters?"

"No. I was a mistake."

"How would you describe the relationship between your father and mother? Or were you too young to notice up to the time he passed on?"

Pru laughed.

"Lousy," she said.

"What evidence brought you to that conclusion?" Dr. Porter asked.

"They lived apart most of the time," Pru said. "But whenever they got together – wow!"

"And on those occasions?"

"Screams in the night. The crash of porcelain and glass. Bloodstains in the bathroom. I was a pretty sensitive kid. Somehow I knew the honeymoon was over."

"You surmised that there was scant remaining mutual respect or fondness?"

"Scant as hell," Pru agreed.

Dr. Porter read the next question carefully, braced himself, and went on.

"The next section concerns your own acquisitions of sexual knowledge," he said. "Now please remember that you can speak out quite candidly, without any fear that anything you may say will ever leave this Institute identified with your name."

Pru calmly nodded.

"Can you tell me of your first awareness of your own sexuality – that is, your earliest memory of sexual experience or gratification?"

"Yes. One summer when we took a house at East Hampton I had this governess, nanny, or what-have-you – she was really a young Danish woman who'd come over for a year allegedly to improve her English."

"Yes?"

"She was one of those great-looking Scandinavian blondes. Like in one of those Swedish art films with midsummer outdoor love scenes. Terrific-looking. I was very impressed. I suppose I was, let me see, yes, nearly eleven years old. She taught me to do the back stroke. I was already quite a good swimmer. We had a pool that summer. There was a boathouse beside it. I can remember Birgitte, that was her name, sort of *posing* a lot when we were chang-

115

ing before and after swimming. Even the first time, I realized that she enjoyed being naked and being admired. I can still see the sun-bleached yellow hair, the suntan, the white flesh where the bikini had been. I was fascinated by the fact that we were alike but so different. I wanted to look like her. That was the first stage: I used to stare at her whenever I got a chance. And suddenly, I remember, suddenly I became aware of those incredible blue eyes, staring at me staring."

"Did either of you verbalize these initial experiences?"

"Talk? I'll say. She took the initiative. I didn't really know what it was all about. She was one of those nuts who use a lot of made-up baby-talk names for everything to do with sex. She really was so cute – when I think of it I almost have to throw up. But it was fun at the time. She told me about all the men she was meeting on her days off, and how naughty they were and all the naughty things they tried to do to her: they tried to touch *these,* and feel *that,* she said. And she'd take my hand and put it against her and press herself against my fingers."

"And you were only ten?"

"Yeah. Nearly eleven. And then she used to come to my room to say good night . . ."

"What did she do then?"

"She showed me how to while away the lonely hour of twilight. She gave me a hobby."

"You mean . . ."

"What else? She taught me about do-it-yourself sex. How to feel myself up."

There was a pause.

"Could you, would you, describe the method she showed you to use?"

"Nothing fancy," Pru recalled matter-of-factly. "Softly stroking the outside. Softly stroking, and then not-so-softly stroking, rubbing, squeezing."

"The mons area?"

"You make it sound like a geography lesson," Pru said.

"I was referring to the mons veneris," Dr. Porter informed her.

"Yes, I know you were referring to the mons veneris," Pru said. "I've read a few books. The Mount of Venus. It's really a very romantic phrase, until you start lousing it up.

Maybe you were referring to the mons area. I was referring to my twat."

"Please, Miss Griswolde!"

"Miss A, to you."

"Miss A," Dr. Porter said soothingly. "I'm sorry, but I'm making a scientific record. Inevitably, the terminology must be somewhat –"

"O.K., O.K., take it easy," Pru said. "Do you want to go on?"

"Yes, please, of course. Now, let me see . . ."

"Meanwhile, back on the mons," Pru said, trying to be helpful.

"Oh, yes. Quite."

"That alone was quite a kick," Pru said. "But then she taught me all about it. That was when I fell in love with my clitoris. We've been going steady ever since."

Dr. Porter cleared his throat again. "Did you attain orgasm?" he asked.

"Sure. A million of them. It was like the Fourth of July. After that, I could hardly wait to get to bed at night. It didn't matter though. Nobody noticed. They didn't give a damn. If anybody thought about it, they probably thought I was tired from all that swimming."

"How many times, how many nights, a week did you practice masturbation?"

"Seven."

"Were these masturbatory episodes accompanied by any sexual fantasy? What did you think about during this activity?"

"In the beginning I used to think about Birgitte's ass."

"Her posterior."

"The sun used to filter through the slats of the bathhouse Venetian blinds. I can still see it. The striped brown-and-white flesh. The brown, straight back, the slender brown waist, and the incredible roundness and whiteness – the white, white ass. It was beautiful. . . ."

Dr. Porter was silenced and immobilized by Pru's hushed voice of fond reminiscence.

After a moment, she continued.

"Then," she said briskly, "I began to think more about the expression on her face when I touched her. She was very physical. She had about as much poetry in her as some

117

housewife drooling over a TV food commercial. And then I used to think about myself, about the sensations I was feeling, and that became enough in itself. I didn't need anything more."

"Did your masturbatory techniques become more sophisticated? Did they vary in any ways? Did you ever make use of foreign objects?"

"I did it every way I could think of. I used anything that I could get. A hairbrush handle, candles, bananas – all kinds of goodies."

"Did you think of them as substitutes for the penis?"

"No. I thought of them as a hairbrush handle, candles, bananas, and so on."

"I see," Dr. Porter said sagely, making a quick note. "How long did this phase continue?"

"It hasn't finished yet," Pru said, smiling. "But there have been many distractions and interruptions. One of the most dramatic ones was when my mother caught me at it. I was in her bedroom, wearing one of her silk negligees, lying on her bed. Her bedroom was full of mirrors. Lovely big, formal mirrors in gilded frames. The sort of formality that makes you want to do something outrageous. I'd been doing a sort of *femme fatale* act, spraying myself with perfume, powdering myself with a big powder puff that she kept on her dressing table, parading around and looking at myself from all angles. The room smelled to high heaven. Like a New Orleans whorehouse on Sunday morning, as they say. And there I was, lying on the bed, the silk bedspread all wrinkled, my head pressed back in the silk pillows, my eyes shut, working away. Busy, busy, busy. I was using a liverwurst sausage, a great discovery."

"Liverwurst?" Dr. Porter said, his pen poised.

"Yes," Pru said. "Salami had an interesting texture, but at that age you don't go for garlic. I got the sausage idea in a local delicatessen, one of those de luxe gourmet places, where they have whole rows of sausages hanging from the ceiling like meat stalactites – phallic organ pipes. All sizes, from cherub to Tarzan. I was fascinated."

"Had you, at that age, actually ever seen the male genitalia?" Dr. Porter expressionlessly inquired.

"No," Pru said. "At the time, I didn't see the sausages as symbols, although I suppose there must have been instinctive recognition. To me, they were simply a whole assortment of the implements I was always looking for. Hey! I just thought of something. Maybe it's sausages and pickled gherkins that are keeping the small, independent delicatessens in business. I'm surprised the big chain stores haven't taken that over – meat dildos at the check-out counter. Sausages can't be illegal, can they, however suggestively they're shaped? Can you see some guy sueing his wife for divorce and citing a frankfurter?"

"Come now, Miss A," Dr. Porter scoldingly pleaded. "We really must keep to the point. You were telling me about your mother."

"This is the point, isn't it? How to ball in a society of dead-beats. I thought that was what you wanted to know. So put sausages on your list. Or how about *soap* dildos? I thought about that, too. A nice, perfumed, pink soap one for milady's bathroom. Kind of clever, when you think about it. It'd get smaller with use. People would always be buying new ones, long before the old ones were used up. Isn't that the kind of product we want in a consumer economy? Listen, Dr. Porter. I'm not so dumb. I always read the Time Essay."

"We know about your academic background," Dr. Porter said. "Nobody's denigrating it. But please."

"My mother," Pru said. "As I was saying. This sausage and I were making mad love. My eyes were shut. I was far gone. The whole world was dark blood-red and pounding like some sort of giant machine. A huge pile driver, thudding away. You know?"

Dr. Porter gritted his teeth against the question and noncommittally nodded for her to proceed.

"I don't know how long she must have stood there, the old bitch, taking in the scene," Pru said. "Perhaps she was learning a trick or two. But anyway suddenly she flipped. She screamed my name. '*Prudence*! What *are* you doing?' Is there a single person in the whole world – anyone – it could be a saint – I don't care who it is – that could honestly claim not to know?"

Dr. Porter had an uncomfortable pinned-down look. "The incidence of masturbation, in both males and females, at some time or another in their lives, is known to be high," he conceded.

"Like a hundred per cent," Pru said. "Including the janitor and the chairman of the board. Anyone who denies it is a liar. I still get mad when I remember my mother's phony scandalized voice: 'What *are* you doing?' What did she think I was doing? Embroidering a sampler, 'God Bless This Home!' She frightened me half to death. There's nothing worse than being frightened by an unexpected intruder when you're about to come. Your heart almost stops. I just about died of fright and shame – and anger. I covered myself with the negligee and just lay there, hoping she'd go away. But she didn't. She stayed and really let me have it."

"The chastisement was severe," Dr. Porter said.

"It was murder," Pru said. "She didn't beat me up or anything like that. She never laid a hand on me. Never. We were never that close. She tore me to shreds with words. On and on and on. I thought she'd never stop. It was like a seventeenth-century sermon rehashed for soap opera. I was completely bad. I had betrayed my heritage. So this was the way I was repaying her for all the years of devoted upbringing. I had desecrated womanhood – and that perfume cost sixty dollars an ounce. She lectured me in words a yard long on moral degeneracy, physical self-destruction, the meaning of marriage, and what a rotten, sneaky little rat I was. And where had I learned such a monstrous, diabolical perversion? She predicted social damnation, banishment to skid row, a state insane asylum, an early, painful death, and everlasting hell-fire. You can imagine how shaken I was. I, who had been counting on joining the Junior League one day."

"This experience clearly had a traumatic effect on you," Dr. Porter said. "What were the immediate results?"

"It was a revelation. I had always thought my mother was indifferent to me. Now I realized that she hated my guts. I think I even recognized the reason. I suddenly understood that she was jealous. So jealous she could hardly see straight. This awareness saved me from being completely destroyed. Getting it all down to that level, I saw that the main part of the criticism was practically meaningless. So I just kept the valuable part of the lesson she had taught me and threw the rest away."

"What do you mean?" Dr. Porter asked.

120

"She had taught me that when you're having sex in a hostile world you should always lock the door," Pru said.

Dr. Porter frowned, made a note, and valiantly carried on in his best clinical manner.

"Perhaps we had better be getting on," he said. "All we need is a factual profile. Would you tell me now of your experiences, heterosexual or homosexual, if any, during puberty?"

"The next historic turning point was falling in love for the first time," Pru related.

"At what age was this?"

"I was twelve, nearly thirteen."

"With a member of the opposite sex?"

"Yes, a boy," Pru said.

"Did intimacy take place?"

"Oh, yes. We were very intimate."

Dr. Porter nodded eagerly. "Please try to recall some details of the case," he said.

"We had moved to Bronxville," Pru began.

"In the Bronx?" Dr. Porter said, surprised. "Had there been a financial reverse?"

"No, Bronxville in Westchester County," Pru said. "My mother had remarried. A producer. He had to spend a lot of time in New York."

"I see."

"Again I was left alone a lot. My mother was firmly opposed to my being sent to boarding school, because she said I was the kind of girl that needed the reassurance of home life. As it worked out, though, I didn't see them very often. Our servants were nice to me, a childless couple, not young. In fact, they let me do anything I wanted."

"And the boy?"

"He went to the local high school. So did I. He was about two years older than I was. I was surprised that he'd even talk to me. He was crazy about football, baseball, basketball, track – everything. And I was only in the eighth grade."

"But . . .?"

"We fell in love."

"Please be specific," Dr. Porter said, a trifle testily. "The intimacy? What happened?"

"We used to write each other long, long letters. Twenty

121

or thirty pages sometimes. He wrote poems about me. His model was Herrick, I learned later. 'Jenny Kissed Me' — that kind of thing. I wish I still had them. Of course I haven't. Perhaps it's just as well."

"Did intercourse occur?"

"We kissed a lot."

"Oral-genital contacts, you mean?"

"No. On the face."

Dr. Porter looked puzzled.

"He used to kiss my mouth with his mouth," Pru explained, "and I used to kiss him back."

"That's all?"

"It seemed tremendous."

"And that, I presume, led to petting. Did you pet to climax?"

"No, it wasn't like that. But we went bowling quite often. Duckpins. He was marvelous to watch. Beautifully coordinated. Usually he took me for a soda afterwards."

"But nothing happened? Did you employ his image in masturbation during this period?"

"I don't remember doing that. I don't think so."

"Hmmm," Dr. Porter said. "How long did this go on?"

"About a month," Pru said. "We were very serious, but then it was summer, and we were sent to different summer camps. That's one of the great modern tragedies, separate camps. Romeo and Juliet isn't in it. My mother had changed her mind about family life. She said I needed a more impersonal discipline. They took off for Venice. I went to Maine."

"Feeling a deep sense of loss," Dr. Porter said. Pru shrugged.

"You'll like this next bit," she said brightly. "I was only at camp a few days, a few nights, when I had my first gang-bang."

"Your what?" Dr. Porter said. The alarmed expression on his face indicated that the term was not an entirely unfamiliar one.

"It was like getting my revenge against my mother," Pru said. "That's the way a head-shrinker might look at it. I had just received a letter from Ward. That was the name of the boy that I'd pledged eternal fidelity to. But he had fallen out of love with me and into love with some girl at *his* camp. I didn't blame him, not really. I felt it was my mother's fault. It *was* her fault. I had asked to go to the same camp. She had known about him. She had refused. But I fixed her. Or so it seemed. One of the counselors – a college kid, about eighteen – got me into a tent after lights out. There were three other counselors in the tent. Two or three. I couldn't see much. They had flashlights and they dazzled me. It was quite an initiation."

"Are you saying they had carnal knowledge of you?"

"Three, or however many there were, held me down and held my legs open while the other one screwed me. Then they took turns. I thought they'd never finish."

"You were supine and they assumed the superior, face-down position?" Dr. Porter said.

"The so-called 'Missionary Position'," Pru said. "You've got the picture. I lay on my back and they lay on top. Quite conventional boys. From very good families. This was no cheap camp."

"This must have been a profound shock to you."

"It hurt. But that was the way I figured it'd be like. Remember the words Bessie Smith used to sing? 'When he got through teaching me, from my elbows down was sore'."

"And what was your attitude towards males afterwards?"

"I'll tell you," Pru said, smiling again. "That summer, I really had a ball. You know why?"

"I'm surprised to hear it," Dr. Porter said.

"The next day, when I woke up in my own tent – I shared a big tent with nine other girls – I felt sore all right, but –"

"Physically?"

"Physically. But I felt surprisingly unchanged. I didn't feel at all crushed. I didn't feel defeated. Just the opposite. I thought to myself, 'O.K., fellas. If you want it that much. . . .' I went around to see the counselor who had instigated the whole thing. He was terrified! He practically went down on his knees and begged me not to turn him in. He'd had some beers, he said. He hadn't known what he was doing. Like hell he hadn't. I said I was ruined. I'd have to think it over. Maybe it was my duty to report them all to the police. On the other hand. . . ." Pru smiled at the remembered moment of triumph. "What did I want? he asked. He'd do anything, give me anything. Well, we came to terms. It was quite a summer. I came to the conclusion that sex was a very valuable commodity. The word is sex, and sex shall make you free. Everybody was happy."

"There were further experiences of heterosexual intercourse at the camp?"

"You know it!" Pru said.

"Did you derive sexual pleasure from them?"

"It's hard to say. Some maybe. But I certainly enjoyed the feeling of power. And I got more money than I knew what to do with."

"Yes," Dr. Porter said. He looked rather depressed for a moment, but rallied his professional faculties once more and continued. "Was intercourse always practiced with multiple partners?" he asked.

"Not always," Pru said. "Usually one at a time. They preferred it that way. Boys of that age are fantastically virile, of course, but they have very little confidence. They were afraid of being laughed at if they didn't perform well. I almost felt sorry for some of them. Almost. I had to help them. They were awkward and clumsy. I found myself, a young girl, teaching *them*. I learned a lot that way. You've no idea what it can do for a thirteen-year-old's self-esteem, the realization that all these hot-shot big-time-operators will give you anything you want if you promise them good sex. It's the sort of lesson that can carry a girl right through life. I was even able to face up to the thought of going back home."

"At what age did menstruation commence?"

"It had already started. I started quite young. When the time came that first month in camp I thought, 'Oh, hell!' But it did nothing but good. It forced me to develop other techniques. I bet it wasn't Helen of Troy's beauty that launched a thousand ships. She probably did the best blow job in town."

"Fellatio," Dr. Porter said pedantically.

"A rose by any other name!" Pru replied cheerfully.

"You practiced fellatio on these young men," Dr. Porter said.

"Almost drove them out of their tiny minds," Pru recalled. "I used to get quite a charge out of it myself. Working them up to the point of coming, and then keeping them there, straining on the brink. It's nice to know who's boss. They'd beg for mercy in the end. I loved that. The

124

muscular legs, shuddering and trembling. That was always a good time to talk about the price. I felt like Cleopatra and Madame Pompadour – 'Just give what you can, kid. Like your empire, some little knickknack like that. . . .' Never failed. I felt like Little Red Riding Hood."

"Little Red *Riding* Hood!" Dr. Porter said, his eyebrows raised.

"I have my own theory about her," Pru said, "and a lot of other characters in so-called children's stories. 'Oh, Grandma! What a big –' "

"I see, I see," Dr. Porter interrupted.

"Jack and the beanstalk," Pru said. "That beanstalk! Who do they think they're kidding?"

"We must remember that we're trying to conduct a scientific study," Dr. Porter said, as though reminding himself of some task that was eluding him. "Let us get back to what you were saying about – you were telling of various methods that you employed to give sexual gratification to young men at your first summer camp. Were there any other methods?"

"Nothing spectacular," Pru said. "Of course, it wasn't always possible to get away from the camp directors and the other kids. There were some narrow escapes. It was a challenge, getting in a quick feel, *en passant,* as it were. Do you play chess, Dr. Porter?"

"No, I do not," Dr. Porter said irritably.

"Too bad," Pru said. "Anyway. There were some funny incidents. The occasional grope under the table in the dining hall. In the camp movie theater in the evenings, trying to jack off your date without causing a commotion. 'Finger-tip control,' as they say in the automobile ads."

"You manipulated the penis while seated side by side, ostensibly watching a motion picture?" Dr. Porter said.

"You got it in one!" Pru congratulated him. "Haven't you ever done that in a theater?"

"Really, Miss A," Dr. Porter said. "I wish you would confine your statements to answering my questions."

"Don't lose your cool, doc," Pru said pleasantly.

"Would you now explain how you happened to enter your present occupation?" Dr. Porter asked. The question had a sobering effect, but Pru wasn't easily subdued.

"For that I have to thank my stepfather," she said.

"Indirectly, at least. I breezed through the rest of high school. I enrolled at Sarah Lawrence. For one thing, it was right there. And I liked the idea of a school with a liberal regime. Intellectually, I mean. And the emphasis on the arts. Plus the fact that it was so easy to get into New York from there. I was becoming interested in the theater. My interest seemed to flatter him, my stepfather, as though it had been a personal compliment to him. What an ego!"

"So?" Dr. Porter said, glancing covertly at his wrist watch. Pru saw him look.

"So after a couple of years at Sarah Lawrence, I was spending so much time with theater people, my academic career began to come apart at the seams. I goofed off. They gave me every encouragement to leave. There were a lot of little things, too, like getting into trouble with my car. Some wild nights. The authorities started nagging. My mother was giving me a hard time. I had another affair that turned sour. One too many. I moved into the city. Greenwich Village – what else?"

"It was in Greenwich Village ..." Dr. Porter said, but faltered at the thought of all that Bohemian irresponsibility.

"At first," Pru said, "my stepfather gave me an allowance. A good allowance, long enough for me to get used to the idea of living in a well-furnished apartment in a nice street. I wasn't getting any place in the theater – I never got a speaking part even *off*-Broadway, let alone on. But I was meeting a lot of swingers. Then things began to go wrong, or wronger, between my stepfather and my mother. He got the incredible idea that I found him attractive. What a scene *that* was! I told him to take his allowance and get lost, and much to my chagrin, that's what he did. I was almost broke. I borrowed some money from a young director. Then I borrowed some more. The loans somehow changed into gifts. At about the same time he somehow moved in with me. It didn't last long. I don't know if I gave him his money's worth. The next time I asked a man for money the period of self-delusion was shorter. Not that the man seemed cynical. In fact, I think he was one of the ones that wanted to get married. It's amazing how many of them do, even nowadays. The poor things get scared in the big city. I wasn't about to get married though. Someone offered me a big break in a little summer theater workshop near Cleveland. Lucky me! He drove me out in his car and we shared a room. My big break turned out to be painting scenery all day and listening to him read scripts at night – In addition to the usual sexual chores. I left him. I could be choosy. I was self-supporting now. I had a trade."

"But really it was just a matter of circumstances, a series of accidents," Dr. Porter said consolingly. "You're an amateur, really."

"We all are, really," Pru said, grinning at him. "You don't think there's a union, do you? 'The American Association of Lady Sex Operatives'? Where have you been?"

"Anyway," Dr. Porter said, looking openly at his watch. "That's a good stopping place for our first session, isn't it? I hope you're going to find *this* project worthwhile. I think you will. And now I must ask to be excused. I have a working lunch with Dr. Schumann."

"Tell her I'll give good value for money," Pru said. Dr. Porter smirked nervously as he ushered her out of the interview room.

EIGHTEEN

THE sky of early springtime arched high and radiant over the Digby campus.

Richard Doughty, wearing an old raincoat, a sand-colored corduroy suit and a carefully loosely knotted dull Paisley bow tie, had visited the site of the Symington Building that morning and had seen how the construction workers were beginning, in their matter-of-fact way, to commit his paper thoughts to reality. Turf was being cut away in squares in conformity with long pieces of string tautly stretched between pegs driven into the ground; his plan for the foundations was being established in the naked mud. While making the drawings Richard had imaginarily looked up, to see the grand columns and masonry blocks of the completed structure. These first scratches in the top-soil were so insubstantial, so tentative; they seemed to proclaim the frail personal base of his architectural aspirations. He said hello to the foreman and hurried away as soon as possible.

Alone, he had a cup of coffee at the Elite and looked at the local newspaper. He abandoned it and went for a walk.

The mild weather was reassuring, promising growth. The grass of the campus, green and wet with spring rain, was softly resilient under foot. The pale sun ascended brightening, warming the fresh air. Close to the horizon the sky was almost white; immediately overhead it was a deep blue. There were thin white streaks of high cloud. A great airliner, a small dark-silver arrowhead, moved slowly, silently across the top of the sky. Richard took off his raincoat and carried it over one arm. Looking through the trees, he saw a light yellow-green mist of opening leaves, the sudden downward flight of a black bird, a yellow beak eagerly probing the dark-brown earth. At noon, the day felt as though it would go on for a long time, full of possibilities. It was too bad that Camilla had to work. He imagined her lovely head dutifully bowed, as though praying, over a microscope, a long yellow lock of hair prettily swinging down beside the brass eyepiece, her impatient fingers combing the hair back, out of the way. He envisioned her as a shining Joan of Arc of science, unselfishly dedicated to a cause, tired to the bone but unflagging – stubbornly brave. He remembered the fair silken down on the slender nape of her neck and felt a sweet pang of lust mingled with pity. What had he got himself into? And how could anyone so obviously constructed for love seem to be interested only in revolting worms the diameter of spaghetti and several miles long? And yet he knew he had somehow committed himself in some unaccustomed way that he did not wholly understand.

It wouldn't be worth meeting for lunch, she had said gravely. There wouldn't be time. She'd have something quick at the lab. She'd get off as early as she could and meet him at the gallery. He went to the Faculty Club self-service snack bar and got a grilled-cheese sandwich (hot, peppery rubber between slices of asbestos) and a chocolate malted (cold, sweet, molten plaster of Paris) and was morosely pleased that they were bad. He had a grievance; she would have to be extra nice.

After lunch he went to the club reading room, sat in a deeply upholstered black-leather armchair, started reading, in a literary quarterly, a minutely detailed analysis of "The Semantics of Romantic Love in Psychedelic Poetry," and was soon comfortably asleep. He dreamed about Camilla in a floatingly inconclusive pastoral chase, and awoke feeling vaguely irritable, until he became aware that it was late enough to go to the gallery; he was going to see her soon.

Richard picked up his car and drove over to the Art Building, a recent innovation that looked like an ambitious Balkan republic's pavilion in a low-budget international industrial fair. The white-stuccoed concrete roof, low-lying and roundly streamlined at one end of the building, rose, at the other end, steeply aslant to a sharply triangular peak. The whole essential circular edifice was supported on un-polished-aluminum-plated cylindrical stilts that raised the single floor about two ordinary stories above ground. Entry was gained centrally by a large shallow spiral ramp raising up into the middle of the main exhibition hall. H. G. Wells or Flash Gordon might have approved.

At the top of the ramp Richard was confronted by a

stark gray rectangle of acoustic baffle board, on which, in lower-case white lettering, was inscribed the title of the current show, "instinct and intellect: a contemporary stereoview of the world we live in." He walked around the obstacle and found himself in a polished white-stone hall littered, as though by chance, with disturbingly unclassifiable mobile electronic constructions. Some of them were smoothly encased in pastel-colored plastic, and only a low internal mechanical hum, as of a computer at rest, seemed to promise the possibility of communication; others were as blatant as the exposed innards of a clock, precisely intermeshing, silently interacting complexes of cogs, pawls, clicks, ratchets and detents. One elaborate machine, apparently otherwise unproductive, was busily blowing soap bubbles, which, caught in the gentle upcurrent of convection heating, were wafted almost straight upward, glinting with tiny deformed rainbows, like the confused colors in oil smears on rainy streets.

"Aren't they beautiful?" Camilla said, coming up behind Richard and enthusiastically squeezing his arm. "I love them. But I don't understand them. You'll have to explain."

"Hi!" Richard exclaimed, turning to beam at her. "You look terrific!" Her hair was tied back with a plain, broad, blue-silk ribbon and her hair was hanging as demurely as Alice in Wonderland's. Her eyes were as calmly intense, as profoundly blue as the sky. The impression of Victorian innocence was not, however, entirely sustained by a blue polo-neck cashmere sweater, a tightly-belted short white raincoat, the soft, pale nakedness of her calves, and short white rubber boots. Modestly, her gaze fell for an instant, and then she looked up again and returned his smile.

"I hope you haven't been waiting long," Camilla said. "I tried to hurry."

"I've been waiting all day," he said gallantly.

"What do you think of the gallery?" she asked. Her expression became earnest. "No, *really*."

Richard looked around as though appraising the place for the first time. "Oh, I don't know," he said lightly. "All right." He noticed her disappointment. "Fine, I suppose," he said. "Very good lighting."

"Now, please," Camilla said. "You promised you'd show

me everything and explain. This new exhibition is fascinating. I've heard some very good things about it. But I'm such a dope about anything nonrepresentational. Often I like something and I don't even know why. It makes me feel thick in the head."

"Wouldn't you rather go for a walk or something?"

"Just a quick lesson," she said.

"All right," Richard said. "And then a walk?"

"Then a walk," she agreed.

They smiled at each other again, as though they had achieved an intimate understanding.

Richard bought a catalogue with a highly glazed black cover and started reading aloud from the introductory essay: "'Red corpuscles and gray matter'," he read. "'Nature's strongest allies, yet how often in conflict! The eternal dichotomy of body and soul, id and superego, is poignantly exemplified in this exciting new exhibition of works by some of our most passionate, most thoughtful, young Ohio artists.' There," Richard said. "Does that help?"

"Not much," Camilla said. "It's so general, isn't it? It applies to everything."

"Jekyll and Hyde? Laurel and Hardy? Ham and eggs? Yes, I suppose you're right. I'll skip to the next page. How about this? 'Organic growth and mechanical synthesis'? No, we've already had that. Let's see. 'The self, the infinitesimally small central point, seeks to project the pattern of its mind, imposing order on the surrounding universal chaos. That is the function of artist and scientist alike. Here, then, twelve young Ohioans offer twelve working hypotheses. Consider each of their abstract constructions as a symbol of that limitless external chaos, rendered finite, manageably small, personal. They –'"

"But what do *you* think?" Camilla asked.

"Me?" Richard said. "I like the one that blows bubbles."

"So do I," Camilla said. "Let's go for a walk."

Hand in hand, they walked together slowly down the spiral ramp, down to earth.

NINETEEN

"I'VE always been attractive to men," confided subject B, settling back comfortably in one of the interview room armchairs. "I'm on their *wave* length. They seem to *sense* that. They seem to know that I really *appreciate* them, themselves, as men. I really *like* them. I can honestly say that *sexually* I'm *quite* unselfish. They're grateful for that. As soon as they recognize my genuine interest, they absolutely *blossom*. Prize fighters and musicians alike, all sorts, quite *surprising* sometimes. They're so used to being guarded, you see. Most women, most of the time, are out for what they can *get*. Let's *face* it. I'm a nonprofit organization."

Rollo Hawkins smiled disarmingly, trying to put Dr. Porter at his ease.

"But don't let me run *on* like this," Rollo said. "You must be very *strict* with me, when we're working. Tell me what you *want*." He supported the back of his head with interlocked fingers, and crossed one outstretched ankle elegantly over the other. "This really is *fun*, isn't it? I *adore* fortune tellers and psychiatrists and people like that, don't you? Tarot cards, crystal balls, tea leaves, bumps on the head, palms, stars – I believe them *all*, don't you? No, you probably *disapprove*, you stuffy old thing. I admit they're madly *unscientific*, but it's such a relief, believing in fate. It saves one from that awful, boring sense of responsibility, doesn't it? One relaxes. Can science accomplish as much? I'm willing to be convinced. But you, Louis, *you* don't seem relaxed. That's your *trouble*, isn't it? Though I've seen you relaxed, haven't I? Goodness *me*, yes. . . ."

"We'd better start now," Dr. Porter said anxiously. "Dr. Schumann very much wants to get these preliminaries out of the way as soon as possible."

"To hear is to obey," Rollo said. "But do you think you could get us some *coffee*? It's frightfully early in the morning to be talking about one's *sex* life. I've made it a strict rule with Lawrence: not a *word* about sex before I've had a chance to compose myself for the day. The problem is,

132

of course, that so many people wake up such an absolute *tower* of strength. I've always had the *greatest* respect for people who can *leap* into action the very moment the cock, so to speak, crows. Alas, I am not one of them. And that Dr. *Schumann*! Hands of *iron*! The embarrassment! I shriveled away almost to *nothing*! Wouldn't it have been more conventional to have a *male* doctor doing the physical? I *mean*! *Really*!"

"Dr. Schumann and I discussed that," Dr. Porter said. "She pointed out that it's necessary to maintain total uniformity of techniques and standards in all our procedures, for the sake of comparative evaluations."

"But a woman doctor examining *men*," Rollo said. "There's a lack of *sympathy*."

"Dr. Schumann pointed out further that most doctors are male. Women are usually examined by male doctors. Nobody objects. Why should anyone object in the converse situation? She happens to be a first-class doctor. By the way, did she give you an injection – a tranquilizer?"

"No, she didn't," Rollo said. "Don't get me wrong; I was a perfect *lamb*. I wasn't *fighting* it. I like it here. The college library is really very good. I only said I wanted a cup of *coffee*."

Dr. Porter rang for Camilla and a few minutes later she brought a small tray bearing two large cardboard cups of coffee.

"*Dixie* cups!" Rollo exclaimed raising his hands in mock delight. "How deliciously *collegiate*! Oh, I wouldn't have missed this for the *world*!"

Camilla left the room, looking uncharacteristically a little sulky. The door closed. Dr. Porter shuffled some papers, and switched on the tape recorder.

"Now," he said in a determinedly genial voice. "Mr. B. What was your date of birth?"

"Oh, *dear*," Rollo said. "*Must* I? I promised to tell all, but I have an awful thing about my age. I left that bit blank in the form."

"It's a vital part of the history," Dr. Porter said. "Who ever heard of a case history without the subject's age?"

"All *right*," Rollo said petulantly. "Forty-five."

"Is that your true age?"

133

"Forty-*nine* then. I hope you're satisfied. In the evening, I'm *often taken for forty.*"

Dr. Porter elicited the basic biographical information. Rollo had been born in a small town in Indiana, an only child, brought up mostly by a doting mother. His father had been a traveling salesman, not very successful, dealing in agricultural machinery. Rollo's education had been limited to high school. He had left home early to get a job as a waiter in Indianapolis.

"You couldn't call it Paris," Rollo said. "But I learned *plenty* there. I was *devastatingly* handsome at the age of eighteen. When Lawrence and I quarrel – we sometimes have *terrible* quarrels; he claims he forgets to phone when he's coming home late; sometimes he stays out all *night* – I find it most *consoling* to get out my album and look at some of the old photographs. I may seem like a tired old queen, to you, now. But I really was *divine.* When I look at myself as I was then, I positively *yearn.* She was *gorgeous.* It's like looking at pictures of some *marvelous* person one met long ago, and somehow accidentally lost. Very sad, of course, but a *romantic* sort of sadness. Quite a relief from having abuse screamed at one by a very ungrateful, *vain* young man."

"What happened in Indianapolis, sexually speaking?" Dr. Porter asked.

"Heavens to *Betsy*!" Rollo exclaimed, rolling his eyes comically. "What *didn't*! Have you read Petronius? The *Satyricon*?"

"Greek isn't my field," Dr. Porter said.

Rollo looked up at the ceiling, but there were no sudden thunderbolts of outrage.

"What we want to do," Dr. Porter explained, "is to record your own experiences, as an individual."

"I was at their mercy, the mercy of everyone in that *ghastly* kitchen, and there *wasn't* any mercy. A restaurant is a world of its *own*, with *laws* of its own. A complicated, inflexible hierarchy. The chief cook was a *dictator*, a cruel and whimsical voluptuary. A *Nero.* I was the low man on the totem pole. He made my life hell, at first. But it was very instructive."

"He was a homosexual?"

"*Must* you use that word, darling? It's *so* dreary."

"I'm trying to –"

"All *right*. He was a *homosexual*, if you *insist*. He was an *ape*, really. Did you read *The Hairy Ape*?"

"I don't have time to read novels," Dr. Porter said.

Rollo shuddered, with his eyes closed.

"He had been a cook at sea. An absolute brute, terrorizing the forecastle. He bullied me *abominably*. I can still smell that *awful* smell of an institutional kitchen: warm grease, with a faint whiff of ammonia. He started me off as *dishwasher*! My hands got all red and wrinkled. I used to run to the john, and lock myself in, and just *weep*."

"Why didn't you quit?" Dr. Porter asked gently. The expression on his face had momentarily softened.

"*Quit*?" Rollo said. "I *couldn't*."

"Why?"

"I'd fallen head over *heels*. He was a *monster*. He had black hair all over his shoulders and chest and back. He wore T-shirts that got so soaked with sweat that his *nipples* showed through. He had hairy *ears* and hairy *nostrils* and his *eyebrows* grew together in one thick black *bar*. His hands were like bunches of big *toes*. Most of his back teeth were gold. When he laughed it was like a *bull* roaring. I loved him."

"You loved him?"

"Hopelessly. Ecstatically. You know what it's like to be in love, don't you?"

"We're not talking about me," Dr. Porter said. "Were you able to cause his attitude to change? What did you *do*, that's what I'm trying to get at."

"I couldn't deliberately *make* it change. It doesn't happen like that, sweetheart. But we both changed. For what seemed *ages* we went through this strange bullying-teasing-flirting sort of – well, *courtship*. He liked *humiliating* me in front of the waiters and busboys. It was tolerable, though, because I knew *instinctively* . . . there was a secret, private tension between him and me. I knew that *he* felt it, too, and I knew that *he* knew that *I* knew. One of *those* situations. Enough for a whole Russian novel. Don't you read *anything*, Louis? Don't worry, I haven't forgotten about the Ph.D. But I've learned more from reading for *pleasure* than I ever learned at school."

"Perhaps our interests are different," Dr. Porter said.

135

"Touché!" Rollo said. "But are our pleasures?"

Dr. Porter looked a trifle flustered.

"Were you practicing masturbation at this time?" Dr. Porter asked, taking refuge in his brief.

"Yes," Rollo said, puzzled by what apparently seemed to him to be an irrelevancy, but patiently adjusting himself to it. "Though I say to myself, I have a certain *flair*. There's masturbation and *masturbation*, I always say."

"I don't understand."

"You don't? It can be done reluctantly, or defiantly, or savagely. Or with a sense of what I can only call *poetry*. No doubt there are narcissistic poems on the subject, under lock and key at the Library of Congress."

"How often did you do it?"

"God! *I* don't know. It depended on the phase of the moon, a chance glimpse of a particularly yummy *traffic* cop, or what I had for dinner, for heaven's sake. What *odd* questions you do ask!"

"Please try to estimate the average weekly incidence. We have to know all this. There are good reasons for every question. This whole questionnaire has been very carefully worked out."

"Two or three times a week? A *dozen*? *I* don't know. I honestly don't. I'm not one of those people who keep *score*. Once a week, perhaps, if I happened to be devoting my attention to someone else, or if I was feeling un*physical*. *No* times, even; there are occasions when I prefer to listen to *Bach*. There was an era, at one point when I was living alone, and on the wagon, when I used to have the most *extraordinary* lovely wet dreams."

"That's very interesting. The literature on nocturnal emissions is meager. They are rare these days, other opportunities being as abundant as they are."

"No doubt. But an underrated sexual experience. Underexploited."

"In what way?"

"Well, *surely*, if one really *worked* at it, it should be possible to influence the nature of dreams, shouldn't it? Plan them, plot them, script them, according to your own special ideals and desires. I don't know anything about biochemistry, but couldn't someone come up with a new kind of pill? Or couldn't hypnosis be used to *program* the part

136

of your mind you dream with? Or couldn't there be a custom-made personalized tape, whispering suggestively from your pillow? *Brave New World*."

"I wouldn't know about that. That's not in my field," Dr. Porter said.

"I get most of my technical knowledge from the "Reader's Digest," Rollo admitted. "But I don't see why there couldn't be a whole *library* of subliminal tapes. New dreams every week. It'd be *fabulous*. Sex fantasies for every taste — Oriental harems, musical-comedy dressing rooms, military *academies*. There'd be none of the common unpleasant side-effects of sex in real life, such as difficulties with the police, debts, disease, *marriage*."

"But we mustn't speculate," Dr. Porter said. "Let's get back to that cook. Did any physical intimacy take place?"

"Yes, I finally got lucky."

"Would you please tell me what happened?"

"It was a *fiasco*," Rollo said. "Several of us went to a bar on payday. I was careful not to drink too much. It was their custom to get blind drunk as fast as possible every Friday night. One by one, the others gradually faded away. My hairy ape was going through his usual routine — affectionate insults. But this time I felt his hot hand on my knee. My heart was beating like *mad*! At *last*! He asked me back to his room for scrambled eggs. He lived in the most *sordid* imaginable rooming house. *Definitely* the wrong side of the tracks. I was already becoming quite fussy about such subtle nuances. But one has to make sacrifices for love. I loved —"

"Never mind about the love," Dr. Porter said. "Just relate the facts."

"You can't separate the love," Rollo said. "That's what this is all about, isn't it?"

"We're concerned with sexual phenomena per se," Dr. Porter said primly. "Physical and psychological sexual stimuli and reactions to them. Love is something else."

"How on *earth* do you think you can have one without the other?" Rollo said. "You don't think I'd have got *involved* with this ape if I hadn't loved him, do you? You don't seem to be using your imagination. Here I was, Adonis, going down into the underworld with this *beast*. It was quite magical."

Dr. Porter compressed his lips and said nothing.

"All right," Rollo said. "It won't take long. We reached his rooming house. We went up to his room. Landladies are very tough on men taking women up to their rooms, but they don't object to men taking men. I've often thought about that, how hard society is on heterosexuals. Anyway, he told me to fix a drink. He had a bottle of rye there. He said he'd be right back. I got undressed as soon as he left the room. I was shaking like a *leaf,* fumbling with buttons and zippers. I lay in the bed, waiting. I must have dozed off. Suddenly the light went on. I was startled. I sat up. There he was. I'll *never* forget it. What a *sight*! He was wearing a silk kimono – 'Souvenir of Hong Kong'-type thing – all scarlet and gold and black dragons. And his *face*! It was a strawberry shortcake! *This* thick with powder and rouge. A *clown's* lipstick. And one of those *awful* geisha wigs, shiny with lacquer – *stiff* with it. It was *quite* a moment. Nothing in Emily Post quite covers the situation. Here was I, the trembling bride, expecting to be overwhelmed, bruised, torn. And all the time he had been counting on *me* to master *him*."

"You ordinarily assume the passive role then," Dr. Porter said.

"Why, Louis," Rollo exclaimed delightedly, "sweetie, you sound quite *disappointed*! But you're not, are you? You inscrutable old sphinx, you! Don't tell me I've come all the way to Digby for nothing!"

TWENTY

"Love is a form of sexual fantasy that cannot be entirely disregarded," Dr. Schumann said with a tolerant smile. "Even hallucinations have a reality of their own. To that extent, Dr. Leary is right. Any belief, however ill-founded, is a factor that cannot be left out of the personality equation. I'd be the first to go along with that. On the other hand, love is also an expression of escapist sentimentality that can have a very real repressive anaphrodisiac effect. It's all very well for our Subject B to profess what he conveniently calls 'love' for the physically superior, intellectually inferior id-figure with whom he had fabricated a possibly imaginary sado-masochistic relationship. But don't let's go overboard, not by a long chalk. Mightn't this profession of love perhaps have been a post-factum rationalization of a failure whose real cause should be described mechanistically?"

"I think you're right," Dr. Porter said. "The latter. That's what I thought."

"Hold it, Navy!" Dr. Schumann exclaimed. "I'm not going out on any limb. Let's wait till all the evidence is in before we make any categorical value judgment on that."

"Heck, yes," Dr. Porter agreed.

"But, for what it's worth, how about a guideline? Nothing binding. Here's a thought that you might keep in mind. What if the wig alone set up a sufficient block – wig equals mother equals childhood – to cause instantaneous detumescence? No, wait! It's too early to say. Let's wait till we see Subject B in action. The proof of the pudding's in the eating. Explanations will reveal themselves."

"I certainly have to hand it to you," Dr. Porter said. "You're right on top of this whole thing. Frankly, I was a little rattled during those first two interviews. I began to realize that there is no sure way we can check up what these people are telling us. I suddenly began to wonder. Hey, look out, Dr. Porter, I said to myself, this could mean trouble! Scientifically speaking, of course. I wondered how we could ever separate fact from fiction."

Dr. Schumann smiled affectionately at his expression of earnest anxiety. "Like all dedicated scientists engaged in advancing the frontiers of human knowledge, you're bound to have occasional moments of misgivings and self-doubt," she said. "If you didn't, I wouldn't want you on the team. But on this score, you have nothing to worry about. If I'd been Dr. Kinsey I'd have worried plenty. I respect his memory – don't get me wrong; he helped prepare the way for what we're doing here at Digby – but he was maybe a bit too dependent on verbal testimony. I hate to criticize a former colleague in medical science who isn't here to answer for himself, but sometimes we scientists have to rise above our personal feelings. Kinsey's interviews were as thorough as he could make them. There's a limit to the practical extent of any statistical cross section, but nobody could say he didn't work at it. It's too bad, though, among scientists and laymen alike, there has always been a small, poisonous suspicion: what if those people weren't telling the truth? Or what if they exaggerated somewhat, for example about the number of partners with whom they had had intercourse, the number of times they achieved orgasm per intercourse unit. Suppose that a significant number of men and women, in order to bolster their sense of sexual normality and prowess, lied quite a bit? Wouldn't you say that Kinsey's conclusions were neither stronger nor weaker than the reliability of his data? Naturally. However, consider the program of the Digby Institute. Case histories, based on interviews, you say? Just like the Kinsey reports? Sure – *so far*. But with him that was everything, with us it's just the beginning. And you want to know something, Dr. Porter? As far as we're concerned, the beginning doesn't mean a thing, except for the fact that it *is* the beginning."

Dr. Porter looked lost.

"The reliability of the testimony itself doesn't mean a thing," Dr. Schumann said. "I don't care whether Miss Griswolde and Mr. Hawkins and the rest of them have been telling the truth or not. They probably have been, with a little self-protective editing here and there. There isn't a drug in the world that can penetrate all the ego's defences. But the tapes seem plausible enough. It doesn't matter. What does matter is that getting them to talk about

140

their sexual experiences helps us in two ways: one, they reveal their sexual predilections and interests; and, two, they become accustomed to the idea of revealing them, not in some hidden back bedroom some place, but right here, in a brightly lighted laboratory."

"So it's helping them to relax," Dr. Porter said.

"And it's helping us to assign them roles," Dr. Schumann said.

"Roles?"

"Yes. One of the ways in which we can constructively profit from the altogether admirable pioneer sex-lab demonstrations arranged by Masters and Johnson is by encouraging sexual practitioners to develop their sexual-performance rating through drama. In my opinion, sexologists have been woefully neglectful of the potential of sexual dramaturgy. Everyone, whether consciously or not, is physically and temperamentally best suited to play one certain part or another, if only in fantasy, in his sexual activities, be they solitary or in association with one partner or more. Think of the stimulus that could be provided by externalization of the fantasy roles, a deliberate acting out of inner tendencies. I'm quite sure that the histrionics of sexuality could be systematized, so that seeming and being could coincide. Sex is a happening. But don't forget that the liveliest spontaneity can be, must be, given its proper opportunity to occur. Environment and the assemblage of personnel are susceptible to planning and control. The biggest, most powerful rockets can be launched only from the most stable pads. I think I'm right, historically, in saying that the most extravagantly frenzied sexual orgies have almost always been enacted by members of the upper social classes in formal settings. Much of the allure of such events evidently resides in the participants' simultaneous sense of fantasy – the extreme unorthodoxy of the group situation makes it seem unreal – and their sense of actuality, witnessed by, vouched for the very persons whose presence and activities strain conventional credulity. Are you with me?"

Dr. Schumann's eyes were shining with zeal that made Dr. Porter uneasily restive. "You're not suggesting," he said, "that the Institute –?"

"I wasn't suggesting anything," Dr. Schumann said, "ex-

141

cept some ideas of the kind that you should be examining."
She laughed merrily. "Just idle shoptalk. However," she
added earnestly, "it's good mental exercise to consider the
possibilities. That's how progress is made."

"Yes," Dr. Porter quickly agreed.

"Speaking of shoptalk," Dr. Schumann said casually, "I
was a little concerned this afternoon. That Fairbank girl
came to see me in my office. She was upset. She seemed
to have the feeling that you were treating her as some
sort of waitress."

"Because I asked her to bring me some coffee? That was
for Subject B. He was in rather a nervous state after the
medical. What's wrong with asking for coffee?"

"Don't you start!" Dr. Schumann said. "Simmer down.
There's nothing wrong with asking for coffee. But you
know how students are. She's very touchy, very thin-
skinned. She's exceptionally well qualified academically.
She's good in the lab. We're going to need her later. We
don't want to lose her. I've been just as much to blame as
you, so take it easy. She complained that all she's been
doing so far has been acting as a receptionist and waitress.
I pointed out that we'd only just started. But I saw her
point. I think we'd better give her something to do as soon
as possible. Got any ideas?"

"We ought to have the automanipulation tests under
way by the first of the week," Dr. Porter said. "The photographic equipment is set up. She could work on those."

"Maybe," Dr. Schumann said. "I think we should super-
vise the first ones. But she could certainly help. She's a
nice girl and I want her to feel assured that she is one of
us."

TWENTY-ONE

"THERE are only two movie theaters," Camilla said apologetically. "Most of the kids watch television. There's an old movie theater in town, the Apollo. It's very *convenient*."

"Do you know what's playing?" Richard asked, not that he cared. He was observing that in the light of the setting sun her blue eyes were illuminated with uncanny flecks of amber.

"A musical version of *Scarface*," Camilla said. "*Scarface* was a movie based on the life of Al Capone, I think. Al Capone was a gangster who lived in Chicago during Prohibition. Prohibition –"

"Thanks," Richard said. "I know about Prohibition. What's the other choice?"

"We could go to the College Drive-in," Camilla said doubtfully.

"You don't sound too enthusiastic."

"It's very *good*," she said. "But people sometimes behave kind of oddly there. It has a reputation for that. As far as the shows are concerned, though, it's great. It's an egghead drive-in. Mostly European movies – very *nouvelle vague*. You know – narrow screen, black and white; it's always night-time and raining, and nothing's in focus but the subtitles."

"Would you rather see the happy, up-beat gangster musical? *Everybody's Doin' the 'Lectric Chair*."

"No," Camilla said. "Let's go to the drive-in. It isn't very far. Just beyond the town limits."

Camilla leaned over and quickly kissed his cheek. Richard awkwardly seized her and kissed her mouth, hard. Camilla immediately pushed him away and kept her hands against his chest, holding him off at arm's length. Her lipstick was slightly blurred. She was breathing as though there weren't enough oxygen in the air.

"Richard!" she said. "We're right in the middle of Digby!"

"So what?" he said, angrily pushing her hands away.

143

Camilla nervously laughed.

He pressed the starter and released the brake and trod heavily on the accelerator, and the car surged forward with a squeal, while Camilla sat back looking slightly dazed, in awe, with one hand against her face, her finger tips cautiously touching her lips.

He was staring straight ahead at the darkening road. He was driving very badly.

The movie was conventionally avant-garde, a Victorian melodrama modernized. Most of the action took place in a laundry in Naples. Laboring in the white steam hissing from neglected old-fashioned boilers in the nonunion shop, the girl fell in love with a courageous young man who was trying to organize their fellow employees. The usual love scenes duly ensued in the usual tenement bedroom – her hand clutching his naked shoulder and so on; he lying on his back on the bed, smoking a cigarette, proclaiming his dreams; her cheek against his naked chest and so on; two pigeons soaring, a fountain gushing, a factory whistle blowing.

In the car, Richard's hand found Camilla's. He gently thrust his fingers, one by one, between hers, warm skin against skin. When their fingers were interlaced, Camilla's hand gently squeezed his.

The owner of the laundry was a bald, obese, cunning sensualist of the kind that gave cigar smoking a bad name. The young man stormed into his office and made a socialist speech. The owner fired the young man and sinisterly picked up the telephone. In the steep, cobbled alley on the way to the girl's tenement (she had put flowers on the table and was cooking his favorite dish, to celebrate their engagement), the young man was horribly beaten up.

Camilla tightly gripped Richard's hand.

The laundry owner told the girl that her lover could have his job back and the union would be recognized only if she would renounce him and become the owner's wife. Otherwise the young man would never work in another laundry. She felt faint. She said she would give her answer that night. She walked the entire length of the Bay of Naples, and the cameraman walked with her, as she tried to make up her mind. She collapsed. Was she pregnant? She went to a hospital. The last scene was agonizingly slow and inconclusive: she walked along a brightly lighted, straight hospital corridor, toward a closed door. Well, was she pregnant? What was her decision? Would the door open? There were some worrying flashbacks of bed sheets and pillow cases tumbling about like tortured ectoplasm in a washing machine. The camera moved right in among the laundry, spinning, falling, around and around. And that was the end.

Camilla disengaged her hand. She softly blew her nose. Other cars were beginning to move away.

"You weren't crying, were you?" Richard asked.

"It *was* sad," Camilla said. "Didn't you think so? What did you think of it?"

"Let's get out of here," Richard said. "I'll tell you then."

He got out of the drive-in compound as fast as he could.

"You should have turned left," Camilla said. "This is the way away from town."

"I want to get away for a while," Richard said.

"There's a Howard Johnson's not far from here, if you want," Camilla said. "The turnoff's about ... there! You missed it. Why are you driving so fast, Richard?"

"It seemed so damned ridiculous, sitting in a car, surrounded by other couples in cars, all those rows of cars lined up in rows, gawping at moving pictures of another couple in bed making love. An actor and actress *pretending* to make love, that is. While we just sat there, holding hands, quietly watching. Jesus! Doesn't it seem slightly insane?"

"Now we're on the parkway," Camilla said with a sigh.

"What if we are?"

"It's all right for you, but I'm not allowed out after midnight, unless I get a pass from the house mother. They're very strict about weeknights."

"Don't panic. I'll turn around soon."

"There are no U-turns."

"Then I'll turn off and go back some other way."

"There isn't another exit for about ten miles."

"Then I'll turn off in ten miles. What's the matter with you, Camilla?"

"You're the one that's irritable. I enjoyed the movie very

145

much. I thought it was very symbolic. I thought the photography was terrific."

"Look," Richard said. "Do you mind if we skip the movie?"

They sat in silence, except for the loud hum of the motor, as the car rushed smoothly around gradual curves, up and down gradual gradients, between obscure landscaped embankments. The moon and a few big stars were out. The sky looked cold, but the interior of the car was almost stupefyingly warm.

"We'll be in Kentucky soon, at this rate," Camilla said.

Richard jammed on the brakes. The car slowed down uncomfortably abruptly. Camilla fell forward and stopped herself by putting out her hands against the dashboard. Richard pulled over to the right, onto the shoulder of the road, and stopped the car. He twisted Camilla around to face him, leaned over her, bent her backward, loomed over her. The closeness of his face blotted out the sky. In the warm darkness, his mouth angrily devoured her lips. She momentarily automatically stiffened in resistance, but then her whole body softened and sagged passively in his arms.

Their lips were warm and moist. Time was suspended. Her lips softly opened. His tongue wetly slipped in between them. Warm and moist. A blank abstraction of pure sensation. A profound, slow throb of pleasure. His hand fumbled with the front of her coat. The spell was broken and reality flooded in. Camilla fought as though suddenly drowning in it. She pulled herself free.

"No, Richard!" she cried. "Please don't! The State Police!"

"The what?"

"You're not allowed to stop on the parkway, unless it's an emergency."

"This is an emergency," Richard said grimly.

"No, please no. Richard, please! We mustn't."

"What was I doing wrong?" he asked.

"Let's go home," she said. "I'm sorry. Please take me back."

A car, driven fast, flashed past them.

"There's an enormous fine," Camilla said. "Come on, Richard."

146

Richard straightened his tie and started the car. "I love you," he said.

"I love you," she said.

"But really. I mean it. I do."

"So do I. But let's go."

"O.K.," Richard said. "I guess there are better places." The car moved slowly back into the right-hand lane.

"Thank you," Camilla said, sitting up straight and adjusting her hair.

They drove along steadily until the headlights were reflected by a giant sign offering a list of places, distances, compass directions and route numbers. Richard swung the car up a steep, abruptly curving concrete ramp, east, north, west, and south again, as the moon revolved above their heads.

"We're still heading the wrong way," Camilla said wearily but without reproach. "We have to go north."

"I know we have to go north. I was trying to go north."

"You should have made a right. To get to the lower level westbound. Then left and up."

"How romantic!" Richard said. "You and me, alone at last, on Lovers' Lane."

"It's only a cloverleaf interchange," Camilla said. "That's nothing to get mad about, is it?"

"Oh, a cloverleaf," Richard said. "Thanks for explaining. I thought it was a conspiracy."

"You are a nut!" Camilla said affectionately, giving him a cheerful, sisterly kiss on the cheek. "Make a right now, and bear left."

Richard silently did as instructed. Before very long they reached the Digby turnoff, and soon Richard recognized the road past the drive-in.

"Is the clock right?" Camilla asked.

"Yes."

"Thank goodness. I hate having to make excuses."

He said nothing, only clenched his hands on the wheel.

"Richard?"

"Yes."

"You aren't angry with me, Richard, are you?"

"Me? Angry? With you? Ha! Why should I be?"

"What's the matter?"

"Nothing's the matter. Which is the way to your dorm?"

"Oh, dear, you *are* angry."

"No I'm not."

"Yes you are."

"I know when I'm angry and when I'm not angry. I'm *not* angry."

"I don't have to be in for nearly forty minutes," she said.

"So?"

"I wondered if you'd like to have a cup of coffee before I go back."

"Coffee!" Richard exclaimed. "We seem to spend all our time together drinking endless cups of coffee. I'm full up to here with coffee."

"I'm sorry," Camilla said.

"There's nothing for you to be sorry about," he said. His tone assumed an unconvincing casual heartiness. "Let's just sit somewhere quiet. Smoke a cigarette."

"We could drive through the Arb," she said.

"The Arb?"

"The Arboretum. It's a park. Trees mostly. There are specimens from all over the world, including the South Pacific. It's very popular."

"How about a place that's very unpopular?"

"Nobody bothers you at the Arb," Camilla assured him. "It's patrolled."

"What about a quiet place where we can park and talk? There doesn't have to be a great view or anything."

"There are some places around the stadium," Camilla said. "You could take the next turn on the left."

Richard turned left. A few moments later she told him to turn again. The car crunched across the cinders of a parking lot and along a narrow gravel drive, passed through the echoing obscurity of a short tunnel beneath the stadium, and emerged into moonlight behind home plate, overlooking the pale-gray grass of the empty field.

"You certainly know your way around," Richard said. "Come to a lot of ball games?"

"You needn't be sarcastic," Camilla said. "This *is* my fourth year at Digby."

Richard kissed her again, as vehemently as though trying to extract a secret. His lips fiercely writhed, but again she broke away, panting, as though a referee had separated them after vicious in-fighting.

148

"Camilla," Richard said.

She only connected their mouths together again. Their kisses smelled of carnations and shaving soap. They tasted of double-mint chewing gum, with a faint hint of salt, blood and brutality.

He and she separated, to gulp air.

Richard muttered something incomprehensible, and bowed his head to kiss her throat, her ear, warm under silken, lanolin-scented hair. Camilla fell back limp against the leatherette car seat, her head tilted far back. Her fingers ruffled and clutched the hair at the back of his head, pressing him closer to her.

"Oh, darling, darling Richard!" she mumbled fretfully. "Oh, Richard, darling. You won't forget the time, will you?"

He found her mouth again with his and silenced her.

Red comets roared silently in flashing arcs through the hot darkness of their blood. Her hands convulsively grasped his shoulders. His hand slowly pried her knees apart. Her hands released his shoulders and her head moved away from him. He tried to reach her mouth again, but she evaded him.

"No," she said. "No, Richard."

His hand reached the warm, smooth, ponderous flesh of her inner thighs, the soft, naked, humid skin above the nylon.

"Please," he said.

"No!"

She violently pushed him away. He grappled with her hands, but one escaped and hit the side of his face. Her desperate strength dismayed him. She moved along the seat, away from him, as far away as possible.

"Camilla," he protested uncertainly. "What's the matter? I didn't hurt you, did I?"

"I'm sorry," she said with deliberate calm. "I'm very sorry. It's my fault. I wanted you to kiss me."

"What's wrong with that, for heaven's sake? I wanted you to want me to. I wanted to kiss you. It isn't a crime."

"I should have let you take me straight back," Camilla said. "Please take me home now. I'm sorry, Richard."

"You can't brush me off that easily," he said. "I want to know what I did that was so terrible,"

149

"Please don't make it so difficult for me," Camilla said. "I feel awful. I shouldn't have encouraged you like that. I'm sorry. That's all there is to say. Couldn't we go now? If you won't take me I'll have to get out and walk."

"Don't get all melodramatic," Richard said. "I'll take you in a few minutes. Don't worry. You're still all right for time."

"To hell with the time!" Camilla said unhappily. "The time doesn't matter all that much. It was an excuse. I didn't want to hurt your feelings. And I didn't want a lot of complications."

"Is there something repulsive about me?"

"Richard! Don't be insane. You're a dream. You're the most attractive man I've met at Digby. The most attractive ever! Everything about you's attractive. I love the way you look, the way you walk, the things you say. It's not that."

"Well, then," Richard said. "Come here!"

"Please no," Camilla pleaded. "No, don't touch me. It'll only start all over again. I'm sorry. I must go back to the dorm. I know you couldn't possibly understand. Nobody can. You'll find another girl. There are lots of them around, and not so many men."

"I don't get it," Richard said. "I know there are lots of women in Digby. There are lots of women everywhere. But not like you. It's you I want. Please let me just . . ."

He reached out to her.

"Don't do that!" Camilla ordered him. "I mean it."

"I can tell you mean it," he said, rather crossly. "That's apparent. But why? It didn't feel as though you didn't enjoy being kissed. You weren't just pretending to like it, were you?"

"It was wonderful," Camilla said. "But as it can't go any further than that, it's better for both of us if we quit right there. I shouldn't have let it go so far. I was carried away. I'm sorry, Richard. Look, there are only five minutes to go."

"To hell with the time," he said. "You said so yourself. Let's get this thing out into the open. What do you mean, 'it can't go any further'? Is it something physical?"

"There's nothing wrong with me as far as I know, if that's what you mean."

150

"What's the matter then? Have you got the curse? If you have, just say so. Why shouldn't you have it? It's nothing to be ashamed of. I'll survive if I have to wait. Is that it?"

"I hate that term," Camilla said. "And it's not the sort of thing I want to discuss. I want to go home now. I really do."

"That's it," Richard said. "You're menstruating. That would explain everything. Poor Camilla. How frustrating. You are a funny girl. You're so solemn about it. It doesn't change anything that matters. I love you."

"It isn't that," Camilla said exasperatedly. "You men are all so vain. I don't want you to go any further because I don't want you to go any further. Is that too simple for you to understand?"

"It doesn't fit in with the other things you've said," Richard said patiently. "It felt so right, you and me. And then, suddenly – whammo! A right to the jaw. Naturally I was surprised. Camilla . . . ?"

"Yes?"

"Is it that you're afraid of getting pregnant? I thought all coeds knew everything there is to know about contraceptives."

"They do," Camilla said. "They never stop arguing about the diaphragm versus the pill."

"Even if you haven't anything with you, you needn't worry about it. Why didn't you explain? It's nothing to get all fussed and bothered about. As it happens, I have one of those quaint, old-fashioned devices. I think they should have gone out with high-buttoned shoes, but you know the Boy Scouts' motto. . . ."

"Oh, Richard," Camilla said. "To save time, and to save you making a fool of yourself, let me make a confession."

"You're secretly married," Richard said.

"No," Camilla said.

"You're not a Lesbian," Richard said. "I know that."

"No, I don't think so," Camilla said. "It's something much more difficult than that. I suppose you were bound to find out sooner or later. It may as well be now, but I was hoping our little affair would last a bit longer."

"What is it?"

"I'm a virgin," Camilla said.

151

"I've been thinking about intra-anal intercourse," Dr. Schumann said, immediately after Dr. Porter had closed her office door and they had exchanged the customary early-morning civilities.

"In what context?" Dr. Porter asked guardedly.

"It's a fact of sexual behaviour," she said, "and, as such, it cannot be swept under the carpet. We have undertaken a comprehensive study, and we must not shirk any aspect of it. The anus, of course, let's face it, is a considerable secondary focal point of sexual stimulation. The gratification of straining at stool is an experience common to all. The anus exists. We cannot be ostriches about it, burying our heads in the sand and expecting it to go away. It has an undeniable place in male and female interrelationships. But I've just been playing back the second Hawkins tape, the tape of your second interview with Subject B. His rhapsodic tribute to the joys of direct stimulation of the prostate gland should be considered with caution."

"I was going to consult you on that," Dr. Porter quickly assured her. "The question of editing the tapes. He's sometimes difficult to control." Dr. Porter looked down into his coffee cup while Dr. Schumann appraised him. "Conversationally," Dr. Porter added.

"It is our duty to record every variety of sexual act," Dr. Schumann said. Her head was high, and the spring sunlight, shining through the window, gleamed on her upswept copper hair. "To do so is our vocation. We are not cowards. Facts are facts. Some of them may not be pretty – who is to say which? – but the truth itself is beautiful. Check?"

"Check," Dr. Porter intoned devoutly.

"I'll emphasize that line of reasoning in the introduction to our first published work," Dr. Schumann said. "There's no ethically valid argument against it. The debate inevitably degenerates into a dialogue on aesthetics. So that's all right. We are going to have to contemplate some bizarre human activities during the days that lie ahead. We cannot risk fellow scientists' accusations of evasiveness. Intra-anal intercourse exists; therefore we must record its existence. We must photograph it, calibrate it, analyze it, and evaluate it, just as we must record every other sexual act. Certainly."

"We've always agreed on that," Dr. Porter meekly confirmed.

"This is a scientific operation we're performing here," Dr. Schumann went on. "Nobody is better aware of that than I am. We are scientists. However . . ."

"However?"

"I had another telephone call from Turner Symington yesterday. He wanted another run-down on how we've been getting along. He's not impatient really, he's not anxious, but he is concerned. The building contractor's supplementary budget to take care of escalating labor costs was higher than expected – that kind of thing. Nobody's really worried. Dr. Essen's no problem. Why should he be? But still, I know it'll be a big relief to Mr. Symington when he can come down here and see for himself that real progress is being made and all the financial expenditure can be justified. I persuaded him to postpone his first visit a little longer, until we can show him something concrete. Not merely the tapes of the interviews, though I told him I've been pleased with the way they've been progressing."

"Thanks," Dr. Porter said. "I appreciate that."

"Incidentally, how much longer are they going to take?"

"We're on schedule," Dr. Porter said. "I hope to be able to wind up the current series by the end of the day. Miss Daventry's the last one."

"Let's keep our fingers crossed," Dr. Schumann said. "We'll try to push her through fast. Then we can start getting some data on film. I'm counting on being able to screen some representative film sequences by the end of next week."

"That'll mean hustling," Dr. Porter said, "but I think we can do it. We can certainly do something. It's difficult to predict quality though, isn't it? We're still groping our way."

"The quality matters. This is the point. When I cited some of the material you had gleaned from the interviewees, to indicate the breadth of scope of experience of

153

the pilot group, Symington made an observation that I think is quite valid."

"What did he say?"

"He said, 'Science is science, and public relations is public relations,' and he hoped we wouldn't have to sacrifice either one to the other, but to begin with public relations was of paramount importance."

"You didn't let him get away with that?"

"Just a minute. Listen. I reacted badly initially too, like you. But he set me straight, and I want to set you straight. He said that what we had already accomplished sounded very important, from a scientific viewpoint, but he, speaking as an interested layman, didn't want us to jeopardize the future of the Institute by publicizing any of its more controversial findings too soon. Get the program properly, securely established and accepted first, he said. Then the sky's the limit."

"There's some sense in that," Dr. Porter admitted. "It depends partly on what he means by controversial."

"I'm glad you accept the basic proposition," Dr. Schumann said dryly. "As I see it, one of its clear immediate applications is that, while evading nothing, we accentuate the positive aspects of our research."

"Would you explain that?"

"I intend to," Dr. Schumann said. "As I have said time and time again, we are scientists, with responsibilities primarily to science. But the Digby Institute has been created partly in order to sustain the college, and to do this we have to propagate public understanding, appreciation and approval of our scientific work. The public is eager for sexual enlightenment, for the sake of total exercise of today's sexual freedom. But the public is also equally eager for sexual encouragement. Through no fault of their own, there are faint hearts in our society, Dr. Porter, and queasy appetites. We would be doing more harm than good, as Mr. Symington instinctively perceived, harm to people at large, harm to Digby, harm even to ourselves, if our publications offended the delicate and deterred the timid. He said of course he didn't want us to censor or distort our data in such a way as to paint a falsely rosy picture of sexuality; on the other hand, he felt the Institute and Digby might suffer if we plunged too deeply, too soon, into the melancholy complexities of sexual inadequacy and aberration. Dale Carnegie and Norman Vincent Peale, though toiling in other vineyards, had their fingers on the public pulse. Let us endeavor to raise hope where before it has languished. We can find it within ourselves, in good conscience, to offer compensation to the glandularly deficient, the petty, the lethargic, the infirm and the old, the halt and the lame, nature's sexual dropouts. I know we can! Let us proclaim the universality and equality of sexual opportunity! 'Equal orgasms for all' was the way Symington put it. He's such an enthusiast. I found his enthusiasm infectious."

"You don't think there's any risk of professional compromise in this upbeat approach?"

"Not if we handle it right," Dr. Schumann assured him. "There isn't going to be any falsification, only emphasis on success and satisfaction. The effect will be entirely beneficial. If people begin to think orgasm, they'll live orgasm."

As always at the conclusion of one of Dr. Schumann's rhetorical pep-talks, Dr. Porter's momentary spasm of exultancy was followed promptly by numb enervation.

"I guess so," he said. "I can see that positivism is likely to pay off with readier acceptance." He thought about the prospect. "Sure," he said. "That figures. And once we are recognized, then we can explain some of the awkward exceptional difficulties."

"I knew I could count on you," Dr. Schumann said. "So let's get the anal data. We need it for the archives. But if you can, as a personal favor, will you try to play it down?"

The direct, intimate appeal hit Dr. Porter where he lived. He clenched his jaws and smiled and his eyes filled with tears. They shook hands like two men.

TWENTY-THREE

"CAMILLA FAIRBANK!" Mary exclaimed, on returning to the dormitory after her nine-o'clock seminar on comparative philosophy. "Do you know what time it is?"

There was no reply from the untidy mound of blankets and pillows on Camilla's single studio couch. Mary went over to it and shook the recumbent body, gently at first, and then with increasing urgency.

"Camilla! Wake up! Hey, Camilla! The morning's half gone! Camilla! Are you all right?"

The shapeless mound stirred and heaved. A hand appeared at the hem of a blanket and pushed it aside, revealing tangled yellow hair and a reproachful pink eye, half open.

"No, I'm not all right. Can't you leave me alone?"

"Phew!" Mary said brightly. "You had me worried there for a minute, kid. The sweatheart of Sigma Chi cutting two classes in a row! How many sleeping pills did you take? It isn't like you. Those are powerful pills. Did the lab give you the afternoon off?"

"I didn't take any pills," Camilla said. "Go away." There was a slow convulsion under the blankets as Camilla rolled over, with her knees drawn up, to face the wall.

"Camilla! What's wrong? There's some mail in your box. A telegram, it looks like. I thought you were out and you'd pick it up on your way back in. Do you want me to get it?"

"I don't want anything," Camilla said, and pulled the blankets up over her head. She sounded so much like a petulant child that Mary indulgently shook her head and smiled.

"That old devil moon," she said. She filled the percolator, plugged it in, and hurried out of the room. A few minutes later, slightly breathless, she returned, carrying a Western Union envelope.

"What is it, your birthday or something?" she said rather nervously. "Come on, wake up! Camilla? Oh, all right. Just lie there and sulk. See if I care."

156

Mary turned on the transistor radio on the low coffee table in the middle of the room. A pop group were hoarsely screaming the number-one love song of the week, but they were soon interrupted by a bulletin from the Far East.

Camilla sat up. Hair hung over one eye. Her cheeks were flushed. "Can't you let me die in peace?" she asked.

Mary refused. "The coffee's nearly ready," she said cheerfully. "A big cup of black coffee, that's what you need. You look awful."

"Thanks a lot," Camilla said ironically. She got out of bed. She was wearing a short, translucent white nightgown with small yellow flowers embroidered at the neck. She reached over and snapped off the radio, leaving a sudden void of silence, except for the inexorably bubbling percolator. "I don't do this to you when you feel depressed."

"Yes you do. Always. I count on it." She gently pressed Camilla into an armchair. There was no resistance. "Open the wire," Mary said. Camilla shook her head.

"Well, it's all over, with Richard," Camilla said. "It's not a record for the course, but it's fast."

"I don't believe it," Mary said.

"Oh, yes it is," Camilla said. "*Finis. Finito. Kaput.*"

"Not bad for a science major," Mary said. "Here's the coffee. Do you want me to open the wire for you?"

"I don't care. No, don't. Give it to me."

"Do you want to talk about last night?"

"No. It was awful. I've never felt so humiliated in my whole life."

"What happened?"

"The usual. But a million times worse. Because this time I really cared."

"He actually dared to kiss you, you mean?"

"Very funny."

"I'm not trying to be funny, Camilla."

"He isn't worth it," Mary said briskly.

"Yes, he is," Camilla said. "That's what's so ghastly about it. With other men I've never minded this much. Not nearly this much. I really loved him."

"Loved him?"

"Love him. I love him."

157

"Then don't just sit there," Mary said. "Do something about it."

Camilla pulled a Kleenex from a box on a nearby radiator and blew her nose. She always relied to a great extent on nose-blowing at times of emotional crisis.

"I couldn't ever face him again," she said in a low voice.

"Was it that bad?" Mary demanded. "Did he go berserk? If he wanted to get you into bed that isn't exactly an insult, you know."

"At first I encouraged him. I didn't mean to. It just happened. I never kissed anyone that way before. Never. For a while I hardly knew what I was doing."

"That doesn't sound bad."

"It was wonderful, in a way. But it was frightening."

"He got out of hand?" Mary said. "What did he do?"

"No. But I shouldn't have misled him like that. I felt like a cheat. Leading him on and then slamming the door in his face. It was so embarrassing, having to explain."

"Why? You could have said anything. What difference could it have made? At a time like that, if it's no, it's no, and that's it."

"But he looked so baffled," Camilla said. "It seemed so unfair. I felt I owed him the truth."

"What did you say?" Mary asked. She was fascinated.

"What could I say? I just said I wouldn't; I couldn't; I never had. I even used that word that amuses you so much, I told him I was a virgin."

"Oh, Camilla!"

"I didn't want him to think I was discriminating against him."

"You'll be the talk of the campus – of Ohio!" Mary said. She was unable to refrain from laughing. "You'll be pointed out in the streets. People will drive for miles. You'll be bigger than Disneyland. Oh, Camilla, really! Why did you have to tell him?"

"I know. It's the end. Well, as far as I'm concerned, men can all drop dead. I'm a virgin, and I'm not ashamed of it, and I'm going to stay a virgin until I'm married."

"Who's going to marry you if they all drop dead?"

Camilla ignored that splitting of hairs. "And I'm not going to get married till I graduate," she said. "I want it to be a marriage of equals."

"Mr. Right has to be a virgin, too? What a man! There isn't even a proper word for him. Celibate sounds so monkishly dried up. Is that what you want?"

"I meant academic equals," Camilla said.

"I'd quit school tomorrow if some guy gave the word," Mary said. "You're crazy, and about fifty years out of date. You're a victim of suffragette propaganda. Why don't you call Richard up and say you were kidding? You could have an operation. Snip, snip – and no more hymen. Any gynecologist would do it for free, just for the rarity of it."

"I wasn't kidding, that's why. He can pick up some life-of-the-party sophomore. I'm not going to try to stop him."

"Camilla, for someone so smart, you're sometimes so dumb."

"It's a matter of principle," Camilla said. "Anyway, arguing with you always makes me feel better." She smiled. "Thanks, Mary. It must be very draggy for you, hearing all my sad tales of woe."

"Forget it, stupid."

They sipped coffee. Camilla casually opened the Western Union envelope, unfolded the telegram, and read it. Then she uttered a high-pitched howl of delight.

"What is it?" Mary asked.

"Mary!" Camilla cried incredulously. "Listen to this: 'O.K. IF YOU INSIST I WILL APPLY JOB ITALIAN LAUNDRY STOP IN MEANTIME HOW ABOUT ANOTHER CUP OF UGH COFFEE QUERY' – and it's signed with *love*, Mary, from Richard."

"Great!" Mary said. "Is it in code?"

"Hug?" Camilla said, avidly rereading the message.

"She's gone," Mary informed the room in general. "Cupid strikes again."

"What did you say?" Camilla asked.

"I only wondered what it meant, that was all," Mary said. She was no longer playing the part of the older sister. Without the role she was nobody, and she was slightly irritated.

"It's too complicated to explain," Camilla said. "But it's wonderful! Look at the time! I must get dressed. I must telephone. Oh, Mary! You have to meet him!"

"I'll be maid of honour," Mary said.

"Can I use some of your perfume?" Camilla asked.

TWENTY-FOUR

"As long as I can remember, everyone said I was the best-built girl in my home town," Marcia Daventry related. "At the age of fifteen my measurements were thirty-eight, twenty-four, thirty-six. That's a fact, and I can prove it. If you like I can send for my scrapbook. The press clippings are all there."

"I believe you," Dr. Porter assured her. "Now, if you would only–"

"I won all the beauty contests," Marcia said. "It got so some of the girls refused to compete if I was going to be in it. I was Miss Dairy Milk three years in a row. They gave a beautiful silver trophy and a weekend for two in Cleveland, all expenses paid. I took my mother. Did we have a time! That was a county-wide contest sponsored by the 4-H Club. You had to be judged for deportment in a full-length evening gown, and then you paraded in a bathing suit, and finally there were points for personality and talent, where you had to sing or dance or something like that."

"That's very interesting," Dr. Porter said impatiently. "But I'd appreciate it if you would get back to the subject of your early sexual experiences."

"This had a lot to do with it," Marcia said. "Wait till I tell you! I was only fifteen, going on sixteen, the first year. Most of the kids sang songs from *South Pacific* and stuff like that, but I outsmarted them. I did a very patriotic recitation – the Gettysburg Address. I'd memorized all the words perfectly. I didn't get a word wrong. You should have heard the applause!"

"But –"

"I'm getting to it. I have to tell it my own way."

"I didn't mean to rush you, Miss Z-4, but you know how time flies. Do go ahead."

"I don't like to be pressured, I don't care who it is, that's all," Marcia said, wrapping her mink coat defensively tighter around her pink angora sweater. "When Dr. Schumann gave me the shot in the arm, she said I could relax. You got to relax if you're going to tell a stranger everything about a lady's intimate personal love life."

"Excuse me," Dr. Porter said.

"O.K.," Marcia said haughtily. "But I don't have to do this, so just remember that. Where was I? Oh, yes! One of the judges — a good-looking fellow; you know, husky, a real man; he was a farmer, like the rest of them, about six foot, a hundred and eighty pounds, maybe a hundred and ninety; I think he was thirty-two years of age — he was really giving me the eye. When I walked past in my bathing suit — I had quite a strut for a fifteen-year-old — I was wearing this fabulous chartroose suit that brought out the color of my hair — it was chestnut then — with a shiny sateen finish and very close-fitting, like skin-tight — I thought he'd cream himself, if you'll excuse the expression."

"Ejaculate, you mean?"

"I don't mean he really came," Marcia said. "But he was breathing hard. You know what I mean."

"I see," Dr. Porter said. "A figure of speech."

"I'm not bragging," Marcia said, "but my bosom really was something. I keep in shape, but when you're a fifteen-year-old girl there's a special bounce, you know? I didn't need any uplift bra in those days. At the reception after the crowning and the presentation of the scroll — it was a very luxurious, catered affair, in a big tent, in case of rain — as soon as I got there, I saw him out of the corner of my eye, making a beeline right over to me. He got me out of there so fast it would of made your head spin. He took me to a motel. No finesse about it. He wanted it and there wasn't any fooling around. He was terrific. He had the biggest one I ever saw. Sometimes those big guys can fool you. They look like Superman in their clothes and then when they get it out it's nothing. Also the other way around. I once had a fellow in Toledo — we met in this exclusive cocktail lounge — they wouldn't even let you in if you weren't dressed right — he worked in a bank over in Elyria, he said — he was so short he wore elevator shoes — a real little fellow — except he was hung like a bull down there. You never can tell. Some women think if a man's got a long nose or long hands that means he's got a big one — or if he has a deep speaking voice — but don't you believe it. That's all a lot of hooey. There's only one way to find out for sure. But anyway, I was telling you, this was the

161

biggest one of all time. It would of won a blue ribbon at the county fair – I kid you not. I could only just hold it in both my two hands. The first time he put it in, I thought the end of it would come out of the top of my head."

"You have made your point," Dr. Porter said, frowning. He looked rather cross, and yet the way he was biting his lower lip suggested a different sort of agitation. "What did he do?" he asked. "It would be a valuable contribution if you would try to recall the methods by which he stimulated you, the erogenous zones to which he paid special attention, and so forth."

"He screwed the living daylights out of me, was all," Marcia said. "Pardon my French."

"What position did you assume?" Dr. Porter enquired.

"You name it. We tried everything. We started with him on top. Then we switched – he lay back there and I did the work. Sometimes we would watch ourselves in the mirror. One look and I came. It was fabulous."

"That's very interesting," Dr. Porter said solemnly, as he jotted down a memorandum. "You found the mirror image more stimulating than direct appraisal. It's curious, but, I believe, generally true, that two-dimensional image makes a greater and more memorable impact than the three-dimensional. I'll have to bring this up with Dr. Schumann. I'm sure she'll be most grateful to you."

"You sure can sling the words around!" Marcia said. Dr. Porter smiled modestly. The interviews seemed to be going better with practice. But he must not allow himself to become complacent. There was so much to learn. The more he found out about sex, the more the subject seemed to expand; every answer seemed to raise two more questions. Would they ever encompass everything? They must. He compressed his lips determinedly.

"Did you achieve a number of orgasms on this occasion of which we have been speaking?" he asked.

"Yeah," Marcia said.

"And your partner? By what means did you maintain him for such a lengthy period in such a state of tension?"

"What's the question? Come again?"

"The activities you have mentioned must have taken a considerable time."

"All evening and half the night. I remember I caught

162

hell when I got home."

"As long as that? Would you tell me how you managed to sustain your partner's efforts?"

"It was just one of those times when you meet someone and it kind of explodes," Marcia said. "You know – everything's right. A trip to the moon on gossamer wings. Of course, it helps when you go down on a man. It keeps things interesting."

"You stimulated him?"

Marcia looked perplexed.

"Fellatio?" Dr. Porter said.

"That's what I said," Marcia said. "It's the quickest way. If a man can't get it up that way you'd better call the mortician. There's a knack to it, though. Those fancy books don't tell you that, do they? I guess I have a natural talent. Some things you're just born with.

"You know, for years – I'm not kidding, about five years – there was a gentleman – he was a very distinguished lawyer – he had a beautiful two-hundred-thousand-dollar home in the Shaker Heights section – he wasn't making out so good with his wife – a very gracious hostess – he was devoted to her – he had to entertain some very important contacts – but in the sack she was nothing – like I say, for four years, every Monday afternoon at four, like clockwork, he used to drive over to my place. He said without it he couldn't have gone on – he'd of walked out on her or something. That was all he liked, me going down on him – he said when his wife tried it it didn't mean a thing. Every week he drove over. I remember he used to come quick like a bunny." Marcia snapped a finger and thumb. "Bingo! Just like that, it was all over. That was the way he liked it. I really liked the guy – a real gentleman – he was very generous – he even gave me Christmas presents. But no. It was all over in a minute, and I got my check. He always paid by check. Can you imagine? Made out to cash. Not one of them ever bounced. You could trust him. A wealthy man. I asked him wouldn't it be better if he paid in bills – you know, it might look bad, a lady endorsing all those checks, the same name once a week, what if his wife saw his canceled checks? And you know what? He said she knew anyway, and she didn't mind. She figured I'd saved her marriage. How about that?"

"What terminated this liaison?" Dr. Porter asked. "Did his sexual needs diminish with aging?"

"He never changed. You could set your watch by him. But he passed on – God rest him. You don't meet many like him."

"One outlet per week, right to the time of decease," Dr. Porter said. "How old was he then? We're concerned with the geriatric aspects of sexual response. Any data of this sort are most welcome."

"He was sixty-eight," Marcia said. "I know that's right, because we had a laugh over the idea of his next birthday – sixty-nine. Get it? He liked a laugh."

Marcia opened her snakeskin handbag and took out a dainty handkerchief with which to prevent the warm tears of reminiscence from streaking her mascara.

"That's quite a tribute to the effectiveness of your ministrations," Dr. Porter said consolingly. Marcia bravely smiled.

"Like I said, technique is something that comes naturally. But you can help it along. I owe a lot to the years I spent in the dance. After a while on the semiprobeauty-contest circuit, I met this wonderful guy who became my personal manager, and he groomed me personally as an exotic dancer. He taught me a lot, but he never laid a hand on me – strictly business. He had me billed as an *ecdysiast* – that's a fancy word for 'stripper' – he said *stripper* sounded cheap, and my act was a class act – I had my own script – special musical arrangements, lighting cues. There was one very artistic routine I did with a boa constrictor. The A.S.P.C.A. got a complaint from some jerk in St. Louis, Missouri, and sent over an inspector. We gave him drinks on the house. He watched my act three times – got real loaded – and came back to the dressing room for a closer look. That wasn't being cruel to the snake, he said, the routine I did with it; he wouldn't mind being the snake, any time. It was quoted in all the papers – Earl Wilson wrote a cute column on it. There was a bit in *Variety*. I got a lot of offers. We went all over – London, Paris, Panama City, Cairo, Egypt, even – Alexandria, Port Said – the Egyptians have some fabulous dancers – I learned a thing or two in Egypt – in the end I was beating them at their own game. We stayed there for two years. Some of the managers thought I should change my name to one of those gag strip names, like Norma Vincent Peel – get it? – or Helen Bedd.

"But I kept to Marcia Daventry. If you keep your dignity nightclub audiences respect you for it. I wouldn't mind going to Egypt again one day, for a visit. It's real romantic. You know some of the Egyptians have skin as light as you or me? That's a fact. I had one Egyptian boy friend – he owned one of the biggest nightclubs in Port Said – he could speak English like a movie star – all his suits were custom-made, and after he wore them a few times he threw them away. He wanted me to try hashish – that's a drug they use over there. I wouldn't, but sometimes I wish I'd tried it. When he used it he could make love for hours at a time without stopping. He was fabulous."

"You're very good," Dr. Porter said, making another note. "It's subjects like you that are going to make all the difference to the Institute."

"You're entirely welcome," Marcia said graciously. "You know the other day I was saying to Billie – she's my personal maid; she's been with me for years – I wonder if I could take a couple of courses while we're here – something artistic maybe. I'd really go for that."

"I don't know," Dr. Porter said. "I'm new here myself. But I don't see why not. I could speak to the registrar. Perhaps he'd let you audit freshman art appreciation or something. You don't care about the credits, do you?"

"I'd really appreciate that," Marcia said. "I've always had an urge to take some courses. I've done all right. But money isn't everything, is it? I've always thought it would be nice to go to a nice school and take some courses."

"We can help each other then, can't we?" Dr. Porter said. "Now, I'd like to go back to that experience you mentioned at the beginning. The Undinist episode. Undinism must be comparatively rare these days. I'm alluding to the elderly lady in Schenectady who used to pay you to urinate on her head."

That evening, before she went to bed, Marcia wrote a letter to her daughter, Joanna, telling her of the wonders of Digby. Since Joanna had gone over to the South of France with her sponsor, a wealthy Greek, in furtherance of her budding career as a motion-picture starlet, Marcia was always casting about for ways of impressing her.

TWENTY-FIVE

"CHASTITY has no intrinsic worth," Richard patiently argued. "There's no percentage in hoarding it. It's a negative virtue, like abstaining from dancing on Sunday. What's the point?"

"Chastity's the innermost, most secret part of your individuality," Camilla said. "It isn't a thing, it's a state of mind; it's your heart. You can only give it once, and then it's committed, or maybe lost. It should be saved until you know what you're doing and you're really sure."

"And you're not sure."

"Even if I thought I were, that sort of love is something I believe should be saved for marriage. That's what marriage means, doesn't it – giving yourself completely to another person? If you go ahead before you get married, why bother to get married? You might as well just sleep around with anyone who comes along."

"You don't have to go from one extreme to the other," Richard objected. "There's such a thing as discrimination and taste."

"Where do you draw the line though?" Camilla demanded. "If you leave the morality out of it, what do you decide by? Just the way you happen to feel at the moment? What kind of commitment is that?"

"If two persons meet, and they are attracted to each other, and nobody is involved, so nobody else can be hurt in any way, what's wrong if they make love? Making love's a good thing. It's the best way of expressing affection. It's beautiful. It's healthy. It's fun. It beats ping-pong. What's wrong with it?"

"We'll never agree on this," Camilla said. "There's a conflict of basic standards. Maybe it's old-fashioned of me, but that's the way I was brought up. My father and mother were brought up the same way. She says marriage is a sacrament, and if you don't accept that you're really just fooling yourself."

"I don't even know what a sacrament is," Richard said. "It sounds like some sort of ointment, an old-style patent medicine or something. Don't let's bring religion into this I thought you believed in facts. I thought you wanted to be a scientist."

"You have to have hypothetical principles as well as facts," Camilla said. "Anyway, I was only talking about my father and mother. They went steady in their junior year. They were engaged for two years. They got married after they graduated. Marriage was very important to them, but so was graduation. It made their marriage better. They never wanted anyone else. Waiting a year or two couldn't kill anyone. They've always been very happy. Don't you believe in self-control?"

"We're not a couple of kids," Richard said. "You've said so yourself. We're adults. These are supposed to be the best years of your life. Do you want to devote them to staring into a test tube or through a microscope or into a cage of white rats or whatever you do in that damn lab? The pleasures you pass up now are gone for ever. Do you want to be a saint?"

"There's no need to exaggerate," Camilla said. "I want to be able to give myself to my husband without feeling ashamed of anything that's happened before."

"Giving yourself!" Richard said. "It sounds like *Little Women* or something on afternoon TV. That isn't what making love is. It's not some sort of blood sacrifice, laying yourself down on a stone slab to have someone carve you up with a knife. It's a lot friendlier than that. At least, it should be. We'd both be giving but we'd also both be taking. What harm could it do?"

"Please let's change the subject," Camilla said. "It's turning into nothing but a lot of words." She sipped some of her lemon Coke and smiled cajolingly. "Please, Richard."

"How can I?" he asked. He broke the ring of doughnut on his plate. "Everything reminds me of it." Ruefully, he held up a piece of doughnut as evidence.

"*Poor* Richard," she said.

"It's no joke," he said. "Camilla?"

"Yes?"

"Do you really love me?"

"Yes."

"Well, why don't we then?"

167

"Oh, Richard! Come on, let's walk over and see how they're getting on with your building."

"Camilla."

"Yes?"

"If only you had some idea of what it's like to be a man."

Camilla's eyes widened.

TWENTY-SIX

"LET'S get the show on the road," said Lawrence da Silva. He was naked, standing in an insolent Gothic slouch, pelvis tilted up at one side, one arm akimbo, smoking a cigarette, in the demonstration lab. The blond hair on his head, as always, was exquisitely brushed back in gleaming, silky waves, contrasting strangely with the tufts of black hair under his arms, the black curls on his chest, the black hair that grew downward from his navel, spreading out in thickening whorls across his abdomen, to form a dense entanglement above the junction of his thighs. "We've been waiting a half hour," he complained. "I could have had half an hour more sleep."

Pru Griswolde, sitting naked on a small upholstered chair against a nearby wall, lowered her magazine and looked up over her reading glasses, but said nothing.

"We're almost ready," Dr. Schumann said. Her manner was more conciliatory than usual. She was bustling about in the flustered way of a stage manager just before the curtain eventually rises late on opening night. "Is that light all right now?" she asked the cameraman.

"Let me take one more reading," he said. "This should do it, but I'd better make sure. It's fast film, but it may not be all this fast. If we were shooting in black and white it wouldn't be any problem."

"We won't go through all that again," Dr. Schumann said. "I've already explained at considerable length the importance of accurately recording skin colours as an index of varying intensity of response. It's no use merely writing the colours down – pink, red, purple. What red? Vermilion, scarlet, cherry? It's not good enough. We're aiming for precision. Please hurry with the light meter."

The relationship between the Institute and the college's economically captive cameraman had already altered, however. The cameraman, having rightly perceived the importance, the indispensability even, of his function and of his discretion, was now behaving with the calm, confident,

169

obstinate sluggishness of all journeymen craftsmen in a sellers' market.

"You want me to do it right, don't you?" he said.

"Yes, yes, yes, of course," Dr. Schumann irritably replied. "Go *on*."

"If you don't like the way I'm operating, you can always get someone else," he said.

"Please, Mr. Vaughan," she said.

He walked slowly over to the large square bed encircled by floodlights, spotlights, microphones, electrocardiograph machines and other equipment in the middle of the starkly aseptic room. He held a light meter close to the taut, smooth, white sheet, and examined the dial thoughtfully.

"Better have them over here," he said. "The reflection will be different with them here."

"Very well," Dr. Schumann agreed. "Subject A, Subject M! Take your places! Mr. Vaughan wants to make the final camera adjustments."

With a sigh of resignation, Lawrence stubbed out his cigarette in an ash tray. Pru stood up and put down her magazine, face down to mark the place, and walked over toward the bed.

"Shouldn't she remove her glasses?" Dr. Porter asked.

"I always keep my glasses on," Pru said. Closer acquaintance with Dr. Porter had not increased her regard for him.

"The optical observations should be made without any artificial impediments, shouldn't they, Dr. Schumann?" he suggested, not even looking at Pru.

"Did we decide that?" Dr. Schumann asked absentmindedly. She was busy looking through her notes.

"Pupil dilation during the excitement phase," Dr. Porter reminded her.

"What?" Dr. Schumann asked. She looked up at him. "Oh, that's right. No glasses. No glasses, Subject A."

"And Subject M," Dr. Porter said, speaking now in an altogether more persuasively friendly voice. "You'd better take off your identification bracelet, if you don't mind. It may seem unduly cautious of them, but the insurance company was quite specific about wrist watches, rings, and other metalware worn on the person during demonstrations. Sorry."

Lawrence tossed his fair head back pettishly, but took

the engraved silver bracelet off his wrist.

"All right," he said. "Then keep it for me, will you till after? It has great sentimental value." He handed the bracelet to Dr. Porter. Halting an automatic movement to put it in the side pocket of his white lab coat, Dr. Porter was about to read the inscription inside the bracelet, when Lawrence, pausing on the way to the bed, with a knowing smile waggled a reproving finger.

"Naughty, naughty!" he said. "We all have our little secrets!" Dr. Porter flinched slightly and put the bracelet away.

"All right," Dr. Porter said, with the ostentatious authority of an assistant director in a film studio. "Places now! Quiet, please! No talking, technicians! That means you, too, Miss Fairbank!"

"Would one of you two sit on the bed, please?" Mr. Vaughan asked. "Would you, Miss, just for a minute?"

Pru sat on the edge of the bed and the cameraman held the translucent white glass bulb of the meter close to her chest.

"That's good," Mr. Vaughan announced. "Right, Dr. Schumann. Whenever you say."

"Has anyone got a comb for a minute?" Lawrence asked. "I left mine in the dressing room."

"What now?" Dr. Schumann said.

"It'll only take a second," Lawrence said. "I can feel a bit sticking up at the back. I washed my hair last night and I must have slept on it the wrong way. There's nothing that looks more ridiculous than hair sticking up at the back."

"Here you are," Dr. Porter said, handing his own comb to Lawrence. Lawrence gratefully smiled, picked a loose hair from the black plastic teeth of the comb, deftly made himself, by his own standards, presentable, and gave the comb back. He moved closer to the center of the warm, white glow of the lights.

The penis was beginning to stir. As slowly as some sort of soft mollusk emerging with surreptitious purposefulness from shelter, it smoothly progressed, lengthening almost imperceptibly at first, centimeter by centimeter, down between his thighs.

"Now," Dr. Schumann said. "I want each of you to pretend that the other is an ordinary, conventional, heterosexual client. Get on the bed, please, both of you. Lie back in a side-by-side reclining position. That's it, supporting your weight on one elbow, Subject A. Very good. Subject M, you lie all the way back. Subject A, you can lean over him a little. Subject M, I don't want you to do anything for the moment, except lie back and relax. Now, Subject A, with your free hand, will you please manipulate your partner – not yet; I'll give the signal – in such a way as to cause it to achieve erection without your hand obscuring it from the camera? In other words, our initial concern is with the process of male arousal. That's what this initial sequence is all about. Mr. Vaughan here is going to take a close-up of Subject M as tumescence occurs. All right? Are there any questions?"

"O.K.," Pru said.

"Dr. Schumann," Lawrence said. "Wouldn't it show better from the side? My right profile is better than full face."

"We'll do it our way, Subject M, thank you very much. Ready, Mr. Vaughan?" The cameraman nodded.

"Roll 'em!" Dr. Porter said. "This is a take." He had been reading an old technical handbook on cinematography in the college library.

Pru, leaning on her left elbow, moved her right hand across Lawrence's leg. Her red-lacquered fingernails glittered prettily in the bright lights. Her finger tips moved gradually up over the gray-black fuzz of his thigh. The penis began noticeably to increase in size, thickening, and lengthening in tiny, regular spasms, moving in miniature, slow, rhythmical leaps up from the horizontal, like a mortar being elevated to an angle of menace.

"Excellent!" Dr. Schumann said.

The cameraman, with his eye to the eyepiece, twisted the camera turret to align a longer, more intimate lens and twisted it into focus.

Lawrence lifted his head to admire himself and to look into the camera.

"No!" Dr. Schumann protested in a voice of painful chagrin. "Stop!"

"Cut!" Dr. Porter said, and the camera stopped its smooth, low whirring.

"Subject M!" Dr. Schumann said. "That's one of the

172

elementary principles! Everyone knows that, surely? Please, no looking into the camera. This is a medical record we're compiling. There must be no feeling that subjects are in any way communicating with the viewer. We simply want an objective study of sexual action and reaction."

During the utterance of adverse criticism, the penis quickly deflated, softened and subsided. Noticing its abashment and shrinkage, Dr. Schumann, like a shrewdly tactful athletic coach, added a few words of encouragement.

"You two got off to a very good start, though. Let's have that again now! And this time please concentrate on yourselves and each other – nobody else. Just behave as if there were nobody here but you. Here we go! Right, Mr. Vaughan."

"It wouldn't have happened if you'd shot it in profile, like I said," Lawrence said.

"No further conversation," Dr. Schumann said, "unless it genuinely pertains to the responses you experience to sexual activity. That's what the microphones are for, Subject M – for that and nothing else. Please start once more, Subject A."

"O.K.," Pru said.

Her clever fingers soon again raised her partner to his full stature; indeed, on his second occasion, the girth and height were possibly somewhat greater. Pru serenely smiled with the modest gratification of a snake charmer who had successfully performed the Indian rope trick in front of an audience composed principally of fakirs who, despite knowing the inner workings of the mystery, surprisingly found themselves marveling at her stylishness. Dr. Schumann stared more intently than any of the others. Yet it was she who resolutely broke the spell.

"Good," she said briskly. "Calibration please, Miss Fairbank! Then, Mr. Vaughan, we can move in for the final close-ups of the climax and resolution. Hurry, please, Miss Fairbank!"

Camilla, wearing an immaculate clinical coat like the others, was standing near the back of the room. She was in a strange state of calm bewilderment, both slightly relieved and slightly let down, as a medical student is at once elated and depressed by the feeling of accomplishment and

173

anticlimax after having witnessed his first surgical operation, or as a soldier feels after having survived his first action under enemy fire. She had been afraid of fear and disgusted by the prospect of disgust. She need not have suffered such agonies of self-doubt. She needn't have gone to Dr. Schumann, again and again since acceptance of the appointment, to ask her for assurances that the work would be scientifically significant and academically valuable.

Now Camilla steadily walked across the room, gazing tranquilly ahead at the body on the bed. It was only a body, a specimen. The fact that it was alive did not matter.

So that minor shaft of muscle and those two small globular appendages were what the awful apprehension, the secret enchantment, the exultant poetry, the gossip in the dorm were all about! She told herself that that rather ludicrous toy flagpole, that insignificant-looking organic totem, was supposed to be the fountainhead, the root, of all human creativity. How dare men make such presumptuous, conceited, overbearing fuss about it? And yet she also felt a certain sense of wonder, a dispassionate thrill of scholarly interest in a biological phenomenon, if not the glow of aesthetic bliss as advertised, when the flaccid little pipe had been pumped large and vertical. It *was* kind of weird. But anyway, this wasn't a man; it was something in a lab. Camilla got the calipers out of her pocket.

TWENTY-SEVEN

JOANNA DAVENTRY opened her lovely hazel eyes, vaguely aware that something was wrong. Nothing threatening. Nothing invigorating with the sharpness of urgency. Something tiresomely not quite right.

Although it was almost noon, she was only half awake. She had the slight headache, the uncomfortable feeling of congestion, that results from boredom. Her dissatisfaction made her feel rather guilty; she should have been appreciative and grateful. He was a kind man, really. Perhaps she was merely tired. She hadn't got back from the Casino until well after three that morning. And the night before. And the night before that. She had felt slightly aggrieved because last night he had sent her back to the hotel escorted by one of his young yes-men. It only took two minutes to walk from the Casino to the hotel, but she thought that he himself should have taken her. Those young men always seemed to be sneering behind their polite smiles. She wasn't being reasonable, she knew. He had been thousands down again, God only knew how many, and he always hated leaving when he was down. But still. . . .

The curtains were drawn and the bedroom was dim and cool, but outside the day was undoubtedly perfect. It always was perfect in Monte Carlo in the spring. It was difficult, though, to keep appreciating the weather. After a while, it wasn't enough.

She sat up and arranged a heap of pillows at the head of the large double bed, to make a sort of throne fit for a lazy queen. She pressed a button on the table next to her side of the bed. In a few moments there was a gentle knock at the door.

"Come in!" she called. She refused to try to speak French any more. When she had tried, his friends had applauded her efforts as good-humoredly condescendingly as though she had been an idiot child with a cleft palate trying to recite Shakespeare. She knew a lot more Shakespeare than any of them did, not that the knowledge had ever done her any good. It certainly hadn't got her a suite of

175

her own at the Hôtel de Paris. And that was quite an achievement for a twenty-year-old, she kept reminding herself, with decreasing conviction.

The waiter was one of those suavely swarthy middle-aged middle European hereditary servants difficult to imagine out of uniform and off duty. He reported the sunshine to her as obsequiously as though offering her an exotic fruit out of season. "The curtains open, madame?" he suggested.

"Sure," she said.

He wheeled the service tray close to her bed.

The usual fresh orange juice, like a great topaz in a setting of crushed diamonds in a silver bowl. Two flaky croissants, warm enough to melt the butter. Clear honey, for which countless bees had labored in the flowery hills of Provence all the past summer. A large silver pot of strong black coffee. And the Paris edition of the *Herald Tribune & Washington Post,* whose comic strips made her feel less remote from the States. And that was all.

But no – it wasn't quite all. Underneath the paper, there was a letter, air mail, with American stamps, addressed in her mother's generously large, round, illiterate scrawl.

"Hey, thanks," she said to the waiter, who was already soundlessly withdrawing.

"It is a pleasure, madame," he said.

How could it be? she wondered. He had probably been up since sunrise, working. How could he stand bringing breakfast to a young woman yawning at midday? The moment of remorse was fleeting. She felt a small squirt of pleasure at the thought of opening the letter.

"Oh, and waiter!" she said, catching him at the door.

"Yes, madame?"

"I think I'll have some figs."

"Very good, madame."

"Green figs."

"Yes, madame."

"And plenty of cream – not one of those little jugs."

"Right away, madame."

"And some cigarettes."

"Benson and Hedges, madame?"

"That's right. You have a good memory."

"*Thank* you, madame."

She tore open the envelope and heard the closing door

click. The day was suddenly picking up. She didn't much care for figs, except for the sweet syrup mixed with cream, but she liked the idea of them. They sounded luxuriously unnecessary. She had taken to Benson and Hedges cigarettes because Alex smoked them and she now associated them with privilege.

The letter was enjoyably long. Several pages, with several lines to a page. Having been educated and housed in a horsy boarding school for girls in Virginia since her mother's divorce, Joanna had hardly ever seen her mother for nearly ten years, and it suited both of them not to define or in any way acknowledge her mother's activities and way of life. Joanna had, since early childhood, evolved such a complicatedly detailed make-believe identity and character for her mother that it was possible for them to exchange the most delightful extravagances in their occasional correspondence with each other without any sensation of straying from the truth about their lives. Joanna was delighted but hardly surprised to hear that her mother was at present taking some courses in art appreciation at Digby College and had begun to give a series of lectures at the Digby Institute. Joanna had long been aware that her mother was interested in the dance and interior decoration but she hadn't realized that her interest in the arts was so broad and so academic. Joanna felt proud but a bit uneasy. Her own career, in motion pictures, still had not reached the stage of actually appearing in one of them, and her stay in Europe, "considering scripts," was becoming more and more difficult to account for, even to herself. Joanna's mother concluded by saying that the spring weather was not too warm and she had never seen southern Ohio looking more beautiful. Joanna felt a pang of homesickness for a small town she had never known.

She got out of bed and stood by the long windows, looking down on the white yachts tied up in the small port far below, and she remembered how impressive they had seemed even a few weeks earlier. She turned to the writing desk and, on a small sheet of paper heavily embossed with a crown, wrote to tell her mother of the cultural marvels of the Principality. Ballet at the Sporting Club, a guided tour of the Musée Océanographique – one thing after another; there seemed to be no end to it.

177

Joanna went down to the hotel's private swimming club and swam twice across the large indoor pool. She had a massage. She sat on an almost horizontal deck chair on the terrace and sun-bathed. Soon it was time for lunch. She had very little appetite, but she was cheered up a little as she stood in her bedroom and contemplated the array of new clothes in the wardrobe. At last, she was dressed, simply, in cream-colored silk, which seemed to enrich her tan and intensify the soft blue-blackness of her long hair, and she went down and took her usual table, among flowers on the terrace, with a commanding view of passersby in the Place du Casino. She sighed when the menu was presented and ordered a chicken sandwich and a glass of milk.

Alex's pale-beige Rolls Royce convertible, driven by a chauffeur in a pale-beige uniform with a brown-leather-peaked cap and brown riding boots, arrived at three o'clock, exactly on time. Joanna, still sitting at her table, messing about with some chestnut ice cream, saw the car come majestically slowly to a halt, far from the curb, in front of the main entrance. She was ready to leave but she kept the chauffeur waiting for ten minutes so that he wouldn't think she was the sort of girl who would jump on demand.

Joanna spent most of the afternoon at the golf club, looking through old copies of *Paris-Match*, waiting for Alex to finish his round.

On the way back down the hill afterward, he asked her how her day had been. Had she been shopping? Fine, she said. No, she hadn't. How had his golf gone?

"Very well," he said. "Seventy-three. Soon I shall be able to beat the pro."

Alex Philopoulos, a forty-eight-year-old Greek with prematurely gray hair and a permanent deep tan, a multimillionaire in several currencies who was proud of the fact that he had never owned a merchant ship in his life, spoke with that ruthlessly direct self-interested candor that some people find charmingly boyish, especially in the very rich.

"On the sixteenth," he told her, "four hundred and ninety yards with a dog-leg to the left, Colonel Rodney-Stewart and I both got into trouble. We hooked around the water all right, but our approach shots landed in the

178

sand trap on the left of the green. What do you think I did?" He chuckled at the thought.

"You won it?"

"I got there ahead of him. I hadn't planned it, it happened like that. So – I stepped on his ball! You should have seen the look on his face! He had a hell of a time."

"But didn't he complain? Isn't that against the rules?" Joanna asked.

"He didn't see me do it, stupid. It was only a joke. I was going to tell him in the clubhouse."

"You didn't?"

"Why should I? You should have seen the way he walked into the bar. As if he owned the place! To hell with him. He's such a snob. He deserves to lose."

Joanna's laughter was hesitant and inadequate, and he changed the subject.

"Did you have lunch at the hotel, darling?" he asked.

"Yes," she said.

"What did you have?"

She told him and he looked shocked.

"You must eat proper meals," he said. "Look at you!"

"Ouch!" she cried. "I wish you wouldn't do that. I'm black and blue." He laughed, showing most of his splendid teeth.

"Darling," he said a little later.

"What?"

"Did you miss me today?"

"Yes, of course I did," she said. "I hate sitting around waiting for you all day."

"Ah, Joanna, darling! You missed your Alex."

His helicopter was waiting for them on the pad between the hotel and the sea. When the pilot saw the car approaching above he started the engine. The rotor was slowly chopping the fragrant, cool, golden air of late afternoon by the time Alex helped her aboard.

The flight to his yacht, *Aphrodite IV*, took only ten minutes.

Dinner for two was served with elaborate formality on the after deck, beneath a royal-blue canvas awning with golden tassels.

"The orchids come from Hawaii," he said. "Green orchids for green eyes."

179

"That's very dear of you," Joanna said.

By the time she was trying to eat her raspberry mousse and he was lighting an enormous cigar the moon had risen over the calm Mediterranean.

"Are you happy?" he asked her. "Do you love me?"

"It's beautiful," she said, indicating the moon's white reflection on the ripples.

A flamenco guitar plinked sweetly from concealed stereophonic speakers.

"You go below now," he told her genially. "I'm going to enjoy my brandy. I won't be long."

In the silken grandeur of the captain's stateroom, he committed his customary amorous atrocities.

"Was it good for you?" he asked her. "Did you like it? Are you happy?"

Joanna burst into tears. He was amazed.

"I'm homesick," she said. "I got a letter from my mother. I wish I could see her. I'd like to visit her."

"Where is your mother?"

"At Digby College. That's in Ohio, Alex. She's taking courses there and lecturing in Art Appreciation."

"Digby? Digby College? Are you sure?"

Wasn't that where that idiot Symington had set up some sort of foolish experiment utilizing Buckeye's, rather than his own funds? Not that the money mattered, so long as Symington eventually agreed to a merger, and it was a legitimate tax dodge, which Buckeye could damn well use. Besides, it might help the sale of the new pill. He looked at Joanna and smiled and patted her on the bare flank.

"Why not?" Alex said jovially. He hugged her shoulder. "But for the moment, let us once more.... This time, I wish you to do it the way I explained to you."

The fact that he was very nearly wholly impotent made her evenings quite arduous.

TWENTY-EIGHT

DURING the following few weeks the cause of medical science was served at Digby strenuously and heatedly. What grapplings, what thrustings, what enfoldings, what thumpings did then ensue! Day after day, evening after evening, the steamy gymnastic labor continued. Dr. Schumann was always right there in the very thick of it, amidst the warm, musky exhalations of mammalian exertion, an inspired and inspiring taskmistress, a knight leading a crusade against sexual obfuscation and incompetence, persuading, encouraging, exhorting, commanding, and, if necessary, sometimes goading the thirty personnel of the pilot group to demonstrate in front of the camera all the multifarious possibilities of human sexual experience. Ingeniously, intricately fitted with electrodes connected by flexible, rubber-covered wires with instruments that recorded their pulse rates, blood pressures, rates of respiration, temperatures, and nervous impulses, the assortment of anonymous, naked men and women performed every feasible sexual act, from the better-known orthodox practices prescribed by the marriage manuals to some of the more fanciful, esoteric, athletic, prodigious sexual tours de force of the specialists, singly, in pairs, in threesomes and in foursomes.

"We are not concerned at this time with the arbitrary ethics, aesthetics and mores of our society," Dr. Schumann kept pointing out. "All that we wish to accomplish is to determine the body's sexual capabilities and capacities; that is to say, the what, the how much, and the how many of sex – the facts."

In her eyes and judgment, no enterprise was too ambitious, no call on the stamina, the patience, the sense of balance, and the sense of decorum too demanding, if it helped to enable her to delineate sexual limits, to decide that in this direction or that it was physically possible to go no farther.

There were minor casualties, as might have been expected – one or two strained ligaments, a severely wrenched knee, a painfully tweaked frenulum, that petty vestige of the foreskin that remains after circumcision. In every case, however, a few days' rest alone in bed enabled the subject to return to lab duty.

Dr. Schumann drove herself harder than any of the pilot group or her own staff. Many a time, in the course of a difficult experimental exercise, she seemed to forget all about her own needs for rest and sustenance. Dr. Porter or Camilla had to remind her, and then she accepted scrappy impromptu meals of sandwiches and coffee, reluctantly, and only on condition that she consumed them on the job, without interrupting the filming. After the last orgasm of the day, as late as ten-thirty in the evening (the beginnings of coital engagements could be scheduled but not their conclusions), Dr. Schumann stayed in her office even later, to work on her notes and to make preparations for the following morning.

Dr. Schumann often used the quiet hour before midnight to study the Polaroid stills that she took as a handy reference guide to Mr. Vaughan's motion pictures. She also pored over classic works of erotology, such as *The Perfumed Garden* and *Kama Sutra* and photographs of erotic sculpture, such as the statues decorating the eleventh-century temples at Khajuraho. Those remote Indian sexual acrobats, depicted at their arduous devotions, challenged Dr. Schumann to devise even more complicated mutual entwinements for her subjects at Digby.

"You're not going to let a bunch of Indians have the last word, are you?" she said, and her team rose to the challenge. Lawrence particularly distinguished himself in emulating various statuesque amorous yogis. During *Bhairavichakra,* an early Indian saturnalia in which the grossest sexual excesses were encouraged by the spiritual authorities in order to liberate the soul from the flesh, even the most respectable of families participated in open communal orgies. The collective libido was greater than the sum of the private parts. Even before Dr. Schumann had completed her pedagogical presentation of the historic precedents for proposed attempts to perform certain startling sexual feats, Lawrence was aflame with enthusiasm.

After only a few days' practice, he became able to copulate effectively for many minutes at a time while standing on his head. His partner in this vertiginous enterprise was supported astride him by two other women, standing the right side up, one on each side, like acolytes.

"That'll give Masters and Johnson something to think about!" Dr. Schumann said exultantly to Dr. Porter when she showed him the graphs. "We have enough data here for a whole chapter on the effects of physical inversion and the stimulus of the unexpected."

Unfortunately, however, though hardly surprisingly, Lawrence's successes went to his head. He read a paperback book, purchased from the revolving rack at the Elite, on traditional Indian sexual customs, and began referring knowingly to the *kakali* posture and *amrachushaka,* much to Rollo's annoyance, especially when he read the book himself and realized that the exotic terms denoted nothing more than a familiar routine.

"If you mean sixty-nine, why can't you *say* sixty-nine?" he asked irritably.

"It's not quite the same," Lawrence said in a superior, smirking manner of Oriental philosophical inscrutability.

"Balls!" Rollo said.

"You say I'm the one that's crude," Lawrence said. "I think you are."

Rollo tried to josh Lawrence out of his new pose by teasingly singing a satirical song fragment of his, Rollo's, own composition, "If I were the yoni girl in the world, and you were the lingam boy," but this approach to the problem led only to door slamming and sulkiness.

Worst of all, Lawrence's narcissistic tendencies, never noticeably kept in check by his own efforts, now began to affect his work in the lab. His attempts to upstage his collaborators were sometimes very distracting, as Pru, for one, complained to Dr. Schumann. And, as he performed more and more blatantly for the camera, repeatedly spoiling otherwise first-class takes by juvenile leering, grinning and winking right into the lens, it became apparent that the camera itself was assuming, for him, a potent sexual significance in its own right. Because of his apparent indefatigability, which was becoming more obviously valuable as some of the other subjects' energy was beginning to flag, Dr. Schumann hesitated to reprimand him too severely, but the afternoon that just one glance at the Polaroid camera caused immediate, premature ejaculation she had to face up to the fact that the time had come for an emergency conference.

"I'm not criticizing you," Dr. Schumann said to Dr. Porter. "I'm as much to blame as you are. But I realize that we made a mistake when we failed to recruit as many men as women."

"Male prostitutes willing to perform bisexually aren't so easy to find," Dr. Porter said.

"I'm sure that's true," Dr. Schumann tactfully agreed. "The trouble is that even the eight we have are unreliable. Subject J is clearly obsessed by transvestite experiences. We tried to encourage him by allowing him to wear high-heel shoes and silk lingerie in the ready room, as you will recall, but he took advantage of us."

"I know," Dr. Porter said. "Worn out by the time he was called! It was very embarrassing."

"Until we found out what was going on out there, some of his partners thought his failures in the lab were unfavorable reflections on their ability."

"He was a good verbal source though," Dr. Porter said.

"I agree," Dr. Schumann said. "But . . ."

"You're right," Dr. Porter said. "You're right. At this stage, he isn't pulling his weight."

"Subject P is virtually useless, except with other males," Dr. Schumann continued. "He means well, he does his best, but the women find him unstimulating. 'Creepy' was the word that one of them used."

"I tried to persuade him not to wear false eyelashes," Dr. Porter said. "But he refused. He said he'd feel naked without them."

"I wish you'd told me about that earlier," Dr. Schumann said grimly. "I wondered what was wrong."

"It's no use making an issue of the eyelashes, though," Dr. Porter said. "A lot of men are wearing them now. Straight men, as well. I understand there was a television program about them the other night. Man-in-the-street interviews. One of them was with a Marine sergeant, and he said why not, if they gave a man confidence. Some very eminent leaders of the business community wear them when they have to make speeches."

"In Subject P's case, though, this grooming has gone too

far. One of his partners said his skin's too smooth and the lotion he uses doesn't have enough of that outdoor he-man briskness. That reminds me: there's a lot of work to be done on olfactory stimulation. It may be that some women need the smell of masculine sweat to trigger vaginal lubrication. It's just a thought we should come back to some time."

"I don't think you'd be able to sell the idea of natural body odors to the man of today," Dr. Porter said. "The armpit is the ultimate taboo zone. Maybe it would be possible to synthesize a body odor and present it attractively packaged as after-shave. Or maybe use it in subtle subliminal quantities in body talc, and call it something else. But I'd have to think about that."

"All right," Dr. Schumann said. "Let's get back to the point. We have this urgent problem. What are we to do about male subjects? At the moment, it looks like we have only six, at the most, who can even begin to perform with females, six men who aren't actually profoundly hostile. Maybe only five. Subject B is always too tired to be of much use."

"Rollo?" Dr. Porter said.

"Your friend," Dr. Schumann said.

"Without my friend, as you call him, we wouldn't have Subject M, your golden-haired boy."

"Let's try to discuss this rationally," Dr. Schumann said. "Yes, that brings us to Subject M. Perhaps I was over-impressed by his vitality. In contrast with his colleagues, he was very encouraging at first. His masturbation tests were 'way ahead of the rest of the group."

"With him it's a question of discipline, isn't it?" Dr. Porter said. "It's too bad you were so complimentary to him during the first days."

Dr. Schumann did not even attempt to defend herself against that charge.

"I have been trying to look at the situation in a constructive way," she said. "And I think I have come up with a couple of ideas that must be put into practice without delay. First, we must reorganize the physical lay-out of the lab itself. I'm convinced that the photographic equipment in particular is much too obtrusive. It would be better if subjects were not continuously reminded that their activities are being recorded on film. Awareness of the camera has impaired Subject M's usefulness to a great extent."

"You're not going to do away with the movie camera, are you?" Dr. Porter said.

"Of course not. But I have ordered some simple structural modifications that should boost lab efficiency."

"What are the changes?"

"There will be two large one-way observation windows," Dr. Schumann said. "From the inside of the lab, they will appear to be mirrors. From the observation rooms, to which the subjects will have no access and whose existence will be unknown to them, filming will be able to proceed without provoking self-conscious histrionics of the sort that have invalidated so much of Subject M's participation."

"That will be a big help in normalizing the lab environment," Dr. Porter said.

"Thank you," Dr. Schumann said. "And to further that process, we're going to have the bed made more like a normal domestic bed, in more normal surroundings. More than one of the female subjects have commented that the lab décor makes them feel uncomfortable. We're going to move the bed close to the corner opposite the observation windows, put a thick wall-to-wall carpet on the floor, move the spotlights closer to the ceiling, put up a decorative chandelier, cover the bed with pastel-colored sheets, and install a TV set beside the bed – in other words, make the place seem like a typical real contemporary bedroom."

"But the instruments? They'll still be there, won't they?" Dr. Porter said.

"Naturally. And so will we. But the instruments are going to be in pale-pink cases, and we're going to wear pink lab coats. Everything extraneous is going to be made as unobtrusive as possible."

"Pink lab coats?" Dr. Porter said.

"The coats will be a deep, neutral shade," Dr. Schumann assured him.

"I see."

"That's one decision. Two: we definitely need fresh blood – a lot of it. We'll keep the pilot group on, because they'll be safer here, and they'll be useful, many of them, as catalytic agents, so to speak. But the time has come to broaden the scope of our investigation. There's no use trying to pretend that the subjects we've been examining so far represent a cross section of the average population. I want to study some perfectly ordinary, normal men and women."

"Yes," Dr. Porter said.

"You sound skeptical."

"I'm only wondering . . ."

"Whether the normals are available? Certainly they are. You're not forgetting your Masters and Johnson, are you? They had no difficulty getting volunteers."

"But that was largely through a teaching hospital," Dr. Porter reminded her.

"So much the better for us! Volunteers from a liberal-arts college, representing the arts and sciences, will be all that much more normal."

"I hope you're right," Dr. Porter said. "About being able to talk them into it without a big outcry."

"You leave that to me," Dr. Schumann said. "I'm not going to announce it over the air. I'll talk to some individual wives discreetly, in private. Once I explain the set-up to the wives the rest will be easy. And once we get a couple in the lab, you don't think they'll go around shouting about it, do you? They'll have as much interest in security as we do. Don't worry."

"I'm not really *worried*," Dr. Porter said.

"Can you imagine a member of the faculty admitting that he's against progressive scientific research?" Dr. Schumann said. "And can you imagine any Digby wife passing up a chance for some legitimate polyandry?"

"I guess not."

"I know. I've been sounding some of them out. They are *ready*, believe me."

"That'll take care of the fatigue of our males then," Dr. Porter said.

"The balance of the sexes will undoubtedly help," Dr. Schumann said. "But even so the program would be much too slow if it were not for a couple of other provisions I've made."

"Other provisions?"

"Mechanization," Dr. Schumann said firmly.
187

"You found a company to manufacture a mechanical dildo?" Dr. Porter said. "Won't that seem like plagiarism?"

"There's no such thing as plagiarism in scientific research. We will willingly give the fullest credit to Masters and Johnson. All scientific endeavor is built on earlier structures. There's no need to apologize for benefiting from the findings of Newton and Einstein. I wasn't able to get the specifications of the machine that Masters and Johnson employed, but we will go one better than them, anyway. Now that it's a fait accompli, I can tell you that we will soon receive a hermaphrodite robot capable of participating in sexual intercourse with men *or* women. It's due to arrive from Tokyo any day now."

TWENTY-NINE

"RICHARD, darling! You're getting yourself all wrought up again. Please, just kiss me gently. I love it when you do. You kiss so beautifully."

"Please, Camilla. Camilla, darling. Please."

"Please, Richard, don't let's go through the whole thing again, Richard. Darling Richard."

They were sitting in his car, parked in a dark, sparsely populated residential street a few blocks from her dormitory. Dinner had been a somber occasion of desultory exchanges of small talk and long silences.

"But I love you," Richard insisted miserably.

"I'm glad," Camilla said soothingly. She held his hand, and toyed affectionately with his little finger.

"I want you," he said. "It's becoming an obsession. It's a good thing the building can take care of itself. I can't get to sleep for hours. I get up in the middle of the night and smoke cigarettes. Then I doze off at dawn, and dream about you, and wake up feeling awful – lonely, aching for you. I feel like a teenager. It's ridiculous."

"If you really love me, you'll be patient," Camilla said. "It'll be worth it, darling, I promise. If we get married, it'll be for a long, long time. Forever."

"What do you mean, 'if'?"

"Sometimes I wonder whether men are capable of controlling themselves. I'm not saying it's your fault. I don't think most men can. But I don't believe I could marry a man who didn't love me enough to wait."

"Oh, Camilla," Richard groaned. "If only you knew what we're missing."

"Richard, darling," Camilla said. "Try to think about other things. We used to talk about so many things when we first met. Do you remember those first long talks we had? It was so exciting."

"Oh, Camilla," he said. "I wish I didn't love you. I wish you weren't so perfect in every other way."

"Richard," she said, fondling the hair at the nape of his neck, smiling calmly into the darkness over his bowed head,

189

"I'm not sleeping as well as I should be," Dr. Leo Plesch apologetically told his physician.

"That's something that's easily fixed," the doctor said, briskly swivelling his chair to face his desk. "Go by the Elite on your way home and pick up some of these." He scribbled on a prescription form. "Mild but effective. No side-effects. They'll soon ease you back onto the rails. Anyway, there's nothing to worry about. It's normal to cut down on the hours of sleep at your age. You don't need as much now as when – as you used to."

"When I was active, you mean."

"When you were more active. I only hope I'm riding a bicycle all over the place when I'm your age."

The doctor solicitously escorted his old patient to the front door and waved from the top of the steps. Dr. Plesch carefully mounted his upright black bicycle and slowly rode away.

"In every old man there's a young man struggling to get out!" his wife, Penelope, used to say, affectionately teasing him when he seemed to be trying too unrealistically to resist the passage of time.

"It's all very well for you," he would say. "You're only fifty-nine. Wait till you're my age." He kept reminding her and himself that he was almost as old as the twentieth century. But that was neither biologically nor psychologically very old nowadays, according to the gerontologists, the psychiatrists, the insurance actuaries, and Penelope.

"Think of Bertrand Russell," she said. "Think of Charlie Chaplin."

"Yes, think of them," he said.

She always reassured him as well as she could, as a matter of habit, except on the unusual days when there seemed to be some danger that wishful thinking might delude him into acceptance of the sort of advertisements that promised that he too could be a subtropical Peter Pan, a Huck Finn in a straw hat and a Hawaiian shirt, fishing in the sunshine in retirement at the age of sixty-five.

"Fishing would never agree with you," she said. "Who would bait the hooks? And what if you caught something? You know how squeamish you are. Let's stick to reading."

"Yes," he said. "That's about my speed."

"Leo, stop this self-pity!"

"The great lover!" he said. "When was the last time I made love to you? I mean properly."

She simply kissed him.

Dr. Plesch smiled gratefully as he pedaled along, thinking of her. After the brief stop at the drugstore, he went to the florist's, and – rare extravagance! – he bought her a hyacinth in a glazed earthenware pot. The stalk and the leaves were crisp and fresh. Spring! He had met her forty springs ago. The blossom was purple, which Penelope in recent years had adopted as her favorite color. It had always seemed to him that she had been better able to adjust to the dignified colors of advancing years, better able to accept many of the changes that were reducing the variety and intensity of their activities together, until by chance one evening he had seen the expression of tragic dismay on her face when, believing herself to be unobserved, she had been peering intently and sighing at the reflection in her dressing-table mirror.

He now wheeled his bicycle almost eagerly along the short concrete pathway to the front door of their small white frame house. Penelope opened the door even as he was fumbling with the key in the lock. He was becoming quite a fumbler, he thought.

"You're so late," she said. "Is anything wrong? Why, Leo – how lovely!" She took the hyacinth pot in both hands, as if it had been precious. She looked up again, to search his face for signs. "What have you been doing? Why didn't you telephone? I thought you'd forgotten all about tonight."

"Tonight?" he repeated guiltily. He noticed that her head was lumpy with curlers wrapped in a silk scarf and knew that some sort of social encounter must be imminent.

"Yes, Leo, tonight!" she said with a short laugh of controlled annoyance and good-natured resignation. "You're quite impossible. Sometimes I think the absent-minded professor role is overplayed. But come on, you can still get ready in time, if only you'll hurry. Oh, goodness – of course you didn't bring the sherry?"

"It isn't our anniversary, is it?" he asked, tugging with agitation and imprecision at the buttons of his raincoat.

"Oh, Leo! Is that why you got the flower?"

"Certainly not. I mean – I have just returned from a medical consultation. I was thinking about you." As he had anticipated, the defensive distraction proved to be an effective one. In fact, it was too effective, and he had to assure her so insistently that he was in the very best of health in order to ease her clamorous anxiety that he realized, with some regret, that he would have to forgo the anticipated comfort of being coddled later.

"It's nothing," he said. "Just a checkup. He gave me some sleeping pills. I told him about my recent restless nights. He said – Oh, dear."

"What is it?" Penelope asked, alarmed again. Married life in the advanced years was becoming a series of increasingly frequent sympathetic disturbances.

"Did you say we were having guests tonight?" he asked.

"You know we are, Leo. Don't you remember we decided we should do something about the Kilmartins? Only a little sendoff. It's the least we can do. I've asked the Shapiros and the Edgertons and that young architect you said you liked. The young man you met at the faculty club?"

"An architect?" Dr. Plesch said. "Do I know a young architect?"

"Really, Leo! Doughty his name is. Richard Doughty."

"Oh, yes. Bright young man. But why did I ask him? It'll be too much."

"It's only a quiet little buffet supper," Penelope said. "Nothing elaborate. They won't stay late on a weeknight."

"Oh, God," Leo said.

"Don't be that way. It isn't as though we entertained so very often. You like the Kilmartins."

"I suppose so. It isn't that. I –"

"If it's the money, don't worry about it. I have a new casserole recipe. I saw it in the *Journal*. I could feed the whole of Digby for ninety-nine cents. It doesn't matter about the sherry. They can drink beer."

"Hush, my dear. Let me get a word in. It's very embarrassing. But the thing is I've already taken two of the pills. I thought I'd just have a sandwich and get a really good, long night's sleep."

"Oh, *Leo*."

"I'm sorry."

"Maybe if you phoned Dr. Schaeffer –?"

"I couldn't do that. He'd think I'd gone crazy if I asked for something to keep me awake. They're not very strong pills though. Give me some black coffee. The Shapiros, you said? Make it very black. Anyway, nobody expects me to be very lively these days. 'Old Plesch'."

"Now, Leo, don't be like that. They're really very nice. He worships you. You must promise to try to be kind to them."

"I'll walk around quickly to the liquor store," he said. "The walk might help. They can't drink beer. They look upon it as a drink for students."

"Do hurry then, dear. Everything else is almost ready. They'll be here at seven."

The Shapiros arrived at 7:01, he smoothly pale-blue-gray under talcum, with an oily back crew-cut and thick rimless bifocals, she earnestly, wholesomely unmade-up, with a glossy brown rope of braided hair encircling the top of her head like a heavy halo. They were terribly nice: she wove cloth and played madrigals on the recorder; he made wine with wild flowers according to medieval monastic recipes and played chess by mail; they believed in the therapeutic benefits of natural pain, and the paradox of collective guilt and individual innocence (every man was guilty until proven guilty in court), and every time Dr. Plesch saw them enter a room he felt that some of the oxygen had been simultaneously withdrawn from it.

"The *ambiance!*" cried Mrs. Shapiro, standing in the living-room doorway, with her flat ballet slippers arranged at right angles, in a *T*, the front foot pointing at Dr. Plesch, her long, white hands tightly clasped together at the waist of her dirndl skirt. *"Muy simpatico!"* she said. "It couldn't be anybody's home but whose it is! The honesty, the solidity, the simplicity of it! The friendliness of the colors! The genuineness of the furniture! The flowers! Aren't hyacinths the most innocent of flowers? – and trying so hard to look grown-up! – like little girls at a party! And the water colors! Very conservative, Dr. Plesch, quite charming! I didn't know you were a painter."

"The paintings are not genuine, unfortunately," he said. "They're Constables. But you're right about the furniture. Grand Rapids, 1934. A great year for American sofa design. They don't make springs like those any more. I dare say they'll endure the holocaust. They'll give archaeologists of the future a clue to the nature of our civilization."

"I wish you wouldn't make jokes like that!" Mrs. Shapiro protested, shuddering and tightly closing her eyes against an unbearable apocalyptic vision that she alone was sensitive enough to imagine. "We mustn't *let* it happen, Dr. Plesch! We had a very stimulating debate on this very subject at this month's meeting of the foreign-affairs committee of the Faculty Wives Association, and I'm glad to say that sanity prevailed."

Dr. Plesch felt the genesis within himself of what, but for a mighty act of will, would have been a cavernous, roaring yawn. He clamped his jaws together and clapped a hand over his mouth. The contained yawn, expanding inside his head, momentarily deafened him and filled his pale-blue eyes with tears.

"I'm sure we can count on Dr. Plesch's moral support," Mr. Shapiro hastily assured his wife. "I've brought a bottle of our new wine," he added. "It's not *new,* but it's the first batch ready to drink. We bottled it last summer. I'd like to know what you think of it."

"That's very good of you," Dr. Plesch said, cautiously accepting a large, gray stone jug. "I remember having heard you speak of it. I'm most curious to sample it some evening soon." Too late, he attempted to check an ascendant yawn, and, once it had effected its extrusion, the warm, moist rush of air kept his mouth open and his eyes closed for several seconds. On regaining his composure, he perceived an expression of disappointment on Mr. Shapiro's face. "My!" Dr. Plesch said, "Forgive me! Just before you two arrived, I was reading some particularly turgid essays by some of my freshmen."

"I know what you mean," Mr. Shapiro said.

"Maybe Dr. Plesch doesn't like wine," Mrs. Shapiro said, smiling sweetly.

"Of course I like wine," Dr. Plesch said. "Now, Shapiro,

when would it be best, do you think? Penelope's concocted one of her celebrated casseroles, and after that, I expect, there'll be some fruit and cheese. Or perhaps we might try some as an *apéritif?*"

"It's one of those wines that go with anything," Mr. Shapiro said. "If you're a connoisseur, you might not think much of it. But it's an interesting wine. It's supposed to have been made first by a small splinter group of Dominicans who fled from France in the seventeenth century and settled, more or less by accident, in Nova Scotia."

"Did the wine come before or after their secession?"

"There are documents in Halifax that indicate that they brought the recipe with them," Mr. Shapiro said, gaining enthusiasm. "The local historical society has published some interesting excerpts from the transcripts of the legal proceedings of that era. It's a strong wine. In the course of those long, cold Northern winters, the lay brothers of the order sometimes went a little berserk."

Dr. Plesch felt a yawn coming, fought it, and lost.

"Don't let him get going on *this* subject," Mrs. Shapiro said. "Dr. Plesch isn't interested in a lot of drunken Canadians."

"They drank this stuff and ran amok, eh, Shapiro?"

"There were altercations and one or two serious fires."

"I think we should open the bottle without further delay," Dr. Plesch said, rising decisively to his feet. "I'll get a corkscrew."

"You won't need one," Mr. Shapiro said. "I use screw tops. Corks proved less satisfactory."

"He means they exploded," his wife explained tersely. "The garage was ankle-deep."

"Well, well," Dr. Plesch said, observing, by means of a fortuitous glance in a mirror, that as soon as his back was turned Mrs. Shapiro angrily pinched Mr. Shapiro's upper arm, and Mr. Shapiro pinched hers about twice as hard. "I'll get some glasses," Dr. Plesch said.

The doorbell rang.

"That will be the others," Dr. Plesch said. "All right, dear, I'll get it," he called, gently halting the distraught figure in a chintz apron who had emerged from the kitchen.

"Ah," he said, opening the front door, "Mr. and Mrs.

Kilmartin, Mr. and Mrs. Edgerton! And Mr. Doughty! How nice! All of you together!" He raised his hand and partially stifled a yawn.

"I'm sorry we're late," Mrs. Kilmartin said. "Are we *very* late?"

"Not at all," Dr. Plesch said, quite unable to minimize the next yawn, which was of Great Dane immensity. "I had an eight-o'clock this morning, but I am in the very best of spirits, delighted to see you, and you're just in time for some of the Shapiros' very latest vintage." He yawned unashamedly. "No doubt it'll refresh us and whet our appetites."

"Camilla asked me to apologize for her," Richard said. "She couldn't make it after all. She had to work late at the lab. Sometimes they don't give her much notice."

"Ah, science!" Dr. Plesch said.

"She's writing to Mrs. Plesch," Richard said.

"We understand," Dr. Plesch said.

They all settled down in a small circle of chairs in the living room. Although Mr. Kilmartin and Mr. Edgerton were of different departments (Romance Languages and Physics), they and the others had as much in common as castaways on a desert island or trusties in a penal colony. That they were all together in Digby was a common condition transcending all idiosyncrasies.

"About this wine!" Dr. Plesch said with assumed heartiness. "Now, Shapiro. I think you should tell us what's in it. Or is the formula secret?"

"The ingredients may sound somewhat on the sweet side," Mr. Shapiro said. "In fact, it *is* rather on the sweet side. The Dominicans have always been noted for their sweet tooth."

"Perhaps the best thing is to try it," Dr. Plesch said. He ceremoniously twisted the stopper of the jug and there was a fierce, brief hiss of gas. "Sounds alive, all right."

"It becomes effervescent after the first few weeks," Mr. Shapiro explained. "That's normal. It's a sparkling wine."

"Sparkling" was possibly not quite the word to describe the thick gout of opaque brown froth that then spewed forth onto the silver tray.

"We're so sorry," Mrs. Shapiro said crossly.

"It sometimes does that," Mr. Shapiro admitted. "It doesn't travel very well."

"How many blocks is it from your place?" Mr. Edgerton asked pleasantly, in a spirit of scientific inquiry.

"That was my fault," Dr. Plesch said. "I must have shaken it. My hands are not very steady. Here we go, however. Your beakers are charged."

"A real Digby wine!" Mr. Kilmartin said, holding his glass up against the electric light. Illuminated, the wine looked like amber alabaster.

"Let's drink to the Kilmartins and their trip!" Dr. Plesch said. They raised their glasses, and carefully moved the rims against their lips, and soon the room was loud with coughing.

"One feels a definite glow," Mrs. Edgerton managed to comment magnanimously at last.

"It certainly packs a wallop," Mr. Kilmartin agreed. "Good for Digby!"

Dr. Plesch felt very tired.

"The ingredients are remarkably simple really," Mr. Shapiro said, already refilling his glass.

"Oh, yes?" Mrs. Edgerton said.

"The basis of the whole brew is ordinary vetch."

"That's some kind of cattle fodder, isn't it?" Mr. Kilmartin said.

"It can be fed to cattle," Mr. Shapiro conceded. "But added to that, that rather subtle *second* taste comes from fermented Queen Anne's Lace."

"How fascinating," Mrs. Kilmartin said. "And it's such a pretty weed, isn't it?"

"And the sweetness?" someone asked.

"That's real Vermont maple syrup," Mr. Shapiro said.

"The whole garage is sticky with it," Mrs. Shapiro testified.

Dr. Plesch yawned and smiled wearily and stood up, holding two glasses.

"If you'll excuse me for a few moments," he said, yawning, "I'm going to leave you to this technical discussion. I must take Penelope a glass or she'd never forgive me."

In the kitchen, yawning, he promptly sloshed the brown foam fizzing into the sink and sluiced it down the drain with cold water.

"This evening's going to be worse than usual, I'm afraid, dear," he told his wife. "That, by the way, was some of Shapiro's wine. I have saved you from that at least. It's like licorice cough medicine spiked with lighter fluid. Somehow we've got to save the Shapiros from fighting before dinner. He seems to be intent on getting tight as fast as he can, and I can't say that I altogether blame him. She's an awful woman. Isn't it strange that so many academic people can be at once so neurotic and so dull?"

"What's happening out there, for goodness sake?" Penelope asked apprehensively. "What about the young man and his girl? Are they all right?"

Dr. Plesch sighed and kissed her moist forehead.

"She couldn't come," he said. "Duty called. He's all right. Rather quiet. He probably wonders what he's doing here." Dr. Plesch smiled. "Every time I see other faculty wives," he said, and he kissed her lightly again, "I am overcome by a sensation of relief that you're not like them." He yawned, leaning heavily against the refrigerator. "Wouldn't it be nice if we could go straight to bed?" She accepted the rhetorical question as a compliment, which was what it had been.

"You must go back," she said. "Would you tell them that dinner is served. I'll be right in. Put the young man between the Shapiros."

"What a fate!" Dr. Plesch exclaimed, shaking his head.

Nearly three hours, three long hours, slowly passed, tick by tick. Mr. Shapiro, his speech thickening, began making mildly suggestive remarks about coeds in short skirts, in spite of, or perhaps partly because of, his wife's sternly glaring eyes.

"Have any of you met Dr. Schumann?" Mr. Shapiro asked with a strange, malevolent smile. He looked around the table. "We have, haven't we, dear?" he said to his wife.

Mrs. Plesch stopped eating for a moment, her fork hesitating halfway between her plate and her mouth.

"Did you say Dr. Schumann?" Richard asked.

"We just met her the other day," Mrs. Shapiro broke in. "What's she like?" Richard asked. "I hear she's quite dynamic. A girl I know – Camilla Fairbank – she was supposed to be here tonight – works for her."

Mr. Shapiro seemed to find that notion amusing. He

giggled until he choked and the giggle became a bad attack of hiccups.

"Try drinking some water from the wrong side of the glass," Mrs. Plesch said, looking quite nervous.

Everyone had a special hiccups cure to suggest, and by the time the paroxysms had been subdued the subject of Dr. Schumann apparently had been forgotten.

At last Dr. Plesch stood at the front door waving good-bye. Although his eyes were drooping almost shut, he insisted that Penelope should go ahead to their bedroom, while he slowly clumsily removed dishes and glasses and silverware from the dining room to the kitchen. By the time he had finished this chivalrous chore, she was sitting at her dressing table, with her gray-auburn hair straggily hanging to her plump, white shoulders, patting small clots of yellow cream into the pale-blue pouches under her eyes.

"It's hideous stuff," she acknowledged with a guilty smile, "but please try not to notice. It's supposed to do wonders for the complexion."

Dr. Plesch yawned and picked up the small white ceramic jar from the glass table top.

" 'With royal jelly'," he read, " 'for the lovely skin of youth.' Maybe. I must say, though, I like you better un-oiled. You've always had lovely skin." He yawned. "It was one of the first things I noticed about you." He yawned. "It's lovely now. I'm the one that needs royal jelly, what-ever it is." He yawned. "Who is Dr. Schumann?"

"You're such a flatterer, Leo," she said. "That's one of the things I love about you."

"Who's this Dr. Schumann?" he said. "Come on, what are you keeping up your sleeve? I saw that look on your face when the name was mentioned. Who is it?" He yawned.

"She's the director of the Digby Institute," Penelope said.

"Oh, science," Dr. Plesch said. "I've had enough of that from Edgerton tonight to last quite a while. He and his space nonsense! Anyone would think that he himself personally invented the universe. They're so damn proprietary about their subjects, these scientists."

"Yes, dear," Penelope said.

"Do you think that wretched Shapiro was sick?" Dr. Plesch asked. "He was in the bathroom for ages."

"The casserole wasn't a huge success, I'm sorry to say," she said.

"It had nothing to do with it," he said. "It was very good. You're the best cook in Digby. It was delicious." He yawned. "I was too" – he yawned – "tired to eat" – he yawned – "too tired; that was all." He sat on the bed and began pulling off his socks. "The wine was horrible," he grumbled, half to himself. He yawned. "Even our pathetic Californian sherry would have been better."

Penelope was brushing her hair, with her head tilted to one side, like a girl's. "It doesn't matter," she said.

"It was nice of them to bring it, I suppose."

"Of course it was," she said. "Go on, get into bed."

"You sound quite amorous, dear," he said. She laughed, and he yawned. He yawned again. "I don't know what I'd do without you," he said. He climbed onto the bed, crawled on it, turned with an effort, and, with a profound, grateful groan of relaxation, straightened his legs under the blankets.

"What was it you were going to tell me about that Dr. Schumann person?" he asked in a blurred voice.

Penelope gently reposed the perfumed, soft, white barrel of her flesh beside him.

"It can wait till tomorrow, if you like," she said. He was silent. "Do you want me to tell you now?" she said, softly caressing his back. She paused.

"M-m-m," he murmured.

"You know you've been saying recently that perhaps there might be some way of ... sort of ... well, pepping ourselves up? Well, I got a telephone call from Dr. Schumann this afternoon. She's the director of the Digby Institute. Maybe you'll hate this idea. It seems that she's been approaching several faculty wives and their husbands. She didn't mention any names. Names are never mentioned. It sounds sort of *odd*, but maybe it would be worth trying. She said that one of the things she's specially interested in is the problems of the late-middle-aged. The sexual problems. She said that that's what the Institute is really all about. Did you know that? It's some kind of sexual research unit. Are you listening to me, Leo? Leo!"

200

She leaned over his shoulder and looked closely at the pale deeply lined, motionless head, and saw that he could not respond. If he had not begun faintly to snore he would have seemed dead.

"Poor baby," she said, stroking his brow. "So tired. Sleep well."

Leo smiled.

THIRTY-ONE

"THAT was a near thing," Mrs. Shapiro said crossly. "What did you have to talk like that for?"

"What's wrong now?" her husband asked.

"Don't drive so fast," she said. "You can't afford any more tickets. Why did you have to mention Dr. Schumann? You know it's all meant to be highly confidential."

"Nobody can even mention her name?"

"You and that ridiculous wine," she said. "You're tight. You might have said anything."

"I knew what I was saying," he said. "I wanted to see what their reactions would be, that was all. I'm curious to know how many of our colleagues are going to be in on this project. There might be some surprises. Did you notice that look on Mrs. Plesch's face when I mentioned Dr. Schumann? I bet the Plesches have been approached."

"That's no concern of ours," Mrs. Shapiro said. "You can count me out if you're going around Digby blabbing to everyone."

"I'm not going around blabbing. I'm not the blabbermouth in this family. But if you don't want to go through with it, then don't. That's O.K. with me. I'll go alone. There'll be some other single men and women."

"You would, wouldn't you? You think it's a chance to have a big romp with a lot of faculty wives. How typical! Eddie Shapiro, campus Casanova!"

"What were you hoping to get out of it?" Mr. Shapiro inquired with an unpleasant smile.

"It is supposed to be a serious, responsible, sober scientific investigation," she said haughtily.

"You have to keep on telling yourself that, don't you?" he said. "You couldn't do anything for kicks, could you? It's your lousy puritanical, reactionary, bourgeois background coming out again. There has to be a serious reason for everyone."

"Sometimes you sound like the *Daily Worker*."

"Sometimes the way you talk makes me feel like an anarchist. It isn't as though you didn't like sex. You want to have it and get a medal for it too."

"I do wish you wouldn't talk like that," Mrs. Shapiro said.

"Well, you do want it, don't you? When you're through with all your committees and debates and petitions and folk dancing, what you really want is a good blow-through."

"You never used to talk like that," she said, but her reprimand lacked severity. "That wine must be stronger than you realize."

"Don't worry about me, Sarah Shapiro. I can handle my wine and handle you."

"Eddie, you're really terrible."

He stopped the car with a squeal in front of their house.

By the time she came to their bedroom, he was already settled in his single bed, sitting up against a couple of pillows, reading a book. He didn't look up as she walked over to her bed. She was wearing a transparent black silk nightdress.

"What are you reading?" she asked.

"Huh?" He looked over. "That Victorian novel that was reviewed in *Time*."

"Is it . . . interesting?"

"Not bad."

"Can I come and read over your shoulder?"

"I didn't think you approved of books like this. Sure you can, if you want." He moved over in the bed and she walked toward him.

"That's quite a nightdress," he said.

"Thank you," she said.

"What's the occasion?"

"Must there be an occasion? Listen, Ed, I know the fighting's sometimes my fault. I've been thinking about it. We didn't fight like this when we were first married, did we?"

"I'm not the easiest man in the world to get along with."

"But I should make things nicer for you."

"What things?"

"Lots of things," she said with a coy smile. "Will you read some of it aloud to me?"

"This stuff?" he said.

"You like it, don't you? It looks as though you do."

He followed her gaze and smiled. "Come here," he said.

"Eddie,'" she said.

"Yes?"

"Stop for a minute. Just lie still. I want to talk about it. Have you thought about what it'll be like at the Institute?"

"In what way?"

"Doing this, with people watching."

"Of course I've thought of it."

"Think of us, darling, naked, like this, and them all dressed, watching. Will you mind that?" she asked.

He started moving again.

"No, wait!" she said.

But it was already too late.

THIRTY-TWO

"SUBJECT M. is good," Dr. Schumann said, "but he's not nearly as good as he thinks he is. Come to the observation room. Have a look and you'll see what I mean."

Dr. Porter followed Dr. Schumann and sat beside her at a one-way window.

Lawrence was lying face down on Marcia Daventry. She was lying on her back with her plump, white thighs parted and her knees upraised, grasping his waist. The large muscles of his rump were rhythmically rising, swelling roundly, and plunging down, tensing in hard, shallow concavities. His yellow forelock was hanging down over one eye, and sweat was dripping from his face down onto Marcia's neck. His back was wet and striped with claw-marks.

Speakers in the observation room enabled Dr. Schumann and Dr. Porter to hear the rapid creaking of the mattress-springs, the stertorous panting, the grunts of exertion, the quiet, calm voices of technicians recording readings from the machines and describing symptoms — "hyper-ventilation ... maculopapular rash ... considerable myotonic tension in both subjects' arms and legs ... Subject M.'s heartbeats now one-five-seven per minute. ..."

"What's wrong?" Dr. Porter asked. "It seems to be going very well." He looked around at Dr. Schumann and his forehead corrugated in puzzlement. Her mouth was set in a thin, straight line.

"Would you say the same if I told you they've been going on like this for the past fifty-five minutes?"

"That's a long time."

"I'll say it's a long time," Dr. Schumann said. "This is only his second episode today. We've been counting on him for three. Our schedules are going completely haywire."

"What's his difficulty?" Dr. Porter said. "Do you think we may have been pushing him too hard?"

"With all that vitamin E he's been getting? All the protein supplement? The stimulative literature? No, it's perfectly obvious that he is deliberately withholding."

"He wouldn't do a thing like that, would he?" Dr. Porter said. "He knows how much time matters to the program."

"That's precisely what he is doing though," Dr. Schumann said.

"Is she orgasmic?"

"On and off for the past fifteen minutes."

"Then why? Why?"

"I've been checking up," Dr. Schumann said. "Screening some of his early film footage. He's been achieving better erections in episodes with this subject. Look at it now — seven point two-five if it's an inch. But the episodes are getting longer and longer."

"If it really is deliberate, it's practically subversive," Dr. Porter said. "I can hardly believe it."

"There's no question about it," Dr. Schumann said. "He's been prolonging the episodes for the sake of pleasure. There's been a lot of vocalizing. He derives gratification from her vocalization."

"What sort of things does she say?"

"At first it was only practical directives," Dr. Schumann said. "They increased his efficiency. She was able to expedite her own tension increment by as much as fifty per cent. But then she began praising him. That's what slowed us up. He doesn't seem to be able to get too much appreciation. This morning she said she loved him."

Dr. Porter slowly shook his head and clicked his tongue.

"I took her aside at lunch break and warned her to adhere to the briefings," Dr. Porter said. "She promised to comply. But this afternoon they're just as bad. I haven't heard her say anything out of line, but I suspect she's signaling to him by means of facial expressions."

"It's too bad," Dr. Porter said.

"There's always someone who takes advantage if you treat them with consideration," Dr. Schumann said.

"Are you going to have to let him go?" Dr. Porter asked anxiously.

"No," Dr. Schumann said. "I've decided to give both of them another chance. Maybe they'll pull themselves together and operate better with other partners."

"One day they'll look back and realize what you've done for them," Dr. Porter said.

Dr. Schumann smiled at him. "Thank you," she said. "Ah!" she said, indicating the tableau on the bed. "And about time too." Watching the final convulsions, she added: "To give credit where credit is due, he *is* a worker."

THIRTY-THREE

RICHARD hoisted the wicker picnic hamper and the tartan plastic ice bucket into the car. He looked at his watch. On time. Five off eleven. He had already been around to the building site, where it was becoming increasingly difficult to think of convincing excuses for his continuing presence in Digby. There had been a letter from Washington suggesting it was about time he tore himself away from the self-indulgence of watching his building take shape – not a severe letter but a sharp one. He had successfully stalled for the time being with a vague explanation about certain difficulties over the landscaping that he wanted to clear up. He couldn't consider leaving Digby until his own prospects were clarified. The rest of the day was entirely free. Camilla, much to their surprise, had been offered an afternoon off from her duties at the Institute.

When he arrived at the dormitory, she was already waiting outside the front entrance. Richard saw her again, as he often did, with an inner tremor of delight, as though for the first time. Her blonde hair was tied in a ponytail and she was wearing white stretch pants and a loose navy-blue polo-neck sweater. This apparently was her nautical gear. He had told her about going out to a lake. When she recognized his car, her face lit up and she waved and shouted "Hi!" and she looked so young that he felt a surge of love, pity, and protectiveness, almost remorse.

"You should have let me make some sandwiches," she said, as she got into the car. She kissed his cheek. "Hi!" she said. "I only had one class this morning. Isn't it a great day?"

"You look terrific," he said, starting the car. "Everything's taken care of. We have everything we need. Everything!"

"When I saw the forecast on the late news last night, I thought, Oh-oh – there goes the picnic. But it's just great."

"Meteorologists are like other scientists," Richard said,

"They're not infallible. They may even be human, deep down."

"No propaganda!" Camilla protested with a grin.

"But I'm surprised you didn't bring a raincoat," he said. "It's as hot as summer now, but those clouds might build up."

"Fractocumulus," she said. "Nothing! Anyway, today I live dangerously!"

Richard turned and looked into her eyes. He was about to say something but then decided not to.

After half an hour or so of rolling through gently undulant farmland, Richard turned off the highway onto a small road, and then, driving through a dense plantation of conifers, turned off again, between the stone pillars of an open gateway, down a long dirt drive.

"Where are we?" Camilla asked.

"Nearly there," Richard said. "I think. This is my first time."

The woods ended and they passed open meadows where horses were grazing. On one side there were stables, barns, twin aluminum silos, and a large farmhouse.

"Here?" Camilla asked.

"Not yet."

Beyond the farm there were more trees, oak, beech, elm and silver birch. The car rounded a bend and came suddenly to a wide panorama of natural lakefront. The only sign of humanity was a small timber boathouse, weathered gray, and a rickety-looking old wooden jetty.

"It's beautiful!" Camilla exclaimed.

"It is, isn't it?" Richard modestly agreed.

Some water-fowl, large white birds with long necks and wide wings, disturbed by the sound of the car, slowly flapped up from rushes near the bank, and glided low across the calm water toward a wooded island about half a mile away.

"Wouldn't it be wonderful to be able to fly like that?" she said. "Skimming along between the warm, blue sky and the cool, green water. Birds are lucky."

"Do you sail?" Richard asked.

"I never have," Camilla said. "I've never even seen the sea. I'd love to though."

"We will, before too long. There are a lot of things I

want to show you. I have a small boat on the Chesapeake Bay, near Annapolis. Nothing very much, but you really get a feeling of being part of the boat."

"I wish we had a boat today."

"We have," he said, indicating the back of the car. "In the trunk."

"Oh, Richard!" Camilla said disappointedly. "For a moment I really thought. . . ."

They got out of the car and he unloaded the picnic things, and then opened the trunk and unloaded the boat, a large olive-drab canvas case containing an inflatable rubber dinghy.

"Help me get it closer to the water," he said. "Good, this is near enough. Now. It's easy. Just undo these straps – like this, and this, and the ones on your side. This comes off. This comes ... out. Right. Now I pull this cord – like this." There was a powerful hiss of carbon dioxide from a metal cylinder, and, within seconds, a large orange-rubber doughnut-shaped raft grew at their feet.

"What fun!" Camilla said.

"We use these little paddles," he said. "There is a sail, but let's not bother. It isn't far."

They slid the dinghy onto the surface of the lake, put the hamper and ice bucket aboard, and carefully climbed in beside them.

"Such a wonderful idea!" Camilla said. "If only there were some music."

"The radio's in the hamper."

Camilla opened the basket and found the small transistor set and tuned in some inoffensive Musak paean to Arcadia, played by harp, flute, glockenspiel and a thousand violins.

"There!" she said.

"You'd better paddle," Richard suggested, "or we'll just keep on going around in circles."

"But not too fast," Camilla said. "Let's just sort of drift along in the sunshine. Isn't it great?"

Richard smiled like an indulgent father, but there was an incestuous glint in his eye.

"You're going to get very warm in that sweater," he said.

They put down their paddles for a moment while

Camilla pulled the sweater up over her head. While her arms were upraised and her head was covered, Richard looked at her breasts, which seemed softly free to move inside a snow-white T-shirt. When her face began emerging, from the chin up, he looked away.

"That's better," she said casually. He conscientiously clenched his jaws and then managed a small smile.

There was silence, except for the slow, irregular plash of the paddles in the water, the small barking of a dog miles away, and an announcer selling cigarettes. Minutes passed.

The dinghy softly bumped against the low grass-tufted bank of the island. Richard jumped out and held the painter while helping Camilla ashore. He pulled the dinghy safely up onto land.

"It doesn't look as though we're very welcome," Camilla said apprehensively, pointing at a hand-painted sign nailed to a tree near another jetty, another boathouse. "Private," it said. "Keep Out. Positively No Fishing or Shooting. This Means You."

"It's all right," Richard said.

"Are you sure?"

"Yes. You feel strongly about rules, don't you?"

"I don't believe in looking for trouble," Camilla said.

"There won't be any trouble," Richard said.

"It's a beautiful island," Camilla said with a conciliatory smile. "Doesn't it make you wish we were children? Think of playing Robinson Crusoe. I could be your Man Friday."

"Not very convincingly," Richard said. "The wrong figure. Let's play grownups."

"I'll unpack the lunch, shall I?" Camilla said brightly. "Where shall we have it? On that small rise, at the edge of the trees? There'd be sun *and* shade there."

"I'm not hungry yet, are you?"

"Starving," she said with a lovely smile.

"O.K.," he said.

He took a blanket out of the hamper and spread it out on the soft, grassy slope. The blanket was dappled with gold-and-green sunlight shining through the leaves of the branches overhead.

"A good spot," he said. "I think I'll just lie down here and watch you work."

Camilla knelt and sat back on her heels and unpacked

the lunch – cold chicken, cold cuts, small cardboard tubs of lobster salad, Russian salad, cole slaw, a long French loaf, several sorts of cheese, a bunch of green grapes, a couple of peaches and pears.

"Nothing fancy," Richard said, "but the Digby Delicatessen did its best."

"It's elegant!" Camilla exclaimed. "I'm drooling."

"There are some paper napkins," Richard assured her. "Pepper and salt. Paper plates. Genuine glass glasses. Open the ice bucket. There's a bottle of Rhine wine in there. It ought to be good and cold by now. The corkscrew's in the hamper, with the knives and forks."

"Richard!" Camilla exclaimed. "You're so efficient!" She handed him the dewy wine bottle and the corkscrew and he reached up and grabbed her around the waist.

"No, Richard!" she protested. "Please," she pleaded. "Really I'm so *hungry*! I'll faint!"

The fight went out of Richard almost instantly. He released her. She leaned forward and softly kissed his mouth and withdrew from his reach before he could change his mind. He rolled over onto his face, theatrically groaning aloud and pounding the ground with his fists.

"The lobster's out of this world!" she reported. "Wouldn't you open that wine?"

So he sat up and opened the wine and they had a delicious lunch.

Afterward, they lay side by side, almost a yard apart, on their backs, looking up at the yellow-green, green, blue-green leaves shimmering against the blue sky.

"Camilla?" Richard said at last.

"Yes?"

"I enjoy being with you."

"I enjoy it, too, being with you."

"I love you, Camilla."

"I love you too."

"Camilla."

"Yes?"

"Look," he said. "No hands. Notice the way I'm not attacking you."

"You're really a very dear person."

"I'm just asking you, very calmly. How can a young woman of your age simply lie there, asleep, unless she finds the man she's with completely unattractive?"

"I wasn't asleep."

"Well, it was a very realistic imitation. I got up. I got within an inch of you, but I thought you were asleep. I went for a walk. I came back. You still certainly looked asleep."

"Perhaps I may have slept a little. I've been working very long hours. Sometimes eighteen hours a day, if you include time at the Libe."

"That's what really gets me. You're working like a slave. For what? In June it'll all be over, won't it, your academic career? Why knock yourself out? Do you really think it matters whether your average was C-minus or A-plus?"

"Nobody gets an A-plus average," Camilla pointed out reasonably.

"Who gives a damn?"

"It isn't the average itself that matters," Camilla said. "It's what it represents. Anyway, I don't think it will be over in June. It's virtually a sure thing now that I'll go on and get my master's at least. Dr. Schumann says she's very pleased with the way I've been working. She's going to use her influence to help me. I'll probably get a fellowship to stay on at the Institute."

"Then getting married this summer is absolutely out?"

"I wish you'd try to understand about my academic career," Camilla said. "It's very important to me. It's the way for me to become a fully rounded and integrated person. You wouldn't want a dropout for a wife. You may think you do now, but later things would get different. You'd want the companionship of an intellectual equal."

"You're no dropout," Richard said. "You're graduating next month, for heaven's sake."

"A bachelor's degree now is only the basic qualification," Camilla said. "It's like a high school diploma when my parents went to school. It isn't enough."

"Camilla," Richard said resolutely. "They're planning to have the building finished – the outer shell, at least, enough of it – in time to hold the dedication ceremony on Commencement Day."

"That's wonderful!" Camilla said. "I'm very glad for you."

"It took a lot of pressure from one of the trustees.

Anyway, they're doing it. I have to leave Digby soon. I may be able to hold out until next month, but I'm not too sure. Even if I do go though, I'll be back for the dedication."

"Richard. Please kiss me."

He crawled awkwardly over to her.

"Camilla," he said.

They kissed. She gently stopped him.

"Camilla. You could transfer to a university in the Washington area. You could go on with your studies."

"That wouldn't be any good. It's the department at Digby that I care about. They've been so encouraging. They've given me so much responsibility. Not every student gets the opportunity I've been given."

"What, to examine some ridiculous sea slug trying to get through a maze?"

"You know I can't discuss the work of the Institute," she said primly.

"I can assure you I don't want to," Richard said. "I'm an architect. And a good one, too. All right, I'll tell you what I'll do. When this building at Digby is finished, I'm sure I could join a good firm in Ohio. There's plenty going on here. You could stay at Digby. I could get an apartment here, and I could commute. How would that be?"

"Richard, darling! I couldn't let you do that. After a while you'd resent not being in Washington. You'd hate me. It would never work."

"What if you got pregnant?" Richard said. "Then would you marry me right away?"

Camilla laughed.

"There isn't much danger of that, is there?"

"Who knows? Perhaps this is a good time to mention that we're stuck on this island till tomorrow."

"What do you mean?"

"I just happened to notice when you were asleep that all the CO_2 has leaked out of the boat. It's flat. We're stranded."

"We can't be!" Camilla said, leaping up.

"Go and look for yourself," Richard said, smiling. "We are."

Camilla saw that he was telling the truth.

"What'll we do?" she demanded. "How will I get back? We can't stay here!"

"Don't look so alarmed," Richard said. "There's a shooting lodge. We'll be very comfortable."

"How do you know? Did you plan this?"

"Calm, Camilla! I know because it was offered to me. The owner happens to be one of our chief contractors. A very nice guy. I'm sure he has excellent taste in hideaways."

"Richard! You're disgusting!"

"Importunate, perhaps. Don't exaggerate. I just happen to love you."

"Call this love?" she said. "Ah, a telephone! There must be a telephone! Give me the key! I'll call for help."

For a moment, Richard looked rather disconcerted. He rallied. "I'm sorry," he said. "No telephone. He uses this place to get away from it all. And even if there were one it wouldn't be turned on. Tomorrow's going to be his first weekend here this year. And besides," Richard added, smiling again, "I don't have a key. We'll have to break a window. I didn't expect to be staying overnight."

"I hate you!" Camilla said. "All right! I'll swim!" Before he could stop her or even make a move, Camilla kicked off her loafers, took a short run, and dived neatly into the lake. When she surfaced, she incredulously gasped at the cold. "I never want to see you again!" she said, and began swimming slowly away from the island. Richard shouted for her to come back, but she ignored him. He pulled off his sneakers and hastily dived in after her. He was a far more powerful swimmer and soon caught up. As they swam side by side, there was a breathless conversation.

"It's too far," he said.

She didn't answer.

"It's too cold. You'll get a cramp."

"You should have thought about that," she said.

"Turn back," he said.

"What for?" she asked, as bitterly as it is possible to speak with a mouth half full of water. She spluttered and splashed on.

"I'll take you in the boat," he said. "There's a spare cylinder of gas. Come on. Turn back."

Camilla seemed to hesitate.

"Please," he said. "I'm sorry."

"Are you sure?"

"Cross my heart."

Now she was treading water.

"Come on," he said more confidently. "Let's get out of this. I'm freezing."

"If you promise," she said.

"I promise."

They swam back to the island faster than they had left it, but even so, as they clambered ashore, their clothes heavy with water and dripping, they were shuddering with cold. The clouds had accumulated in great white piles during the early afternoon, and the sun's rays were diffused whitely through the massive summit of one of the biggest cloud banks in the sky.

"I'll tell you what," Richard said soothingly.

"What?" Camilla asked. Her expression was both relieved and wary.

"Let's get these clothes dry first. There's no point in going back like this. We'll catch pneumonia or something."

Camilla, miserably hunched forward with her arms folded, clutching her wet sides, and her teeth chattering, looked doubtful but tempted.

"We can't just break into his place like that."

"I hate to admit it," Richard said. "But I have a key."

Camilla was too uncomfortable to complain about this evidence of conspiracy.

"He told me there's a big fireplace," Richard said. "And lots of blankets."

Camilla nodded.

The lodge, an elaborately crude pseudo-rustic split-level pioneer home-away-from-home, was a long timber-and-fieldstone structure with a steeply gabled clapboard roof and big picture-windows. Even at that moment of emotional stress and physical discomfort, Richard the architect was unable to refrain from sneering.

"Walden à la mode!" he said.

Camilla mutely waited for him to open the door.

"God!" he exclaimed, following her in. "Look at it! A bamboo bar and the biggest television set in the world! A real nature lover, isn't he?"

"Let's light the fire," Camilla said. "It's cold in here."

"Courvoisier!" Richard said behind the bar. "He's not all bad,"

"Richard, light the fire."

"A brandy would help in the meantime," he said.

"I don't want any more to drink," Camilla said.

"All right, all right. I was only trying to help."

The fireplace was fully prepared, a wide stone hearth with quaint old oiled-walnut-and-red-leather inglenook seats on each side of a large black wrought-iron grate laden with neatly matched birch logs. Beneath the grate there was a perforated gas pipe for easy ignition. Richard turned on the gas and felt for his cigarette lighter in his sodden trouser pocket. Camilla moved closer to the fireplace and gazed expectantly at the logs.

"Hurry, Richard," she said, "or you'll blow the place up."

Richard went down on one knee and flicked the lighter.

Nothing happened.

He tried again.

Nothing.

Again.

No.

"I'm sorry," he said. "The flint's a little wet still. Wait a minute. I'll get some matches."

Several minutes elapsed. He returned from the kitchen looking irritable and sheepish. "I don't seem to be able to find any," he said.

"Turn on the stove," Camilla said. "Light a piece of paper."

"I thought of that. It's an electric stove. The electricity is turned off. I can't find the switch."

"You must be able to," Camilla said.

"You look then," he said. "I'll try the lighter some more."

"You're supposed to be the architect," she said. "Surely you know something about wiring."

"All I can say is, I can't find it. I want a fire as much as you do. Maybe more."

"Oh!"

Camilla angrily flounced out of the room into the kitchen and there were sounds of drawers being pulled open and shut and doors opened and slammed. Richard knelt in front of the fireplace, impotently thumbing the abrasive tiny wheel of the lighter, until his thumb was grooved red.

Camilla came back, wrinkling her nose and sniffing,

"You'd better turn that gas off," she said. "This room smells awful."

"One more try," Richard said.

It failed.

Richard stood up and guiltily smiled. "Did you see that movie in which the couple gets caught in the mountains in this snowstorm and—"

"And they find a cute little log cabin," Camilla said, "and she rustles up a cute little meal of bacon and eggs and coffee, and they sit in front of this wonderful log fire—"

"No, in the one I saw the main thing was they got out of their cold, wet clothes, and he found her some pajamas — a man's pajamas—"

"And she looked so cute in those long sleeves and legs," Camilla said. "Thanks a lot. Nothing doing."

"There's no need to be so sour about this situation," Richard said. "I didn't tell you to jump in the lake."

"You might as well have though."

"Well, we're here, and we're miserable, so let's find some dry clothes, whether they're cute or not."

There was a flicker of hope in Camilla's eyes.

"And don't be such a grouch," Richard said, heading for the bedroom. Camilla stood for a moment in front of the dark fireplace and then went after him.

One entire wall of the bedroom, opposite the double bed, was a single built-in closet.

"His wife probably has her sport clothes custom-made in Rome!" Richard said encouragingly. He pulled sideways at one of the wardrobe's sliding doors.

"Locked?" Camilla asked with controlled, ferociously sarcastic sweetness.

"I'm very sorry," Richard said. "It is." He looked around desperately. "The bed!" he said.

"No thanks," Camilla said. "I'll stay cold."

"Don't be silly," Richard said. "I didn't mean that. I meant we can borrow a couple of blankets." He pulled off the pink quilted silk bedspread and the pink electric blanket underneath.

"I think you'd look better in the silk," he said.

"Very funny!" Camilla said, but she took it and wrapped it around herself, with a sort of cowl over her head. Only her face showed. It was scowling, but its prettiness made it

218

very difficult to take it seriously. Richard wore his blanket like a Roman toga and made a few classic Shakespearean gestures.

"How do you like it?" he asked.

Camilla tried hard not to smile. "We may as well get going," she said, forcing a sound of disapproval.

"Wouldn't you like to undress and dry yourself?" Richard said. "At least the bathroom isn't locked." He pointed a blanketed arm toward the open door.

"If you'd just get the boat ready," Camilla said.

"Yes, madam," Richard said. He turned abruptly and walked out.

The rubber dinghy took only a few seconds to reinflate.

By the time that Camilla, still wearing the quilt, which was now noticeably more smartly swathed about her body, had joined him at the shore, the first heavy, wide-spaced drops of warm rain were beginning to fall.

Halfway across the water, the shower became a downpour, a torrent, a monsoon deluge, a cataclysm.

That was when Camilla started to laugh, and Richard started to laugh with her.

By the time they regained the security of the car he suggested, perhaps out of desperation since he had exhausted his resources, that they get married.

THIRTY-FOUR

"GERONTOLOGY begins at forty," Dr. Schumann said, twinkling merrily, as she always did when citing one of her favorite aphorisms. "Of course, the aging process begins long before that. Like life insurance – the sooner you acknowledge the facts, the better. It's never too early to prepare for death. It's a pity so many of our senior citizens neglect to prepare themselves sexually. Some of them – present company excepted, I'm sure – are stubborn in their refusal to face up to their mortality in sexual terms. On the other hand, Professor Plesch," she added encouragingly, "better late than never. And once one recognizes where one is, gonadwise, it is perfectly right and proper – indeed, medically speaking, a *must* – to make a place in one's life situation for sexual activity. Sex in diminuendo, perhaps; but sex to the end.

"Masters and Johnson," Dr. Schumann said, her eyes lighting in the reflected glory of the very names, "were justifiably proud, very proud, of one of their subjects, an eighty-nine-year-old man, who was able to achieve penile erection and spermatic expulsion during an observed laboratory episode. Imagine!" There was a hush in the room as they both imagined.

"Dr. Aslan," Dr. Schumann continued, "the well-known Rumanian gerontologist – we've had our differences in the past, the Iron Curtain sexologists and we of the West; but, after all, sexually, we live in one world; in this respect, Wendell Wilkie was undoubtedly right – Dr. Aslan, as I was saying, once told a visitor to her experimental home for the aged in Bucharest that subjects of hers undergoing H-3 therapy – basically novocaine, with certain vital additives, injected intramuscularly; I won't bore you with the technical details – some of these subjects were sexually potent at ages in excess of one hundred years. In some cases, in fact, the sexual function was the last over which subjects were able to exert any reasonable control. Let us never forget, Professor Plesch, that under the right nursing supervision, there could and should be all sorts of means of sexual expression as long as the body endures. Psychiatrically, such activity is essential. Even if the subject himself or herself is no longer able because of various handicaps, mental and physical, to take the sexual initiative, it is up to us, of the laboratory, to ensure that none of anybody's sexual potential is unrealized.

"Dr. Aslan introduced the visitor to one couple, a man of one hundred and eight and a woman of ninety-one, and said that they had just got married. Special quarters had been established for them close to the institution's operating theater, and an emergency first-aid unit was put on twenty-four-hour stand-by with oxygen, plasma, glucose, copies of Eichenlaub's treatise on 'The Marriage Art,' and so on. The marriage, Dr. Aslan reported, was 'a *real* marriage' – a richly rewarding physical union. The Hunzas, who live in the Himalayas, I might add, play volleyball at the age of one hundred and twenty!"

"A game that has never appealed to me, I must confess," Leo Plesch murmured.

"But, don't you see?" Dr. Schumann said. "If they can play volleyball – it is a well-established fact that all sports are sexual in motivation."

"Aesthetically, though, I wonder," Dr. Plesch said.

"People can adjust themselves to anything," Dr. Schumann pointed out. "Think of some of the faces you see in buses and stores. There are people living behind all those faces. Every day they get up and wash them and look at them in mirrors. And every day, whether consciously or not, they search for sexual outlets, and if they don't find them one way they'll find them another. It's all a question of libido channelization."

"It's true that one continually makes adjustments to the contemplation of one's own physical development and decay," Dr. Plesch agreed.

"There's sex for everybody!" Dr. Schumann affirmed. "Sex for everybody forever! If the Digby Institute can make the world accept that fact our work shall not have been in vain."

"There *are* worse campaign slogans," Dr. Plesch said.

"But there I go!" Dr. Schumann cheerfully chided herself. "Off on my hobbyhorse again. And I invited you to

221

the Institute to talk about you. It's very good of you to accept our invitation. We appreciate your help.

"We must all help each other," he said.

"I'm afraid I wouldn't be of much use to you on the subject of Mayan temples," she said, with a short, formal snort of pedantic hilarity.

"Egyptian," he said. "You're thinking of poor Dr. Hay. Jacob passed on in El Peten, in Guatemala, three years ago."

"I'm sorry," Dr. Schumann said. "I hadn't realized that Digby was such a hotbed of archaeology. One of my assistants was mentioning having taken a course on Mayan temples. But that's all water under the bridge. To business! Are you quite comfortable here, Professor, or would you rather go into one of the interview cubicles? Our confessionals." She chuckled in a friendly manner. The hint of blasphemy, like a whiff of gunpowder, tickled the nostrils of her imagination.

"I'm quite comfortable here," Plesch said, boyishly rubbing his nose. "I'm ready to fire away as we are. Ask me anything you like and I'll do my best to answer."

"Well, then, we'll begin, shall we?" she said as brightly as a kindergarten teacher addressing a child.

"Yes," he said.

"First of all, I must ask you when you were born."

"I'll be sixty-four next February twelfth."

"Aquarius!" she exclaimed jovially.

"Do you believe in astrology?" he asked.

"Professor Plesch!" she protested, slightly pinkening.

"I just wondered," he said. "I've often wondered whether the moon has any influence on human behavior. All behavior. Haven't you ever felt a strange thrill when you've looked up at the sky at night, having *felt* the moon, to find, as you had expected, that it had suddenly become full?"

"The myths about the moon are fascinating," she said indulgently.

"The Indians of Peru called the moon Mama Quilla," he informed her. "They believed she was the cause of all generation. On the other hand, according to Brinton – Daniel G. Brinton, a Philadelphian who wrote his great work, *The Myths of the New World,* in 1896 – the Mexicans were of the opinion that the moon was at the same time a baleful creature."

"Really?" Dr. Schumann said politely. Her smile was fading.

" 'She engenders the miasmatic poisons that rack our bones' – that was the way he put it, as I recall. I admire his felicity of phrasing, don't you?"

"Most felicitous," she said rather bleakly. She made an effort to resume command, sat straighter, and said, "Now, perhaps, if I might just –"

"The Algonquins, according to van Helmont," Dr. Plesch mildly insisted, "used to believe that it was she – the moon – who kills men, otherwise they would never die; she eats their flesh and gnaws their vitals, till they fall away and miserably perish."

"That's *very* interesting," Dr. Schumann said in her kindergarten-teacher voice. "But I mustn't take too much of your time, so we really should get on."

"It's all right," he said. "Men's ideas about the moon should come within the scope of your investigation, if I may say so, Dr. Schumann." Avuncularly reproachful, he peered at her over his Benjamin Franklin spectacles. "Let us not forget what the Aztecs said: 'Beware when the moon assumes the form of a beautiful woman. A few moments of pleasure in her embrace cause death'."

"It's true that there is a certain dread of sex," she said.

"I think of the emotion as awe," he said. "Xochiquetzal, as the Aztecs called her, was the patroness of love and childbirth, yet drove men mad."

"One of the purposes of this Institute," Dr. Schumann said, "is, of course, to eliminate popular delusions."

"I'm sure it is," he said kindly. "Don't mind me. Go ahead and ask your questions. I merely thought that you might wish to bear that curious ambivalence in mind."

"I'll make a note of it," she assured him, and ostentatiously wrote a few words on her note pad: "Plesch is senile."

"The Greeks regarded the day of the full moon as the most propitious day for the marriage ceremony," he said.

"I'm so glad you've called this to my attention," Dr. Schumann said. "How did we get started on the moon? Oh, yes! I said you were Aquarius, didn't I? The trouble with me is that I'm sometimes too frivolous. The question I wanted to ask you, Professor Plesch, if I may –"

"Anything you like," he assured her. "Before I forget, though, while we're discussing the moon, I must recommend that you look up Bunce's *Fairy Tales*. John Thackray Bunce, London, 1878. An extraordinary work, Dr. Schumann."

"Is that right?" Dr. Schumann looked surreptitiously at the clock on the wall.

"It seems that the Danes used to believe in moon folk," he continued. "Elves."

"What, Professor?"

"I said, 'elves'."

"Oh, of course."

"They went in pairs. A man and a woman, you know. The woman was always very beautiful, in front. But behind she was hollow – 'like a dough trough.' I have always remembered the phrase. I wonder what that must have been like?"

"A dough trough?"

"Yes. Bunce was the sort of man who knew what he was talking about, but I must confess that in this instance the precise significance eludes me."

"You're getting me confused, Professor."

"I'm sorry, my dear, but nothing in the world is simple. We must use our imaginations. It is safe to assume, anyway, that a dough trough was something not very beautiful when made flesh, don't you agree?"

"In that context –"

"Exactly, Dr. Schumann."

"But –"

"Anyway, she had a sort of harp or lyre."

"Who had?"

"Really, Dr. Schumann. The moon-folk woman elf."

"Couldn't we –"

"I'll get to the point soon enough, if only you'll let me," Dr. Plesch said patiently. "She used it to lure young men to her abode. It was not by any means without a certain hedonistic charm, her abode. She lured men inside, made love to them, and, afterward – while they slept, of course – she killed them."

"Do you feel antagonism toward members of the opposite sex, Professor Plesch?" Dr. Schumann asked shrewdly.

"Goodness, no," he said "As you know, Dr. Schumann, I am married."

"In some cases," she said, "the most antagonistic of persons get their revenge through marriage."

Plesch looked at his watch. "My dear Dr. Schumann, we really must be getting on with the questionnaire. I have enjoyed our talk, but time is running on."

Dr. Schumann bit a fingernail in anguish. "I'll skip the routine questions, shall I, Professor Plesch?"

"My understanding was that you wished to conduct some sort of interview concerning sexual love," he said. "As a member of the faculty, I felt it was my duty not to refuse."

"You have no objection, have you?" Dr. Schumann asked.

"Not if I can get home at a reasonable hour," he said.

"Sexual behavior," she corrected him. "Yes, that's what I asked you to come here to talk about," she said.

"Why don't you go ahead?" he asked.

"We're investigating the role of fantasy in sexual stimulation," Dr. Schumann said, assuming a more domineering manner. "The essential question is this. And please answer quite spontaneously. The first response that comes into your head. Speak right out, without evaluating your impulsive reaction. What image do you imagine when I ask you to think of the sexually most exciting thing in the world?"

"Dogs copulating," he said without hesitation.

"Really?" Dr. Schumann exclaimed delightedly. She scribbled a note. "That's *very* good. What is there particularly about that concept that you find stimulating?"

Having perceived what sort of answer pleased the woman, Plesch relaxed and spoke freely. "It reminds me of me copulating," he explained with mock diffidence.

"Good, good," Dr. Schumann coaxed him.

"The motion of it, you know," he said. "The to and fro movement. The ... urgency. Dogs always look in those circumstances as though they expect the world to come to an end at any moment. They hurry. I sympathize with them. I think I know how they must feel."

"I see, I see," Dr. Schumann said. "Yes, of course. And

225

now, Professor Plesch, I wonder if you would tell me what human spectacle you consider most stimulating?"

This question evidently was more difficult.

"Some glimpse of the anatomy, perhaps," Dr. Schumann suggested in the fawningly wheedling manner of a pander.

"A woman's eyes when she's in ecstasy," he said.

"When she's achieving an orgasm?" Dr. Schumann helpfully translated.

"You may put it in those words if you wish," he said.

"What about the eyes specially?"

"The look of a martyred angel. The fixed expression of total surrender. The beautiful tears."

"That's a very masculine approach," Dr. Schumann said.

"One had always hoped so," he said unreproachfully.

"Now," Dr. Schumann said, quite at ease, the interview having progressed so well after its inauspicious beginning. "I want you to describe, if you will, one or two human situations or incidents which you consider to be sexually stimulating."

"You want a couple of titillating vignettes?" he said. He looked faintly amused.

"You might call them that," she said.

"Cameos," he said.

"All right," she said, her pencil poised.

Dr. Plesch closed his eyes. He looked like a medium in a trance. "The garden of a house on the Nile," he began.

"Egypt again!" Dr. Schumann said to herself. "What is it about Egypt?"

"A fine night," Dr. Plesch said. "The moon shining on the dark river. A diplomat garden party. Strings of small colored lights festoon the trees. Near a house, a nineteenth-century mansion, Regency, there is a small orchestra of Viennese persuasion, and dancers in evening dress, on a terrace of polished mosaic tiles. There is champagne."

Dr. Schumann looked a trifle restive but she did not wish to interrupt the old man's flow of thought. He sighed and lapsed into silence. It was possible to hear the ticking of the clock.

"Yes?" Dr. Schumann said. "And then?"

"That's the scene," he said.

"And the stimulation?"

"A scent of orange blossoms," he said. "The cool fragrance of orange blossoms in the moonlight, the loveliest scent in the world. Some would argue in favor of jasmine; I will not succumb to their blandishments. The scent must be orange. A balmy breeze, scented. The sound of music. The moonlight. A young man in white tie and tails is seated on a comfortable upright garden chair in the darker part of the garden, away from the house and close to the water's edge. A young lady, wearing a long, white evening gown, is seated on his lap."

"Is that all?" Dr. Schumann asked.

"Don't you think it's romantic?" Plesch asked.

"Very romantic," Dr. Schumann said. "But . . ."

"Well, you see," he went on mildly, somewhat lowering his voice and speaking slowly, "the thing about it is this. The piquancy, as it were, resides in the fact that under the cover of the exquisitely embroidered white lace of her long, flowing ball gown, which is artfully draped over him, the young man's and young woman's private parts are conjoined."

Dr. Schumann caught her breath.

"Other couples, strolling about the garden, encounter the interlocked pair, and pleasantly converse with them, unaware that under the gown his person is inserted into hers."

"Remarkable!" Dr. Schumann exclaimed.

"The proximity of friends and casual acquaintances making conventional small talk, at the very moment of the seated couple's most intimate contact, you see," he explained. "The young lady makes fatuous remarks about the weather, while slyly shifting her weight, slowly, from, if I may say so, hip to hip."

"Please speak quite freely," Dr. Schumann urged him.

"The stimulation is thus maintained steadily, at quite a high level of sensuous enjoyment, over a considerable period of time. A prank of rare voluptuousness. The music and the animated conversation and laughter – not too loud – continue to resound from the terrace. The air is sweet. The moonlight gleams. Her hair is like perfumed silk against his cheek. More friends amble over, chat a while, and amble on. The sensual glow under the gown becomes gradually almost intolerably gratifying. Her movements become rather less furtive. He grasps her waist. She tries to

227

keep up the pretense of social conversation with the young man, but her words are mumbled incoherently. She stifles a cry with the back of her hand. He grunts. Another man and woman saunter elegantly over and exchange with them a number of pleasantries about the fine evening."

Again there was silence. Dr. Schumann sat temporarily speechless.

"Any other scenes of that nature?" she asked expressionlessly.

"Oh, my, yes," he said.

He paused. He cleared his throat.

"A midsummer evening in Venice," he said. "A gondola glides along a dark canal in faint moonlight. The gondolier is silent, having been paid well not to sing. A young man is sitting back, almost lying, between two young ladies, against many large cushions. The evening is cool and they have a large woollen blanket drawn up over their outstretched legs, over their waists, up to their necks. He feels the warmth of their legs pressing against the full length of his.

"He is reciting some lyrical verses of his own composition – romantic trifles of old-fashioned formality. Georgian, I suppose, one might call them. As he speaks, and the gondola silently proceeds, beneath low bridges and between dark buildings, he becomes aware of a hand, a warm hand, moving as stealthily as a small rodent, tiptoeing, so to speak, up between his thighs. He doesn't know which of his charmingly solemn listeners is so boldly misbehaving. He looks first at one and then at the other, but as they are almost entirely concealed by the blanket, he cannot detect the miscreant. He continues to speak the words of poetry as though nothing out of the ordinary were happening, and now the hand, whose he knows not, is burrowing most provocatively into the apparel, as though trying teasingly to cause him to forget his lines. The hand, of course, succeeds. He mutters some sort of apology for his forgetfulness. 'Are you feeling all right?' one of the young ladies asks him. As the hand is now quite shamelessly, unambiguously active, its smooth skin delicately stroking his, he finds the question ironic, and wonders whether the questioner has any cause to appreciate its irony. He sighs in irresponsible resignation, and settles farther back in the cushions, looking up at the clouds sailing slowly across the moon. In the distance, there is a sudden golden explosion of fireworks."

"Extraordinary!" Dr. Schumann said. "Quite extraordinary. The vividness of the fantasy is quite exceptional."

"Fantasy?" Professor Plesch said. "I thought you were interested in facts. I was recounting summaries of incidents I experienced in 1927."

"You mean to say that the young man in the garden was you? And the young woman . . .?"

"The young woman became my wife," Dr. Plesch said.

"And the young woman in the gondola?"

"I think that was my wife," Dr. Plesch said ."Not an easy sort of question to ask on one's honeymoon."

Dr. Schumann looked quite shocked.

THIRTY-FIVE

IN the bedrooms of faculty homes all over Digby, married couples of all ages were searching their hearts, trying to decide whether to give their services to medical science.

"I don't mind answering their questions in an impersonal way, in writing," said a thirty-five-year-old associate professor of mathematics. "But intercourse in a lab ... Gee, honey, I swear. I don't know about that. I think we have to consider the ethics of the deal."

"This isn't back in the nineteen-fifties," said his wife, one of those small, neat, alert, beaky women with quick reflexes and voracious appetites. "What's the matter with you? You won't get in on anything that's new and different."

"It's a question of ethics," he said, stepping into his pajama trousers with all the dignity that that maneuver permits.

"Where do ethics come into it?" his wife demanded scornfully. "It's officially sponsored by the college. It's not some crazy drunken wife-swapping party or something. And it's all strictly confidential. Dr. Schumann guaranteed that."

"But is it – I don't know – *right*? I mean, honey, gee whizz. And I wish you'd stop referring to those parties. I don't want to hear any more about them."

"Take it easy about the parties. When I talked about them at the Kilmartins' that time, I was only kidding, for heaven's sake. Learn to take a joke."

"If you expect me to be amused by the thought of my wife throwing her car key in with a lot of other wives' keys and having one of my lecherous colleagues –"

"I've told you a thousand times, it never happened. I was only trying to needle you. You'd been fishing some place all weekend, remember?"

"You don't think that I would do anything out of line, do you?"

"No," she said. "I don't."

"Don't you forget it."

"How could I? Darling, you know who one of the volunteers is?"

"No," he said. "I thought nobody was supposed to know."

"Professor Plesch."

"He is? I don't believe it. How do you know?"

"Naomi Fairlie saw him going into the Institute yesterday afternoon."

"That doesn't prove anything. All kinds of people go into the Biology Building every day. That doesn't mean he's a volunteer. You shouldn't say things like that. That's the way rumors start."

"Then there'd be no harm in our going into the building, would there? Just to discuss the program with Dr. Schumann?"

"I'm against it," he said. "What do you think Junior would think of us if he found out when he grew up? He wouldn't be **very** proud of his mother and father, would he?"

"By the time he grows up it won't mean a thing. He'd wonder what all the fuss was about. Even today the kids at Digby treat sex very casually, as one of the amenities, like hot water that pours when you turn on the faucet, taken for granted. You only worry about it when you turn the tap and there isn't any hot water."

"That's a false analogy, and you know it."

"It's beginning to seem truer and truer," she said with a sigh. She brightened. "Why don't you come over to my bed, and we'll talk it over?"

"Not tonight, honey," he said, pulling back the sheet of his own bed. "Tomorrow's Wednesday. You know I have an early class. It's a big class, fifty students, and I have to stay on top of the situation."

"I'm not going to do a Delilah," she said banteringly. "I don't like talking across the room. Come on over."

"For a little while then," he said. "But I must get some sleep."

He got into her bed. It was like submitting himself to an octopus – eight hands and a predatory beak.

"Let's just lie quietly, honey," he said. "Seriously, honey,
231

No, don't do that. Honey, hold on a minute. We have to get this thing settled."

"Go ahead and talk," she said slyly. "Don't let me bother you."

"How can I when you do that? I'm serious, honey. We'll have to let her know tomorrow. You said she said it was urgent."

"I'll talk on one condition."

"And that is?"

"You know."

"Couldn't you wait till tomorrow, honey? Wednesday's my best night!"

"About the Institute," she said briskly. "I think it would be good for us. Remember how I once said, half kidding, I thought you ought to go away to Cleveland some night and get yourself a call girl?"

"A shocking suggestion."

"It wouldn't kill you. It might broaden your horizons, break down some of those inhibitions – get rid of Mama."

"I'm going right back to my bed if you mention her name in this connection."

"Calm down," she said. "Nobody's criticizing her, even if she did scare you half out of your mind about sex."

"Cut that out," he said.

"You're so out of date," she said. "It's nothing to be ashamed of. It's only how you were brought up. You have this hang-up about red-light districts and the dangers of fallen women and disease and being arrested by the police. You even feel guilty with me, don't you, now honestly, admit it?"

"You're something special," he said.

"No, I'm not, goddammit. I'm not. Nor are you, if you'd only look at yourself clearly and see. You're not at all special. You're absolutely normal, when you let yourself go. You couldn't be more normal. The dividing line between normal and abnormal is finer than a human hair."

"Who wrote that?" he asked sardonically.

"We have a duty to the Institute. We owe something to posterity. But, more than that, the main reason I want you to go is to find out about yourself and me and other people. I think it would help."

As she spoke, she gently, persuasively kneaded his arm,

232

Without arousing him, the repeated squeezing kept reminding him of arousal.

"Will you do it?" she asked. "For my sake?"

"We don't need them," he said, turning on his side and clumsily fingering her breast. "Let's not talk any more now."

"You never like to talk when you're making love, do you?" she said sadly. "I'd give anything to know what goes on in your mind when you're doing it."

"I think about you," he said.

"Like hell you do," she said, but her tone of voice did not seem to deter him. His hand had moved down to Foreplay Erogenous Zone Number 2, and she waited for the duly allotted time to pass that invariably preceded the brief unconscious frenzy of his passion.

"I'm going to call Dr. Schumann first thing in the morning, whether you want to volunteer or not."

"That was wonderful, darling," he said.

THIRTY-SIX

"The more sophisticated the game playing, the more restrictive, of course," Dr. Schumann pointed out. "That much is self-evidently axiomatic. You might have expected higher I.Q. levels to mean more sensitive sexual suggestibility and thus an enhanced orgasm yield. But it isn't quite that simple, is it?"

She and Dr. Porter were in an observation booth watching a young anthropologist laboring to gratify Mrs. Shapiro. They were two of several faculty subjects who had been prompt to volunteer for extramarital cross-pairing, but the stimulus of novelty apparently had not wholly compensated for the uncoordinated awkwardness of their inexperience as a copulative unit. She was standing, bent forward from the waist and holding on to the back of a chair, with the ample white cushions of her posterior provocatively outthrust. He was standing immediately behind her with his legs slightly apart and his knees flexed and trembling. His face was contorted and shiny with effort. She was frowning with concentration, as though straining her consciousness to focus it on a distant point of mystical enlightenment, and she was licking her lips nervously, as though that point kept moving out of reach, just beyond comprehension. They both appeared to be staring straight at Dr. Schumann and Dr. Porter, but the appearance was illusory; the subjects were in fact looking at their own reflections in the mirror on their side of the one-way observation window. As his muscular agitation failed to engender the paroxysm of bliss, his ardor verged upon numb desperation, and her frown deepened. Now he looked as anxious as a jockey who has made his move so early that he fears his mount may fail him before reaching the end of the home stretch.

"Subjects of higher intelligence are more complicatedly conditioned to reject as well as to accept the variations of sexual congress," Dr. Schumann said. "The intellectual's self-awareness can make or break him sexually." She looked down at a stop watch on the shelf in front of her.

"Some of our pilot group certainly could have attained climax several minutes ago, and they are self-conscious enough, goodness knows. These amateurs make one appreciate the Marcia Daventrys of this world, don't they? With all her faults, she is wonderfully adaptable. The way she can switch from Sapphic to orthodox activities is a wonder to behold. You can see that these subjects are overcerebrating. Marcia would never do that. If they don't watch out, they may set up cortical blocks that could prove insurmountable. More film wasted! They don't seem to be able to escape from consciousness of our critical surveillance, even though they cannot see us, by each other, and by themselves. Each awareness intensifies the other's and drains off nervous energy that might be more usefully spent on sexual response. He is standing aside, that man, outside himself, watching and worrying, imperiling his performance; and so is she. We must do something about the mirrors. I was wrong about them; they are less of a help than a hindrance."

"But at least he seems to have reached a higher degree of tension with this subject than with his spouse," Dr. Porter said.

"She too," Dr. Schumann agreed. "I should hope so! With their marital partners they were severely handicapped by negative feelings of seduction-lack, a difficulty experienced in many marriages. If we had time to spare, I might consider conducting a minor investigation of the castration-effect of legitimacy, but we have our hands full without that."

"So many snags!" Dr. Porter lamented. "Sex sometimes seems to be riddled with them."

"Do you think so?" Dr. Schumann said, glancing curiously at him. "You know, Louis, as we sit here together, day after day, doing our work, I sometimes watch you appraising the subjects in action, making notes in that neat handwriting of yours, and I think back to the days of our childhood, when you lived next door – the times we used to have, you and I. And I wonder whether you remember too."

Dr. Porter smiled uneasily. "Of course I do," he said, wondering what she was leading up to.

"Do you really?" she said. "I wonder if you remember

the same things I remember. You were a funny boy in some ways. Very shy sometimes. But we had fun, didn't we?"

"Children get up to some funny games," he said, remembering one day in particular.

"Beatrice!"

In the dim light of the miniature shack, not much more than a hutch, an improvised structure of corrugated iron, wooden planks and grocery crates, between the outhouse and the back fence, the pale face of the small boy looked fearfully in the direction of the unseen house.

"All right, everything's quiet," the girl said in a curiously brisk, efficient, adult manner. "She must be feeding the baby."

"Couldn't we go some place else?" the boy asked. "Someone'll come and find us."

"There's nothing to be scared of," Beatrice said. "The baby's getting its milk. She can't leave it now. Come on, are you going to do what I say or aren't you? You're a very sick boy. I think I'd better check on your temperature."

"Oh, Beatrice!" the boy feebly protested, but he allowed her to stick a pencil into his mouth, under his tongue. Beatrice took his frail white wrist between finger and thumb, and gravely looked at her dime-store wrist watch.

"Hmm," she said. "That's what I figured. Yes."

Though they had been through the whole routine on countless previous occasions, the boy's expression became authentically anxious. "I don't want to," he said.

"Don't *want* to?" Beatrice echoed contemptuously. "You've heard of yellow fever, haven't you? There isn't time to fool around."

"Oh, please, Bea," the boy said. "Please don't let's. Couldn't we do it another time? Please?"

"You know you're not supposed to call me 'Bea'."

"Please, doctor."

"Come on," she said, slipping the pencil into the pocket of her faded cardigan. Her voice was irresistibly authoritative and her mouth was set in a firm, straight line. "There's going to have to be a complete examination. Get undressed."

The boy's eyes gleamed with moisture, but he didn't dare allow it to become tears. He fumbled with the buttons on his shirt front and his cuffs and got them undone. When he pulled the shirt off and bared his torso, his collarbones, his breastbone, his ribs prominent under the smooth, white skin, it looked like the carcass of a plucked pullet. The Ohio spring morning was mild, but he was shivering. For a moment, he stupidly stood there, his meager, bony shoulders rounded, his thin arms folded, his hands clutching the undeveloped biceps.

"What are you waiting for?" Beatrice asked.

"It's cold in here," he said. "I'm cold."

"Well, hurry then," she said. Almost kindly, she added, "You know it doesn't take long."

"Oh . . ." he pleaded. "You've already seen it." Beatrice's face hardened again.

"Don't talk like that," she said. "You don't know how to do anything right. Come on, and fast."

The boy seemed to grit his teeth, and obediently he tugged at his belt to open the buckle. Then he disengaged the top button from its buttonhole, and then, reluctantly, the second button, and then, still more reluctantly, the third . . . Beatrice stood immobile, a pretty twelve-year-old with auburn curls, long eyelashes, a short, freckled nose, angelic, round cheeks, softly pouting pink lips, a long, slender, white neck, intently staring. Her eyes glittered fixedly, as though hypnotizing his fingers.

"Go on," she murmured. "That's a good boy."

The divided front of his brown corduroy shorts fell open, revealing a white triangle of underwear, and he had to grab the shorts to prevent them from falling down.

"Shoes and socks," Beatrice said, tersely encouraging him. "I have to examine everything, don't I? You want me to make you all better, don't you?"

The boy said nothing. Crouching primitively, with his knees almost level with his shoulders, he automatically undid his laces, removed his blue-and-white canvas sneakers, pulled off his thick white sweat socks, and stood up, allowing his shorts to fall about his ankles. He lifted one foot free and then the other. Now he was wearing only his elastic-top white cotton jockey shorts.

Beatrice nodded in rapture.

The child automaton hooked his fingers inside the elastic and peeled away downward the last shield. The elastic left a faint pink imprint in the soft white skin of his waist. Beatrice held her breath. The shorts were off. The boy looked straight ahead as numbly steadfast as a somnambulist. Beatrice stared at the penis, smaller than a little finger, curled in under itself, wrapped around the daintily wrinkled pink scrotal sac, as modestly withdrawn as a statuary cherub's. Free from the constriction of the tight underwear, the penis timidly, infinitesimally stirred.

Suddenly the shack was loud with Beatrice's hooting laughter. The boy, shocked, covered his betrayed parts with his hands. Beatrice angrily tore the interfering fingers aside.

"What's the matter, baby boy?" she demanded. Again, she burst out laughing, and the boy, twisting around so that his naked back, his sardine spine, protected him, began silently sobbing.

"You didn't really mind anything I did, did you?" she asked.

"Of course not," he said. "Kids are kids. They aren't responsible the way adults are." Dr. Porter looked a trifle uncomfortable.

"I don't believe in things like fate, of course," Dr. Schumann said. "But it almost seems as though it was fate, doesn't it? The way we lived next door to each other. The understanding between us. The friendship. The intimacy. And now the Institute."

"We have known each other for a long time," Dr. Porter acknowledged. "A long time."

"You have done very well academically, Louis," Dr. Schumann said. "I would hate to see that changed."

"What do you mean?"

"You needn't get all nervous," she said. "I merely meant that I value having you here with me."

"I'm not nervous," he said. "It's just that . . ."

"Oh, you've already had feelers? Well, I suppose that was inevitable. Our work here is important and no matter how hard we've tried to keep it hush-hush I expect the word has gotten around. Well, who wants you and for how much, Louis?"

Dr. Louis Porter did not answer, though he shifted uneasily in his seat.

"Oh, I shan't twist your arm, Louis. It's just that I'd hoped you'd be a bit more open about it. After all you do owe me *some* loyalty. By the way what did you mean when you said sex seems to be riddled with snags?"

"From an investigative point of view," he said hastily. "You can set up any number of controls, and yet beyond a certain point there are so many variables, you know?"

"Are you still fond of me, Louis?"

"I respect you very much," he said.

"But what are your feelings as a human being?" she asked. "Is there anything between you and Rollo Hawkins?"

"Dr. Schumann! How could you say such a thing!"

"Beatrice," she said. "You used to call me Bea when we were little."

"You used to make me call you 'doctor'," he blurted out.

"Only when we were playing that game," she said, smiling at his small outburst of old indignation. "When you protest like that, suddenly it all seems like yesterday."

"But I'm a man now," Dr. Porter said. "Things aren't the same any more. The difference in our ages is no longer significant."

"I'm so glad to hear you say that," Dr. Schumann said. "But I already knew it. I've been watching you more closely than you may realize."

"What do you mean?" Dr. Porter asked.

"Oh, just noticing your reactions during episodes," she said vaguely. "You react more to some things than to others. What is there between you and Rollo Hawkins?"

"There's nothing between him and me," Dr. Porter said with pompous gravity. "We're merely casual friends. He has quite an unusual mind."

"I'm sure he has," Dr. Schumann said. "Is that why you took him to the Digby Theater Workshop and introduced him to the director?"

"Who told you that?" Dr. Porter asked. "What's wrong with it, anyway? He happens to be very interested in the theater. He asked me to arrange a meeting."

"Don't get upset," Dr. Schumann said. "I don't mind

239

who your friends are. So long as we understand each other. We do, don't we?"

"Sure," Dr. Porter said.

"Fine," Dr. Schumann said blandly. "A program of this sort requires the closest cooperation. I can count on you, can't I? I mean, you won't take too seriously any offers to leave here. I want you here with me, Louis, and you know a word dropped here and there about your friendship with Rollo could do you incalculable harm. Not that I would, of course."

"You needn't doubt my loyalty to the Institute," Dr. Porter said.

"That's all I wanted to hear you say," Dr. Schumann calmly assured him.

"When is the robot getting here?" Dr. Porter asked. "If you'll give me a little warning, I'll keep my evenings free."

"That's very nice of you, Louis," Dr. Schumann said. "It's already overdue. We've had some difficulty with Customs. Our poor robot is at present languishing in custody in Seattle. Some absurd, antediluvian objection about obscene artifacts! But Mr. Symington has been on the telephone to Capitol Hill, and they've promised to get the robot cleared right away, as a work of art."

Mrs. Shapiro, her face red and bloated with some strong emotion, suddenly began frantically to wag her hindquarters. Dr. Schumann notified Camilla over the intercom that everybody could take a fifteen-minute break.

THIRTY-SEVEN

"No, Billie, no more, no. It's wonderful, but I can't stand it. I think I'll die. Oh, Billie. . . ."

Marcia made no physical effort to stop her. Billie was adhering to their customary routine, providing her mistress with her usual refreshments and comforts on her return from the rigors of an afternoon at the lab – two large vodka martinis, a small sirloin steak, charred outside and almost raw within, a green salad with oil and vinegar, a cup of black coffee, a long soak in a sweetly perfumed, deep, very hot bath, and a meticulously thorough massage on the silken bed. The massage always began therapeutically, an efficient, systematic gentle kneading of every muscle from the neck to the toes and up again. It was so relaxing, at first, that it made Marcia groan in pleasurable surrender. Therapy became an act of amorous devotion. Billie's tireless erotic tenderness and skill seemed to alter the very quality of Marcia's skin. At last she became one quivering stripped bundle of nerves in an agony of delight.

"Billie!" Marcia squealed. "Oh, God, Billie! I love you."

Billie sat back on her heels at the foot of the bed and happily surveyed the inert, spread-eagled body, as proudly as though she had created it.

"Ain't you something?" she said.

Marcia opened her eyes and dazedly smiled. "Wow," she said. "They don't make them like that down at the lab."

Billie smiled. "Bad day?" she asked.

"There was some old professor," Marcia said. "A nice old guy. A real gentleman. He was very polite. But it just didn't seem right."

"I hate to think of a dirty old man like that, slobbering over you, touching you."

"It wasn't like that. You couldn't help liking him. I know what you mean. When you see old people, old men and women, in the street, it's difficult to imagine them undressed even – impossible to think of them at it. You can't even imagine them ever having done it. Or even think of them *thinking* about it. You look at them and somehow

241

you think they don't know what's going on in the world. You forget they've been young once, and they've made it, and they've had children and grandchildren. You just think to yourself there's a poor old guy, all dried up, almost dead. What has he got? What has he got to look forward to? A walk in the park, an evening in front of the television set, picking out his false teeth? I had an uncle like that. All he did was talk about football and baseball. But you know something, Billie. In fifteen or twenty years, I'll be getting old. In twenty-five years, even you will. That's what that professor made me realize. He didn't say anything about it. I felt it. He showed me there's a connection."

"You won't be old," Billie said indignantly. "You know how to look after yourself. There isn't a wrinkle. You have a real young body. I wouldn't kid you."

"It's in the mind, Billie. Young, middle-aged, old."

"You don't have to get old if you take care," Billie said.

"He seemed so young in some ways, his ideas, that getting old didn't seem bad," Marcia said.

"But wasn't it kind of depressing? After you'd got through talking?"

"I felt bad about it," Marcia said. "He seemed so dignified. I felt sorry for him, he was so friendly. It didn't seem right for him to show himself in front of all those people. I felt . . . bad about it."

"You're too softhearted, that's your trouble," Billie said, reassuringly stroking Marcia's flank.

"But I've got news for you," Marcia said more cheerfully. "He came out of it all right. He wasn't like some of those men in their fifties, trying to prove something. He was really nice. I liked the way he talked to me when Dr. Schumann introduced us. You know, I've told you the way she acts."

"Big time operator, trying to push you all around?"

"Yeah. She was talking up a storm – a real snow job, all her theories and all that stuff. He was polite to her, too, but in his quiet way he really cut her down to size. I felt like kissing him. I don't know what he said, but when she used a word this big he used one twice as long. You should've seen her face! The more serious she tried to get, the more he somehow kidded her out of it – quietly – nothing you

242

could put your finger on. After a while it was like she didn't know what to do with him."

"What did you do then?"

"I didn't know what to do. A lot of it was going over my head."

"You're a whole lot smarter than you think," Billie said.

"Thanks, Billie. Common sense, maybe. But I'm not smart. Let's face it. So it was time for action. Dr. Schumann told us what she wanted us to do. Nothing wild, only the regular things. She explained how we work. Then she said she'd have someone conduct him to his undressing room and we'd meet up in the ready room for orientation."

"Don't *you* start with the sixty-four-dollar words."

"Like getting acquainted. It makes it easier for some of them if you neck a little, feel them up a little, before doing anything in the main demonstration room."

"What was he like?" Billie asked, rather resentfully.

"Wait, I'll tell you," Marcia said. "He told Dr. Schumann he wanted to talk with me for a minute."

"Before getting undressed."

"Dr. Schumann was getting impatient – she often does – but she didn't dare refuse him any special request. You could see she was almost scared of him in a way. He's a real brain, Miss Fairbank said."

"Who's she?"

"That doesn't matter. A kid that works in the lab. So the professor took me aside, away from everyone. 'I want you to know I like you,' he said. 'You mustn't think it's anything to do with you – you're a good woman.' He really said it! I didn't know what was up. I started to cry almost, he was so nice. He said, 'I've decided to tell Dr. Schumann I'm not going through with it. I'm withdrawing from the program. There's nothing at all wrong with you. You're a very attractive woman.' He said, 'If I were a bachelor things would be different. But I'm not. So you see it's impossible. I'm a silly old man. I shouldn't have listened to my wife. She persuaded me to come here for my sake; I'm going back for hers – and that's for my sake too.' I couldn't help crying! I gave him a big fat kiss on the cheek. What a nice guy! He's the kind of guy you'd want for a father. And I bet he's quite a man."

"But what did Dr. Schumann say?"

243

"Dr. Schumann? Dr. Schumann about blew her top!"

"Was she mad at you?"

"How could she be? It wasn't my fault. But she was fit to be tied."

"Marcia, aren't you getting tired of Dr. Schumann and all that jazz?"

"I can't quit now," Marcia said. "Not until Joanna's visit is over. I've got to wait for that. It won't be long. She thinks I'm really something at Digby."

"You'd be something anywhere!" Billie said. "You don't have to put on any act. Let's get out of here and you be your own self. You don't have to take anything from that Dr. Schumann. You can be independent any time you want."

"Dr. Schumann doesn't bother me, Billie, believe me. The minute she does we'll pull out. Don't worry about that."

"Do you get a charge out of balling with all them cats in the lab?"

"Billie!"

"Do you like them as much as you like me?" Billie asked.

"I'll try to answer that if you lie down," Marcia said. "I never heard of such jealousy."

"Ain't never been nothing to be so jealous about," Billie said.

"Maybe this will convince you," Marcia said.

She convinced her exhaustively.

THIRTY-EIGHT

THE parcel was delivered to the Institute the next morning, a long, rectangular aluminum box the size of a coffin, secured with steel tape and plastered with red-and-white labels proclaiming, in Japanese and English, the fragility of the contents and the urgency of the consignment.

"What's in here, a body?" asked one of the delivery men, as they slowly eased the box onto a counter in the lab, in obedience to Dr. Schumann's eager but cautious instructions and exhortations.

"This is a serious matter," Dr. Schumann said. "It's nothing to joke about."

"Don't listen to him," the other delivery man said. "It's a warm day though." He lifted the peak of his cap to scratch his sweating scalp, and produced a receipt book from a pocket. "Do you want to look the goods over before you sign?"

"No, that isn't necessary," Dr. Schumann assured him. "Let me sign. I'm sure it's well packed."

"I thought maybe you'd want to," the man said. "With that kind of insurance.... There's a lot of dough involved."

"She said it's all right," Dr. Porter snapped. He was almost as impatient as Dr. Schumann.

"O.K., mister," the delivery man said. "O.K."

Dr. Porter got a hammer and screwdriver from the janitor's workshop in the basement and began levering open the steel tapes.

"Hurry!" Dr. Schumann urged him.

"I am hurrying," he said.

There were several screws that had to be undone to release the lid.

"I wonder if it's fitted with standard plugs," Dr. Schumann said. "I hope the voltage is right."

"Don't let that worry you," Dr. Porter said. "Those Japanese don't miss a trick when it comes to modifying designs for export. Think of the fantastic speed with which they responded to your order. Think of the problems of

245

design and manufacture."

"It isn't the first sexual robot they've ever made," Dr. Schumann said. "They were proud of that. It's an industry based on generations of experience of making full-scale sex dolls for men. Some Japanese officers had them when serving far from home during the war. The sales manager told me they had made something like this robot for a certain South American president, and another's on the drawing board for NASA, for astronauts on long space probes – simpler models than ours, though; theirs don't have to be bisexual. They wouldn't say which South American president, and you know how tight security is in the space program, but the Japanese were probably telling the truth. Why not? They certainly didn't need me to spell out any of the specifications for them. In fact, they suggested several minor refinements and extra added features that I hadn't even thought of."

"This is the last screw," Dr. Porter said. The screwdriver slipped and he carefully adjusted it in the groove of the screwhead.

"Of course," Dr. Schumann continued, "the Japanese have always been far ahead of us in the fabrication of mechanical sex aids. There's a small mail-order house in southern California that sells artificial vaginas, offered, according to the ads, to collect sperm from any male animal, including, one assumes, Homo sapiens. But it isn't a great product. I commissioned a young graduate student at U.C.L.A. to examine it for me. His report was disappointing. Kobe, a thriving seaport on Osaka Bay, is the site of the most celebrated sex shop in Japan, and that means the most celebrated in the world. That woman in Hamburg's a beginner. The Japanese craftsmanship! Their exquisite taste! Their synthetic phalluses are beyond question the best you can get anywhere. Their bride's pillow-books, practical guides to marital sexual congress, copiously illustrated with paintings on washable cloth pages, are collectors' items. But, unfortunately, Kobe hasn't kept up with developments in the field of electronics in this connection. The transistor has revolutionized sex machines. It's too bad our newspapers and news magazines don't keep us up to date on this front. Things are moving very fast. Even our own A.M.A. *Journal,* so sympathetic in other ways, has

246

been remiss on this score. I've written to them often enough, but it still seems to be a blind spot."

"Here we go!" Dr. Porter said.

They lifted off the lid and put it down on the counter. The box was padded inside with pale-gray foam rubber and filled with protective, aromatic cedar shavings. Dr. Schumann quickly swept some of them aside with an impatient hand, and she and Dr. Porter found themselves looking down at the face of one of Hollywood's most popular, most beautiful young actresses.

It was life-size and uncannily realistic, a photograph portrait cast in the round in material that looked exactly like human flesh, tinted in natural hues heightened with cosmetics.

"A marvelous likeness," Dr. Porter said. "But wouldn't she sue if she somehow found out? I mean, if she found out what the robot was being used for."

"Can you see anyone going to court over that? It is amazingly like her, but it's not the kind of publicity she'd want. Look at the texture, the finish!" She touched the robot's lovely cheek and uttered a small cry of wonder and admiration. "Feel it!" she said. Dr. Porter, fascinated but wary, did so and marveled. "But I hope the obvious identity of the face doesn't have a bad effect on our subjects," Dr. Schumann said. "In the letter confirming the order, I merely stipulated that the faces had to be Caucasian, to obviate any possible racialist reactions. I didn't wish to introduce extraneous factors of any kind."

"And how about the closed eyes?" Dr. Porter asked. "Won't there be a danger of necrophilic undertones?"

"The eyes open," Dr. Schumann replied with regained confidence. "So does the mouth. You can vary the lids' blink-rate. And the lip movements can be programed to synchronize with the vocal tapes. The sound system has been so well miniaturized that the robot has quite an extensive repertoire of phrases and breathing effects. There's even a tongue, which can be activated in a number of useful ways, and lubricated with something chemically indistinguishable from saliva. They have been most ingenious in devising controls to regulate the flow of bodily secretions. For instance, the simulated sweat glands are coordinated with the thermostats that govern temperatures in various parts of the body. The robot's internal fluid levels are topped up as part of routine servicing between episodes – an operation that takes only minutes."

"Let's have a look at the rest of it," Dr. Porter said.

Dr. Schumann and he brushed away more shavings to disclose prominently conical white breasts, like twin volcanoes, surmounted by immaculate pink nipples.

"The Japanese, like many other people, still have a somewhat exaggerated, old-fashioned notion about the American male's breast fixation," Dr. Schumann pointed out. "But it doesn't matter. The breasts are adjustable, by inflation and deflation. These are obviously at maximum. The facial, torso and pelvic components are disconnected and replaced by male components, as required. Ah! Here's a letter. It looks like it includes operational and maintenance instructions. 'The Venadonis Company of Tokyo congratulates you!' it begins. 'We wish you will be completely satisfied with your custom-made specially modified de luxe model Copu-Doll.' I'll let you read the rest yourself later. I think I already know the technical side of it."

"And here's some kind of brochure!" Dr. Porter exclaimed, picking up a glossy, multicolored booklet from the robot's chest and blowing the sawdust off the cover. "Is this robot a commercial product?"

"Not yet," Dr. Schumann said. "Anyway, certainly not this one. This is a special, custom-made research model, as the letter says. It would be far beyond the means and requirements of the ordinary individual. As it happens, the company was able to give us a very generous discount, on the understanding that on the satisfactory completion of our work with it we might be able to see our way clear to giving the robot the Institute's seal of approval. The suggestion was mine, and their response was immediately favorable. It would be our first such endorsement. I believe the robot will prove worthy of it.

"Think of the immensity of the market for these robots in this country alone!" Dr. Schumann said. "Sexual gratification without infidelity and social and legal risk! What could be a safer, more effective way of initiating and training the adolescent, of soothing the bachelor and consoling the widow, of inspiring the blasé and appeasing the over-endowed? I am quite convinced that the time will come in

248

the very near future when there will be a Copu-Doll in every home. Perhaps several of them – one for Mom and Dad, one for the kids, and one in the guest room. Diplomats, G.I.'s and traveling salesmen, to name only a few, will take collapsible, battery-powered Copu-Dolls when they are separated from their dear ones. Every hotel room will contain a Copu-Doll, ready to plug in, with appropriate charges indicated on a chronological meter, like in a taxi. Would five dollars be excessive for half an hour in the arms of your favorite star of stage or screen, pop singer, ballplayer, or society leader? The interchangeable portrait masks are among the less costly accessories. You could even have one made of your own husband or wife, if you so desired. It'd make a very thoughtful anniversary gift, wouldn't it – a robot mask modeled from a wedding photograph."

"If we award the Institute seal, will the Institute receive any sort of royalty payment on sales?" Dr. Porter asked. Dr. Schumann smiled.

"In its male form," she said earnestly, "like Masters and Johnson's relatively primitive coital mechanism, this robot is fitted with an artificial penis made of shatter-proof transparent plastic, as optically true as plate glass, containing a camera and lighting equipment for clinical photography inside the vagina during simulated sexual intercourse. I don't mean to detract in any way from Masters and Johnson's pioneer work, of course, but our robot could be compared to their apparatus much as next year's space capsule could be compared to the first Model-T Ford. Penis for penis, there may not initially seem to be very much in it; both are responsive to the subject's changing demands for variations in penile size, rate of motion in and out of the vagina, and depth of thrust. But there the resemblance ends. Their device was a penis in the abstract, a penis unattached, in limbo, requiring of the subject herself a degree of imaginative sexual initiative and response far in excess of the norm; this robot, on the other hand, is a complete corporeal entity, sexually stimulating, and, what is more, reliably following through, with all the excitement-inducing vigor, dexterity and persistence, the weight, solidity, muscle tension, facial expressiveness, tactile, visual, auditory and olfactory stimulation of the ideal human partner.

Just imagine, Louis! Quality control and indefatigability! What a difference this is going to make!"

Dr. Porter was clearing away the shavings that concealed the robot's lower abdomen.

"You won't be able to tell it from the real thing," Dr. Schumann assured him, nodding with a smile of rather smug approval at the gradual revelation of a dark pubic toupée.

"See how exactly they've matched the wig?" Dr. Schumann said. "Every detail is right."

One of the delivery men entered the room again, staggering under the weight of a wooden packing case.

"This one's for you, too," he said, dumping the box on the floor.

"Careful!" Dr. Schumann said. She insisted on opening the box to make sure there was no damage before signing.

" 'Extra faces and spare parts'," she said, reading the Customs declaration. Dr. Porter levered the top open.

"Hey! That's all right!" the delivery man exclaimed admiringly, as the topmost face was revealed. "The spittin' image of him!"

"Thank you, you may go now," Dr. Schumann told the man.

"O.K., lady, take it easy," he said, turning and leaving with a shrug of the shoulders.

"The trouble with the Japanese," Dr. Schumann said irritably to Dr. Porter, "is they have no sense of propriety. How would they like it, I wonder, if an American manufacturer of this kind of equipment sent them a portrait head of their prime minister?"

"Maybe it's meant to be an honor," Dr. Porter said. "Don't get upset. We don't have to use that one."

"I should hope not!"

"Now show me how this thing *operates*," he said.

It was not much more difficult to figure out than an electric mixer and its accessories, but somehow the time sped by, and suddenly it was time to go to the Faculty Club for dinner.

"You go ahead," Dr. Porter said. "Don't wait for me. I'm going to tinker around some more."

"No, you'd better go eat," Dr. Schumann said. "I'll dismantle him and put him away."

Dr. Porter could hardly decently make an issue of it.

THIRTY-NINE

"MARY and her date have gone on to another party," Camilla said. "She said they'd see us there later. It doesn't matter when we arrive. It isn't formal."

"I like your dress," Richard said. He shut the car door behind her and walked around to the driver's seat.

"Are you sure you want to go to the party?" he asked her as he started the car. "I thought you wanted to see that Eskimo tragedy at the drive-in."

"Mary said it was time we did something," Camilla said. "She's afraid I'm missing everything. She said I ought to see how the other ninety-nine per cent live, whatever that means. She said I owe it to you."

"All I want is to be with you," Richard said, leaning away from the wheel and kissing her.

"Mary thinks it's some kind of sacrilege not to be with the rest of the kids on Saturday night. She says I'll get old before my time if I keep on this way."

"You don't look very old yet."

"It isn't far from here. Maybe it'll be fun."

She directed him along quiet streets, and soon they reached a gateway to a drive and a large Georgian-style mansion in half an acre or so of overgrown garden. All the lights appeared to be out, but many cars were parked in front of the house and there was a loud, thudding emanation from it of drums and electric guitars.

"This is it, all right," Camilla said.

Nobody answered the front-door bell. Richard tried the door, and it was open, so they went in.

Inside, it was not absolutely dark, but heavy purple-black velvet curtains, hanging from ceiling to floor, minimized the dim red light from Chinese paper lanterns suspended in mid-air. Richard and Camilla gradually perceived that they were in a hall, with a broad, curved stairway crowded with obscure seated figures, whose faces were all but invisible, except momentarily, irregularly, here and there, when one of them was faintly illuminated by the glow of a puffed cigarette. The air was thick and sweet with

251

smoke. Richard had an uneasy feeling that Camilla and he could be seen more easily than they could see, but he suspected that this was merely the self-consciousness of the maladjusted latecomer.

"Let's go where the music is," he said. "I'll find you a drink."

"Do you mind if I have a Coke?" Camilla said. "You have something, but all this noise and everything."

"You'd better have a gin and tonic," he said. "In self-defense. If I can find anything. I can't see much."

They passed through an open double doorway into a sudden black furnace of sound.

"Wait here!" he shouted close to her ear.

"What?"

"Wait . . . here! I'll . . . get . . . the drinks!"

He felt the pounding of the bass in his entrails and the thin wires of the guitars repeatedly slicing his brain. As he hesitantly made his way across the hot room, he was jostled and bumped by the jerking arms of the mass of solitary dancers.

Richard found someone leaning against a wall.

"Where's the bar?" Richard asked.

"Bar?" the girl said.

"I'm trying to get something to drink."

"Blowing pot," she said. "Want some?"

"Isn't anyone drinking?"

"Want to turn on?"

"Isn't there anything else?"

"Only if you go upstairs," she said.

Richard forced his way back through the maelstrom to Camilla. "Upstairs!" he shouted.

"Don't you want to dance?"

"Come on!"

He took her hand firmly and led her slowly up the crowded stairway, apologizing right and left as they pushed past the bodies.

The noise diminished surprisingly quickly as they walked along a dimly red-lighted, thickly carpeted corridor, with several closed doors on either side.

"Don't you want to dance?" Camilla asked.

"Down there?"

"Isn't that what we came for?"

"But not to that! Let's have a drink. Then perhaps later."

"I wonder if Mary's arrived yet," Camilla said doubtfully.

"Who's her date?" Richard asked. "Some party!"

"He's very nice. He's a philosophy major, but very nice. This is their first big date."

The corridor came to a dead end.

"I wonder where everyone is?" Camilla said.

"I'll find out," Richard said. He knocked on a door. There was no answer. He opened the door and looked inside.

"Oh! Excuse me!" he said, and quickly closed the door. He turned to Camilla. "Perhaps we'd better go."

The bedroom door opened again, and a middle-aged man emerged, knotting the sash of a dressing gown.

"*Hi!*" he said. "Were you looking for *me*?"

"I'm sorry," Richard said. "No. That is to say, we were trying to find our host. The only catch is, we don't know what he looks like. I – is this your party?"

"Don't *fret*," the man said. "I guess you're not a regular, are you? Tony's in *there*," he said, indicating the next door down, "but I imagine he's far gone. You know how it is. Or *do* you? What's your *name*? I'm Rollo Hawkins."

"We're just guests of guests," Richard said.

"Mary Charlton invited us," Camilla said. "But we were just going."

"Miss *Fairbank*!" Rollo exclaimed. "I didn't expect to see *you* here!"

"You know each other?" Richard said.

"We work in the same building," Camilla said hastily. "We must be going."

"*Going*?" Rollo said. "Don't be *insane*! We just *got* here. What's your name?" he asked Richard. "Have you ever had a psychedelic experience? It's really *something*. Why don't you turn off your *mind*, for heaven's sake? Relax, and float down*stream*!"

"We have to go," Richard said. "Tell Tony we're sorry we missed him – Camilla Fairbank and Richard Doughty. But he wouldn't know. Friends of Mary Charlton's."

"Don't be so *snooty*!" Rollo said. "I like your face. Come on in. We could use you. Lawrence is being *impossible*. He's supposed to be in the Second *Bardo*, for heaven's sake, but

253

you wouldn't *know* it. He wouldn't accept Final Reality if it was handed to him on a platter, that one!"

"Thanks a lot, but no," Richard said. "No, thanks. I don't know what you're talking about, but thanks, no."

"I'm talking about lysergic acid diethylamide, baby," Rollo said. "I'm talking about making it through the doors of *perception*. I'm talking about kicking your *ego,* for heaven's sake. What do you think I'm talking about? Why are you *here*?" He turned to Camilla. "What's *his* problem?"

"Let's go and dance," Richard said.

"Let's just *go*!" Camilla said.

"*Square*!" Rollo said.

Richard hurried Camilla away.

FORTY

DR. PORTER, unable to sleep later that evening, dressed and drove to the Biology Building and let himself in at the Institute entrance.

Someone had left the lights on in the foyer. He selected another key from his key chain and unlocked the door to the laboratory. He paused. He could hear a voice in the demonstration room. He opened the door.

"I love you, I love you, I love you, I love you, I love you," a man's voice kept repeating in a faintly Japanese accent.

Dr. Porter cautiously peered around the door. A single spotlight shone on a powerful nude male figure, lying on its back, manifestly in a state of extreme sexual excitement, raising and lowering his hips spasmodically in time with the words.

It was the robot. Dr. Porter walked close to the bed and stood motionless beside it, staring at the unreciprocated passionate thrusts of the artificial lover.

"I love you, I love you, I love you, I love you, I love you," the robot said.

Dr. Porter sat on the edge of the bed and looked closer. He slowly reached out his right hand.

A door opened beside him, and his hand froze. He turned his head. Dr. Schumann.

"You!" she said. "I didn't know who it was. You scared me."

Dr. Porter stood up. "I saw a light," he said. "I was passing by. I wondered if anything was wrong."

"I love you, I love you, I love you," the robot said.

"I don't seem to be able to turn it off," Dr. Schumann said, fingering a button at the neck of her blouse. "It seems to be stuck. Some minor thing, I suppose. You have to expect a few bugs at first."

Dr. Porter went to the wall switch and turned it off.

"I love –" the robot said, stopping rigidly in the hips-raised position.

"Thanks," Dr. Schumann said. "Don't bother now. We can work it out in the morning."

"A faulty relay some place," Dr. Porter said.

"Yes, no doubt," Dr. Schumann said. "Thanks for looking in."

"Well, I'll be going then," Dr. Porter said.

"Right," Dr. Schumann said. "Good night."

"Good night."

As soon as Dr. Porter had left the room and closed the door, Dr. Schumann hurried back to the observation booth. Turner Symington appeared to be much amused.

"A very conscientious young man," he said. "You shouldn't have stopped him."

FORTY-ONE

HITHERTO sedate academics and their circumspect wives were startlingly transformed into melodramatic extroverts when separately introduced to the robot. The youthful bloom of its pastel-pink rubbery-plastic flesh, the silken gleam of its hair, the clear sparkle of its glass eyes, the candidly sensual flattery of its vocal utterances, and the unflagging vigor of its electrically powered pelvic thrusts aroused its human partners, male and female alike, to an extravagance of activity.

One gray, desiccated political historian, noted for the somberness of his tweeds and the nagging pedantry of his lectures, alarmed Dr. Schumann, when the camera was whirring, by leaping and bounding around the laboratory bed, whooping like a ruttish Tarzan. He explained afterward, gloating and still rather breathless, that he had been unwontedly encouraged by the opportunity to gain physical gratification without any inhibiting sense of obligation to gratify another.

"After nearly a quarter of a century of unselfishly abiding the directions of the marriage manuals," he said, "I find it refreshing to do exactly what I want, when I want it, no more, no less, without any regard whatsoever for the efficacy of my performance." The substance of his explanation, stated more pithily, was echoed, curiously enough, by his wife, when interrogated after her own romp with the robot.

Carefree self-indulgence built up confidence; confidence, however, grew lamentably soon into tiresomely fulsome over-confidence, verging in many cases on arrogance.

One corpulent dowager, discreetly fragrant with talcum and cologne when she reported for duty, a lady respected throughout the community as the quietly authoritative program chairman of the Digby chapter of the League of Women Voters and admired far and wide for the subtle daintiness of her flower arrangements, took to mechanical intercourse with the ponderous gusto of a runaway steam engine. Her enthusiasm reached such a pitch, indeed, that she seemed to lose all sense of the passage of time, let alone decorum. She absorbed the robot into her great maw like some vast, ravenous amoeba, taking the machine's maximum caliber, extent, depth of penetration, and tempo, until the scene assumed the farcical frenzy of one of the works of Mack Sennett. Dr. Schumann eventually felt compelled to intervene, terminating the bout by jerking the electric cable from its socket. The resulting flood of angry tears and recriminations caused the volunteer much chagrin when she regained her self-control.

"We're worse off than we were before," Dr. Schumann commented grimly to Dr. Porter at the end of the tumultuous afternoon. "The robot's too good. It induces hysteria. I don't mind admitting that it's got me good and worried."

"It seems to bring out the ham in people," Dr. Porter agreed.

"The exhibitionism factor," Dr. Schumann said. "A subject worthy of study. But not now. First things first. The Copu-Doll evidently releases a long-pent-up desire for exhibitionism. There's a flamboyant excessiveness about it that I don't like. The pilot group was bad enough. The faculty volunteers are even worse. Years of respectability have taken their toll. There must be some happy medium in between these two extremes. But we have no access to it. How valid are our statistics going to prove when related to the normal connubial sexual situation—"

"What's it going to do to us at Atlantic City?" Dr. Porter asked uneasily, bringing out into the open an anxiety that had been growing for some time in their minds.

"The A.M.A. leans over backward not to find fault with members' papers presented at the convention," Dr. Schumann said. "But professional courtesy only stretches so far. It isn't unlimited. The Association has to protect itself. Frankly, we don't have a foot of film in which exhibitionism doesn't stick out like a sore thumb. Some faultfinder is bound to comment."

"Would it be better to stay away from the convention this year?" Dr. Porter suggested.

"We can't afford the time," Dr. Schumann said. "We need publication, and we need the security of prior official approval. Without the Association's backing, our position vis-à-vis the trustees wouldn't be worth a plugged nickel."

"Now you've got me really worried," Dr. Porter said. "Exhibitionism's an ugly word."

"Very ugly," Dr. Schumann said.

When she discussed the situation with Mr. Symington that evening he too seemed disturbed.

FORTY-TWO

"WHAT is it?" Pru Griswolde asked. Although she was as well groomed as usual, wearing a frilly white blouse and a spring suit of primrose-yellow linen, her face was pale and there were blue shadows under her eyes. "I'm not supposed to be on the early schedule this week."

"My apologies for sending for you like this," Dr. Schumann said with an earnest smile. "But I need your help. The Institute needs your help. I want to request your cooperation."

"God! Haven't I been cooperating?" Pru said.

"Please sit down," Dr. Schumann said, indicating a chair near her desk. "I'm just going to order some coffee. Would you care for some?"

"O.K., thanks."

"Cigarette?" Dr. Schumann said, holding forth a silver box.

"Thank you."

Dr. Porter got to his feet and leaned forward with a lighter.

"Hey, what is this?" Pru asked. Her brief grin was skeptically lopsided. "I'm not used to being pampered around here."

"If we sometimes seem brusque, it's only for professional reasons," Dr. Schumann said.

"We've been watching you with interest," Dr. Porter said.

"Thanks a lot," Pru said. "For an encore I get to be burned at the stake."

Dr. Schumann frowned at Dr. Porter for silence.

"I'm appealing to you as someone of high intelligence and wide experience," Dr. Schumann said. "You combine some of the most valuable characteristics of both categories of subjects, both faculty volunteers and the professionals of the pilot group."

"Quick on the uptake," Pru said, "with the morals of an alley cat. That's me."

"You mustn't speak of yourself in those terms," Dr Schumann said. "After all, what are morals? Ethical systems are man's most subjective and arbitrary inventions."

"I may not know much about sin, but I know what I hate."

"You should have been a playwright," Dr. Porter said, beaming ingratiatingly.

"What do you know about plays?" Pru asked sharply. Dr. Porter's smile evaporated, leaving an expression of nervous hostility. "I've seen you around the Theater Workshop, but I didn't think it was for the plays."

"Really!" Dr. Porter protested, turning to Dr. Schumann for support.

"I don't think you should address my colleague in that manner," Dr. Schumann said, but her rebuke was perfunctory. "But let us proceed with our discussion. As it happens, we thought your background in the theater, and in acting, could be very helpful."

"It's a long way in the background," Pru said, but she looked faintly pleased.

"I'm sure you have real ability," Dr. Porter said, managing another smile, a weaker one.

Dr. Schumann noticed the glare that Pru gave him in return.

"Perhaps it would be better if I talked to Miss Griswolde alone," Dr. Schumann said. "If you'd excuse us, Dr. Porter."

Dr. Porter petulantly withdrew from the room.

"That Theater Workshop!" Pru said after the door had closed. "Cliquey old queens!"

"Acting still is a great interest of yours, isn't it?" Dr. Schumann asked pleasantly.

"It's a kind of disease," Pru said modestly. "I don't think anyone ever gets really cured. If you ever become interested in the theater, you're hooked for life."

"I have a very important part for you," Dr. Schumann said. "I can't overemphasize how much it means to us."

Pru sat up, brightening.

"Well, perhaps not a part exactly, not in the conventional sense. But it's quite a challenge. I'm prepared to pay you a substantial bonus. It'll mean some extra work."

"Never mind the money part of it," Pru said with eager impatience. "What is it? I didn't know you were interested in the theater."

"I want to make a convincingly naturalistic film to illustrate a paper I'm preparing," Dr. Schumann said. Pru looked puzzled. "I've selected you to perform in it. I want to take some very special, realistically underplayed film sequences of you and the robot."

Until then, the robot had been paired exclusively with faculty volunteers, and Pru had heard nothing about it, so it took several minutes of Dr. Schumann's eulogistic description of the robot and its function for Pru's disappointment to boil up into indignation and anger.

"Thanks a lot, Dr. Frankenstein!" Pru exclaimed. "I'll say it's a challenge!"

"Please don't take that emotional attitude," Dr. Schumann urged her. "This is a very carefully designed mechanism. There's no danger involved. It's all well insulated. There are sensitive fuses. Everyone's fully insured."

"There's a terrific danger that I might throw up though," Pru said. "I've been wanting to pull out of this deal since the very beginning. I'm ashamed I didn't. Blame my coming along on laziness or debt or curiosity or something. Somehow the squeaky-clean building fooled me – or helped me fool myself. And now a monster! That's it, Dr. Schumann. If anyone's going to get herself screwed by a monster around here, I'll tell you who ought to be number one."

Dr. Schumann's face was pale but outwardly absolutely calm. "We're trying to serve humanity," she said.

"Don't make me laugh," Pru said. "You're insane. I've served humanity better any Saturday night." Pru stood up, trembling with fury.

"Please, Miss Griswolde, there's no need to shout. Why don't you sit down and get hold of yourself? I don't see why you should object to performing with a scientifically designed automaton. You, of all people!"

Pru remained standing. "What do you mean by that?" she demanded.

"Your history of masturbation," Dr. Schumann gently reminded her. "It's no ordinary history. The penis surrogates that you have employed. That was one of the reasons we thought you would be so suitable. Dr. Porter said –"

"Screw Dr. Porter!" Pru cried. The strain of recent weeks was suddenly too much for her. "Screw Digby College! And screw you too!"

"That's quite enough!" Dr. Schumann said. "I think you had better return to your quarters." She pressed a button on her desk. "If you wish to apologize after you've gotten over this little outburst, you may telephone this office for an appointment tomorrow morning. For the sake of the program – we don't want any unpleasantness – I'm prepared to overlook your intemperate language. Otherwise, of course –"

"Shut up!" Pru shouted. "Don't you know how lousy this whole rotten setup is? Are you crazy?"

Dr. Schumann pressed the button again, sharply, several times in succession. "All right," she said. "You can go straight to the cashier." She raised her voice. "And don't worry about the Institute. The Institute will survive your departure. There are plenty of women in your line of work – better women than you – who will be grateful to take your place."

"There won't be," Pru retorted. "Not when I get through with the Institute."

"What can you do?" Dr. Schumann asked.

"There are laws in this country," Pru said.

"I suggest you go and study them," Dr. Schumann said, "If you think the College lawyers don't know what we're doing here, you must be even further out of touch than I imagined. Didn't you read your contract?"

"I don't care what it said."

"You'd better care. No – go to the police. It'd do you good. I'd like to hear how you make out – a common prostitute complaining to the police about immoral behavior at a medical institute."

"You wait, that's all!" Pru said.

"Too bad you're so unstable," Dr. Schumann said. "It'll make it so difficult for you to adjust when you get back to your customers. It'll be too late then to wish you hadn't messed up your chances at Digby."

There was a tap at the door.

"Come in!" Dr. Schumann said.

Camilla entered.

"There's such a thing as public opinion!" Pru said.

"Show this person out," Dr. Schumann said.

Pru left without being shown. Camilla hurried after her.

Watching Camilla's lovely back, Dr. Schumann snapped her fingers in a gesture of discovery and elation, and her face relaxed in a warm smile.

"Miss Fairbank!" she called. "Of course!" she said aloud

to herself. "Why not?" Why hadn't she thought of it sooner? Two young people in love would be far better than anything involving the robots. Far more natural, and absolutely no chance for a show of exhibition. The girl was certainly not sophisticated, but the fact that she so desperately was counting on a grant would overcome any reticence.

FORTY-THREE

THE office of *The Digby Intelligence & Advertiser*, founded 1887, paid circulation 1,972, "Personalized Job Printing A Speciality," was situated on Union Street, down at what most of the well-to-do local people called "the wrong end".

The walk across the campus and through the town did nothing to blunt Pru's anger. She had seen enough old movies on television to know, as though by instinct, what any public-spirited citizen must do when a heinous civic wrong, festering under cover. required the antiseptic cautery of communal indignation.

Pru pushed open the dusty glass door, causing a brass bell to jangle above her head. She found herself at the entrance of a long, narrow, drab office, to which her way was barred by a counter and a low swinging door. A gray-haired woman wearing rimless glasses and a maroon cardigan was sitting on a stool against the wall at one end of the counter, intently knitting another garment of some sort with more of the same maroon wool.

"You're much too late," she said, still looking down at her wooden needles. She looked up. "Unless you want to place an ad."

"No, I haven't come for that," Pru said. "I want to see the editor."

"Too late," the woman said dismissively. "Club notes were closed yesterday at five-thirty. How often do we have to tell you people?"

"I don't know what you're talking about," Pru said. "I have something most important to tell the editor. It's something he should know about."

"Do you have an appointment?" the woman asked.

Pru noticed a young man sitting at a typewriter. He had stopped typing to listen. He seemed to find the conversation entertaining. The other desks were empty but there was a rhythmic rumble of machinery from the rear of the building.

"No," Pru said. "But this is urgent. I'm sure he'd want

to know about this. It's a scandal that concerns the whole College, the whole town."

"You don't say?" the woman said. "What's it about?" She put down her knitting for a moment to blow her nose. Its contents sounded inexhaustibly copious, but she stopped and briskly wiped her nostrils. "We don't report divorce news until it comes out in court. You can get sued if you're not careful."

"Please let me see him," Pru said. "I must."

"Oh, you must, must you? Well, I'm Mrs. Robertson. You can tell me." She relented a little. "Mr. Robertson isn't in."

"Is Mr. Robertson the editor?" Pru asked.

"Yes," his wife said wearily. "He's the editor and publisher, advertising director, linotype operator and circulation manager. But he's also the chief reporter, and he's out on a story."

"I can wait," Pru said firmly. "When do you think he'll be back?"

"It depends on how lucky he is. He's playing poker dice next door."

"Thank you very much," Pru said.

"He won't be pleased to see you," Mrs. Robertson said.

The bar next door, an old-fashioned saloon that smelled of stale beer, extinguished cigars and hot cooking fat, was almost empty. The bartender, a fat man in a white apron, was standing behind the bar near the door, looking up at a quizz show and absent-mindedly wiping the bar with a wet rag. A small group of men in shapeless dark business suits were standing at the far end of the bar, drinking draught beer. One of them was shaking dice in a leather cup.

"Excuse me," Pru said to the bartender.

He sadly looked at her.

"Excuse me," she said.

"No unaccompanied ladies served at the bar," he said. "You can sit in a booth at the back. It's not my rule. I only work here."

"Please would you tell Mr. Robertson I have some very important information," Pru said. She looked at the group at the other end of the room. She half expected to see a man in shirt sleeves and a dark-green eyeshade, smoking a pipe. "His wife said I could find him here."

"Hey, Ace!" the bartender bawled. "Lady to see you!"

The men at the other end of the bar looked up from their game. One of them must have murmured a ribald comment, because a couple of the others laughed that distinctive laugh, a loud, hoarse guffaw, that often greets ribaldry in small-town bars, especially when a woman is present, preferably alone.

"Knock it off," one of the men said, and walked over to Pru. "Yeah?" he said. "I'm Mr. Robertson. What do you want?"

"I have a story for you," Pru said.

"We come out tomorrow. It's too late, unless it's good enough for the front page."

"It's about sex research at Digby," Pru said in a low voice. "I can't talk here. Some very strange things are going on in this town."

"O.K.," he said. "Let's go."

"To your office?" Pru asked.

"There's a private room at the back," he said. "No one will bother us there."

There were whistles and catcalls from the other drinkers as the editor guided Pru out into the street.

"Don't let them bother you," he said.

"It takes a lot more than that to bother me," Pru assured him.

"If there are any phone calls for me," Mr. Robertson told his wife, as he opened the low swinging door for Pru, "I'll take them in the back."

"Yes, Mr. Hearst," his wife said.

FORTY-FOUR

"I WONDER what she wants to talk to me about?" Camilla asked.

"Don't worry about it," Mary said. "You'd better get some sleep or you'll be a nervous wreck."

"How can I sleep? I know I've been taking too much time off – arriving at the lab a little late, leaving a little early. She must have noticed."

"Don't be silly, Camilla. You're probably the most conscientious person she has working for her. You're probably the most conscientious person in the whole of Digby. It's probably just some routine matter she wants to discuss. Anyway, why shouldn't you take some time off to see Richard? What matters more to you – him or the lab?"

"That's the sort of question that Richard keeps asking," Camilla said. "It's not a fair question. Nobody's forcing me to choose."

"I don't know about that," Mary said. "His patience can't last for ever."

"Oh, Mary! Can't you think of anything else but that?"

"Everything will be all right in the morning," Mary said. "You'll see Dr. Schumann and she'll give you the Nobel Prize."

"Oh, dear!" Camilla said. "If only I'd worked harder. What would I tell my mother if I flunked biology?"

"How could you flunk at this stage? Don't be insane."

"Not flunk maybe. But Dr. Schumann could refuse to recommend me for a fellowship. I wrote home to tell them I almost certainly wouldn't need any help from them next fall."

"Tell them you're getting married. They'd be delighted."

"Mary, why do you refuse to take me seriously?"

"Because you're such a square about school. A few years from now you'll wonder what you were making all the fuss about."

"You don't understand, Mary."

"I can tell time, though," Mary said. "It's late. There are some sleeping pills in the bathroom closet."

"What are you suggesting?" Camilla asked. "I'm not the sort of person who'd do a thing like that."

"I thought maybe you were the sort of person who'd take a pill and let me get to sleep."

"Oh."

FORTY-FIVE

"GOOD morning, Dr. Schumann," Camilla said.

"Yes, another beautiful, sunny morning!" Dr. Schumann said. "We at Digby sometimes forget our blessings, don't we? Sit down, Miss Fairbank. You look tired. Are you well? I hope you haven't been overdoing things."

Camilla sat down and nervously smiled. "Finals are so close," she said. "I'm sorry if you've missed me sometimes late in the afternoon. I've been studying a lot."

"You aren't unhappy at the Institute, are you?"

"Oh, no, Dr. Schumann!" Camilla exclaimed, aghast at the very idea. "Is anything wrong?"

"You have been with us long enough to know by now, deep down, whether you have a true sense of vocation for this sort of research."

"I've learned a whole lot since I joined," Camilla said.

"You seemed anxious at first, unsure of yourself. You are gaining confidence, aren't you?"

"Haven't my reports been all right?" Camilla asked.

"I would have let you know if they hadn't been. I'm talking about your over-all adjustment to this field of study. Do you feel in your heart that it's really worthwhile, this investigation?"

"Oh, I'm sure it is, Dr. Schumann. It's very basic, isn't it?"

"You don't feel any sense of loss, getting away from microbiology?"

"You aren't suggesting that I may have to leave the Institute, are you, Dr. Schumann?"

"Whether you stay on the Institute team depends largely on you yourself and on your degree of commitment," Dr. Schumann said.

"There *is* something wrong, isn't there?" Camilla said. "I knew there was. You're letting me down easily, aren't you? What is it? How am I failing? Please tell me."

"I didn't say you were *failing*," Dr. Schumann said. "Do you remember our first conversations?"

"Yes, of course. I even wrote down some of the things you said. In my diary."

"Then you do realize that it is an unusual privilege for a young undergraduate like yourself to be singled out for a job of such responsibility?"

"Yes, Dr. Schumann."

"You remember I told you that there was a very real chance of your achieving great academic distinction after only a short time as a member of the Institute staff."

"Yes, Dr. Schumann. I'm very appreciative of the fact. Truly."

"And you haven't forgotten what I said about the possibility of my using my influence to get you substantial financial aid as well as professional recognition and prestige, if we decided that you fitted in?"

Camilla gulped and nodded.

"Final exams and all that are not unimportant," Dr. Schumann conceded in a smooth, level voice, "but in these days of increasingly intensive competition, to be quite frank with you, Miss Fairbank, exam results are less important than personal recommendations from the right people. Honors, appointments, promotions – these often go to outstanding scholars, certainly, but most often to scholars considered to possess outstanding *potential*. And how can that be measured? How can it even be detected? Not by averaging grades alone, Miss Fairbank, you may be sure. I wonder if I am beginning to make my meaning clear to you?"

"I think so," Camilla said.

"I think so, too," Dr. Schumann said. "I think we understand each other. You want to graduate *summa cum laude*. You want an important graduate appointment. You deserve these prizes. You've worked for them. I merely want to help to put them within your grasp. How does that sound?"

"Well, gosh, Dr. Schumann, you know, just *wonderful*, of course," Camilla said. "I'm very grateful to you."

Dr. Schumann smiled and held up a cautionary, silencing hand. "Just a minute," she said. "I haven't quite finished. There's one thing I want you to do for the Institute."

"Sure!" Camilla assured her. "Anything!"

"You're engaged, aren't you, Miss Fairbank?"

271

"To be married?"

"Yes, I meant to be married."

"Yes, I am," Camilla said. She was flustered. "That is to say, no – not officially, formally, actually *engaged*."

"But the young man I've seen you with. You and he have some sort of *understanding*, I suppose?"

"Well, yes. We're *kind* of engaged. We're almost engaged. But we're planning to wait. Our relationship needn't interfere with my academic program. I've explained to him how important that is."

"Very wise of you, Miss Fairbank. Now what I want you to do is really quite simple. You're already well aware of how discreet we are at the Institute. I trust you, and you can surely trust us."

"Of course, Dr. Schumann."

"Good. As you know, our lab samples, the two groups of subjects, have been small. We had to start somewhere, didn't we? We've been under a certain amount of pressure to get quick results, in order to get the Institute established. Perhaps our cross section hasn't been quite wide enough. Perhaps our controls require some sort of modification. We don't claim to be perfect. Research techniques take time to develop. I'm sure everything will work out satisfactorily in the end. But the trouble is, Miss Fairbank, we don't have much time. The A.M.A. convention isn't very far away, and it's essential for administrative reasons that we should be strongly represented there. I am preparing a paper that I believe we will all be able to take pride in."

Dr. Schumann paused and shrewdly scrutinized Camilla's face for signs.

"But what can I do?" Camilla asked.

"Ah, what can you do? We need some really good film of normal, unself-conscious, heterosexual intercourse. Where, I asked myself, could we produce the sexual services of a normal couple, an intelligent and photogenic pair, of whom the female would be susceptible to scientific discipline, and the male wouldn't even be aware that certain scientific observations were being made? And then – eureka! – I got it! The next evening you and your young man plan to make love, you simply inveigle him into doing so in the lab!"

"Dr. Schumann! What are you saying? What a proposal!"

"I know you would do it, Miss Fairbank. I have complete faith in you! No histrionics. No hysteria. Nothing complicated. A simple, straightforward demonstration of our methods."

"Dr. Schumann, how could I? It's out of the question!"

Dr. Schumann seemed taken aback. "Why not?" she asked. "What's the matter with that? It's the answer to our problem."

"Richard and I in the lab?" Camilla said. "I couldn't do that! It's impossible!"

"What do you mean 'impossible'?"

"Well, for one thing ..." Camilla hesitated, blushing.

"For one thing what?" Dr. Schumann was beginning to look vexed.

"I'm a virgin," Camilla said.

"A *virgin*? I don't believe it. You can't be."

"I am," Camilla said.

"There's nothing ... physically *wrong* with you, is there?" Dr. Schumann said.

"No," Camilla said.

"A virgin!" Dr. Schumann exclaimed, brightening again. "Why, Miss Fairbank! What a fantastic stroke of good fortune!"

"It is?" Camilla said, her eyebrows raised in perplexity.

"Of course!" Dr. Schumann said. "Don't you see? Think of it! the actual defloration of a virgin! What a splendid coup for the Institute! What a first! I do most heartily congratulate you, Miss Fairbank! You're a very fortunate young lady – *summa cum laude*, without a shadow of a doubt!"

"And if I decline?" Camilla asked.

Dr. Schumann walked around her desk and patted Camilla reassuringly on the shoulder. "You won't decline," Dr. Schumann said. "You can't. There's too much at stake. What's wrong with making love with the man you're going to marry – especially if doing so means saving a very promising academic career? You may be a virgin, due to some atavistic superstitious dread, Miss Fairbank, but remember: first and foremost, you are a scientist! Think as

273

a scientist, Miss Fairbank! Think rationally! Weigh the pros and cons!"

"It's very difficult," Camilla said. She looked down at her hands in her lap.

Dr. Schumann smiled. "No, Miss Fairbank. Not if you really love him. If you love him, Miss Fairbank, it's very easy."

"But what if someone should recognize me?"

"Oh, have no fear of that, my dear. The film would never be shown here on campus. Only at the A.M.A. convention in Atlantic City, so it's highly unlikely, isn't it? I'll destroy it after that one showing, if you wish, so you see your fears are really quite unfounded. And since I can sympathize with your feelings, I have another suggestion. I'll even arrange to have the camera start automatically, activated by the turning-off of the switch that controls the overhead lights. Why I won't even know what night you are going to nip into the lab! No one will be there, you see, the two of you will be completely alone. And I know how important that is, believe me."

Camilla agitatedly bit her lip.

"And think of your parents," Dr. Schumann said. "They expected so much of you. You wouldn't want to disappoint them, would you? I mean about the grant. I understand they aren't too well off."

FORTY-SIX

PRU GRISWOLDE told Ace Robertson plenty. As they sat in his small, private office, with the door locked, chain-smoking cigarettes, she described the personnel, policies and activities of the Institute in minute, malicious detail, as he avidly scribbled notes, pausing only to make comments such as, "That's the most disgusting thing I've ever heard!" and "They ought to be strung up!" or to ask questions such as, "What did they do then?" and "Can you beat that?"

When he had a notebookful, he put down his ball-point pen and leaned back in his editorial swivel chair and thoughtfully rubbed his nose.

"In all my years as editor of this paper," he said, "what you have just told me is without doubt the most sensational, the most shocking exposé it has been my privilege to take the lid off of. Miss Griswolde, the people who care about Digby will be grateful to you. To think this state of affairs has existed in the very heart of the college all this time, and I hadn't even heard a thing about it." He looked at his watch. "Is this scientific orgy still in progress right now?" he asked. "It's not that I don't trust you, Miss Griswolde, but you understand, a newspaperman has to be sure of his facts – check and double check. Especially in the case of a situation like this, in which the impairment of the morals of the young may be involved. I can't take any risks."

"They'll be at the lab for hours yet," Pru said. "Sometimes they hang around there till far into the evening. There's almost always something nasty going on."

"You don't say?" he said. "That's terrible. So O.K., fine, thank you, Miss Griswolde. I'm very grateful to you. It was very courageous of you to come over to the *Intelligencer* and we really appreciate it. Now it's time for me to hit the old typewriter – and I can tell you this is going to be the roughest, hardest-hitting item that ever hit the streets of this town. The whole front page – how's that? O.K.? How will that be, Miss Griswolde? And we can just make it by press time. I'll run over to the Institute now with a copy. Anything your Dr. Schumann has to say will be rich."

"I'd like to see her face," Pru said. "And she's not my Dr. Schumann."

"Right," he said, getting up and showing her the way out. "You just leave it with me then."

"When will the article appear?" she asked.

"First thing tomorrow," he said. "I'll run off an extra batch. Everyone in Digby will want to buy one."

"Richard?" Camilla asked on the telephone.

"Camilla! Where are you?"

"At work."

"Oh."

"I thought maybe . . ."

"What?"

"I wondered if this evening . . . whether you were doing anything?"

"Yes, I have big plans," Richard said. "I was going to sit here and read a book. Don't tell me they're breaking down and letting you have a whole evening off?"

"I can get off in about half an hour."

"I'll be over there in twenty-nine minutes."

"No," Camilla said. "I want this to be a specially nice evening. I'd like to go back to the dorm and change into something a little different. Could you pick me up there?"

"Where would you like to go?" Richard asked. "Would you like to drive over to Cincinnati or somewhere?"

"What I'd really like is a quiet, early dinner at the Digby Inn," Camilla said, speaking more rapidly than usual, rather breathlessly. "If you'd pick me up at about six-thirty. Maybe we could have a couple of cocktails, could we?"

Richard ironically whistled.

"Why not?" he said.

"Dwight Robertson, of the *Intelligencer*," he told the secretary in Dr. Schumann's outer office. He held up a sheaf of yellow copy paper. "I have an article here I have to check out with Dr. Schumann." The secretary looked doubtful. "You'd better tell her it's urgent."

"I know Dr. Schumann doesn't wish to be disturbed," the secretary said, unwittingly indicating her employer's whereabouts by looking at one of the inner doors. A red light was shining above it. "She's in the projection room, briefing a member of the Board of Trustees. Is there any information I could help you with? Or would you care to make an appointment for the morning?"

"You're a doll," Robertson said, "but right now you're not the person I want." He saluted, bringing the sheaf of papers against the brim of his corduroy porkpie hat, grinned, and opened the forbidden door. The secretary stood up, holding out a supplicatory hand, but the editor was already inside.

On the screen, in ripe-peach flesh colors, like an animated Ingres houri performing a horizontal belly-dance, Marcia Daventry was having a bit of a go with Lawrence Da Silva. Robertson, whose wife opened the saline pulp of her charms to him twice monthly with all the abandon of a Chincoteague oyster, stared open-mouthed at the human cornucopia.

"Nora?" Dr. Schumann's voice crossly demanded. "What is it? Is that you? Who is it? Turn on the lights!" The bounding curves of the two-backed beast were paled by sudden fluorescent brightness.

"Who are you?" Dr. Schumann demanded. "What do you mean by bursting in here like this? Didn't you see the red light was on? I must ask you to leave immediately."

"The red-light Institute!" Robertson said. "I like that! Digby's shame!" Mockingly he harangued her in headlines of scandalous revelation. "Digby's secret sex-school! Now I've seen it with my own eyes."

"Get out of here!" Dr. Schumann said. "Who let you in? Who do you think you are?"

"I think I'm the editor and publisher of *The Digby Intelligencer,* that's who," Robertson said triumphantly. "The paper that has kept Digby safe for decent citizens since 1887. You must be Dr. Schumann. Well, lady, I'm going to bust this little smut factory of yours wide open – blast it off the face of the campus. What do you have to say about that?"

"I –"

"Wait a minute," Turner Symington said, laying a cau-
277

tionary hand against Dr. Schumann's arm. "*The Digby Intelligencer* is a very fine newspaper. It's highly spoken of state-wide." Dr. Schumann stirred restlessly and began to make a grumbling sound, but Symington again silenced her with a touch of the hand. "There's no fundamental conflict of interests here that I can see."

Robertson already looked considerably mollified, but wary. He didn't want to relinquish his apparent tactical ascendancy. "The Institute must be able to explain the arrival of Alex Philopoulos and companion," he said with a knowing leer.

"Who?" Symington asked.

"Alex Philopoulos, the millionaire and international playboy. They checked into the Inn today. Dr. Schumann isn't going to try to tell me that's just a coincidence, are you, Dr. Schumann? What brings the jet set to Digby? The daffodils?"

Symington chuckled at the witticism. "Mr. Philopoulos is in town, is he?" he said urbanely. "Well, Dr. Schumann, it looks as though we'll have to take Mr. . . . ."

"Mr. Robertson. Dwight Robertson."

"Of course – someone was mentioning your name at the National Press Club only the other day. Mr. Robertson –"

"They were?"

"You mustn't be too modest, Mr. Robertson! You and your crusades! The thing we must keep in the forefront of our minds, Mr. Robertson, Dr. Schumann, is that all of us are working to serve one purpose – to build a greater Digby. Isn't that correct, Mr. Robertson?"

"Well, sure. But how can this Institute you have here –"

"Dr. Schumann," Symington said. "Let us save time and put our cards on the table. I like the look of Robertson here. I think he's the sort of man of vision who would appreciate what we're trying to do at the Institute. Why don't you leave us to talk things over, confidentially, man to man? I could explain the whole setup, our goals, our ways of doing things. I could explain the program to Mr. Robertson, show him some of our laboratory data, perhaps screen a couple of films. Would that be of value to you, Mr. Robertson, just for background?"

"Is that wise?" Dr. Schumann asked.

"The press always finds out in the end," Symington said. "Doesn't it. Mr. Robertson?"

Robertson smirked.

"That's why we must cooperate, to make it possible for Mr. Robertson to help Digby by giving the community the facts about the Institute – the truth, the whole truth, and nothing but the truth. Right, Mr. Robertson?"

"Yeah, I'd understand a lot better if you'd ... present some of the Institute's findings."

"All right," Dr. Schumann said. "You know best, Mr. Symington."

"Please tell the projectionist to run a selection of the Daventry series," Symington said.

Robertson settled back in a comfortable chair and took off his hat and placed it on his lap.

Dr. Schumann left the room.

"Have a drink," Symington said. "There's some bourbon in that cupboard over there. I'll join you. Good. Now I'm not going to talk for a while. We'll let the pictures tell their own story. A man of the world like you doesn't need anything spelled out." Symington raised his glass in a silent toast. "O.K.!" he shouted to the projectionist. "Go ahead as soon as you're ready!"

Robertson took a long sip and stared at the screen. The overhead lights went out and the demonstration began.

When it came to an end, a considerable time later, and the lights went on again, Robertson was very quiet.

"Of course," Symington pointed out gently, "if you were willing to serve science, you, too, might volunteer for future tests. Quite anonymously, you understand." Symington gave Robertson a moment or two to contemplate that possibility, and then added genially, "Now, tell me about this article you're planning to publish. Perhaps I could help you get the approach right, eh? There's a lot at stake here, you know. The college. The economic betterment of the town. Buckeye Pharmaceutical is backing this, you know. Big company, one of the biggest. I don't doubt they'd be grateful for the P.R. Wonderful business, public relations. Ever thought of going into it, Robertson? I'm sure I could help you get started."

Robertson looked at his watch and sat abruptly upright with a startled look on his face. "Hell!" he said. "Is there a phone I can use? It's late. It's already edition time. Where's a telephone?"

He called his office. It was already too late. The presses were running, the first bundles of papers had already left the shop.

FORTY-SEVEN

"MR. PHILOPOULOS says to have the limousine over here at three o'clock," the desk clerk said.

"They're not checking out, are they?" the elderly bell-boy asked, his face tense with anxiety. Never before in the Digby Inn's long history had there been such a guest, so demanding yet so prodigally generous, quite demoralizingly generous, with tips. From the moment that the entire male staff, all six of them, had struggled, admiringly grumbling, under the gross splendor of the monogrammed white-leather trunks, valises, hat-boxes and golf bag, it had been apparent that this one and the young lady with him were special. The manageress, a Mrs. Deborah Krebb, ordinarily noted for her aloofness and inflexibility, had been moved somehow, after a brief, murmurous conference with Mr. Philopoulos at the front desk, to adjust her schedule of reservations to provide him with a double room for the young lady and the coveted Taft Suite, whose curtains were made of dark-red velvet, instead of flowered chintz. She herself had led the way upstairs and had personally supervised the unprecedented, heretical rearrangement of furniture to satisfy Mr. Philopoulos's exacting requirements.

Much to the disappointment of the waitresses, who had been curious as well as hopeful, the new arrivals never appeared in the hotel dining room, preferring to take all their meals in regal seclusion in their private chambers. And what meals! After the first and only catastrophe, which occurred when room service made the grievous error of taking up the regular table d'hote dish of the day, luke-warm, Mr. Philopoulos made a telephone call to one of his representatives in New York. A distinguished French restaurant there was prevailed upon, for an undisclosed sum, to give its chef a temporary leave of absence, and, having taken the next plane, he soon demonstrated that it was possible to perform culinary wonders with the simple but wholesome local materials. An urgently summoned taxi rushed a shipment of respectable wines from Cleveland to reinforce the Inn's cellar, which that month was featuring Chilean Riesling, New York State Chianti, and a liqueur reminiscent of cherry brandy, but sweeter, that was believed to originate in the back room of an avant-garde pharmacy right there in Digby. A kitchen that had produced nothing interesting since its establishment, except squirrel stew and pickled pigs' feet at the turn of the century, now created a succession of meals that were sumptuous and exquisite.

"That Mr. Philopoulos knows what he wants!" was the way one of the assistant cooks put it. "You should see the bill he's run up just for *cream*!"

"I don't know," an associate shrewdly replied, the dishwasher, who was repeatedly surprised by the plates that came downstairs again. "There's a whole lot of *pickin'* goin' on up there."

The fact of the matter was that Alexander Philopoulos was increasingly unsure that he knew what he wanted. He thought he knew; he was being offered the best that money could buy; and yet, when he actually confronted it, his appetite kept proving curiously, tediously elusive.

"If you'd only relax and take it easy like I told you," Joanna said, with the set, sweet, stoic smile of a tired angel, as she kneeled on the bed, where she had been trying, for hours on end, simultaneously to soothe and inspire him. Unaccustomed to failures in other areas, Philopoulos gritted his strong teeth. He was not so much chagrined as impatient, and becoming increasingly irritated. It seemed wrong that a man of power should be thwarted by a few inches of obstinately rubbery flesh. That it was his own made the insubordination no less inexcusable.

"Ain't that a shame?" said the dishwasher, examining the latest tray.

"Didn't hardly touch the lobster mousse," said the assistant cook. "D'you know that took two whole lobsters? You want to know what they cost, just the lobsters alone flown in from Maine like they was?"

"They say he has millions he hasn't even counted yet."

"What's the use if he can't eat right?" the assistant cook asked piously.

"I read a magazine once where he took over a whole resort hotel, over in Switzerland, with a skating rink and everything, for a private party. People jetted in from all over the world just for the weekend, and he picked up the tab. Everyone had to go to the party as some kind of devil, the worst they could think of. They all had to wear masks, black or red. There were plenty of topless dresses. Can you imagine?"

"But if he can't eat," the cook stubbornly insisted. "If he hasn't got his health . . ."

"He sure *looks* healthy," the dishwasher said. "You could buy a lot of Alka-Seltzer with his kind of money."

"O.K.," Philopoulos said, recumbent in the rumpled linen of the historic four-poster bed in which the late Senator Taft had once slept. "Forget it."

"Alex, darling," Joanna said, pouting with feigned petulance, resting a flushed cheek on the matted whorls of black hair, looking up at him with big, hurt, devoted eyes. "Don't be mad at me. It's only because you're tired. It takes a few days to get used to the time difference."

"I'm not mad at you," he said irritably. He raised himself up onto one elbow, beginning to sit up. Joanna tried to restrain him, but gently, firmly, he pushed her white hand away from his dark olive torso. "I have an appointment. Remember?"

"That's not till this afternoon," Joanna protested.

"What do you think it is now?"

In that curtained room, for her there was no time.

"It's two thirty-five," Philopoulos said, looking at the gold wrist watch on his bedside table.

"No kidding!" Joanna said brightly.

" 'No kidding,' as you say," he solemnly assured her. "I never kid."

"But you said the appointment's for three o'clock," Joanna said, suddenly looking dismayed. "How can I get ready in time? My face! I'll have to use pancake. You're so scratchy! I don't want to meet those people looking just any-old-how."

"Your face is beautiful," he said with sincere gallantry. "But you don't have to worry. You stay here. Go get a hairdo. Telephone, if you like; they'll send someone. I'll go alone and see you later. You can make sure everything's all ready for the party. Your mother should have a very nice party. It's for your sake, Joanna. She is a very charming lady, your mother."

"You're a sweetie-pie," Joanna said gratefully, snuggling into the pillows he had just left.

"A sweetie-pie!" he exclaimed silently with raised eyebrows to the bathroom mirror on the way to the shower.

Punctually the limousine arrived at the front door of the Inn; ten minutes later, Alexander Pericles Philopoulos, at ease wearing the comfortable authority of a well-tailored suit with an alligatorskin-covered checkbook and a slender solid-gold fountain pen in the inside pocket, left for the Digby Institute.

Sweetie-pie! he thought. His smile was urbanely tolerant, but he was shaking his head. "Sweetie-pie!" he said aloud. The chauffeur turned his head.

"Excuse me, sir," he said. "I didn't get that."

"We're late," Philopoulos said.

"Yes, sir," the chauffeur said, discreetly but noticeably stepping on the gas.

Dr. Schumann was in her office. She was wearing a vivid green-chartreuse silk suit that ennobled the gold-glinting bronze of her hair. She looked handsome as she resolutely stood up and offered her hand, but her face was pitifully pale.

"Mr. Philopoulos!" she said, managing a genial, proprietary smile. "We're so grateful that you have been able to find the time to visit our Institute."

"Not at all, Dr. Schumann," he said, courteously bowing his head in recognition of her professional status. "It is I, Alexander Philopoulos, who am grateful. Since I arrived this week, I have seen once more my good friend Mr. Symington. We have had many good talks. He has told me of the excellent promises of your investigation."

"Mr. Symington is a loyal enthusiast," Dr. Schumann said modestly.

"He said you are a great pioneer in your field. He said that he himself is merely a layman. That is why he wanted that I should present myself to you. Tell me, Dr. Schumann. I wish you to explain exactly what it is, your field? Mr. Symington talks very fast, and sometimes his language is very technical."

"There are many pioneers," Dr. Schumann said, reverently clasping her hands together. "We are doing what we can. The task is immense – sometimes it seems almost overwhelming. We are only human. We have our ups and downs. Even in work of this kind, unfortunately, scholars must continually justify themselves. There are difficulties, as you may be able to imagine. Digby College, though highly respected in the academic world, is a college of limited resources. There are many conflicting demands, even jealousies."

Philopoulos was familiar with this sort of preamble. He brushed it aside.

"Money is no problem," he said curtly. "We can deal with that kind of thing. I wish you to tell me about your discoveries. Please, in a few words, tell me what you have learned. I am interested particularly, you understand, in geriatrics, the sexual effects of aging in the case of the male, though not for myself, of course. You see, I have this friend, this dear friend. He has been like a father to me."

Dr. Schumann was unable to answer Mr. Philopoulos in a few words; she did so in many thousands, deferentially, carefully, frankly, and, eventually, encouragingly, starting in general terms, sketching out the broad historical outlines of sexology, and proceeding to describe the purposes and methods of the Institute, its successes, its obstacles, and its prospects, especially the probability, given the proper support, that its investigations in the immediate future might in practical, substantial ways alleviate the anxieties of men of great natural vigor and aesthetic sensibility who, due to no fault of their own, were experiencing a temporary and quite unnecessary sexual block. . . .

Mr. Philopoulos listened with interest. He suspected that some of his most confidential intimations to Mr. Symington had been passed on; but Dr. Schumann alluded to them with such impersonal delicacy and drew from them such warmly reassuring inferences that Mr. Philopoulos easily overcame a momentary feeling of betrayal and injured pride. After all, here was a doctor of medicine dealing with matters of clinical fact. He willingly undertook the leap of faith into the bosom of the new orthodoxy.

"It has already been clearly established," Dr. Schumann

285

was saying, "here and by others, that while there's life there's sex. Life and sex are inseparably coexistent, sex without end, sex evermore. Life *is* sex, and sex is life. There is no age too old for sex. There have been cases of men over one hundred years of age achieving multiple orgasm day after day, under observation. I have read the medical affidavits. We have to trust the Russians on *some* matters, Mr. Philopoulos. There is an international exchange of sexual information that transcends political rivalry."

"Men don't suddenly wear out?" Mr. Philopoulos asked, nudging her back to relevancy.

"Of course not," Dr. Schumann said, with the good-natured chuckle that had put so many of the Institute's employees and volunteers at their ease.

"If the world's greatest specialists examine a man thoroughly, and find nothing wrong with his body, but still he cannot – he feels unable – he is with a very beautiful young woman – and yet...." Mr. Philopoulos eloquently jutted forward his lower lip, turned down the corners of his mouth, hunched his shoulders and spread out his hands.

"In such a hypothetical case," Dr. Schumann said, "the friend of whom you speak is undoubtedly suffering from some sort of psychological handicap – some little thing that, once analyzed by an expert, could easily be overcome."

"How?" Mr. Philopoulos asked, in that sharply incisive manner that on more than one occasion had caused international financiers to quail. Dr. Schumann was not at all abashed. To the contrary, her heart leaped with hope.

"A false relationship, for example. Faulty sexual selection perhaps. There are some men in the prime of their later years who feel that they may be rejuvenated by consorting sexually with a number of women increasingly their junior. Very often, however, the extreme age difference may have quite the opposite effect. The contemplation of a very young woman, no matter how beautiful, may easily have a definitely depressing effect."

"Is that so?" Mr. Philopoulos said.

"Of course, sexual compatability at all ages is really our ultimate goal," Dr. Schumann said. "What that hypothetical friend of yours must do is to try to determine what sort of woman really attracts him, not what sort of woman he feels it is fashionable to display in public. But I am talking far too long. Look at the time! I expect you must want to be getting back to the Inn."

"I have time," Mr. Philopoulos said. "This has been a very interesting chat. There are many aspects of the Institute's work I would like to discuss further. It's possible – I do not promise, but it is *possible* – that I may be able to give you some help over and above the grant from Buckeye Pharmaceutical. Now, where is your Mr. Symington? He said he would be here this afternoon to show me some motion pictures."

"I don't know what arrangements Mr. Symington has made." Dr. Schumann replied demurely. "But I'm sure that if that is what he said he must be waiting for you in the projection theater. I'll show you the way."

As they reached the door of the theater, Dr. Schumann once more formally extended her hand and smiled her most queenly smile.

"How about I come back tomorrow morning?" Mr. Philopoulos suggested. "Early. Ten o'clock. We can have another talk."

"That would be delightful," Dr. Schumann said. "I look forward to seeing you then."

Mr. Symington showed Mr. Philopoulos many, many films of the Institute at work. Mr. Philopoulos was pleased to experience the almost forgotten glow of effortless spontaneous excitement. The mature amplitude and warmly boisterous eroticism of one subject more than any of the others aroused in him a blissful pang of desire akin to pain. He was sure he recognized her face.

"Who is that?" he asked, indicating the pink-and-white Renoir plumpness gyrating happily under the floodlights.

"Ah," said Mr. Symington, "one of the Institute's most adaptable subjects." And he uttered the name.

"Are you one-hundred-per-cent sure?" Mr. Philopoulos asked, hardly daring to believe his good fortune.

"Sure I'm sure," Mr. Symington answered casually. "Who would know better than I? Now take a look at this next series. You may think you know all there is to know about this kind of man, but, believe me –"

"No, that's all," Mr. Philopoulos said. "That's enough."

"Whatever you say," Mr. Symington said. "There's nothing wrong, is there? Nothing I said?"

"No, nothing is wrong," Mr. Philopoulos said. "But why should I be interested? You think, perhaps, because my countrymen, thousands of years ago, were given to pederasty, that I too am interested in the buggering of young boys? No, I have a party this evening – only a little family dinner, really. I have stayed too long as it is. I must hurry back to get ready to greet my guests."

"We'll be seeing you tomorrow though, won't we?" Mr. Symington asked, humbly. Why were all minorities so touchy?

"Of course," Mr. Philopoulos assured him. "Don't worry. You have nothing to worry about. I wish again to see Dr. Schumann. She is very wise, Dr. Schumann."

"You can say that again," Mr. Symington said.

Mr. Philopoulos's evening of entertaining was a great success.

FORTY-EIGHT

CAMILLA'S plain, high-necked Thai-silk dress was the same lovely blue as her eyes, ultramarine, lapis lazuli, with an unfathomable depth of dark turquoise, shimmering and subtly changing in the candle-light. Uncharacteristically, she was wearing her light-yellow hair upswept, making her neck seem longer, slenderer and more girlishly fragile than ever. Her ears were neat and white, with a single simulated pearl attached to each lobe. Her eyebrows and eyelashes were more clearly defined than usual; her eyes seemed very large. There was a long line of small, yellow mother-of-pearl buttons down the side of her dress, from neck to hem. The smallness, whiteness and numerousness of the buttons looked innocent, and yet, as her body softly moved inside the thin silk, they seemed less like a prohibition than a discreet instruction: to remove, tear along dotted line. Richard sighed, as he guided her, his hand lightly touching the small of her back, to their corner table, where he was aware of an unfamiliar, heady perfume.

The inevitable late-middle-aged waitress brought them menus. By now, because she was part of the Inn, where they had spent so many pleasant though inconclusive evenings, they quite liked her; her spinsterish asperity had become amusingly quaint.

"Isn't it a beautiful evening?" Richard asked, knowing that she disapproved of all enjoyable natural phenomena, and knowing that calling attention to them was unkind, yet being unable to resist doing so.

"I wouldn't know," the waitress said, putting down the outsize cards of fare.

Camilla smiled at the success of the minor ritual of their private joke, the usual opening gambit that elicited the waitress's usual sour response.

"It really is beautiful," Camilla confirmed. "It was seventy on the six o'clock news. The stars are huge! It's like Hawaii."

Richard smiled admiringly at the last touch, mentioning Hawaii.

"Myself, I was never west of Chicago," the waitress said disdainfully, suggesting that everything west of that city was as frivolous as weather observation. "Would you mind ordering?" the waitress said. "We've got two girls out sick. There's no lobster."

The game was not one that could be savored long. They ordered.

"She's funny, but she's a sad case that woman, isn't she?" Camilla said, when the waitress was safely in the kitchen. Camilla raised the sugary cold rim of her pink Bacardi cocktail against her pink, full lower lip, and for a moment Richard just stared.

"Not too pathetic," Richard said. "She's quite pleased with herself. Her authority. The busboys are scared to death of her."

"I think she's very sad," Camilla said. "The thought of her life. The loneliness. The waste."

"Waste?" Richard said. He smiled sardonically. "But she has her career, hasn't she?"

"O.K. – touché," Camilla said.

"I wouldn't want to end up alone and embittered," Camilla said.

Richard laughed. "You won't," he said.

"I'm serious," she said.

"So am I."

"But you think I overemphasize the importance of my academic program, don't you? I mean, you used to keep saying so."

"I used to," he agreed. "From my point of view, I was undoubtedly right. But perhaps I was being selfish."

"I don't think you're selfish," Camilla said. "I think you're very patient."

"I'm doing my best," he said. He smiled and drank some more of his cocktail.

"I wish you'd try to look at the situation objectively," Camilla said. "Really objectively. It isn't easy. It's getting more and more difficult for me. But *objectively*, Richard, do you think it's right for me to sacrifice certain personal things I value – would it be right for me to sacrifice something I think matters a great *deal* personally if I thought it was a means to an end? If it could lead to success at Digby?"

Richard sipped thoughtfully and tried to appraise the expression in her eyes. It was inscrutable. For once, he couldn't be at all sure what she wished his answer to be; and yet for once he very much wanted to give her the answer she felt was right; he wanted to reassure her, because he was now sure that he did love her. He had come to see things her way.

"Well," he said, and paused. But she offered no clue.

"What do you really think?" Camilla asked.

"I think you must do what you honestly believe you should do," he said. "I think that in this instance, Digby matters to you so much that you mustn't allow anything else to get in the way. Digby first. Get that taken care of, and then we'll be able to carry on from there. I can wait. I know that now."

"You do really mean that, don't you?" Camilla said.

"Yes. Now you look almost ... disappointed. What's wrong?"

Camilla smiled, and her eyes filled with tears.

"You're too nice," she said. "I don't deserve anyone as nice as you. Please, can I have another cocktail?"

"Yes, of course," Richard said. "And I assure you I'm not being noble. I want you to be happy. I don't want you to look back and wish you hadn't gone through with your work here." He asked the waitress for two more Bacardis.

"I love you," Camilla said. She said it almost as if in anguish.

"I love you too," Richard said cheerfully. He held her hand on the table top until the waitress returned.

The conversation was casual during dinner. They discussed the people at nearby tables and comedians and travel aboard and whether God was dead and fried chicken compared with grilled. While they stirred their coffee to cool it there was a silence. Then Camilla suddenly said:

"Do you still want to sleep with me?"

"What's the point of asking? Don't you know?"

"I want to know. If I'd changed my mind about it, would you still want me to ..."

"To 'give yourself to me' – isn't that the way it used to be said?"

"I don't blame you for being sarcastic," Camilla said.

"But please answer the question."

"Look," Richard said. "I've enjoyed dinner very much. I always enjoy being with you. You know that. I love you. Of course I want you – that's part of loving you. But I've accepted your explanation of how it must be. I don't necessarily agree with you. I don't regard sex before marriage and sex in marriage as questions of absolute right or wrong. But if waiting's very important to you, a test of love, all right, dammit, it isn't easy, but I'll wait. But for God's sake let's just leave it at that, can't we? Let's not go on and on about it."

"Please don't get angry with me, Richard. I can't bear it."

"I'm not angry with you, Camilla –"

"But what if I really had changed my mind?"

"Don't be silly. You haven't. So forget it. Do you want some more coffee?"

"Richard. Let me tell you something. I've been thinking about all the things you've said – you know, how anything's all right, as long as two people really sincerely love each other, as long as the physical thing isn't completely indiscriminate, mechanical, meaningless."

Richard looked at her, but said nothing.

"I know I'm not very clever," Camilla said. Richard began to protest, but she silenced him. "No, wait. I know I'm not. I'm not *un*intelligent. I work hard. I came to Digby with a ready-made moral code, a ready-made set of morals, and I thought that took care of that. I *have* learned a lot, Richard. I really have. I mean, it's on record, in black and white, on a file card in the registrar's office, isn't it?"

"Now who's being sarcastic?"

"But since I met you I've learned a lot of other things. You've broadened my outlook. Maybe, with the right person ... I mean, if we went to bed together before we got married, if we are going to get married, if you don't get tired of me, if you weren't disappointed, it couldn't do any *harm,* could it?"

"I couldn't ever get tired of you, Camilla. You're honest, and sensitive, and funny, and very, very beautiful. But please don't change for my sake. It's very sweet of you, Camilla. I'm very grateful. I mean it. A few weeks ago, if you'd started to show any signs of weakening, I'd have hustled you into the nearest bed, I admit. But somehow now I feel different. I'd rather not do something that you really don't want to do, something that you'd be doing only for my sake. Can't you understand that?"

"Oh, Richard!" Camilla said. "You do love me, don't you?"

"I thought I'd made that clear."

"It seems as though our roles have somehow suddenly been reversed."

"I don't think so."

"How can I convince you?" Camilla asked. "I've thought it all out. You were right, and I was wrong. I wasn't being logical. I was only repeating my mother's lessons – and I suppose she was only repeating hers. We have to think for ourselves, don't we? That's what you always say."

"I've changed my mind," Richard said. "I'm not going to let you change yours. There's no consistency in that. This has nothing to do with logic. It's a simple matter of emotion. You have just offered to make a sacrifice for my sake. I'm too selfish to let you. I'm going to make one for yours. I insist, though it's kind of hilarious when you come to think about it."

"You're being stubborn," Camilla said. "Or else you're trying to let me down gently. I kept putting you off so long you're not interested any more."

"I'm interested, Camilla. Don't worry about that. But old Granite Face obviously wants us to get out of here."

"I'll go and get my coat," Camilla said decisively. "See you at the front door."

Richard paid the bill and the waitress surprised him by smiling. "You're a very lucky young man," she said.

"I know."

"She's a very lovely person," the waitress said.

"Yes," Richard replied. "Thank you."

"Have you fixed the day?"

Richard looked embarrassed.

"Don't let her get away," the waitress said, and left before he could think of any suitable response. He felt slightly ashamed of the things Camilla and he had said about her.

He waited in the pine-paneled foyer, looking at the hunting prints, for what seemed a long time.

"Here I am," Camilla said brightly.

"Are you all right?" Richard asked.

"Quite all right. Ready for anything."

"I thought perhaps — I always feel a bit queasy just looking at those hot fudge sundaes. But you look terrific."

"I don't much like cheese," she said. "You don't think that means we're incompatible, do you?" Her manner was determinedly light. She put an arm through his and gave him a comradely squeeze.

They drove slowly through the small town. Though it was still quite early in the evening, most of the lights of Main Street were already out.

"I wish we were in New York," Camilla said.

"I didn't know you'd ever been to New York."

"I'd like to be in a place that's open all night."

"What would you do?"

"I'd like to go to a small nightclub and dance with you."

"You never cease to surprise me," Richard said, as he turned into the street leading to her dormitory.

"If we were dancing . . ." Camilla said.

"Yes?"

"You would at least be holding me."

Richard drove on.

"You're not taking me straight back to the dorm, are you?" Camilla asked.

"You usually have work to do," Richard reminded her. "Your finals, remember?"

"Stop here for a minute," Camilla said.

Richard stopped the car beside a dark row of elms.

"Kiss me," she said.

He turned to her upturned face, a pale blur in the faint glow from the instrument panel and a distant street light. Gently, he moved closer, until their lips were touching. Suddenly she encircled his neck with warm arms and her lips parted.

The kiss became the whole world, and in its blind red-blackness he felt her tongue. His tongue. Her tongue. Tongues. Tongue. Their heartbeats became a single thudding. Time was suspended. The kiss no longer progressed in a line; it expanded circularly like a star exploding in slow motion. The kiss filled the universe. It was a big kiss.

"Camilla!" Richard whispered hoarsely.

"Kiss me," she said.

He kissed her. This one seemed to enlarge more quickly.

"Kiss me, Richard," she said. He kissed her again. And then abruptly he stopped kissing her.

"What's the matter, darling?" she asked softly.

"You know damn' well what's the matter."

"Please kiss me," she said.

"Oh, hell!" he said, and he seized her.

In a moment he broke away from her. "This is ridiculous," he complained.

"Richard," Camilla said. "We don't have to sit in this car. That's the ridiculous part, sitting in a car. Why can't we go somewhere a bit more comfortable?"

"I can't take you to my apartment," Richard said. "That's out of the question."

"Because of my reputation," Camilla agreed with mock solemnity. "And there isn't a private entrance. But if we were very quiet?"

"Cut it out," Richard said. "You can't possibly come to my apartment. As far as Mrs. Cassell's concerned, you'd be a scarlet woman, and she'd tell everyone in Digby. When I said she was deaf, dumb, blind and indifferent, I was – I wasn't telling the truth."

"For shame!" Camilla said unreproachfully. "I wasn't going to suggest anything like that. I was going to suggest we go to the Institute. I have a key to the lab. It's very comfortable – not a bit like a lab really. I could make some coffee. We could talk. There's even brandy. I don't want to go back to the dorm yet."

"The lab?" Richard said. "I thought it was strictly *verboten* to outsiders."

"Come on, Richard," Camilla said. "Please."

"It's all right with me," Richard said. "The way you talked about Dr. Scumann I thought she lurked there like some kind of fire-breathing dragon in its lair."

"Please let's," Camilla said coaxingly.

"Sure. If you like."

The front of the Biology Building was dark. They walked around to the side. A solitary light, on the ground floor, was extinguished as they approached the side entrance.

"The cleaning woman," Camilla explained. "It's O.K. – she goes out the other way."

"We're not criminals," Richard said.

"No, of course not."

Inside the building, Camilla led the way, turning on and turning off lights as they went.

"It doesn't matter if anyone notices the lights," Camilla said. "We often work late."

"Relax," Richard said.

"I am relaxed."

They came to the hall which passed Dr. Schumann's outer office. Camilla stopped and turned and put a hand to his shoulder, and looked into his eyes.

"You do love me, don't you?"

"Of course I do," he said.

The silence of the building seemed strangely thrilling.

"You're trembling."

"No I'm not," Camilla said. "It is rather chilly."

"It seems warm to me."

"Here's the entrance to the lab," Camilla said. "Don't be put off by the clinical look of the vestibule."

She selected a key from her keyring. She fumbled to get the key into the keyhole.

"I'm almost jealous of this building," Richard said. "You spend more of your time with it than with me."

"Shhh!" Camilla said.

"Is the building easily offended?"

"Here we go," Camilla said, opening the door.

"It's not so bad," Richard said. "Not bad at all. I imagined something all zinc and white enamel. This is more like a progressive dentist's waiting-room."

Camilla looked around quickly and furtively and then turned back to Richard.

"Well," Richard said. Her nervousness was infectious.

"Would you rather leave now?" Camilla asked.

"We just got here," Richard said. "Perhaps some coffee wouldn't be a bad idea."

"I'm not sure the cupboard's open."

"Try it."

"It's in the next room."

"All right."

"But let's not."

"Why?"

"I don't feel like coffee now. Do you?"

"I don't care much, one way or the other."

"I'd rather not."

"All right."

Richard smiled at her. Camilla stretched out her arms.

"Richard."

"Yes?"

"Come here."

"All right."

He slowly moved forward, slowly, slowly, like a sleep-walker. And then, once more, he was kissing her. And she was kissing him.

"Richard," she said after a while.

"Yes?"

"Please make love to me."

"I can't," he said. "I promised I wouldn't."

"No you didn't."

"I promised myself."

"I want you to."

"It doesn't make sense," Richard said uncertainly. "It doesn't fit in with anything you ever said before."

"I want to know what it's like," Camilla said. "I may be a virgin, but that doesn't mean that I don't feel anything. I've often only just stopped myself with you. On the island . . ."

"That would have been ideal, wouldn't it?" Richard said. He looked nostalgic for a moment and then got a grip on himself. "It would be against all your principles."

Camilla kissed his mouth. "Principles are only generalities," she said tauntingly. "You said so yourself. This is a special case."

"I mustn't," Richard said fretfully.

"Maybe I'm no good at making love," Camilla said. "Shouldn't we make sure?"

"You couldn't kiss like that and not be good at making love."

Camilla moved even closer to him, pressed herself against him for a moment, and then stepped backwards, away from him. She took off her coat and threw it to one side. She approached him again.

"It's silly to go on talking about it," Camilla said. "It's

297

spring. It's a lovely night. We're young. We love each other. I want to feel your love. I want to show you how much I love you. I'm all soft and melting with desire for you, Richard."

"Oh, Camilla..." Richard feebly protested. "I shouldn't."

"I've been horribly wrong," Camilla said. "I've tried to split life into a lot of separate categories, like courses in the college catalogue. It isn't like that, is it? Love is everything all at once, isn't it? And everything's part of it? Everything we love is part of the way I feel about you. When you kiss me, Richard, it's like landscapes and the sky and music and everything all mixed up. I want you to kiss me and kiss me and kiss me all over, until I almost pass out. I want to feel you so deep inside me that I can't tell which is you and which is me. Richard..."

He tried to speak, but uttered only a sort of groan.

"I really tried not to," he said.

He put his arms around her and kissed her with tender ferocity.

"Not here!" Camilla said, pushing his chest.

"It's a thick carpet," he said.

"There's a bed in the next room."

She opened a door and he followed her into a large, brightly lighted room. There was a bed in one corner, flanked by various cabinets and what appeared to be an elaborate built-in hi-fi television set.

Richard hesitated in the doorway. Camilla held out a hand to lead him inside.

"Won't you regret this?" he asked.

"I love you," she said.

Richard followed her in.

They sat on the edge of the bed.

"There's nothing more I can say," Richard said. He started systematically and carefully to unbutton the small mother-of-pearl buttons down the side of Camilla's dress. He leaned forward and gently kissed her, as his fingers continued steadily to climb down the miniature ladder of buttons.

When half a dozen or so were undone, his hand slipped inside the front of her dress. He could feel her nipple through the brassière. Camilla disengaged her mouth and caught his forearm and sat upright.

"Wait!" she cried. "There's something I must do first."

"We've got to, Camilla!"

"No!"

"Camilla, please!"

"Wait, darling!" Camilla said.

She jumped to the floor, took off one of her high-heeled shoes and kicked off the other. Brandishing the shoe in her hand, as Richard stared at her, she appeared to go absolutely raving mad.

Using the heel of the shoe like a hammer, she attacked the furniture, smashing panels of glass in the cabinets grouped curiously around the bed. One of the boxes, when she hit it, emitted a flash of blue flame and a wisp of smoke. Another made a noise like Donald Duck jabbering very fast.

Richard was so surprised that he remained on the bed, leaning on one elbow, merely watching.

"There!" Camilla cried, hurling her shoes at a partly curtained mirror on the far side of the room. "That's for you, you dragon."

"Camilla!" Richard protested at last. "What's the matter?"

"I'll be right with you," she assured him as she seized a number of gray-rubber-covered cables and began tearing them away from the wainscoting.

"Camilla!" Richard shouted, getting up from the bed.

"Only two to go!" she said, reaching down and grabbing a double coil of wires, like twin snakes, and violently pulling them out of their sockets.

"Camilla, stop!" he said, as she hurried past him to lock the door from the inside. "Stop!" he said, as she hurried to the light-control console. "Camilla!" he said. Rapidly, one by one, the lights were turned off. Just before the last one went, she turned to him and smiled.

The room was black.

"Camilla!" he whispered when he felt her weight on the bed beside him.

She was naked.

FORTY-NINE

DWIGHT ROBERTSON, carrying a speed-graphic camera, pushed his way through the summer dresses and seersucker suits saying "Excuse me, Press – Press, excuse me," gradually making his way through the crowd to get to the V.I.P.'s. There hadn't been such a large crowd at the college on Commencement Day as long as he could remember. The first heatwave of the summer had started three days before, and he was sweating profusely, but feeling quite pleased with life.

Fortunately, all things considered, his exposé of the goings-on at the Digby Institute had had quite the opposite effect from what he had expected. *The Intelligencer* had been sold out the day of publication – a record. And instead of arousing indignation and organized civic protests, the account of the activities in the lab had brought the Institute eager volunteers from all over the community, so many that Dr. Schumann and her associate could look forward to many years of research and professional distinction. All sorts of men and women, of all ages, in all walks of life, from the wife of the president of the Digby Fidelity Trust Savings and Loan Association to a number of distressed unemployables who hitherto had derived most of their income for Muscatel-type wine by selling their blood to the Digby Clinic. The Institute was going to bring added contentment to every stratum of local society.

Robertson had been surprised again by the reaction of the national wire services, which he served as stringer for the Digby area. They thanked him for his call but only perfunctorily. They said a paragraph or two would be quite sufficient, because that very week, they explained, the nation's news editors had given some little play to reports of the establishment of new sex research institutes in Utah, Idaho, Tennessee and West Virginia. You never could tell with news, Robertson philosophically concluded. Nevertheless, Turner Symington had complimented him upon the "campaign" he had run and how much it had, in the end, benefited Digby College, the Institute, and indirectly Buckeye Pharmaceutical. He had also suggested they lunch whenever practical and discuss the opening of a public-relations service.

Now he was close to the enclosure in which senior members of the faculty and distinguished guests were to witness the laying of the cornerstone of the Digby Institute's grand new quarters, to be known as the Symington Building. Robertson moved around the velvet rope, taking the shots that were scheduled to fill the pages of a special dedication supplement of the *Intelligencer*.

There was popular Dr. Frank Essen, President of Digby, beaming and nodding as he surveyed the friendly gathering around him. It was a great day for him, a personal triumph. And Mr. Turner Symington, with the rest of the Board of Trustees, leading citizens all. At his right hand sat Mr. Alexander Pericles Philopoulos, the philanthropist, who had just been appointed an honorary director of the Institute, in recognition of his unprecedentedly generous gift to the college. He was accompanied by his bride, the former Mrs. Marcia Daventry, of Ashtabula Ohio, and his stepdaughter, Miss Joanna Daventry, and her fiancé, Mr. Lawrence Da Silva, of Cleveland. Mr. Da Silva and his fiancée will soon be on their way to Hollywood; Mr. Philopoulos has purchased a television studio there, and it is understood that Mr. Da Silva will be in charge of production, and that undoubtedly in some of the projects under consideration his fiancée will appear as a featured performer.

There, too, was Dr. Beatrice Schumann, radiant in a two-piece suit of lavender silk with a matching hat trimmed with artificial flowers. Dr. Schumann has just had her contract extended at the Institute and received, from all reports, a substantial increase in salary. She was seen engaged in animated conversation with her assistant, Dr. Louis Porter. Among the faculty was Mr. Rollo Hawkins, the director and critic, the newly appointed director of the Digby College Theater Workshop and the Digby Summer Theater.

The principal speakers were Dr. Essen and Mr. Symington. Mr. Symington deftly troweled mortar around the engraved bronze plaque which would be imbedded just to the right of the multi-pillared front entrance. The inscription read: THE SYMINGTON BUILDING – MADE POSSIBLE BY THE GENEROUS GIFT OF ALEXANDER PERICLES PHILOPOULOS, FRIEND OF DIGBY – and the date. This pleased Dr. Essen as being more dignified than any mention of Buckeye Pharmaceutical. Trustee Symington had offered to relinquish the honor of having the new building named after him and had suggested that that honor be given to Mr. Philopoulos in recognition of the new endowment fund bearing his name, but the generous donor demurred, saying that the building should bear the name of the individual who had made all this possible.

The architect who designed the new home of the Digby Institute, Mr. Richard Doughty, could not attend the dedication ceremony, because he was at present out of the country. According to a press release from the Royal Bougainvillaea Hotel, in Hamilton, Bermuda, Mr. Doughty and his bride are honeymooning there. Mrs. Doughty is the former Miss Camilla Fairbank, an alumna of this year's graduating class.

After the unveiling, the Digby Band played the College song, and there was a reception at the Digby Inn for invited guests. The manager of the hotel, Mrs. Deborah Kreeb, said that one hundred and sixty-five persons were in attendance.

GLOSSARY

Beauty	Physical, moral, or spiritual loveliness.
Dignity	Elevation of character; intrinsic worth; excellence.
Ecstasy	A state of overmastering feeling, esp. joy; rapture.
Fidelity	Careful observance of duty, or discharge of obligations, esp.: *a* Loyalty. *b* Adherence to the marriage contract.
Honor	That which rightfully attracts esteem, as dignity and courage; esp. excellence of character; in men, integrity; uprightness; in women, purity; chastity.
Love	A feeling of strong personal attachment induced by sympathetic understanding. Tender and passionate affection for one of the opposite sex.
Progress	Movement forward. Advance to an objective. Gradual betterment.
Truth	Quality or state of being true; hence: *a Archaic.* Fidelity; constancy.

– Webster's New Collegiate Dictionary
(G. & G. Merriam Co., Springfield, Mass.)

SOME PANTHER AUTHORS

Norman Mailer	Robert Musil
Jean-Paul Sartre	Ivy Compton-Burnett
Len Deighton	Chester Himes
Henry Miller	Chaucer
Georgette Heyer	Alan Williams
Mordecai Richler	Oscar Lewis
Gerard de Nerval	Jean Genet
James Hadley Chase	H. P. Lovecraft
Juvenal	Anthony Trollope
Violette Leduc	Robert van Gulik
Agnar Mykle	Louis Auchincloss
Isaac Asimov	Vladimir Nabokov
Doris Lessing	Colin Spencer
Ivan Turgenev	Alex Comfort
Maureen Duffy	John Barth
Nicholas Monsarrat	Rachel Carson
Fernando Henriques	Simon Raven
B. S. Johnson	Roger Peyrefitte
Edmund Wilson	J. G. Ballard
Olivia Manning	Mary McCarthy
Julian Mitchell	Kurt Vonnegut
Christopher Hill	Alexis Lykiard